THE SEA HORROR

A cabin door on the deck above the fighters slammed open, and a nightmare burst out.

It was an enormous, tailless lizard, half as tall as a man, with a long, fanged head like a crocodile. Its skin was large, rainbow-hued scales, and it carried a forward-curving sword in each four-fingered claw. It moved impossibly fast, leaping down the ladder, slashing into pirates, spinning away from counterthrusts and lunges, squealing all the while.

Gareth shot at it with one of his pistols, missed, and, guts clenching, went for the monster with his sword . . .

Also by Chris Bunch

The Demon King
The Empire Stone
The Seer King
The Warrior King

Available from Warner Aspect

CORSAIR

CHRIS BUNCH

A Time Warner Company

WARNER BOOKS EDITION

Cover design by Don Puckey
Cover illustration by Ciruelo Cabral
Hand lettering by Ron Zinn

Aspect® name and logo are registered trademarks of Warner Books, Inc.

Warner Books, Inc.
1271 Avenue of the Americas
New York, NY 10020

Visit our Web site at
www.twbookmark.com

 A Time Warner Company

Printed in the United States of America

First Printing: May 2001

10 9 8 7 6 5 4 3 2 1

To
Elizabeth Rice Bunch
Not too wee, but fierce

One

"Morning, Mage Radnor," the boy said cheerily. "And could we have a spell for our fishing?"

"If I could summon up the cod, and have them dancing on your doorstep," the rather rotund, balding man said with a smile, "do you think I'd be sitting here worrying about taxes?"

"Probably," said the wizard's wife, Bon, a slender woman some ten years younger than her husband. "Maybe not living here—perhaps with our own fleet, with a fine house in Ticao, like your brother—but you'd still be fretting about the king's share. Just think how much more it would be if you *could* magic up the finnies."

"Probably, probably that's how things would work out," Radnor said. "Plus the cost of the nets, whether my men were happy, whether I needed to build my own salting plant, and so on and so forth. Best we should be happy with what we have.

"Although I *would* fancy a spell that'd bring up a tiny demon that understood addition and subtraction."

He got up from the table littered with scrawled papers and broken-tipped quills, and went to the stairs.

"Gareth! Knoll's a-waiting!"

There was no reply.

"He's been sulking all morning," Bon Radnor said.

"Over what? What's there to gloom about?" Knoll N'b'ry said. "The sun's out, the sea's almost flat, there's near no wind, and the tide is on the turn." He raised his voice. "C'mon, Gareth! Tuck your pouty lip back in and stir your stumps!"

Footsteps sounded, and Gareth Radnor came down the winding stairs. He was just fifteen, taller than his friend Knoll, thin, and if it weren't for his pursed lips and frown, would be considered darkly handsome. He wore heavy canvas pants and a patched sweater.

Without speaking to anyone, he sat by the back door and pulled on tarred canvas knee boots, then stood.

"Don't forget your oilskins, dear," his mother said.

"Good idea," Knoll said. "Bound to be a chop coming back."

Gareth didn't answer, but went out, letting the door bang behind him.

"So it's his business if he gets wet," his father said.

Knoll held up his hands helplessly. "He doesn't listen to me, either," and went after Gareth.

"There is a temptation," Radnor said wearily, "to cast a bit of a weather spell after our only son. Nothing more than a half-hour drenching, mind you."

"Make it a weeklong cascade for all of me," Bon said.

"I'm sure I wasn't that big a pain in the sitter when I was his age," Radnor said righteously.

"And I'm sure you were," his wife said. "Now, what, assuming the boys have no luck, do you fancy for our evening meal?"

* * *

Knoll caught up to Gareth as he went down the cobbled street toward the docks.

"And what's the matter with you?" he asked. "A night-spirit appear in your bed and then leave before you were satisfied or something?"

"Oh shut it," Gareth snapped.

Knoll looked at him, sneered ostentatiously, but said nothing. The street flattened, and they passed mostly empty docks.

"Hope we do as well as the fleet," Knoll said, unable to keep silent for long. "I helped Da load his pots, and said a prayer over every one before dawn."

"Prayers don't do any good with fish," Gareth said.

"And how do you know that? Just because your father's a magician doesn't mean you have the Gift," Knoll said. "Next you'll be saying magic doesn't work either. Maybe we should just put fish guts in the traps and let the crabs' common sense, or lack of it, take charge."

"Probably do as good as anything else."

A small boat was tied up at the last, rickety, half-sinking pier. The boat was old, but neatly kept, white with green trim, single-masted, a bit over twenty feet long, with a tiller at the stern. A third boy, almost as thick as he was tall, not quite Gareth's height, busied himself baiting hooks on a long line and curling the line in a wooden bucket.

"What kept you?" he asked.

"Gareth's got the pouts," Knoll said. "I tried chucking his little chin, but he'd have none of it."

"Can't have a man going out with the pissies," the stocky boy said and, surprising for one of his bulk, sprang athletically to the dock. "Come on, Gareth. We'll need a smile for all the little fishies to admire."

"Dammit, leave me alone, Thom," Gareth almost snarled. "I'll be all right."

"Oh I know you will," Thom Tehidy said happily. "In fact, I guarantee it."

"Thom, I'm in no mood to be trifled with! I said, leave me alone! We've got fishing to do!"

Tehidy picked Radnor up in his thick arms, spun him until he was head down, feet flailing in empty air.

"Now, we dunk him a time or two, nice brackish water down here, look, there's a turd floating, right under your head, and one, and a two, and—"

"All right! All right!" Gareth said. "I'm in a good mood! See? Look at this smile!"

"What do you think, Knoll N'b'ry?" Tehidy said. "Appears to me he's faking it, and needs a good healthy drink of mother ocean."

"Thom, put me back on my feet."

Tehidy obeyed, swinging Gareth around and setting him on the dock.

"Should've just tossed you in," he said. "M' pap always said the day starts best and easiest if you're already wet."

Gareth looked at his two friends, then started laughing. It was a strong, cheerful sound.

"There," Knoll said. "Now you're all better, and we'll even let you man the rudder on the way out."

"So what was the problem?" Knoll asked, as the boat tacked out of the harbor under its single sail.

"Everything," Gareth said.

"Everything like how?" Thom said, from his seat below the mast.

"Look around, dammit!"

Behind them, about a third of a league distant, was

the village, climbing up steep cliffs, houses brightly painted, roofs red, blue, green. Occasional clouds drifted above, and the sky was a solid blue. Behind the village, on rising ground to the high moors, were farmhouses and cultivated land. Here and there were the dots of oxen pulling plows, their owners beside the teams.

Two of the royal semaphore towers could be seen leading off into the distance, connecting the village with the capital of Ticao and the rest of the great island of Saros.

Empty beaches and cliffs were on either side of the village, and other settlements could be dimly made out to the east and west.

The sea was greenish blue, low waves gently lifting the boat, a slight breeze blowing across the boat's thwarts.

"What's to see?" Tehidy asked bewilderedly.

"Only the same thing we look at every day, that's all!"

"What's the matter with that?" Thom said. "Who wants a change when things are good?"

Gareth growled. "What good? We're doing the same thing we've done every week that somebody doesn't want us to work on one of the boats, or else helping some clod kicker with his planting! There's time enough for drudgery in the years to come!"

"That's what we are," Thom said. "That's what we do, what we're going to be doing, isn't it?"

"I know!" Gareth said. "That's the problem! For the rest of our lives, pulling fish out of the ocean or shoving seeds in the ground! Over and over and over!"

Thom was looking at him curiously.

"I remember," he said slowly, "when we were kids, and you were always going on about going off to be a sailor. I mean, a deepwater sailor. Fighting wars."

"Or being a pirate," Knoll said.

"I wish I'd stuck to that," Gareth said sullenly.

"The problem is," Tehidy said reasonably, "none of us know who to talk to about pirating. Nobody at the semaphore station seems to know the routing for the Royal Loyal Evil and Roistering Pirates."

"Plus," N'b'ry put in, "we figured out a long time ago that Old Man Baltit's stories about pirating seem to be mostly made up, since they keep changing, and he's just about the only one who's been away anywhere."

"I know," Gareth said, through clenched teeth.

"You could always run away," Thom went on. "Find a village that's on the king's impressment list, and be taken for the navy. Even though I hear running up and down the mast with some bastard with a rope end hitting you on your butt gets old real fast.

"Or join the coastal guard. Give you a chance to stay in home waters, and prob'ly drown in the first big storm, trying to save some dumb fisherman like me. Or maybe meet real pirates on the wrong end of a cannon."

"What happened?" Knoll asked quietly. "You normally don't go off like this."

Gareth sat staring out at the water. He picked up a bit of salted fish from the bait bucket, chewed at it.

"Dad got a letter this morning, that he's supposed to pass along to the herald so everybody'll hear it," he finally said. "From Vel's father."

"Uh-oh," Thom said quietly. Vel Kese had been the closest thing the village had to a beauty, a year younger than the boys. Her father had run one of the village's two shops until recently, when he'd announced there wasn't any money to be made here and moved the family to another village two or three days' distant. She'd been Gareth's girl since they were seven or eight, and most of the villagers assumed she and Gareth would eventually marry.

Gareth was considered a good catch, being the son of

the village thaumaturge, with seven years of tutoring. Everyone assumed that he'd amount to something more than a fisherman, even though he didn't show any signs of having his father's Talent.

"*Hern* Kese is really damned proud to announce that his daughter has become affianced and will soon be the second bride of some asshole cidermaker, who'll make her very happy and so on and so forth."

"Oh," Knoll said softly.

"Makes me wish Dad had let me go off to Ticao and live with my uncle. Instead, I hung around here, and thought that . . . It doesn't matter what I thought," Gareth said.

Thom reached across and patted Gareth's knee.

"Oh the hells with it," Gareth said. "Let's start looking for a good place to drop our lines."

"I thought," Knoll said, eager for the change of subject, "we'd try back of that seamount you climbed once, to the east, where it shallows."

"Why not?" Gareth said. "It's past time I learn to concentrate on making a good life for myself," he said bitterly. "Whatever the hells that might be.

"I just wish," he said, after a pause, "something exciting would happen around here."

The seas around the huge stack, rising abruptly out of the deep waters, were choppy, almost treacherous. Even though all three boys had been in boats since before they could walk, they still kept a wary eye to seaward for the sudden widowmaker that could smash them into the nearby rocks.

They also watched the horizon as the day grew later, saw the village's crabbers sail home.

Two years earlier, on a dare, Gareth had climbed to the top of the nearby stack, using a grass rope where he could, finding foot- and toeholds in cracks, pulling himself up with the tussocks that grew out of the face. Once a gull had exploded from its nest, almost making him fall. When he reached the top, a tiny plateau not much bigger than his father's spellcasting floor, he'd held firm against the gusts that tried to send him spinning down into the breakers, wondering why the hells he insisted on making such a damned fool of himself, and then wondered how he would climb down.

But he had, and the villagers swore he was the first, well, perhaps the second, to ever climb that seamount, although no one could remember that first man's name.

It was getting cold. Gareth's fingers were sore, salt-burned, and his ears felt like they were the finest porcelain, and would shatter if anyone tapped them with a fingernail.

"Hi," Knoll said suddenly. "Look."

Distant smoke boiled across the water from somewhere behind the seamount.

"Fire," Thom said. "Something big's burning!"

Knoll was reeling in the line as Gareth went to the rudder and brought the boat about as Thom raised the sail. Gareth let the current skitter the boat around the mount, close to a dark cliff and a cave, where the surf boomed in deadly invitation.

"Oh gods," Knoll said softly. Something *was* burning.

It was their village. Sailing out from under that cloud were four ships like none they'd ever seen. Gareth could faintly make out their hulls against the water. They were black, with red lateen sails on three masts.

"What're they?" Thom said.

"I don't know," Gareth said, but the flames gave him the answer.

"Linyati," Knoll whispered. "The Slavers! I never heard of them this far north."

"Gods," Thom echoed Knoll, less a prayer than a moan. "Come on, Gareth! Hurry!"

The village was a shatter of flames and ruin, the only sounds the crackling of the fires, crashes as roof timbers collapsed.

The fishing boats were smoldering ruin, their oil-soaked wood having instantly flared up when torches were thrown.

There were two men dead on the docks, arrowheads coming out their backs. Half a dozen crabs from a broken trap crawled across their bodies on their way back to the water.

Gareth leapt over the bodies, the other two behind him, running for their homes.

A body sprawled at the foot of the street in a pool of blood. Next to him lay a broken boathook, and, with great wounds in their bodies, three dark-complected men in foreign, silk-looking garb. Gareth had time for a flashing thought that perhaps Old Man Baltit hadn't been the colossal liar everyone thought he was, for he'd taken at least these raiders down, then ran on, heart hammering under his ribs, toward his house.

His father lay on his back, just inside the doorway. His hand had been chopped off, trying to push away the spear that had buried itself in his chest.

Gareth's mother sat on the foot of the stairs, and for an instant Gareth thought she was still alive, until he saw the gaping slash across her neck, and the way her head lolled.

He was on his knees, and the only numb thought he

had, over and over, was *I didn't even say good-bye, I didn't say good-bye to them.*

Time passed. He heard footsteps, didn't turn.

Knoll's voice came:

"They took . . . Thom's whole family . . . my father's dead . . . mother and my sisters are gone. They took them all. There's no one left in the village.

"Only the dead, Gareth. That's all they left."

Another thought came to Gareth:

And I didn't tell them that I loved them. I don't remember, can't remember, when I said that last.

Then the tears finally came free.

Two

Gareth Radnor crouched behind a chimney pot, trying not to think about the steep gables on either side of him, the four-story drop if he slid on the slates, and the cobbles below that would hardly soften his fall.

Across the square rose the great temple of Megaris, the favored god of the Ticaons and, by extension, all of Saros. Atop the temple's flat roof were four columns supporting a small stone canopy, and, in the middle, a great gong.

The gong was struck by monks every hour on the hour, its boom resounding across Ticao to the Nalta River, and across that to the slums beyond, one of Ticao's familiar sounds.

But the square below, in spite of the hour—bare moments before middle-night—held three dozen people, staring up in curiosity and awe.

For something was awry with the worship of the god, or, some people whispered, with the god himself.

Ten nights now, instead of twelve strokes, the gong

had sent out thirteen, and no one knew why. Monks and priests had prayed long and hard for an explanation of this omen, but without result.

The priests tried to keep the marvel a secret, but without success. Two nights ago there'd been four people who witnessed the phenomenon, the night before eleven, and Gareth saw more trickling into sight below.

He grinned, took a sling from his pouch, and took out a stone, carefully selected for its smooth roundness.

Across the way, a hatch opened and four monks clambered into sight. One carried the huge padded hammer used to strike the gong, and one of the others held a glass, watching the sands run out.

There should have been only two for the ceremony. Gareth supposed the others to be high priests present to keep demons from making an appearance, some sort of curse striking, or the monks in charge of the signal pulling some sort of tomfoolery.

The monk with the hammer pushed the sleeves of his habit back and lifted the tool. Previously it'd been with a flourish, but Gareth now thought he moved with a bit of trepidation.

The man with the glass lifted his arm, and lowered it.

The monk struck, struck again . . .

Three . . . four . . . five . . . six . . . seven . . . eight . . . nine . . .

Gareth stood, braced against the chimney, fixed his eyes on his target.

Ten . . . eleven . . .

Gareth whipped the sling into life.

Twelve . . .

Gareth released one end of the sling, and the stone hummed across the distance . . .

Thirteen!

Gareth had a moment to see one of the monks drop to his knees in prayer, heard the clamor from the square, tucked his sling in his pouch, and scrabbled back down the slates. He grabbed the knotted rope and slid over the edge, hand-over-handing down, down. Then Labala had him, and Fox was whipping the rope back down from where it'd been looped around the chimney. He was the one who could climb a sheet of glass if you dared him, who'd clambered up a drain spout for eleven nights and fixed the rope for Gareth to climb.

Labala was holding back laughter, great whooping roars that'd ring as loudly as the gong if he let them out.

They turned to run, and a voice called.

"You! You three! Stand where you are!"

It had to be a warder.

None of the three responded, but began to run.

"I said stop!" the warder called, and pelted after them, truncheon raised.

The fourth member of the team, Cosyra, dumped a bucket of slops out from the doorway she'd been stationed in, and the warder shrieked, skidded, and went flat. Cosyra leapt over him, ran after the others.

Even laughing as hard as she was, she caught up in a block.

They ran on a few blocks, ducked into a deserted mews.

"Eleven nights," Labala gurgled, his bulk jiggling with laughter. "They'll be gaoinga in the headbone in another ten."

"There won't be another ten," Gareth said flatly.

"Why not?" Fox asked.

"We almost got caught tonight," he said. "It won't be nearly as funny if we end up in some priestly dungeon after twelve nights . . . or fifteen."

Labala pouted.

"But we had them going so much!"

"Gareth's right," Cosyra said. "Always best to stop when you're ahead."

"Truths," Fox agreed. "So what's next?"

Gareth thought. "I've got a couple of ideas."

"So do I," Cosyra said.

"I'd like a night or two to hammer them out," Gareth said. "Meet here, two nights gone?"

Labala grunted, Fox nodded.

"Two nights from now," Cosyra said, and, without further farewell, went out of the mews and was gone.

Gareth and the others made good-byes, and Gareth made his way through the dark streets, ducking the torch of a warder's patrol once, and spotting two footpads in an alley that he went around to his uncle's house.

The ladder he'd left against the outer wall was still in place, and Gareth went up it deftly. The courtyard on the other side was empty, and he put the small ladder on the wall top, where it'd not be seen, went down the eight feet to the brick courtyard on one of his aunt's flowering vines. He crossed the courtyard, used the jagged corners of the mansion's brick facing to climb two stories, went across to a drain on a windowsill, up another story, and into his bedroom.

He uncovered a lantern, blew it into life, looked at himself in the mirror. A bit dusty, hands and feet dirty. He stripped, put his clothes in a hamper for a laundress, washed, and slid into bed.

His body said it was time for sleep, that the morning's dullness with its quills and ink would come too soon, but his mind was still moving fast.

It'd been close to a year since his parents' murder by the Linyati. The coastal watch had arrived just at dusk, and

Gareth had wanted to rave where had they been, why were they always late?

But his village had been the third raided that day. One guardsman told him, although Gareth didn't absorb the information until later, that this was, indeed, as far north as the dreaded and loathed Linyati had come on their raids, and perhaps this would be enough to get King Alfieri off his ass and declare war on the Slavers.

His mate had snorted, and said nothing would get that lard-butt moving except maybe setting fire to the throne itself. Or, he added, getting a priest to ban all the wenching he did, although that'd more likely get the priest banned.

Gareth didn't care what kings did . . . all he wanted was to have his parents back, to say the words he'd not said that day. Or, failing that, to learn how to use a sword, and somehow find the Slavers who'd brought ruin to his village and kill them all, slowly.

Knoll and Thom, and two other villagers who'd seen the dark ships beach and fled into the moors, would be taken in by the nearest village and raised as one of them, as was common along the coast, where accident, storm, and creatures of the depths not infrequently brought tragedy.

A letter of credit was semaphored from Ticao, and Gareth went by the first coach to the capital, to be taken in by his father's brother, Pol.

All he took with him from the ransacked house, besides what clothes he thought he might need, realizing most of what he owned would mark him for the bumpkin he was, was an ornate wand his father had been given when he completed his studies, a small but very dangerous-looking razor-edged sorcerous dagger used for cutting herbs, wicks, and magical circles, and a ring with a cameo of his mother that his father had made when they'd become betrothed.

The rest, and whatever else was salvageable in the village, would be auctioned, and whatever money raised would go to help support Thom and Knoll in their new homes.

The three boys made hesitant farewells, minds on the pyres burning on the headlands, and the bodies turning to ash on them. They swore they'd meet again, someday, and they'd never forget one another, all three knowing their words to be impossible dreams, no better than lies.

Gareth turned away from the ruins, toward a new life in the great city.

Pol Radnor was eight years younger than his brother, the wizard, and, at least as far as girth and ostensible merriment, very much like him. But where the Mage Daav Radnor had been content with being a minor magician in a sleepy village, helping the people and their animals with their woes and sicknesses, sometimes able to cast a bit of a weather spell, Pol was very ambitious.

He'd spent only three years as a shipper's clerk before becoming a purser on one of his magnate's ships. Two voyages later, he had made enough contacts and profit for his employer to loan him the money for a single cargo. The ship didn't sink, and pirates didn't spot the small merchantman, and Pol had begun his rise.

Now he owned directly or controlled half a dozen ships, had agents in twice that many ports, and was known as a fortunate man. The cargoes he agreed to carry not only arrived at their destination, but not infrequently at exactly the time they could bring the highest profits. Some said Pol had the Gift for the future, but he denied it with a chuckle, saying he was no more than lucky.

However, he was known to say, to his handful of cronies, that a man made his own luck.

It took little time for Gareth to realize that if it was possible to make your luck through hard work and careful insinuation into the right circles, Pol Radnor was lucky indeed, and it should not be long before his uncle would be named a King's Servant, then possibly knighted, and, if he were successful enough, be granted a Merchant Prince's cloak and allowed to wear furs on his robes.

He'd married well, to an older, rather plain woman named Priscian, another magnate's daughter. So far, their marriage was unblessed, but Pol seemed unworried. Priscian's dowry had not only included two ships with their crews and a newly built mansion not far from the river that divided Ticao in half, but a country estate and, most importantly, the gold and servants to operate them handsomely.

Gareth had always been a bit suspicious of Pol's cheeriness, thinking no one could be that honestly hearty that much of the time. But after almost a year he grudged the man's jollity must be sincere. He did notice, though, that Pol seemed happiest when his receivables were for gold, rather than silver.

Pol had allowed Gareth a respectable time, almost a month, for mourning, then announced the young man's future. He would be permitted to follow in his uncle's footsteps, first as a clerk, then as a chief clerk, then, if all went well, put in control of an entire division of Pol's mercantile empire, for empire it surely would be in a few short years, Megaris blessing them.

Gareth asked when he'd be allowed to go to sea.

"Never, if it's any of me, son," Pol said. "I went, twice, and a blasted waste of time it was. Nothing but crude men, storms, seasickness, pirates, and uncertainty.

"I learned my lesson, and am going to do you the great favor of not making you repeat the course.

"As they say, a man with one foot on dry land is blessed, and a man with both feet there is in league with the gods.

"While you live in this house, I'll never allow you such suffering."

And so Gareth joined the household. There were a dozen servants, and everyone rose at dawn. Gareth noted that, even though Pol and his wife went regularly to the Merchant's Temple, having their own box seat high on the walls, they didn't spend time praying when alone.

That suited Gareth well. He'd decided if there were any gods, they were uncaring, or maybe malignant, and most likely nothing but stone statues, mewling priests, and self-righteous canons.

After rising and washing, the household ate heartily, if simply, for Pol believed a man worked best on a full stomach.

Gareth had a tutor come in for an hour each day, for Pol thought his lack of knowledge, particularly of figures, deplorable. Once a week another man came in and talked of music, art, books, for Pol said a good merchant must be able to talk about anything to his clients.

After that, Gareth made his way to Pol's factory along the riverfront, which had offices and clerks' warrens in front, and huge warehouses behind.

That was pure torture for the boy, for the ships of a hundred nations docked along the water, their masts standing close to the upper stories of the Merchant Princes' buildings, bowsprits sometimes nearly blocking the path of the wagons clattering back and forth. Ships that he'd never be allowed to sign on to, ships that would visit strange and wonderful parts of the world he'd never see.

Even worse was when his uncle called a sorcerer in to cast the spell that'd give Gareth the traders' patois. Why, he asked Pol, was he doing this, if he had no intent of letting Gareth go to sea? "We deal with merchants from many lands," Radnor said briskly, "who come to my office frequently. You can generally strike a better bargain if you have a tongue in common with the other party."

At least once a month Gareth asked if he could be loaned to another magnate with a recommendation he be allowed to sign aboard a ship, for seasoning, "for surely, Uncle, how can a man be a good merchant if he has no knowledge of his distant clients and their lands?"

"By reading and correspondence," Pol might reply, "which you've been most slight about. All things can be learned in books, and there's no need to be tossed about in a leaking hulk eating wormy beef and drinking small beer if you can sit in comfort, now is there?"

"But—"

"But me no buts," Pol would say, not unkindly. "Now, to your accounts, and pay more attention there than you have been. Your chief has found, he told me, some twenty errors in your last accounting alone.

"That's not good, Gareth. That's not what can make me proud of you, proud of yourself, now is it?"

Not being able to find a reply, Gareth would slink back to his canted desk, which grew larger and higher from the ground every day, more and more covered with scribbles on paper, his stool taller and taller, stretching toward heavens as dull as the wintry Sarosian skies, when he longed for tropic sunshine and warm blue waters splashing on sandy beaches.

The clerks around him were all older, and all seemed to have found a home, and delighted in telling stories of how they almost sent a cargo of oranges to the tropics, or how they'd gotten lucky, and found an erroneous entry, and saved *Hern* Radnor so many gold coins.

There wasn't even any point in pranking them, for all that happened the two or three times he tried something was a long look and a tired sigh.

At dusk, or after twelve turnings of the glass during the short winter days, the office was closed.

The evening meal was heavy, Pol giving himself two glasses of the finest ale before dinner, three glasses of wine with the sumptuous feast—food from many lands that Pol traded with—and two brandies before bed as he read and responded to his agents' correspondence.

Gareth got drunk once on the ale, didn't like the sickness it brought nor the way he felt the next day, and forever after remained a non-toper, never really minding, unlike most of his countrymen, if he were forced to drink small beer, very watered wine, or even simple water itself.

After the evening meal, no one cared what Gareth did, so long as he was back inside the compound by two turnings before middle-night.

When he discovered the small ladder in a shed, his path was open, and he'd retire early and slide out across the roofs. No one seemed to check on him, and he suspected they would not care much if they did find his bed empty.

Ticao was a magical city to explore.

It had been built long ages past, first as an upriver trading village, sensibly ten leagues from the sea, to guard against raiders. Its river, the Nalta, was wide enough for a ship to tack up, especially after dredges had begun deepening the main channel over the past one hundred years. It continued north into the farming heartland of Saros, and canals had been built from east and west, so most of the goods Saros traded in came through Ticao.

On the northeast bank of the river was the trading heart of Ticao, around and in the old walled city. Beyond that rose the heights, where the king's castle and other noble buildings sat. Pol said that while he certainly wanted to be a Merchant Prince, he would never build on the king's mountain, since one requirement was that in time of war, if the capital were threatened, all these homes would be razed to give clear fields of fire to the cannon in the Royal castle.

Ticao had spread across the river, where working quarters and slums sprawled, just as the city had reached north, beyond the King's mountain, through greater and smaller country homes into the rolling countryside.

Streets, alleys, wound through the city, and it seemed impossible to ever know Ticao completely, for there was always a new shop, tea-bar, or tavern being opened. Here and there through Ticao were parks, spreading tree-spattered grasslands, and it was a royal edict that they be open to any citizen.

And so he explored the avenues and alleys of Ticao, never clambering back into his bedroom before midnight, sometimes not until dawn, after which he would spend a yawning day at his desk, trying to ignore the frowns from the chief clerk.

Ticao was thronged with seamen and traders from foreign parts, including men from Linyati. The first time he saw one of the olive-complected, blank-faced sailors, he asked a beggar who the man was.

"Slavers," the man spat, hand still out for a coin.

"The ones who raid our villages?"

"Th' same."

"Why are they allowed ashore?" Gareth asked in shock.

"'Cause our nimby-namby king doesn't want war with anybody, wants the seaways to be open to all, so Saros can bring home the most gold.

"Damned fool, with all respect. There's some who know the way to deal with scum like the Slavers is at sword point. 'At's how I got all crippled up, lad, in a grand battle ashore with a bunch of them. I fought my best, kept my mate alive, but took a terrible wound. Here, for a copper or two I'll show you, right—"

Gareth dropped a coin, hurried away.

He saw them again, seldom singly, mostly in groups of half a dozen, to prevent the mutterers who trailed them from becoming bolder and hurling cobbles or filth. The things the Slavers bought made no sense. Sometimes it would be a sweetmeat, sometimes a jewel. Anything edible or drinkable was immediately gulped down, as if they were small boys sneaking behind their parents' back.

Gareth trailed them often, trying to figure out what they were, following them back to their strange ships, ships whose portholes were alight from within from dusk to dawn, as if the Slavers never slept.

He asked what they came to Ticao to trade, since slavery had been outlawed for generations in Saros. A clerk from another factory made a face, said the slaves they took, generally from the savage continent of Kashi, separated from the continent of Linyati by a long isthmus, were sold elsewhere, to other countries who still held bondage legal. Those trade goods were perfectly legitimate to bring into Saros.

"Damned shame, too," the young man added. "Our factor's lost three ships in five years, and one or another of our seamen managed to make his way home later to tell us they'd not been wrecked by storms, but seized by the Slavers.

"Good King Alfieri ought to fit out a fleet, and drive them back to their own lands. No one needs dealing with murderous bastards like them."

Twice Gareth hurled a stone at a knot of Linyati, and was breathlessly pursued down alleys, the Slavers waving daggers or the thin-bladed swords they preferred. Their language was a series of coughs, like one of the lions Gareth saw in the King's Menagerie.

Once he lurked on a rooftop, waited until four of the Slavers passed underneath, and tipped a full chamberpot over.

But this was very small beer, he knew, and wanted greater revenge, revenge with a pistol or sword.

His uncle Pol told him he shouldn't bear hatred, for it kept the memory of that murderous day alive. That was fine with Gareth. He wanted not one, not ten, but a hundred dead Slavers for his mother and father, even more for the others of his village who now wore chains on some unknown shore.

But Gareth did not let himself become a dark brooder, like fishermen he'd known who'd lost a son or a brother at sea. He loved pranking, jesting against those he thought were pompous, foolish, or malicious, whether rich merchants, cheating shopkeepers, or pompous citizens, once even a fraud claiming to be a magician, who persuaded an entire street of credulous whores of his talents with love potions.

He made two friends in his ramblings, then a third.

The first was the enormous Labala, whom he rescued from being rolled by cutpurses when drunk. Labala's family came from a distant tropical island, but none of them knew precisely where it was. Labala, like his father, worked as a stevedore on Ticao's docks, augmenting his income by what he could steal.

In return for Gareth's favor, he promised that neither he, nor any of his family, nor any of his cousins, would ever thieve from a Radnor cargo, no matter the temptation.

Labala was two years—or so he thought—older than Gareth, but appeared in his twenties at least. Some made the mistake of not taking him seriously, or thinking him stupid, because of his bulk, the rolls of fat he was quite proud of, and the constant beam on his round face.

The grin concealed quite a nasty temper, as quite a few discovered after the smile suddenly vanished and Labala growled, "Now I'm going to sit on you." Which he would do, after his huge fists had hammered the person's body for a while. Labala was also very fast. Gareth saw a man pull two knives on him one night, lose them both in an armblock and two crashing blows, and then get hurled into the river.

Labala loved pranking as well, without much regard for the target or outcome.

Fox was the second. He never said what he did during the day. Gareth thought he was a cutpurse or perhaps pickpocket, the way his eyes followed money around. He was very small, skinny to the point of emaciation, and his eyes darted about under a mop of unruly hair. Gareth knew little of his family, except he had a mother whom he revered, two twin brothers—"the greatest of heartless villains," he said proudly—and a seemingly endless array of uncles. He never mentioned his father.

Fox's taste in japery ran toward the well dressed and those with purses he might be able to end up with during the hubbub.

The last was Cosyra. She stood just to Gareth's chin, was slender, small-breasted, wore her brown hair very short, dressed like a boy. Her face was heart-shaped, with perfect teeth and a grin almost as frequent as Labala's.

Like the other three, she wore commoner's clothes of leather, wool, or coarse cotton. There was one thing unusual about her appearance: on a silver chain she wore a small icon of a sea eagle.

Cosyra spoke, unlike Fox and Labala, in an educated

tongue, though the cant of thieves and the streets came easily to her.

She never spoke of a family or friends. One of her favorite quick pranks was, when someone realized she was a woman and showed lustful signs, enticing them for a bit, then telling them she was the daughter of a shopkeeper, and would love to tryst later, at a certain address. Since the address she gave was that of the temple of Houf, Goddess of Eunuchs and the Celibate, Gareth wondered if she was a young harlot, sold to one of the many bordellos of Ticao.

None of the three young men ever tried to bed her. For some unknown reason, they all felt that might spoil things.

And so, every second or third night, they'd creep out, either looking for a target, or else putting a plan in motion.

The pranked were generally picked by either Cosyra or Gareth, the other two seeming content to be lieutenants in the schemes.

Gareth thought his japery might be the only thing that kept him from going mad.

Three

I have it," Labala gurgled from the darkness. "Let's paint the statue of the king in Centersquare."

"We did that three months ago," Cosyra said patiently.

"Yes . . . yes . . . but this time, we'll paint his butt blue, instead of pink," Labala said, and almost fell against the stone wall in his mirth.

"Well," Gareth said diplomatically, "we'll consider that as a second option." None of them wanted to get Labala unhappy, for obvious reasons.

"You have somethin' in th' way of a scheme," Fox said, not a question.

"Maybe," Gareth said. "Do any of you know Lord Quindolphin?"

"I do. I mean, I've heard of him," Cosyra said.

Gareth waited.

"Not supposed to be a very nice sort," she said.

"Had a mate of my uncle's drawn an' quartered," Fox

said. "Just for borrowin' one of them gilt eagles off his mansion's gates."

"That ain't right," Labala said indignantly. "Let's do him. Forget about the king's stony arse."

"His daughter's getting married four nights from now," Gareth went on. "There'll be a big party afterwards."

"Of course," Cosyra said. "But his mansion's got big, high walls."

"He's not having it there," Gareth went on. "For some reason, he's putting it on at the Banker's Guildhall."

"Prob'ly owes 'em money," Fox said.

"Could be," Gareth said. "Anyway, I scouted the place on my way here. It's got a big delivery door at the rear."

"So?" Cosyra said.

"A *very* big delivery door," Gareth said, and outlined his idea as Labala's laughter grew, almost shaking the cobbles they stood on.

"An'—an'—an'—" he interrupted, sides shaking like they were in a gale, "there's a ship, come from upcountry, just docked today, with just the right present for old Quindolphie."

"Way for the musicians' gear," Gareth bayed, cracking, rather ineptly, the whip he'd borrowed along with the freight wagon and its horses.

A guildhall worker nodded without much interest, went back inside, under draped red and black banners.

Gareth managed to swing the wagon around, and Fox jumped out of the back. He awkwardly pushed at the horses until they backed up, and the wagon thudded against the building's dock.

Cosyra and Labala jumped off the back, and slid a ramp from its slot under the wagon to the dock. She went to the guildhall's gate, prepared to open it.

Fox and Labala were on either side of the ramp, and Gareth unbarred the wagon's rear door.

Two dozen pigs saw freedom, squealed happily, and ran down the ramp as Cosyra opened the guildhall entrance.

Someone shouted, a woman shrieked, and the pigs boiled through the kitchen—no doubt smelling in horror their former colleagues revolving on spits—knocking a wine steward aside, into the middle of milord Quindolphin's daughter's reception.

The squeals were louder, human, and there were shouts and frenzy.

Gareth let himself listen to the cacophony with great pleasure, then came back to reality.

"Come on. There's trouble building," he shouted, and the four, abandoning the wagon they'd "borrowed" some hours earlier, ran down the side of the guildhall and into the street.

There was a man, rather foppishly dressed, dismounting at the main entrance, handing his horse's reins to a servitor.

"Here, you," he shouted. "What's going on in there?"

Paying no attention, the four ran on.

Gareth looked back, saw the man draw a sword, come after them. But they had him by ten lengths, and in another two hundred feet would be able to dart into a winding, mazelike alley.

Then Cosyra slipped, skidded on the cobbles, and lay flat, her breath knocked out.

"I have you, shitheel," the man shouted, blade lowered. "Damned footpad that you are, stealing from his lordship's wedding—"

Cosyra was on her knees, trying to get up, the blade was no more than a few inches from her chest.

Gareth, without needing to think, saw a loose cobble,

scooped it up, and threw it hard. The stone smashed into the man's head, and Gareth's stomach roiled as he heard bone smash. The man dropped the sword, skidded on his belly against the curb, contorted twice, and lay very still.

Gareth heard, numbly, shouts from the guildhall, as he helped Cosyra to her feet.

Horses' hooves rang on the stones, and he saw riders galloping toward him.

Fox had stopped, crouched against a building; Labala was running back toward him.

"No," Gareth shouted. "Go on. Better they get one of us than all."

"But—" Cosyra managed.

"Go, dammit! Or they'll have us all!"

Cosyra worked her lips, then ran, grabbing Labala by the sleeve.

A pistol went off, and a ball ricocheted off the stone near them, then the three were gone.

Four riders were around Gareth, three with drawn swords, the fourth, with a ready pistol, slid out of his saddle. He went to the body, knelt, and turned it over, his eyes and pistol barrel hard on Gareth's chest.

He glanced down for a minute.

"It's Sir Wyeth," the man said. "He's dead."

He looked hard at Gareth.

"Now you're for it, lad."

The warders in the dank, chill Great Dungeon that sprawled just downslope from the east side of the king's palace weren't any more cheerful.

"Killed a man, and noble at that," one of them said, smiling in pleasure. "And what's your class, boy?"

Gareth shook his head, not really knowing.

"That'll determine what happens to you," the warder

went on. "Commoner—which I suspects, seein' how you're dressed—for murderin' nobility, 'specially in the course of a crime, that's having your guts pulled out in front of you an' burnt, then the rope. Merchantman, that's slow hangin', or maybe bein' broke on th' wheel. If you were noble, like Sir Wyeth, it'd be no more'n th' ax.

"But they'll not let you die that easy," he said with glee.

"Best you come up with some silver afore th' day, boy, so you can pay th' headsman to put a blade in y'r heart after he makes the first cut along y'r guts."

The first cell he'd been thrown into had been occupied by two great bruisers. They'd decided to fight to see who'd be first to have the boy as bedmate. The noise had attracted the corridor warder, who jerked Gareth out and put him in a solitary cell. Not, he was careful to explain, that he minded the idea of Gareth being raped, but both the thugs were in for murdering a fellow of his, and he'd see they had no pleasure at all before their death day.

Gareth had stayed in that cell long enough to hear the prediction of his fate and, hating to do it, getting paper and pen and promising a guard he'd be paid for taking a message to his uncle.

When that warder came back, his manner had changed.

"Here, boy," he said. "Your uncle said to make sure you was took care of."

He escorted Gareth out of that section, up flights of stairs into another corridor, and to a very different cell. This had a desk, a chair, even a bed. The bedding, though threadbare, was clean, and the cell didn't smell too badly of shit.

"Anything you want to eat," the warder said, "just call for me. Name's Aharah. You want anything now?"

Gareth shook his head, then asked for water, and could he wash?

A pitcher of clear water and a bucket and soap were brought, and Gareth numbly cleaned himself, thinking of what the first warder had said of his death options.

He went to the cell window, looked out. Gray day, gray stone walls, guards walking their rounds on the parapets. He was high enough to see a bit over the walls, a few streets, then the Nalta River, gray winding to the ocean he'd never sail.

After a while, Aharah brought a tureen of soup, bread, and cheese. Gareth forced himself to eat. The soup wasn't bad, and he forced gloom away.

Perhaps he'd find a way to escape before the execution. He guessed he'd be taken out of his cell and brought before some judge or other. Maybe there'd be a chance then.

Surely! He jeered at himself. Just about as great as the possibility of growing wings and flying out of here.

Aharah came back, with a small box.

"A girl brought this," he said. "Gimme a gold piece to take it to you."

Gareth took the box, untied string, opened it. Inside was a silver sea eagle he recognized, and a note:

This has been ensorcelled, so if you ever are free, think of me, hold the eagle, and it will lead you to where I am.

C

"Wait," he said as Aharah was leaving. "What of this girl? What was she dressed like?"

Aharah shrugged. "Wore a cloak, so I couldn't tell much. Looked like maybe she was somebody's maid or somethin'. Thin. Short hair. Haw, boy. You so popular with the little girlies you don't know who sends you things?"

Gareth didn't answer, but sat turning the eagle in his fingers. At last, he put its chain around his neck, tucked it well out of sight.

Strangely cheered, as if the little icon could somehow help, he lay down, and sleep came.

Two days later, his uncle came to see him.

Gareth had wondered if Pol would simply forget him as a murderous fool, or, if he did come to the prison, only rail at him for his stupidities.

Radnor did neither.

He sat down, heavily, in Gareth's chair.

"These damned stairs take it out of a man," he said.

Gareth sat, waiting.

"I've often said, as I'm sure you've heard me, that I consider myself lucky.

"Son, compared to you, I'm the original cursed one with a black cloud over my head."

Gareth started in surprise.

"The first piece of luck you've had is Sir Wyeth, the man you . . . you killed, is . . . was . . . has a reputation around the city for being a rapscallion and a man without honor. I don't know what he did to gain such repute.

"As an aside, I assume that you killed him in fair fight, although what the hells you were doing out and about at that hour is quite beyond me.

"I do not believe a Radnor, particularly my brother's son, capable of cold-blooded murder. Nor do I wish any explanations.

"As I said, the identity of the man you killed was the first piece of luck. No one seems much to care whether his death is recompensed.

"The second is even greater. The king has heard of what happened."

Gareth could feel the blood leave his face, braced. What kind of luck was that, to have the king aware of him?

"Lord Quindolphin has long been in disfavor with the king. I—and I never want you to repeat these words, since it bodes not well for a man to openly criticize those above him—have found him to be without integrity, especially when he decides to do business with those he considers of a lesser class, such as merchants and shippers.

"I confess to having suffered financially at Quindolphin's hands myself. Why the king dislikes him, I don't know, and don't care to know. But King Alfieri heard of your little sport, and found it most amusing. It gave him, I've been told, the only hearty laugh he's enjoyed this month.

"When I heard that, I ventured to speak to a friend, who has friends elsewhere. Your joke has cost me dearly, Gareth. But there will be no judgment passed on you. If Sir Wyeth's heirs materialize and become noisome, I'll see they're paid for the loss of their relative."

"That means . . ."

"That means you'll not end before the King's Justice and . . . other, less pleasant places."

Gareth slumped back on the bed in disbelief.

"However, this doesn't mean that matters can return to normal," Pol said.

"Oh, nossir," Gareth babbled. "You can rest assured that I'll never again—"

"I am hardly referring to your choice of recreation," Pol said with asperity. "I'm saying that Lord Quindolphin has sworn revenge, and, since he knows whose kin you are, vows he'll go to any extreme to see you punished for making the wedding of his only daughter the joke of the city.

"I hope you didn't know she's considered a rather plain thing, poor lass, and was known to her friends as 'Hoggy.' "

Gareth grimaced.

"So there is no way that you could continue to live with me, let alone work in my factory, without having armed guards convey you everywhere, and my own house would have to be somewhat garrisoned. And I assume that would be of little good, since Quindolphin has far more men under his command who're familiar with blade and ball than I could dream of or pay.

"So Ticao and Saros are lost to you, boy, at least for a couple of years. I've already made arrangements for you to be taken from this prison after nightfall. We'll move quickly, and hopefully fool the lord if he's having this prison watched. You'll go directly to the port, and board a certain merchant ship as purser's assistant. Suitable clothing and gear is being purchased at this moment, and will be waiting for you aboard ship.

"You have found a most peculiar way to secure the position you were always hounding me for. But now you are for the sea.

"And the gods have mercy on you."

Four

Gareth's first ship was the elderly *Idris*, a small two-masted coaster, with two jib sails and a lateen sail on its foremast, a smaller lateen on its main mast, with a crew of twelve. The purser—Gareth's new master, Kazala—was also second mate.

Gareth was at the railing, marveling at all, as the *Idris* cleared the mouth of the Nalta River. He'd had nothing to do thus far, because the *Idris* was already loaded, carrying sacked potatoes to Adrianople, two weeks' sail distant to the south, away from the winter's gray and storms.

He was proud of himself for having no trouble with the *Idris*'s slow roll in the river current, having noticed a couple of hands bending over the side, "praying to the sea goddess," as one sailor put it. But they'd been noticeably debauched-looking when they put to sea.

Then the first ocean swell lifted the *Idris,* in a rather gentle corkscrewing motion. Interesting. Then another, and another. Gareth felt his throat knot, swallowed hastily.

The *Idris* hit a bit of chop, and the motion became a

seesaw, and Gareth lost interest in exactly describing the ship's motion.

He bent over the railing, feeling the entire world coming up, and heard a baying command:

"Boy, if y'puke on m' ship, I'll have the rope's end to your arse! T' loo'ard, dammit!" from the captain in the stern.

He staggered across the deck as ordered, and emptied himself.

Then another shout came, this from Purser Kazala:

"*Hern* Radnor! Below with you! We need to go over the bills of lading!"

He threw up once more, then stumbled toward the hatch.

Belowdecks it was thick, muggy, and Gareth suspected the *Idris* had carried fish not long before. Old fish. He tried to pay attention to the papers Kazala was busily stacking in front of him, felt his guts rising again.

"Don't throw up on the paperwork," Kazala warned him. "Here. Put this bucket 'tween your knees, and I'll get some dry biscuit from the dogsbody. Now, get yourself to work, for there's a hundredweight discrepancy between the factor's claims and what the watch logged as being loaded.

"Try to see whether we're being rooked or if the damned first mate just can't add.

"And stop looking so damned piteous! You think you're the first lubber who's gotten seasick?"

A day later, Gareth got his sea legs, and after that had far less trouble on sailing day, although, to his dying day, he had to busy himself with important work and think about other things when his ship first struck open water after a long time ashore.

* * *

The *Idris* dropped her sails when she came on a fishing fleet from the city of Lyrawise, capital of Juterbog, the sometimes-friend, sometimes-foe of Saros, about a day's sail across the Narrow Sea.

They traded casks of beer for bottled wine, fresh cuts of beef for salted cheeses, fresh produce for salted herring that'd been spell-cast to not only last almost forever, but keep the sailors of the *Idris* free of scurvy.

Then they sailed on.

Kazala, whom Gareth had thought the very model of rectitude, sat with a loaf of bread from the fishing smacks and a fresh cheese.

"This'll not appear on any books, needless to say," he told Gareth.

The boy supposed he showed a bit of shock.

"There's laws on the land," Kazala said. "They don't stretch to sea. We've our own articles afloat."

"Which are?"

"Unwritten and yet to be learned by you, boy. Yet to be learned by you."

Gareth went carefully up the shroud lines, not looking down, not considering how solid the deck below was, trying to keep thinking that it wasn't that far on up to the main yard. The big merchant ships he'd walked past back in Ticao had masts far taller. But that was then, and on dry land. He pushed the thought away, climbing with one arm through the shrouding, making sure of each step.

"Yer takin' all day," the hand hanging precariously on the yard above him said. "When th' skip wants all hands oop th' mast, there ain't no time for caution, y'know."

Gareth ignored him, kept climbing, scrabbled at solid wood above his head. He looked up at the seaman, sitting on the slanting yard holding on with one crooked leg, took a deep breath, and wriggled up beside him.

"Dam' glad you made it," the sailor said. "But y'want t' be careful wi' that hold you've got on th' yard. Don't be crushin' the wood, now, with y'r holt."

He laughed raucously, and Gareth managed a weak grin.

"Y' on firm, boy?"

Gareth nodded.

"Good. Now, get t' your feet . . . use the mast for a hold, and shinny on up t' the headrope's block an' give it a whack, hard 'nough so I can hear it."

Gareth gritted his teeth and obeyed, wondering what he was using for holds on the smooth wood. He reached up, and up, felt the pulley, hit it hard, just as a bellow came from the deck below:

"*Hern* Radnor! What the hells are you doing arsing about up there! We've got a weekly loss chart to make up!"

"'At's a pity," the sailor said. "An' we was just gettin' started." He slid easily from his perch and went hand-over-hand down a backstay to the deck.

Gareth made it back to the yard, decided the long slide could wait for another day, and began a cautious climb back down the shroud lines to his waiting, dreaded quill pen.

"All right, young Gareth," the first mate said. "Why do you want to learn about cannon? Assuming this pipsquirt of a popgun qualifies. Pursers, no matter how crooked they get, don't need guns, at least not at sea."

"Because, sir, I want to learn everything I can," Gareth said, wishing he didn't sound like some saphead in a romance.

"Hmmph," the mate said. "Why not? It's a slow watch,

anyway. Now, this gun's called a moyen. Any smaller, and it'd be a musket. Shoots lead balls, which is better than the stones our grandsires used.

"Big advantage a gun has, besides doing damage at a lot longer range than anything except a siege engine, is it takes a master magician to cast a spell to keep it from going bang. Almost as reliable as cold steel in a fight.

"Normally, the gun's kept lashed to the rail, like it is now. If we spot pirates, and we're stupid enough to want to fight, we'd unlash it so it swings free in its swivel, load it—which I'll show you how in a minute—and then use this little notched vee up on the barrel to sight through.

"Depending on how far away the enemy is, and with this little shiteroo it best not be far, you'll aim high or low.

"If 'twere a *real* cannon, like pirates and warships have, we could load with grapeshot, which is a lot of little balls, and aim at the enemy's crew. Or we could use chainshot, which is two balls with a chain, and try to take down a mast or unrig a vessel."

"But with the single ball this gun shoots," Gareth said, "what would be the target?"

The mate rubbed his stubbly chin.

"Actually, you *could* load with pebbles, and have small shot, and wait until the first boarder tries to cut through the nets we'd drape down, and then get half a dozen, if they were bunched up. Or maybe take down the captain, if you could figure out which one that is.

"Generally, though, with a single ball, and remembering that a lot of pirates come after you in spitkits, aim below the waterline, and hope you hole the bastard. Or, when they're close, pick a target on the quarterdeck—the captain, watch officer, or the helmsman.

"Better idea would be to run up a white flag. There's

enough ways for a sailor to die without getting involved in fighting, when there's always a white flag to be found.

"Unless," the mate said, "unless you're overhauled by a frigging Slaver. You've heard of the Linyati?"

"My parents were killed by them," Gareth said, and once more felt the pain.

"Then you know. Better to go down fighting if we come under their guns. Or grab something heavy and leap overside and drown yourself."

At Adrianople, they sold the potatoes and took on barrels of just-pickled beef for Irtysh.

At Irtysh, they made a small profit, waited for three unprofitable weeks, then filled their holds with crated chickens.

Some sickness struck the chickens that made them smash about their cages pecking at one another's behinds, and a tenth died.

They got rid of the chickens at Badakhshan, scrubbed the holds over and over again, Gareth swearing he'd never be able to look at either end of a fowl without vomiting.

Then they loaded bales of peacock and other exotic feathers for the rich city of Prim.

At Prim, the profit more than made up for the chickens, and they loaded, very carefully, pigs of smelted iron for Killis. Both the captain and the first mate hung over the stevedores to make sure the ship wasn't overloaded. Each pig was weighed, stowed carefully so there'd be no possibility of shifting, and the *Idris* sank lower and lower in the water.

Then they sailed on.

At Killis they lay at anchor for two weeks before finding a cargo, and the one they did find was a nightmare. A pair of magicians, hired for a small squabble by an island warlord, took passage, together with their acolytes and mistresses. Nothing was ever right for them, and finally the cook told them to shut the hells up and eat what was in front of them, or dig out their wands and magic up something better. After that, they could insert those wands in a convenient place. Sideways.

Gareth watched, holding his breath, waiting to see the cook turn into a pig or an albatross. But the sorcerers just swore at him, and growled their way up to the bow, where they brooded until the next meal.

But at least the *Idris* was sailing south, into warmer waters and steady trade winds.

South, ever south . . .

"Normally we don't even need this," the captain told Gareth, "because we navigate fairly close to shore, and take our bearings from landmarks, which I keep close in a book, like all navigators do.

"But when you're out of sight of land, you can get the altitude of a star using this astrolabe, which then, if you consult your charts, gives you latitude, longitude, even the time of day. You want to make sure, though, by taking a couple of sights and averaging them.

"Men make mistakes, and mistakes make wrecks," the man said grimly. "And wrecks are damned uncomfortable, not to mention unprofitable as a son of a bitch."

The soft wind brought jasmine, other scents across the night. The sand was warm under Gareth's bare feet, and strange flowering trees sighed overhead.

He could just make out the dark bulk of the *Idris* moored at the long pier behind them, where the lights of the small port gleamed.

Small waves phosphoresced onto the shore, and music

came, in a tonal scale utterly foreign to Gareth, from the thatched-roof pavilion they'd left.

He put his arm around the young woman, and she nestled closer, smiled up at him, long hair soft, brown skin like silk.

Gareth sighed happily. This was the first port he'd been allowed shore leave in, the first time he'd seen a flying fish skitter across the bows of the *Idris*, the first time he'd tasted tropical fruits. This was what had brought him to sea, the dream of tropic islands, calm under a warm sun, exotic under the night sky.

"Something wrong?" the girl asked.

"Nothing's wrong."

"Good," she said. "You be happy. You see. I worth every copper you paid. I know many things you not know."

Romance teetered. Gareth kissed her, hard, and the reality of the night's rental vanished.

Gareth sat quietly, listening, a bit out of the rope-yarn circle. He wasn't quite an officer, though certainly not a deck hand, which was one explanation for keeping himself apart. The other was that, growing, Gareth had always liked listening to the stories older people told, not the chatter of boys and girls.

The round of tales about the various ways the sea could kill you stopped for a moment, and Gareth chanced a question:

"What about pirates?"

"You hirin', or huntin'?" the seaman who'd helped him make his first mast climb asked. Gareth didn't answer.

"Pirates," another sailor said. "That's even a hard thing to put a label to.

"First, let's say there's two general kinds of pirates.

People-pirates and those godsdamned Slavers." He spat overside reflexively.

"Let's not talk on them," a third sailor said. "Even mentioning 'em's liable to be a summons."

"Damn, Jav, but you're superstitious," another said. "Not like a sailor, 'tall, 'tall."

When the laughter faded, the second man went on.

"So we're talkin' about human pirates, 'cause I'm about half doubtin' the Linyati are even people."

"No need to make 'em scarier'n than they are."

"Like I said," the man went on. "We're not talkin' about them.

"A pirate's somebody who goes out on a ship, and takes something that ain't his for profit."

"Shit," a sailor spat. "You sound like the king's judge, givin' th' law afore he hangs your young ass."

"Now, what's the differments," the second sailor went on, " 'tween a pirate and a navy sailor? The answer is there ain't none, but what one ship flies a country's flag, and the other flies a black flag, or none at all.

"One's ruled by kings and queens, and the other by brethren law."

"Don't forget privateers," a sailor put in.

"Wait," Gareth said. "What's brethren law?"

"When people set out to go a-pirating," the first sailor said, "they agree to certain conditions. Like the skipper gets, say, ten shares of any loot, the quartermaster gets ten, since he speaks for the crew, the ship's carpenter five, the gunners five, and us common deck apes one."

Gareth noted the word "us," didn't comment.

"Other rules, like if you loses a hand or an eye, you get a share on top, rules forbiddin' maybe gambling, maybe women, though that's foolish.

"Another thing is the men elect their captain. If he—

even she, sometimes—does well, he stays atop. If not, they kick him back to where he was an' try again with somebody else."

"Where do pirates come from?" Gareth asked.

There was general laughter.

"Now, don't breathe a word of this, boy," the sailor said, "but from the likes of you and me. Sometimes men have a bad cap'n, and they mutiny. Or sometimes men ashore steal a ship that's anchored, and take after honest merchantmen like us."

"And what happens when you're taken?"

"Gen'rly, not much of anything," the man said. "'Less you were a butthead, and killed some of their friends while the shootin' was going on. Then maybe you'll swim with the sharks. But normally you get a choice, join 'em or be set ashore somewhere, generally somewhere you can make it back to civil'zation."

"Join 'em," Jav said, "an' you've got five years t' run, on average. Then they catches you, and hangs you. Sometimes some navies, who's generally the folks who catch you, figure you should die harder than just a broke neck at the end of a rope. Hard cheese, 'tis."

"Sometimes," another man said. "But there's those who've taken some ships, and then disappeared off the sea. I've heard tales some of the lords upcountry in Saros got their start that way, paid off the King's Justice, and now their shit smells like attar a' roses."

"Somebody said something about privateering," Gareth said.

"Privateer's a pirate that's got the king or queen's warrant to go mess about with some country or people the king's pissed at this week," the second man explained. "This means, in theory, you get treated right if you get caught by whoever you're privateerin' against.

"So you goes out, and takes prizes, and then you and your crew get most of the profit, the king takes his cut.

"But you got to be careful. If you're too successful, the king's liable to disclaim your ass, keep the spoils all for himself, and send all of you to the gibbet. Or if the enemy makes peace with the king while you're out at sea and you come back, all piss and vinegar, on'y to find out that warrant ain't worth shit anymore, and there you are, goin' up the rope neck first, like before.

"'Tis a complicated world," the man sighed.

It was almost a year before the *Idris*, more battered than ever, sailed back upriver and tied up to a wharf in Ticao.

Pol Radnor and his wife greeted Gareth gladly, and hid him in a secluded bedroom. A day later, after Pol had a report from Kazala about Gareth's performance: "Hard-working, very curious, completely honest, but doesn't pay nearly enough attention to his sums," they held a quiet celebration.

Pol apologized for not doing a full-scale party for Gareth and inviting all his friends, especially their daughters, since he was now to be considered an eligible man, but Lord Quindolphin had neither forgiven nor forgotten.

"I'm afraid, son, that you'll have to go back to sea," he told Gareth sadly. "Unless you want to chance staying ashore, and I'll find a place for you on one of my estates, and there'll be no marrying for you for a while."

Gareth hid his sigh of relief about marriage, then noticed that the country estate was evidently one of several now. He happened to see a letter on Radnor's desk.

"King's Servant Pol it is now, Uncle?"

Radnor beamed. "Yes, yes. The King saw fit . . . the last list of honors . . . only a title, you know . . . but still . . ."

Gareth thought Pol's chest might burst his tunic.

"Well, then, uncle," he said, burying a laugh. "I don't appear to have much choice, and it's a rough life, sir. But I guess I'll have to sign aboard again."

He wondered what had happened to Cosyra, Fox, Labala, thought of slipping out and using the silver eagle he still kept hidden around his neck to track her, if the icon had indeed been given a spell.

But something stopped him, and so he took his second post aboard the trading hooker *Zarafshan*, two-masted, gaff-rigged, with two robinets, almost real cannon, and set out once more, this time voyaging to the frozen cities of the north, trading mostly for furs.

"Why," Gareth asked, "don't sailors use more magic than we do?"

The weathered boatswain nodded.

"Good question, lad, and the answer'll teach you more than just what the answer gives.

"First is that sailors are rank superstitious, and dislike having any greater wizardry than they're familiar with. You know how you don't whistle aboard, you don't talk about the land gods when you're afloat, and like that.

"All that's wizardry," the bosun went on, "and it's hard enough being afloat without extra magic. You ever sail with a magician aboard?"

Gareth remembered the two obnoxities on the *Idris* and nodded.

"Your skipper must've been braver, or more foolhardy, than most. Or maybe you were hurting for a cargo, eh? Still, not a good idea.

"Another reason is magic isn't precise."

"I don't understand."

"Did you ever figure why every damned piece of string

on this ship's got a different name? It's not to confuse lubbers, 'though that's not a bad accomplishment.

"Quick. Now, what's that rope up there—sight along my finger."

Gareth obeyed. "Why, one of the lower tops'l clewlines."

"A real specific name, right? So if I holler at you in a blow to haul away on it, you know just what to do? Everything on a ship's like that . . . got to be like that, or else there's confusion and maybe disaster.

"Magic isn't like that. I know. My sister's married to a man with some of the Gift, and everything's a pinch of this, and a beaker of that. How big's a pinch? I've got big fingers, bigger than yours, so a pinch to me's bigger, right?

"Not to mention that when a spell's cast, sometimes it works, sometimes it doesn't, and nobody ever knows why.

"Our provender's got stasis spells on it, so nothing spoils. But there's still a good portion of it that's just salt beef, pork, and dry crackers, like in olden times, in the event the spell doesn't hold."

"You've seen the captain pay for a fair weather spell already this voyage, and what did we get? Damned near dismasted. Now, when we make port, he'll have words with that wizard, and get his gold back.

"But that's magic. Vague, wiggly. And surely not to be depended on."

Gareth asked the captain why he'd insisted on treble payment to carry a cargo of basics—salt, casks of beef, seed, rolls of canvas, bales of cloth.

"Let's just say I'm not trying to turn a profit your uncle won't know about," the man answered shortly. "And I'm sure you'd like to know what's in those cases I've got lashed to the foremast, getting in everyone's way. Gods willing, you can ask that question in two weeks, and then I'll have an answer.

"But more likely, you won't have to ask."

Gareth didn't.

Their course led through a maze of small islands. Half a day after they entered the labyrinth, the first pirates, in craft almost as small as the *Zarafshan*'s boats, attacked. The captain ordered those mysterious crates opened by the watch on deck. Inside were muskets, powder, ball.

The watch below and all non-watchstanders like Gareth were turned to. Heavy cargo nets were draped loosely from the yards down to the deck, to entrap any boarders.

But they weren't needed. A volley was enough to turn the pirates away, and, hooting and swearing, they disappeared in the ship's wake.

The second attempt came the next day. Two larger boats, probably once fishing boats, tacked toward them. This time Gareth saw, with a thrill, the black flag cracking at mainmast of one of them.

Then he felt terribly sick to his stomach, worse than he had when the *Idris* first took spray over her bow.

Something strange was coiling up at them from the depths, some fabulous monster. A seaman screamed.

"Godsdammit, stand to your duties," the bosun bellowed, and again the muskets were loaded and readied.

But this time the two mates loaded one of the two robinets, swung it out, and aimed carefully.

Gareth just had time to see a man in dark robes in the bow of the leading ship when the robinet fired. The ball skipped water past the first boat's prow.

"Load grape, dammit!" the captain shouted, and the mates obeyed.

Gareth stared at the dark tentacles as they lifted from

the water and reached toward him. Then he shouted in pain as the bosun's rope end lashed across his shoulders.

"Eyes on your task, man," and anger rushed through Gareth, vanished as he realized the bosun hadn't even seen who he'd struck.

"Careful, careful," the captain was chanting. "Make sure, gentlemen, be very sure."

Gareth saw the tentacles pass through the shrouds, realized the horrid monster was a magical illusion, and the robinet went off with a thud.

There were shrieks from the first pirate ship, and the robed man threw up his hands, pivoted, and fell overside, where his boat passed over him. Other men where the wizard had stood were down, writhing in pain.

Muskets banged from the second ship, and a man beside Gareth said, "Oh shit," in a very surprised manner, looked at the red seeping, just at his waistline, then screamed and fell, clutching himself.

The other cannon was loaded, and the Zarafshan came about and sailed down on the pirates. They tacked away frantically as both cannon went off. The single mast on the second ship cracked, broke, and sail and shrouds fell overside.

Again the robinets fired, and smoke curled from the stern of the first ship, flames pouring out as the fish-oil-soaked wood caught.

"Bring her about," the captain ordered the man at the wheel, "and take our former course."

"Former course, east by northeast, sir, aye."

A third attempt was made on the Zarafshan—four small boats this time. The Zarafshan had just struck open water, and simply outsailed the pirates. But no one rejoiced.

The sailor who'd been shot had died.

* * *

Gareth had been out for a bit more than a year when he heard, in a smoky tavern, of the disappearance of the *Idris*. "Storm, maybe," the man who told him about it said. "But one of their crew—he went overside before they lifted the hook in Ticao—told me they had orders for the far south. Too damned close to the Slavers' land to suit him."

When he returned to Ticao, he thought about rubbing the icon and thinking of Cosyra, but then thought better. By now Cosyra—assuming she'd been an apprentice bawd or even a seamstress—would certainly have forgotten about him, and would hardly want to play childish pranks again.

But he didn't take the tiny eagle off the chain.

When the *Zarafshan* had a cargo lined up—worked fur robes Gareth might've traded for on his last voyage—he was very ready for the sea.

The woman was certainly not much better than a whore, for who but a harlot or a barmaid would chance the harbor quarter of Irtysh by night?

Still, whatever the three Linyati wanted with her, it should not have involved pushing, growled laughter, and the flashing hint of steel Gareth saw by the flickering taper over the taproom's entrance.

There was no one about, rain drifting across the streets.

"Stop!" he shouted, and the three Slavers turned. Their laughter grew as they saw only one man, a slender youth, outlined against the night.

One carried a sword on a low hanger. It whispered from its sheath. The woman saw it, shrieked, and darted inside the taproom. Not that Gareth expected anyone to come out and help. Not in this part of the city.

The Linyati with the sword started toward Gareth, the other two flanking him. One had a long poignard, the third a brass knuckleduster in his right hand.

They no doubt expected him to run, and would chase him down for ruining their sport.

Gareth stood his ground, feeling his breathing quicken, his vision close until there was nothing but the three men. His hand went to his back, came out with a sheeps-foot mariner's knife not a handspan long, without a point, but honed to a razor edge.

The swordsman laughed harder, closed on the fool. A lunge, the body tossed into the harbor, and they'd no doubt have a goodly tale when they returned to their ship.

He flicked a lunge, but Gareth wasn't there. He'd side-jumped to the wall of the taproom, where a small bench sat for outside drinking in better weather.

He had the bench in one hand, and threw it hard into the face of the man with the sword. The man tried to block, was too late, and the heavy wood smashed his face. He shouted, stumbled, fell back, his sword clattering on the stones.

The Linyati with the knuckleduster made the mistake of looking away, reaching down for the sword, and Gareth booted him headfirst into the wall. Gareth heard the crack of breaking bones.

The Linyati slid down it bonelessly and lay still; Gareth closed on the man with the knife.

The poignard may have looked lethal, but its tapering V-shaped blade was only good for back stabbing. The Slaver knew a bit, but only a bit, about knife-fighting, sidling in on Gareth with his free hand open as a block, the knife held on his hip, point up.

Gareth obliged him by slashing the man's palm open, leaping back before the poignard strike could land.

He circled toward the man's weak side, saw an opening, cut hard into the man's arm, saw blood drizzle down onto the wet stones.

Gareth stepped back, back again, as the Slaver came in on him. Then his foot slipped on some muck, and he fell backward, rolling left as the Linyati pounced. The poignard clashed against the paving stones, and Gareth was on his knees, cutting again, this time down the side of the man's face and deeply into his neck.

The Slaver cried out, rolled on his back.

Gareth got up, breathing hard. He stared down at the semiconscious seaman, saw the blood drain from his body.

If I was a proper bastard, he thought, I'd save the maybes and cut his throat.

But he couldn't bring himself to it.

He wiped the blood from his knife, sheathed it, and disappeared into the night, back toward the *Zarafshan*.

This wasn't the first time he'd fought the Linyati, always remembering his parents' bodies, sprawled in their looted house.

A thin, almost invisible scar now ran from the corner of his mouth up his left cheek, disappearing in the hair above his ear, a souvenir of one encounter.

After that, he'd spent more time offwatch in the foc'sle, learning more than seamanship from the hardbitten sailors. He'd learned to swing a cutlass, fight with the unpointed knives seamen carried, to use a marlin spike, a broken wineglass, almost anything that could be found on a ship's deck or—more often—in a tavern, for a weapon.

The Slavers were getting cockier, bolder. More and more, if a Linyati ship was in port, there'd be a brawl. None of these fights was ever friendly, and most Sarosians had taken to carrying some sort of weapon when they went ashore.

And there were more and more Slavers at sea. Not in Sarosian ports, where they were not met with friendliness, in spite of King Alfieri's continued policy of peace. But they had a dozen or more countries allied with them, which Gareth couldn't understand. Doing business with demons, or men little better than demons, would always end in disaster.

Gareth had been to enough lands now to learn where the Linyati traded their human cargoes. He'd even chanced, when he could, asking these slaves if they were from Saros, but so far all he'd been met with was uncomprehending looks, fear, and, occasionally, the muttered name of another country or city.

He remembered, long ago, a beggar telling him the only way to deal with the Linyati was at swordpoint. He wondered if, with this new round of raids against Saros and its neighbors, enough would finally be enough, and someone would declare war against the hated Slavers.

If anyone did, he thought, he'd find a way to join that expeditionary force.

He knew there was a time coming to stand and be counted, when the allies of the Linyati would also be forced to make a reckoning.

The *Zarafshan* rode the cresting tide up the Nalta, through the center of Ticao. Gareth stood in the bows, feeling more tired than he thought possible.

It had been a good voyage, at least until the last port. Some sort of disease had struck down the purser and both mates. Gareth had not only taken over the purser's duties, managing the unloading and sale of the cargo, but negotiated for a new shipment for Ticao: ensorcelled trinkets he knew would go for a high price when Saros's nobility saw these new toys.

Then he'd stood watch on, watch off with the captain on the three-week voyage home.

During the long sleepless hours, he found himself

thinking of Cosyra. He vowed, if the damned *Zarafshan* didn't fall apart under him, or if he or the man at the wheel didn't fall asleep and the ship go at full sail onto a reef, that this time he'd attempt its magic, find out just what had happened to the woman. She'd be, what, seventeen to his eighteen, almost nineteen?

When they'd entered the Nalta River's mouth, the captain had sent a boat ashore to the semaphore station, to signal to Pol of the voyage.

Gareth was holding hard, counting the yards left to go as the *Zarafshan* dropped all sails but one and turned toward the Radnor factory. As soon as the mooring lines went across and the damned ship was tied firm, he'd hire a carriage to his uncle's house and sleep for a week.

No, two weeks.

There were people waiting at the quay. There was his uncle, surprisingly his wife, Priscian, some servants, and two men, strangers, waving wildly.

Then he recognized the strangers, grown though they were: the last survivors of his native village, Thom Tehidy, a bigger barrel than before, and Knoll N'b'ry, his quick-witted companion.

Fatigue fell away.

Just let him get his feet on solid land, and then there'd be a time to remember!

Five

I did not expect to see either of you again," Gareth said, feeling a little drunk, although, unlike the others, he'd had nothing but charged water with his meal.

His uncle and aunt had cheerfully invited Thom and Knoll into their home, although Gareth thought he detected a slightly quizzical expression from Aunt Priscian over his friends' stained working dress.

They'd eaten lavishly, after Gareth had bathed and ordered his sea clothes to be burned. Then Thom had suggested they go out, seeing Gareth's uncle hiding a yawn.

"That might not be too wise," Pol said, before Gareth could answer.

Knoll had lifted an eyebrow.

"A couple of years ago," Gareth said, "I did something pretty dumb, and I've got a certain lord upset at me."

"Which one, if I might ask?" Knoll asked. "For since we've been in Ticao, we've learned there's some to walk most small among, and others, generally the biggest blowmouths, to never worry about."

Pol had given Gareth a look, signifying he'd said more than enough.

But Gareth cared little for secrets, then or ever.

"Lord Quindolphin," he said. "I loosed pigs at his daughter's wedding."

"Mmph," Thom said. "That's bad, for he's a vengeful bas— pardon, Lady Radnor, not a nice man at all. His son's worse, and they carry goons about with them like body lice, ever ready to do their bidding, as long as it's bloody-handed."

"But we know a tavern," Knoll said, "where not Quindolphin, nor his kin, nor his swordsmen would dare enter."

"Then why should a boy like Gareth be safe?" Priscian asked. Gareth concealed a wince. She would probably always think of him as a babe, even if she lived to see him as a graybeard.

"Which tavern would that be?" Pol asked, interested.

"The Slit Nose," Thom said, a bit proudly.

"I know it," Pol said. "A place of thieves, rogues, villains—"

"And watermen," Knoll said. "Which is what we are."

"I've not been in a public house like that in . . . twenty years," Pol said, just a bit wistfully.

"And well you shouldn't," Priscian said. "A King's Servant, soon to be a Merchant Prince? Highly out of his station."

Pol smiled gently, didn't reply, and, not for the first time, Gareth wondered about his uncle.

"Come, then," Thom said. "I fancy a rough pint, and I see your family's a-yawn, and we keep no one up past his bedtime."

Gareth wondered why he hadn't collapsed two hours ago, nose into the meat pasty, but still felt fully alert.

His friends made their thanks for the meal, were told

there would be a proper feast in the next few days celebrating Gareth's homecoming and that they were more than welcome.

It was a spring night, but there was a chill coming off the river. The three pulled their cloaks about them, and Gareth noted Knoll's was more than a bit threadbare.

Taking side streets, they went to the waterfront, then down a noisome alley.

"Follow the screeches," Thom said, "and you'll never get lost."

The Slit Nose's door yawned open into the night, and music and singing shouts echoed around them. They were about to enter when two men stumbled out, swinging broadsides at each other.

"Here, now," Thom said cheerfully. "Mark your target and ignore the innocent."

One of the men broke away and swung at Tehidy. Thom lifted him by his collar, and tossed him over his shoulder to thud into a stone wall.

"You want to play, too?" he asked the other brawler, who shook his head rapidly, ducked under Tehidy, and was gone.

"I see you've lost none of your strength," Gareth said, as they went through the crowd to a table where only a drunk snored, his head in a pool of wine.

Knoll unceremoniously pushed him onto the floor, whistled shrilly through his fingers, and a barmaid saw him.

"Aye, m'love," she shouted over the din. "The usual?"

"The usual . . . and some iced water?"

"You've not bathed?"

"For my friend here the virgin."

The drinks arrived. Gareth noted that Thom sat with his back against a wall, and Knoll half-turned, to watch the room.

"My uncle told you all of me," Gareth said. "It's your turn now."

With Thom interrupting, when he thought Knoll wasn't being properly fulsome about himself, Gareth learned the two boys had indeed been taken in by another village.

"But 'twasn't like our own," Knoll said. "They thought they'd brought in a couple of servies, almost slaves."

"Busting our ass in the fishhold with the nets," Thom agreed. "And with not a share in the price, but only a handful of coppers and a bit of silver now and then."

But that hadn't been the worst. The village was one of those who owed tribute to the king, and the tribute was paid with two young men, every year or so, for the navy when the impressment officers came along.

"Even if you hadn't been so down on serving the king," Knoll said, "there were enough time-served men in the village with their tales of shipwreck, wormy biscuit, and battle to discourage us."

"'Twasn't the wreck and battle so much," Thom put in. "'Twas that when they were used up and washed up, the king's service threw them out without a coin, without a pension, without anything except the clothes on their back, to make their way back home, and sit damned near begging at the door. Not like pirating, where, if you're lucky, you can walk away from the sea with gold and jewels, eh?"

"Naturally," Gareth said, "you two being outsiders, the minute you got old enough for the king, you were the target."

"You've lost none of your quickness of wit," Knoll said. "And so we ran, ran to Ticao, figuring there'd be chance enough here for everyone.

"There's chance, for certain," he said, a bit gloomily. "Just enough to keep you from starving, not enough to make you rich, and there seems to always be someone in the way."

"Like the godsdamned Waterman's Guild," Thom said. "It's not satisfying to them for us to learn the landings, and the river, and the current, and find a boat that somebody'll sell you at ruinous rates, and then make it pretty so men and women with gold'll sit on your cushions and let you row 'em back and forth and up and down.

"No. You apply to the Guild, and in their own good time, perhaps they let you in. Or perhaps not. In the meantime, you can starve for all of them. Or work the downriver landings, where there's never any custom."

"If they find you pushing your way in at a landing where good fares await," Knoll put in, "they're not above stoving your boat in, or pushing you overside, or even tapping you along the head with a pig of iron and seeing if you can float all the way downriver to the ocean. Face-down."

"Not that they've ever tried any of that shit on us," Thom said grimly. "A couple thought they could, back six months, when we first went on the river, and found themselves wet and overturned. And then, when they thought all was settled, somebody waited on them at their slip and wanted to carry on the discussion."

"But that didn't make us any better loved by the Guild," Knoll agreed. "So we're keeping ourselves fed . . . but look at our clothes. Hardly the finest, which is what attracts the big custom. And our boat could do with a haul out and re-caulking, which we can't afford either."

"And we sure aren't living in a mansion, either," Thom said, then brightened as he upended his jack of ale, and signaled for another. "But if there's beer in the cask, all can't be bad."

"Still, Ticao is far better than being in that damned village," Knoll said, "hauling fish from now to the grave."

Tehidy turned somber.

"Perhaps. Perhaps. But I'll still never forget what drove us out of our homes."

"Of course not," Knoll said. "Once, maybe twice, I thought I could sneak up on one of those damned Slavers and give him swimming lessons. But once the man got away, and the next time there were too many of them, even though Thom said once we got among them they'd think we were a throng."

"I've done a little good in that direction," Gareth said, and, without heroics, told them of his crusade. At the end of his story Tehidy, good humor restored, roared laughter.

"Good, good, Gareth. And it's better seeing you, and seeing how things are going so well for you."

Gareth started to say something that, now he knew where his friends were, things'd be better for them, as well. He had more than a sufficiency of gold saved, and thought N'b'ry-Tehidy Water Ferrymen might benefit from a silent partner.

But that could wait until later.

They talked of other things, including the specifics of what had driven Gareth into his odd form of semi-exile, and Gareth found himself telling them of Cosyra and the charm.

"Damn me," Tehidy said. "That's romantic. And you haven't used the spell?"

"No."

"Why not?" Knoll said.

"I'm ... not sure," Gareth said. "Maybe I'm afraid it won't work ... or that it will, and I won't like what it shows me."

"Reach down," Thom said, "below your belt. Between your legs."

"Why?" Gareth said.

"Just do as I say, dammit!"

Gareth obeyed.

"And what do you feel?"

"Why . . . my balls, of course."

"Good!" Tehidy said. "Thought you'd lost them for a minute. Don't you think it's best to bang 'em together and see what happens?"

Gareth drank water, and nodded slowly, twice.

"It is," he said. "It surely is."

It took Gareth a time to discover how the sea eagle charm worked. At first, he thought Cosyra's wizard had tricked her, and taken her money without providing any service. But then he realized when the eagle's beak was pointed in a certain direction, the amulet warmed. Turned away, it grew instantly cold.

Gareth had waited to make the test for two days, while his body finally wreaked revenge, and he did nothing but eat and sleep.

After sunset on the fourth night, he put on a dark cloak and started out. Then he'd stopped, remembering his enemy—who, most ironically, he'd never even seen—and borrowed from his uncle's extensive armory a short-barreled pistol with a bore almost as big as two of his fingers together. He loaded it, lit the slow match and covered it, and went out into the windy night.

He assumed his quest would lead him toward the river, and possibly even across, into the slums. Instead, the eagle's beak led north and slightly west, toward the great hill which was crowned by the king's castle.

Gareth lost his way twice, following the eagle instead

of the twisting alleys and ending against solid stone walls. He retraced his steps, and then the eagle grew warm, warmer.

He looked about, realized he was in a wealthy district.

If the charm is working, and is real, he thought, *Cosyra is not a whore. Perhaps a scullery maid, or even the daughter of a servant.*

A single lane turned off the road, and the eagle "pointed" in that direction. He followed, until he was stopped by a wrought-iron gate, cast with odd animals and plants climbing up it.

On the other side was a cobbled yard, a gatehouse, and an imposing mansion four stories high, with turrets and a glassed widow's walk atop it that would give a view of the entire city, save what the royal castle above blocked.

There were lights on inside, and lamps flickering in the wind, stronger at this height.

It was quite a house, something a great lord might own.

Of course Gareth wouldn't disturb the household at this hour. But by the gods, he would not give up, and would return on the morrow and ask the head of the household's servants about Cosyra.

Quite a house indeed, he thought, and turned, when a voice came from the shadows beyond the gate:

"It took you long enough."

He jolted, and a slight, cloaked figure came out.

"Cosyra? How did you know I was coming?"

"When I had the charm magicked," she said, "of course I had a small ring linked to it.

"But you didn't answer my accusation, Gareth Radnor. What took you so long?"

"I, uh, was at sea."

"Not all the time," she said.

Gareth decided the only option he had was to tell the truth. There was a silence when he was through, then a tinkling laugh.

"You *really* thought that I'd be a staggering doxy, or else a married barmaid with a dozen lovers?"

"Something like that."

"Well, I'm not."

She stepped into the lamplight, shed her cloak. Cosyra had been a beautiful girl, now she was a woman. She still wore her dark hair short, she hadn't grown more than an inch or so, and she was still small-figured. But she was very, very lovely, lips soft, inviting, eyes smiling.

Gareth noticed all this . . . and something as important. Cosyra wore a multicolored blouse that looked like heavy, raw silk, and black pantaloons. At her wrist were bracelets, each reflecting the lamplight in a different color. No servant could ever afford such clothing or baubles.

"As long as you're listing my stupidities," he said, "add in that I've just figured out that you're not a maid or a servant's daughter here."

"No," she agreed. "This house is mine, or rather held in a trust from my mother until I reach adulthood. Would you care to come in for a glass of mulled wine? I assume, you being a sailor now, you're still not a slave to that vile habit of drinking water."

"Actually . . . yes. I still am."

"I thought you would have learned its evil by now," Cosyra said, as she touched the gate here, there, another place, none of them specially marked, and the gate swung open. "Fish piss in it.

"But come on. I think there's some water about. It rained night before last, and I don't suppose all of it's run off yet."

* * *

Gareth told Cosyra of his voyages and asked what she'd been doing.

"Not much," she said. "Being noble, going to horsy events, masked balls and such. Which takes up all your time, even if it uses none of your mind.

"I've not," she said with a sigh, "been pranking or doing anything useful since that night."

Gareth stirred his tea with a cinnamon stick, chanced asking of their friends.

Cosyra made a face.

"Of that great hulk Labala, I know nothing, although I've searched the waterfront for him. As for Fox, he was taken by the watch for theft and had his hand cut off, that being the third time he'd been found out.

"The wound didn't heal quickly, and he decided his life as a thief was over, which meant life itself was done. I found out the inn he was staying at two days after he died. At least I could pay for proper burial ceremonies, although I'm not one of those who believes the gods give a broken nail about their creations."

"Damn," Gareth said sadly, then caught himself for uttering a rare profanity. "I beg your pardon."

"Why?" Cosyra said. "There was worse said when the watch was chasing us. What should have changed now that you see my proper circumstances, which you must know I had nothing in arranging. I am still Cosyra, gods damn it!"

Gareth looked about the huge dining hall once again, at the portraits of stern men in armor holding swords, of women, some young and pretty, some older and imperious, the paintings of land and sea between them, swords, spears, daggers here and there. On the far wall was a great, constantly turning Wheel of Life. Those who could afford it, and the incantations that made it spin, swore it brought the best of luck.

They were the only two in the room. A servant had listened to Cosyra's commands, nodded without speaking, and, in a few minutes, returned with a goblet of wine and Gareth's tea.

"Five years ago," Gareth said, still recovering from the surprise of Cosyra's station, "I would have never thought I'd ever see a manse such as this, although I'd dreamed of it."

Cosyra sipped her wine without lifting her gaze.

"It must be nice to have dreams," she said softly. "Instead of knowing your life is quite planned."

Gareth waited.

"That was why I went out on the streets," she said. "It was—is—very clear to me that my fate is graven in stone. I'm to be a perfect maiden, stay a virgin, and one of the noble bees that swarm about me—or rather, swarm about what my dowry is expected to be—will take me to wife.

"I'll then have how ever many children he wants, stay close at home, save when we go out for important occasions, while he's allowed to do as he pleases, with mistresses, battles, travel to strange lands . . . whatever.

"Marriage . . . marriage . . . *phaf*!"

Gareth decided to change the subject.

"You said you and your mother live here."

"Lived. My mother passed on three years ago."

"So there's just you in this monstrous heap of stones?"

"Except for eighty-seven servants of various callings. I have an executor of the estate, a certain elderly lord, who keeps me from harm, especially self-intended. Some of the servants are, of course, his agents, so I can get away with little mischief.

"But friends of mine call, and we go out. They all, of course, are noble, but some have a bit of spirit, and we're able to get into trouble.

"Not any as exciting as you led me into," she added.

"You've made no mention of your father."

Cosyra reddened a little, and her lips tightened.

"I'm sorry," Gareth said hastily.

"No, no," Cosyra said. "You had no way of knowing. My mother was even more a free spirit than I am. She chose not to marry."

"Oh."

"She had lovers. Ten, maybe twenty. She kept no diary that I've been able to find. One of those lovers, I know not whether he was noble like she was, was my father. I know nothing of him, and my lord the estate manager swears he knows nothing either.

"All of these noble beards and growing ladies," she said, motioning to the pictures, "are of her relatives. Her line went far back in the history of Saros, supposedly to the first man with a piece of jagged flint who held it at his fellow's throat and announced he was better, and the other had best acknowledge it if he didn't want two smiles.

"The story has it we built on this hill even before the king of Saros did. So of course it's expected of me to marry and carry on the tradition. Perhaps one day I'll get my portrait hung on one of these walls, looking properly pissed."

"Well . . . do you *have* to do just what's expected?" Gareth asked. "I mean, you slipped out with us. Couldn't you, if you wanted, go out of Ticao, into the country?"

"And not have anyone follow me? Not have anyone name me as Lady Cosyra of the Mount, whereupon I'd have to deal with all the tintibullations as my executor huffed and puffed and dragged me back to my proper station?"

"You could try."

Cosyra looked at him thoughtfully.

"Perhaps you're right. Perhaps I could at least attempt something like that, instead of sitting here feeling sorry for myself."

"I didn't mean to be critical."

"Why not?" Cosyra said. "Everybody else seems like they know how to live my life better than I do."

Gareth, uncomfortable, stood, reaching for his cloak.

"I'm sorry," Cosyra said. "That was an unwarrantedly bitchy thing to say.

"Gareth, I'm very glad that you're doing so well with your uncle, and glad that your voyages have been successful. Believe me, I've kept track."

"Thank you."

"I'm just tired," Cosyra said. "I didn't sleep well last night."

"I'm sorry."

Cosyra shrugged.

"It was a long, deadly dull night to begin with. Too much of it spent with someone who, by the way, is not your friend."

Gareth waited.

"Anthon, Lord Quindolphin's youngest son, fancies himself a great one for courting." Cosyra hid a yawn. "I've not told him, of course, that the highest I think of him and his family is what we did to his sister's wedding. Which, naturally, I've made no mention of."

Gareth slowly shook his head. This damned Quindolphin family seemed hells-bent to weasel into his life from every direction.

Cosyra seemed to read his thoughts.

"I'd rather marry that sister—or, for that matter, one of those pigs—than him."

"I'm truly glad of that," Gareth said, and put his cloak on. "I really must go. But may I see you again?"

"Any time you wish," Cosyra said, leading him to the door and opening it. The night wind . . . no, early morning now . . . whipped around her. Gareth went past her to the steps.

"Gareth."

He turned, thought for an instant her green eyes were glowing in the night.

"It is *very* nice to see you again."

He started to smile, and she leaned toward him. On a step higher, she was just at eye-level.

"Very nice, indeed," she said softly, and her lips brushed across his.

Then the door closed, and the gate stood open. He went through it, and as he did, the lamps guttered down into darkness.

Gareth Radnor went down the cobbled streets, not feeling the wind, or the chill.

He knew there could be nothing, of course, between a merchant's nephew—a seagoing clerk—and someone like Cosyra. And of course, as young as he was, he hardly wanted complications and ties.

But he slept well that night, and woke with a smile on his lips.

"Have you considered your next undertaking?" Pol Radnor asked politely over breakfast.

"No, Uncle," Gareth said, buttering a roll over a yawn. He'd been late again at Cosyra's—talking, no more. She'd kissed him that first night, but not again in the three times they'd seen each other.

Occasionally he caught her looking at him with a slightly puzzled expression, which vanished when he turned to her.

He took a bite of the roll, added relish to the slice of ham, cut a fragment.

"I suppose I'll go to sea again in the next few weeks, after I've finished eating your larder bare."

"You'll never manage that," his aunt said.

"Any ideas on what ships, or what ports you'd prefer?"

"Something warm, I think," Gareth said. "That one trip buying furs still freezes my blood. But nothing more specific's occurred to me."

He didn't say that he was thinking of Knoll and Thom, wondering if they'd be interested in going out, wondering how he'd manage to find a berth for them on the same ship, since he still wasn't exactly a hero of the seas, someone a captain would make any concession to sign aboard his ship.

"I find this discussion interesting," Pol said, his face as bland as if he were negotiating for a cargo. "Perhaps we should continue in my study."

"Let me suggest an alternative to returning to the sea," Pol said, without preamble.

"Your aunt is concerned that we've been unsuccessful thus far in having children, in making sure the Radnor name goes down through the ages."

Gareth was a little embarrassed at this frankness.

"Be that as it may, I pointed out to her that you've advanced rather remarkably since you came to live with us. Of course, you've still got more than a bit of wildness, but then, who of us doesn't when we're young? That will pass with time.

"Let me make a suggestion, which will have nothing to do with whether or not Priscian and I have children, for there's more than enough business in this world to richen an entire clan.

"Rather than go back to sea, I would be willing to pay your way for a full course at one of the best seminaries: Tuil, Frenk, even Winhope, although that's most pricey."

"Me, a priest?"

"There are many, many sects, as you should know, many of them not requiring vows of silence, withdrawal, celibacy or diet," Pol said, a bit impatiently. "That should not be a factor in your decision.

"As a licentiate, you would be not only knowledge-able in culture—which never hurts a businessman, as I've never tired of saying—but familiar with the ways of business and managing people, almost as thoroughly as if I purchased you an officer's warrant in the military.

"Better still is the people you'd meet at such a seminary, lifelong friends who'll help you in your rise, just as you'll assist them.

"With such training, you'd be more than competent, after some years of seasoning, of assuming responsibility for all that I've been able to build, now and in the future."

Gareth gaped, thinking about being his uncle's heir. Then he thought on, thought of years—how many he didn't want to think—of listening to dry, dull voices rasp through dead facts and theories. And then, out of the classroom, associating with those whose every decision would be based on how it could benefit them. He repressed a shudder.

"Uncle," he said, seeking the right way to put things, aware of what an enormous gift he was refusing, "I'm afraid the sea has ruined me.

"I don't think I could sit making notes from a book, or checking a ledger when the wind comes sharp off the ocean, and I could hear the gulls' scream and the distant sound of water."

Pol took a deep breath. "I'm not angry, nor even surprised," he said, but his voice was heavy with disappointment. "That was the real reason I fought to keep you ashore: to keep you from hearing the call of the sea, for all too many friends of mine have heard that gull song, water dance, and the land's promise vanishes for them, and they've no need for safety, comfort, or wealth.

"Most likely I was not being honest with myself from the first day you arrived, for growing up in that village might have already . . . no, I will not say ruined . . . worked its way with you.

"Very well, very well," Pol said. "So that's that, at least for the moment, and you'll be seeking a ship. Since you've evidently not decided whose articles you might sign, perhaps you might go to North Basin. There's a new ship, just finishing fitting out, named the *Steadfast*. A little too sleek for a real carrack, but with room enough for a good cargo."

"Where's it bound?"

"The captain's named Luynes," Pol said. "You might be interested in talking to him."

Gareth, eager to be away from this uncomfortable scene, stood quickly.

"One thing, though, Gareth," his uncle said. "Do us a boon, and don't tell Luynes that you're there at my request."

"Why not?"

"Just call it a favor of the moment. Depending on what you think of the man and his ship, I promise I'll give you a full explanation."

Gareth realized his uncle wore an unfamiliar expression: stealthy cunning.

* * *

The *Steadfast* was round-hulled, about one hundred feet long, a quarter of that wide. It was a three-master, fore- and main mast square-rigged, the mizzen mast at the stern, with a lateen sail. Gareth noted a spritsail could be rigged under the bowsprit. He thought, in a cross sea, with its bluff bow and evidently rounded bottom, it would roll like a drunken bitch. But it probably could come close ashore in shallow waters, which was a virtue for a trader.

Gareth saw with some surprise there were four guns on the main deck, each a demi-cannon, eleven feet long, and with a bore almost seven inches in diameter. Those long guns would be hard to load in a seaway, but were longer-ranged than the usual drakes merchantmen carried, more suited for a warship. Gareth concluded the *Steadfast* was intended to go into troubled waters.

In the bows, above the main deck, was a fairly small foredeck, and here were a pair of swivel guns. Astern of the main deck were two higher decks, the quarter deck the ship was commanded from, and above that, just over the stern, was a sterncastle, again with two swivel guns.

Interesting.

There didn't appear to be anyone aboard ship. Gareth went down the wharf, stopped at the gangplank of the *Steadfast*.

"Ahoy the ship."

There was no reply, and Gareth hailed again.

A hatch opened, and a man came out on the quarterdeck.

"Permission to come aboard?"

"Granted."

The man came down the steps to the main deck as Gareth went up the gangplank, dropping down onto the main deck between the two guns. The ship smelt new, of tar, just-aged wood, fresh cordage.

"The name's Luynes," the man said. "Captain. Yours?"

Luynes may have been one of the best-looking men Gareth had ever seen. His hair was dark, worn medium-length, his face square, honest-looking, his eyes penetrating blue. He was tall, taller than Gareth, and built like an athlete. His smile was open, friendly.

"Gareth Radnor."

"A relation of King's Servant Radnor?"

"My uncle."

"Ah. Then you're the purser's man who brought the *Zarafshan* home. A handy piece of work."

"There were others aboard," Gareth said.

"I like a modest man full well. Come into my cabin, Gareth Radnor, and discuss what brings you to the *Steadfast*."

Gareth followed Luynes up the companionway and into his cabin. It was fairly large, but outfitted rather spartanly, with a big desk, a chart table, a boxed-in bunk large enough for two people, a dining table, chairs, two cabinets, and a pair of seachests, very battered, securely tied to a pair of ringbolts in the deck.

"A brandy?" Luynes asked.

"No thank you, sir," Gareth said. "Water if you will."

Luynes looked surprised. "A sailor not drinking, and the sun's well up?"

Gareth smiled. Luynes started to pour himself a dram, hesitated, then set the decanter down and poured his cup half full of wine from a different container and watered it.

He nodded to a chair and sat down behind his desk.

"I'm looking for a berth," Gareth said. "A friend said you might be sailing into interesting waters."

"A friend, eh? Your uncle?"

"No, sir, although he had nothing bad to say about you or the *Steadfast* when I told him my intentions."

"He shouldn't," Luynes said. "He made me a loan, at a ruinous interest I might add, that helped me finish fitting her out. And I suppose, when I return to Ticao, he'll be one of the most interested bidders on my cargo."

"Which will be?"

"Spices," Luynes said. "Your spy told you true. I intend to sail far east, through Linyati waters, to certain islands I've learned about in my travels.

"They have spices beyond any allspice, cinnamon, ganta, whatever, that the luxury markets hawk. One voyage through hazardous waters and I—and those who sign on with me—will be rich for life. That's why I ordered the holds of the *Steadfast* configured differently, with bulkheads that can be moved to create a larger or smaller area, depending on what we choose to load."

His eyes shone.

"That's also why the guns?" Gareth said.

"It is. There are natives in those isles who like men from the sea but little."

"What about the Slavers?"

"Mostly I do not worry about them, having had . . . acceptable, if not joyous, relations with them. But there are exceptions, for the Linyati are an independent race. If we can't outsail those folks . . . as you said, there are the guns, and I doubt if they'd think us worth the trouble.

"For one thing, I'll sail with a large crew. I want forty hands aboard when we cast off."

Gareth whistled. That was almost double what the ship would require to sail.

"Yes, *Hern* Radnor, I've thought things out full well," Luynes said. "And I've already begun provisioning, which is a sore pain, for I intensely dislike having to deal with figures and merchants and fear I might be swindled or, worse, buy garbage that is bad in the barrel, despite the expensive spells I have cast about them."

"I know reliable magicians for that task," Gareth said.

"I don't doubt you do, Radnor, for you have a bit of a reputation, surprising for someone as young as you are. Indeed, I have no purser nor assistant yet signed aboard."

"I would be interested in the position of purser."

"Ah. Ambition."

"Why not?"

"Why not indeed," Luynes agreed. "Without it, we'd all be no better than the cook's punk."

He mentioned the wages and benefits of the side, which Gareth found quite satisfactory.

"One thing I insist on," Luynes went on. "When you sign the articles, there's one that reads you're to give me absolute obedience. If you disobey in battle, you can be punished as I see fit. If you disobey at other times, you'll be chained and put ashore on the first land I deem habitable, whether it's a known port or not."

"A hard rule," Gareth said.

"I expect hard times," Luynes said.

"That seems fair," Gareth said. "I've seen one near-mutiny."

"Not on a ship of mine," Luynes said grimly. "The rope's end to the back or the rope around the neck as soon as trouble bodes keeps that from men's minds."

His smile was a bit unpleasant.

"You said you wanted to sail with a large crew," Gareth asked. "Are you still signing on crewmen?"

"Hells yes," Luynes said. "Either the pimpsy doodles are feared of my destination, or they've got a chance to go aboard a coaster and sleep safe ashore every night or the godsdamned navy has impressed them."

"I know two men," Gareth said. "Neither have blue-water experience, but they're both fishermen, now watermen here in Ticao."

"Ah?" Luynes said interestedly. "My mates and bosun can teach anyone to scamper up a mast. It's a damned sight harder to train someone in a small boat. Anyone who's managed to stay alive on this tidal-damned river is someone I'd welcome aboard, assuming there are no other problems, and there aren't that many king's warrants on them."

"No problems, no warrants," Gareth said, got up. "In two days, no more, sir," he said, "I'll return with my answer to your offer."

"You're a careful man," Luynes said, as he escorted Gareth back to the dock.

"Thank you, sir," Gareth said, touching his forehead.

"Now," Knoll N'b'ry said, wrinkling his nose at the reek as he bailed the wherry's bilges, "hasn't it always been you who led us into schemes?"

"Not true," Thom Tehidy said. "I was the one who found that old wreck of a fishing boat down from the village."

"It was," Knoll agreed. "But who was it who said we could fix it up and make a killing in the crab market? I won't talk about who almost got us killed the first time we dropped a pot too close inshore."

"But didn't I see that wave first, and turn the boat into it?" Gareth said.

"Aye," Knoll said. "So I should ignore who got us in the breakers in the first place?"

"Sweetest crabs are closest to shore," Thom said. "Everybody knows that. But I'm not sorry we turned to long-lining."

"This damned discussion has gotten a long damned

way from whether we're going to let Gareth press us into serving on this carrack that's going trading into mysterious waters, where we're likely to get ourselves killed," N'b'ry said.

"Or worse—trapped by those damnable Slavers, to end with an iron collar around our necks."

"That'll not happen while I can still lift a fist," Tehidy said firmly. "And isn't that a plus, now, giving us a better chance to revenge ourselves on some of the bastards besides hoping one of them hires us to take him across the river and it's dark enough so nobody raises a cry when we boot his ass overboard?"

Knoll's smile vanished, and he sat thinking, or perhaps looking back a few years. Finally he nodded.

"Yes," he said. "Yes, there is that."

"So that's a decision?" Gareth asked.

"Wonder what we can get for the wherry," Tehidy said, and the matter was settled.

"I did, indeed, loan Luynes some money when he ran short, as most ship masters do when they become ambitious and venture into building their own bottoms," Pol said. "He paid it in full thirty days ago, from a long-term grant another factor made him."

"Why, Uncle, didn't you want me to say I was there at your behest? To make me appear less your puppet?"

"I wasn't being that solicitous of you," Pol said. "Look. There are many of us here in Saros who, while thinking the world of King Alfieri, do not think his temporizing with pure evil—I refer to the Linyati—is particularly wise."

Gareth looked at his uncle in surprise.

"Yes, Gareth," Pol said. "There are those who have opinions, even hatreds, we don't find necessary to advertise publicly. Sometimes things like that are best held close, until a moment offers itself."

Gareth nodded in reluctant agreement.

"The problem is, almost nothing is known about the Slavers, about their native lands, about that great continent of Kashi joined to Linyati to the west-southwest, to the spice islands Luynes mentioned far to the east of the Linyati. We also know nothing about their allies and their main customers for slaves.

"It's not possible that they're making a great profit off their pinprick raids in Saros or other countries in the north.

"So somewhere there are, if you will, fields for their human harvest, just as there must be large markets. I have a particularly disgusting theory that the slaves they take and sell may be being used up in terrible ways. No, not necessarily screaming sacrifices on the altars of dark magicians, although I'm sure there's a market there.

"There are worse—or, rather, better—ways to use up mankind. Working men until they drop under a hot tropic sun, or in mines where the air isn't worth the breathing, or in jobs like diving in shark-infested waters for pearls or other gawdies."

"Oh," Gareth said in a small voice, never having thought much about the Linyati other than wanting them dead. Then he recovered a bit.

"Uncle, perhaps you'd best tell me more about Luynes."

"There's not much to tell. He claims to have come from northern Saros, where his family owned half a dozen coastal traders. He says he got bored, took his inheritance and signed aboard a ship headed for distant waters.

"Interestingly, unlike most sailors, he's never been heard to brag of his voyages and the strange people and creatures he's encountered. But he has done well for himself over five years, always to the south, which suggests to me that he's a man of uncommon skills and cunning. Or . . ."

"Or he's made an alliance with the Slavers," Gareth said.

"Just so. Another interesting thing is that he has about half a crew of regulars: men, hardbitten men, who prefer to sail with him, and are as close-mouthed as he is about their destinations and cargo."

"Interesting," Gareth said, and there *was* interest in his voice. Pol smiled, recognizing it.

"Now, like any normal man, I love a profit. So when you decided you didn't wish to become safe, rich, and comfortable, I thought I could provide you with all the adventure you could use."

"As your spy."

"I would not noise that about," Pol said. "You'll be under suspicion as it is, being my nephew, if our good captain has more than one fish on the hook.

"Oh. By the way. Your aunt thinks I'm terrible for letting you go in the way of such danger."

Gareth smiled happily.

"I can think of no nicer present you could have given me, Uncle."

"And I'm glad to have you, Gareth," Captain Luynes said heartily. "For there's many a matter I'd rather delegate, what with this new ship and its ballasting, rigging, and such that's still not right.

"As for your friends, I'll sign them on as well. By the time we return, they'll have enough experience to call themselves seamen.

"You'll be worked hard from now until we sail, for

I've finally gotten the proper connections for the best trading cargo."

"Men are such pond scum," Cosyra said fiercely.

"Well . . . yes," Gareth said uncomfortably. "I mean, I guess so. But why in particular right now . . . and why me?"

"Because not only do you set up the rules for the world, but any time they get uncomfortable, you can run off to sea, or to war, or . . . or to anywhere you please."

"Right," Gareth agreed. "You see a lot of peasants saying padiddle to their lords, and running off to be bandits. Or sailors deciding they want to be landed gentry. Or the lost ones in the Slavers' clutches saying they want to be free."

"All right," Cosyra grumbled. "So there are limits. But you must admit women are even more constricted than men."

"I do freely," Gareth said. "And the minute I'm the king's advisor, I'll have a word with him about that."

Cosyra wrinkled her nose.

"You're determined not to let my bad mood affect you."

"I'm determined," Gareth agreed.

"All right. I'll give up on being a grump. It doesn't fit right, anyway. And besides, you've got a present to open."

Cosyra reached behind the couch they were sitting on, took out a long bundle, and gave it to Gareth. He opened it and found a sheathed sword.

"You'll notice," Cosyra said, "no jewels or geegaws to make some other sailor lust after it. A nice sensible blade-length, straight, double-edged. Double pommel, short, with upturns to catch an enemy blade, not long enough for you to get caught. Ratskin handle, pierced, so sweat won't let the sword turn in your hand.

"That's a nice, sensible murderer's blade, or so the armorer I consulted advised me. Together with a sensible belt, sheath, and a matching dagger."

Gareth was barely listening to her description. He drew the blade, made a few passes in the air, a parry, a jump-lunge.

He tried the edge with a thumb.

"It's sharp," Cosyra said, as he yelped and sucked on the small cut. "And you're dumb."

"This is . . . quite a present," Gareth said.

"It's been given a spell for greater strength, and against ever rusting, since it's layered steel," she said. "Now, give me a coin, for blades must never be given as presents, or they'll cut the bonds of friendship."

"Superstitious wench," Gareth said, digging a coin from his purse. "Here."

She stood to get it, and he pulled her into an embrace and kissed her. It was supposed to be just a grateful sort of kiss, but lasted a bit longer than he'd intended.

Eventually, she pulled back.

"My, sir. You presume."

"I . . . I sort of guess I did," Gareth said, a bit breathless.

"You could apologize by doing that again."

He did, and the kiss lasted somewhat longer. This time, it was Gareth who broke the embrace.

"This isn't a very good idea," he said.

"It isn't?"

"It might give me an idea beyond my station."

Cosyra's voice went flat.

"It might . . . and we both have enough problems without . . . without, well . . . oh the hells with them. Kiss me again, and then I'll throw you out before either one of us can start thinking about there being nobody in this house who could stop things from . . . from doing whatever they might do."

Gareth obeyed, and it was very hard to break away.

"Perhaps tomorrow, instead of your coming up here, I should meet you in a public place, or at your uncle's."

Gareth took a couple of deep breaths.

"Surely. Surely." He looked at her for a long moment. "Don't you hate being so damned sensible?"

"I do . . . and get out before I stop!" Cosyra said.

"Your supplies are doubly, trebly, bound," the small man in rather resplendent robes bragged. Captain Luynes looked at him skeptically.

"Your pardon, *Hern* Perekop," he said, "for I don't mean to be either rude or skeptical. But I've sailed out other times with my comestibles magicked until they squeaked. Yet somehow, after some time at sea, and more significantly being a-port where other spells had been cast, things started spoiling."

"You should have no fear of that from *my* wizardry," Perekop said, a bit pompously.

"My purser here has said his uncle's used your spells with success," Luynes said thoughtfully. "That counts for something. What other spells would you suggest?"

"If you're willing to spend a bit more," Perekop said, "I could also cast a grand spell against the fraying of your cordage for half a year."

Luynes looked surprised.

"That's something that could be useful. Why haven't I heard of that before?"

"It's something I've newly developed," Perekop said. "Of course, it's a bit expensive, and for a new ship of this size I'd expect, oh, ten pieces of gold."

"Five," Gareth broke in reflexively.

"Nine."

"Five."

"Eight."

"Five."

"Shall we settle at seven?" the magician said.

"Settled," Gareth said.

Perekop bobbed in satisfaction.

"It's an excellent spell, indeed it is, using dwarf nettle, elecampane, rare spices I grow, exotic incenses and words of power from the west. As with my other spells, I fully guarantee the results."

"Excellent," Luynes said. "For I have a regrettable tendency to call on those sages who've disappointed me, at a later date. And some men say I have a temper that tends toward the extreme." No doubt by accident his fingers touched his knife, a rather long, curved blade useless as a mariner's tool.

Perekop licked suddenly dry lips.

"I'll doubly seal these spells for you."

"Then I'll be doubly pleased."

"We are loading an interesting cargo," Gareth said.

"Ah?" His uncle looked curious.

"Lead ingots as ballast in the bottom of the hold, which as I've told you can be modified into several different sizes, which I've never seen before.

"The real cargo began arriving today. Crudely fashioned cutlasses first, then long knives that could, Captain Luynes said, be used, like the cutlasses, in harvesting tropic fruit."

Pol Radnor snorted amusement.

"Then came long cases, which were marked as holding pipe. Luynes was very interested in seeing they were loaded well for'rd, where a port inspector's not likely to note them.

"Being your spy, I waited until he was called ashore on other business, found a prybar, and opened one of those cases."

"Spears? Crossbows?" his uncle asked with a bit of a smile.

"Worse," Gareth said. "Muskets. Cheaply made, but still . . .

"Later, we loaded cases of iron tools—which actually were tools, needles, blacksmithy and carpentry gear—and then, most carefully, for'rd in the paint locker, barrels of gunpowder."

Gareth had expected surprise from his uncle, got none. Pol sat, stroking his chin thoughtfully. "It appears Captain Luynes intends to seek out trouble," he mused. "His lading suggests he will go into strange, primitive waters in his quest for spices.

"Don't look alarmed or shocked, Gareth. In my earlier days I, too, was known to send weapons out, praying that the coastal guard wouldn't search the ship. Remember that such cargoes are just legal, even though frowned on, and generally subject to seizure until the situation clarifies itself.

"Unless, of course, it's one of the king's own ships taking weaponry to, ahem, support our allies. That also keeps any of our neighbors from being able to grab such devices for their own use.

"Hmm, hmm. It would appear to me, Gareth, that you may indeed expect adventure from this cruise."

Gareth suddenly found the situation funny, and laughed very hard. When his mirth subsided, he shook his head. "If this were a romance, Uncle, shouldn't our roles be reversed?"

"Of course," Pol agreed. "That's why the foolish, or those who dislike the sharp bite of reality, seek out such trash.

"And aren't you home from your duties early?"

"There was nothing more to load," Gareth said. "We'll board the final items, plus our water and fresh supplies, tomorrow.

"Captain Luynes has set the sailing date for the dawn tide, the day after tomorrow. Tonight I plan to dine with . . . with a friend."

"Where are you taking me to dine?" Cosyra asked.

"A pub named the Heron and Beaver," he said. "They understand fish there."

"You mean, speaking in their tongues and such? How magical." Cosyra giggled, tucking her arm in his. "Let us try not to fall on our butts as we go downhill. Hardly dignified for a rising young officer of the merchant marine and his doxy."

"Doxy?" Gareth asked. "Virgins aren't doxies."

"I've been thinking about that," Cosyra said. "Perhaps, if you ply me with wine, and a fine fish stew, with brandy afterward, when we return to my house, I might choose to invite you in.

"After all, the day after tomorrow you *are* bound for distant shores, where all men carry deadly weapons against you, and all women are seductive sirens."

"I am?" Gareth said. "Tell me again about those seductive sirens. Ouch! That hurt!"

"You are certainly a goatbrain at being romantic," Cosyra whispered.

Gareth turned serious.

"I . . . I know. It's sort of hard to look at somebody

who was a friend, someone to jape with, and then change her into something else."

"There's the problem between men and women," Cosyra said. "We never seem to be able to think of friends as lovers."

"I wouldn't know," Gareth said. "Not having the benefit of a noble education."

"Hmmph. Well, for starters, I would suggest you think of eating oysters."

"I'm shocked," Gareth said. "Rough seamen like myself hear of such things, but not chaste ladies of the court."

"You'd be surprised how few of *them* there are," Cosyra said. "And, truth be told, all I know about oysters—besides their taste, I mean—is what my friends giggle and whisper about."

They'd reached the waterfront, and stopped under a flickering lantern.

"Perhaps," Gareth said, "here's a better place to start with romance, before the oysters."

He kissed her. After a while, she pulled her lips away, breathing a little hard, and was about to say something.

"Get away from that bastard," a voice grated from the shadows. Cosyra let out a little squeal, and spun as four men came out of the darkness.

"Lord Anthon!" she said. "What are you . . . were you following me?"

"I was," one of the men said. He was slender, taller than Gareth, a year or two older. He wore elaborately dyed silks. A sword hung from his side. His face was sharp, his lips pinched over the scraggly beard he was trying to cultivate. The other three wore plainer but still expensive clothes, were also armed.

"Now I see what company you prefer to mine," Anthon said. He looked at Gareth.

"You are Gareth Radnor, the one who shamed my sister," he said. "My father has sought you long, and will be delighted that I'll be the one who revenges our family name this night."

His hand went to his sword, and it flashed in the torch-light.

"You'll kill me where I stand, without a weapon?" Gareth said. "Brave indeed."

"You and you, take him," Anthon said. Gareth's hands came up as the two henchmen came closer. He struck with his right, full weight behind the blow, taking one man below the ribs. Air chuffed from the man's lungs, and he bent. Gareth snapped another blow into the side of the man's neck, and he fell back, gurgling.

But then the other two men had him firm, one on either side.

"Very good," Anthon Quindolphin said. "Very good indeed."

"Anthon," Cosyra said, "you cannot do this!"

"Oh, but I can," Anthon said. "No damned commoner can be permitted such liberties."

"If you don't stop right now I'll make sure your cowardice is known throughout the court," Cosyra said fiercely. "And you'll never be permitted to call on me again!"

"What makes you think I'd want to call again on someone who's proven herself no more than a sailor's whore?"

Cosyra stopped, frozen for an instant.

"Now," Anthon gloated. "We'll start with your face, Radnor. Hold him secure, fellows."

Anthon stepped closer, and the shining point of his sword was just in front of Gareth's eyes.

Gareth collapsed forward, limp—then, held by the surprised toughs, lashed both feet up into the nobleman's crotch.

Anthon howled, and his sword clattered to the cobbles. He clutched himself, bending, straightening, yelping. The two holding Gareth relaxed their hold long enough for him to regain his stance, rake one foot down one man's leg to smash the arch of his foot.

The man shouted, let go, and Gareth half turned, hit the man still holding him in the cheek. The man grunted and let go of Gareth.

Gareth danced free, and the third man was in a fighting stance, fists ready. The first man stumbled to his feet. "We'll get the little bastard," he managed, a knife coming from nowhere.

"Kill him," Anthon managed, panting. "Kill him now and throw him in the godsdamned river!" He staggered about, clutching his groin. The second man hobbled in, a short truncheon in his hand.

Cosyra had Anthon's sword in her hand. "Get away from him!"

The third man had a sword out, dagger in his other hand.

"Sir?"

"Get the damned sword away from her," Anthon ordered. "Don't kill her unless you have to."

The man half smiled, came in on Cosyra.

Gareth was looking about for a weapon as the other two henchmen closed.

Then the darkness bellowed rage, and a very big man with wild-flying hair came out of the darkness, waving a long balk of lumber.

One tough's attention was broken, and Gareth was inside his guard, hitting him as hard as he could, very quickly, three times in the face. The man stumbled back, and Gareth clubbed him down with his fists clenched together.

The man with the truncheon swung at Gareth, missing, and the hairy monster smashed him over the head. Gareth heard his skull crack.

Cosyra lunged with Anthon's sword, blade going home in the swordsman's arm. He screeched, dropped his sword as Cosyra recovered and lunged again, her blade going to the hilt into his thigh.

The man screamed again, turned, pulling the sword from Cosyra's hands. He ran, hobbling, into the night, paying no attention to his master.

Anthon Quindolphin looked at the huge man, ducked under his swing with the wood, and scuttled away, half-bent.

The big man threw the wood after him, heard a thump and a shout of pain.

Then there was nothing but a corpse, an unconscious man, an angry, beautiful woman, Gareth Radnor and the monster, under the lamp.

"I had this *Feeling* I hadda be here," the huge one rumbled.

"Labala!" Gareth said. "It's you! Where . . . how . . ."

"Come on," Cosyra said. "We'll do jolly reunions later. The watch'll be coming in a moment. Back for my house!"

Gareth heard the shouts, the clatter of boots on the stones, saw the flash of lanterns, and the three ran hard.

By the time they reached Cosyra's mansion, her anger had grown into a cold, deadly fury. She summoned her castellan and gave quiet orders. His face showed rage as well, and he hurried away.

Moments later, horses galloped through the gates, and other servants tumbled outside, armed with swords, crossbows, and a scattering of pistols.

About that time another servant arrived with a tray with hot tea, brandy, and other drinks.

"Just in case that mad son-of-a-whore's-get has an idea you might be here," she told Gareth, "my men will back him off. And I've sent for a detachment of the King's Guard, which I was told long ago owes my mother's family."

"What about the man I slew?" Labala said.

"I doubt anyone'll bring that up, but if they do, I can vouch it was self-defense."

Labala nodded. "But can we be sure they'll believe . . . oh." He finally seemed to realize what sort of house he was in.

"Sorry, lady."

"*Dammit!* Why does everybody keep doing that?" she snapped. "It's still Cosyra!"

"Mmmh," Labala said.

"I think," Gareth said, "I'd best, when things clear up a bit, go for my ship. Since the only way Quindolphin found me was by trailing you, he can't have any knowledge of the *Steadfast.*" He grimaced. "But that'll not let me say farewell to my uncle."

"Nor," Cosyra said, "to eat oysters."

Gareth managed a wry smile. Labala's eyes brightened.

"You were going to eat oysters? Damn, but that'd be a fine feast, after an outing and playabout like we just had."

Cosyra giggled.

"Never mind, Labala," Gareth said. "I'll give you silver for a bait of them if you want, later. But first, what was that you said about a 'Feeling'? And can't you brush that mop off your face?"

"Gives me what they call statyur," Labala said, but raked a paw through his hair until they could see most of his face. He drank off his glass of spirits, licked his lips.

"Not my style," he said. "Don't suppose there's any beer about?"

Cosyra signaled for a servant.

"What's this stature?" she asked. "What are you now? Or should I ask?"

"I'm sort of a magician," Labala said. Gareth choked on his tea, got scowled at.

"Don't laugh, Gareth, or I'll sink you. My family, back when they lived in the Eastern Isles, before we come to Saros, generally had some witch in the blood.

"Just after you got took by that lord, giving us a chance to flee—for which I thank you and'll thank you again—I went back to work, stevedoring, and was down in a hold, loading grain, which is dirty and kind of dangerous, especially if the bastard on the winch lets a net slip.

"I was in the hold, as I said, tossin' bags around, and I got this *Feeling* that we better move. I called out, everybody scampered, and a cable went and dropped big heavy bags of grain all over the place, but nobody got killed or anything.

"That made me think, and if I see that damned grin again, Gareth, I'll blat you one, I swear and vow. So I hunted me up a witch, and she showed me some simple spells, and damned if they didn't work for me.

"So I been doing that, casting fortunes along the docks, which sometimes is right, sometimes wrong, maybe a love potion for one of the whores. Making a little gold, some silver.

"An' then tonight I got a real strong sense I better be somewhere, and I saw your faces in my mind, and so I come as fast and hard as I could."

"Saving our lives," Cosyra said. Suddenly she turned pale, said, "Oh dear," and sat down very quickly, almost missing the chair.

Gareth was beside her.

"I . . . I just . . . realized I never stabbed anyone before," she whispered. "It's not at all like fencing, is it?"

Gareth had his arm around her, pulling her against him, feeling her shake. In a few moments the shaking stopped.

"I'm all right. I think," she said. "But maybe some brandy?" She drank it down as they heard the clatter of a dozen or more horses in the courtyard.

"That'll be the King's Guard," she said. "I'll have them take you to the *Steadfast*, and make sure your uncle knows where to go to say good-bye."

"I best be going too," Labala said, upending his mug. "I don't need none of the kingsmen, but perhaps I better have myself hid out for a couple of days, since nobility takes shit like we did seriously."

Gareth was looking intently at Labala. "You really like what you're doing? Being a fortune-teller and all?"

Labala shrugged uncomfortably.

"Better'n heaving big bags of stuff around, I guess."

"I know a ship," Gareth said, "that's looking for crew."

"I dreamed, off and on, of going to sea, like my family used to do, before we got stuck here in Saros," Labala said. "But I never had anybody stand good for me."

"I'll do that," Gareth said.

"Mmmph," Labala said. "That might be all right. See some of the world and all. Gareth, I'll go with you. Maybe we'll have a chance to do some more foolery, like we used to."

"Maybe," Gareth said. "When we're ashore, but not aboard ship."

Labala shrugged indifference.

Gareth turned to Cosyra.

"I'm sorry."

Cosyra made a face. "There'll be other times for oysters."

"You promise?"

"I promise," she whispered, lips parting as she came to him.

From the *Mercantile Posting*:

The carrack Steadfast, 220 tons, Captain Luynes, cargo of trading goods, from North Basin, for Nalta Mouth and beyond, under sealed orders.

Six

The *Steadfast* sailed east-southeast, past Adrianople, Prim, Killis, other cities Gareth had traded with, into the tropics.

Gareth found a new pleasure—seeing friends enjoy something new, things that he'd already discovered: the constant tradewind that now was cooling, instead of freezing the sailors; the blue skies and rolling oceans; the taste of unfamiliar fish netted from the stern yard and grilled on a charcoal brazier and drenched in lime juice; floating coconuts fished up, split and their milk drunk, still unspoiled by the salt water; the warmth of the sun; the soft skies that welcomed a dreamy night watch.

Tom and Knoll learned shipboard routine readily. Labala seemed to have a little trouble at first, but his constant cheerfulness and enormous strength kept him from making enemies.

Gareth watched with amusement. The thought came that he needed but one other friend here to be utterly content, and that brought his mood crashing down.

Cosyra, just a friend? Of course not. He didn't want to sleep with his other friends. But was just basic lust all of it?

He was afraid not, but he refused to countenance love. Love was an anchor, a millstone, that held you back, and tied you to staleness and the land.

Not that he had any particular reason to think that Cosyra was in love with *him*, of course. He knew lust wasn't an exclusively male emotion.

But this made him brood further, about what he wasn't sure. He tried to pay attention to his accounts, which, considering the hidden cargoes, was a little complicated. Gareth was more than happy to be called on deck by Captain Luynes.

He realized it must be a serious matter when Luynes told the deck officer he'd take the watch and took Gareth on up to the deserted stern castle.

"This man Labala," he said without preamble. "You wanted me to sign him aboard."

"Yes, sir. Is there anything the matter with him?"

"Other than he's a godsdamned magician, nothing. Did you know he's a spellcaster?"

"Yes," Gareth admitted. "He told me he played about with some small pieces of wizardry when he was a longshoreman."

Luynes growled.

"I do not like magicians aboard my ship."

"No, sir," Gareth said. "Most seamen don't seem to, either. But I've sailed with them, and had no trouble. Besides, Labala's not much more than a witch, really. Love potions and so forth."

"I'm not being superstitious," Luynes said. "I've a particular reason to not want wizards on the *Steadfast*."

Gareth waited, but Luynes didn't seem inclined to explain.

"Look at him," he said, pointing. "Up there in the foresheets, probably working up some casting or other. You go talk to him, Purser, since you're his friend. Tell him I'm not pleased, for my own reasons, and he's to refrain from any witchery while he's aboard the *Steadfast*. If he's wise, he'll take my warning, and not need any further . . . attention from me."

Gareth remembered the oath of utter obedience in the articles, said, "Aye, sir," and went for'rd to where Labala leaned over the railing.

"And how's the lad?" Labala asked. "All white and like from bending over the accounts, making sure none of us've stolen an extra herring?"

"Better than you," Gareth said, repeating Luynes's orders.

"Superstitious, he is."

"He said there's a good reason."

"Just bein' captain's reason enough for him, I'd guess," Labala said. "And just when I was starting to get some good ideas.

"You know, Gareth, last night, I came up in the dog-watches, and the mist was swirling about the deck like ghosts dancing. And a spell came, and I started saying it, and those fog-ghosts started dancing to it. I think, with a little thought, I could move a whole harbor full of mist."

Gareth shivered. "Maybe the skipper's got a point."

"Aarh, you're superstitious too. It wasn't ghosts, just bits of water-smoke, obeying what I called it to do. Ghosts are another, entirely different thing, which I'm not proposing to fool about with.

"Not yet, anyway."

Labala sighed. "And coming up with new words and

thinking about handling things like water, and fire, and smoke, made the watches pass a lot faster, too. I just wish I could read and cipher, so I could keep track of my ideas.

"But, thinking that maybe the Captain's got enough of the Gift—or somebody on his side does, anyhoo—I'll cut my sails closer to the wind."

He jabbed Gareth in the ribs with an elbow. "Catch that, matey? See how I'm gettin' as nautical as all shit here?"

Gareth recovered his breath painfully. "Gods, Labala. Can't you just make your point with words?"

"And words are what I'm no good at," Labala said. "So you'll have to live with what I am, won't you?"

The next day, Luynes ordered all hands to learn how to fire the ship's cannon. We *are* going to sail into trouble, Gareth thought.

He was grateful that he'd learned all he could on his first voyages. He, and Thom Tehidy, seemed to have a certain talent with the cannon, able to range in on the crates they threw overside for target practice within a shot or two.

Luynes made Gareth a gun captain.

Another thing Gareth found unsettling was the way the crew behaved. Some knew little of Luynes, but a bit less than half of the men had sailed with Luynes before.

These experienced sailors, and this included the two watch officers and the bosun, held their experience close, sharing it with none of the newcomers, as if it was some sort of pleasurable but shameful vice they practiced secretly. Some of these men were not much older than Gareth, but all were most experienced seamen.

Even offwatch, yarning, they didn't mingle with the others.

Gareth asked one of them, when the man had the helm and Gareth was the only other one on the quarterdeck. The man looked innocently wide eyed, and said, "Why sir, it's not that we've secrets or anything. But you should know by now how people tend to hold back when they're around fellows who're yet untested."

Gareth knew that, nodded understanding. His doubts might have vanished if he hadn't seen the way the man looked at him an instant later, under his brows, his expression calculating, shrewd.

The two watch officers were Kelch and Rooke. They were highly experienced, but they seemed more like prison warders than sailors to Gareth, even though they never laid a hand on any seaman. The bosun, Nomios, wasn't much better.

Gareth was glad that he had three completely reliable friends, and hoped he was just being overly suspicious.

A week south of Killis, Luynes ordered the crew to gather on the maindeck, save the helmsman and a single lookout.

Luynes clambered atop one of the cannon and stood looking about for a moment, thumbs hooked in his breeches, appearing very satisfied with the world.

"All right, now," he said. "I'm proposing to finally tell you where we're bound, and what our intentions are. Some of you, who've sailed with me before, have a good idea, for we've dabbled in these cargoes before."

"We're not bound for spices, then?" one of the new men asked.

"That'll be the cargo we finish up with, when we finally sail back north," Luynes said. "And it'll make us all as rich as I promised.

"But first, we'll be loading goods damn' near as valuable.

"Men," he said. "Men and women."

"Slaves?" someone asked, and there was a ripple of amusement from the older hands.

"Slaves it is," Luynes said. "I had the *Steadfast* purpose-built for them. She's shallow-draft, which is why she rolls so bastardly. But she'll be able to cruise up the rivers of Linyati and Kashi—that's the other half of their continent—and take on cargoes the raiders who go into the interior after the natives will bring to us."

"Which," Knoll N'b'ry said, "we then take to the Linyati?"

"Exactly, boy. That bother you?"

"It does, sir. First, I don't like the idea of doing business with the Slavers, second I don't like being a slaver myself."

Mutters of agreement came from some of the crewmen.

"Well," Luynes said, "ain't that tough titty. You signed aboard to follow my orders, remember?"

"I signed aboard," Knoll said stubbornly, "to learn to be a sailor, and trade for spices, I thought. Not to be a murderer."

Rooke the mate growled, and Knoll set his jaw firm.

"You're not going to be murdering anyone, boy," Luynes said. "You'll be going up and down the mast, pulling ropes, standing your watch. What we've got under the hatches, now and later, is none of your damned business."

Knoll was looking at Gareth. Gareth moved his head, very slightly, sideways. N'b'ry looked stubborn, then forced blankness.

"Aye, aye, sir," he said, but his voice still was stubborn. "I'll follow orders."

"Damn' right you will," Kelch snapped.

Labala started forward, then stopped.

"You have something to say?" Luynes said.

"Nossir. Things is just surprisin' to me."

"The only surprise you should concern yourself with is how much more gold you'll go ashore with when we get back to Ticao," Luynes said, and there was laughter and agreement.

"Now, back to your posts. Purser, I want a word with you."

Luynes waited until the crew dispersed, then:

"And what do you think your uncle would think of that?"

"Not my concern, sir," Gareth said. "He's a long ways distant, now isn't he?"

He gave Luynes a gaze of straightforward innocence, and hoped the rakehelly would buy his lie.

"I sort of figured you'd feel like that," Luynes said. "That's why I signed you. I figured any man with ambition like you've shown wouldn't worry overmuch about the laws of a faraway place, particularly when he can get rich by being a pragmatist. Most of the world doesn't agree with this namby-pamby shit anyway.

"Shitfire, Gareth, I'll bet that half the peasants in Saros are nothing but slaves, what with their duties and oaths to their lords and estates."

Gareth thought that was likely true, but the lowest scut at home still called his soul his own.

"Now give me a hand with something."

Gareth followed Luynes into his cabin, and the man opened one of his seachests and lifted out a cylinder wrapped in rags. He unwrapped it, and Gareth saw a very strange-looking lantern, with ornate carvings on it.

"This," Luynes said, "is our safe passage among the Linyati. It took damned near a week of negotiating, and a bit of gold, before they were willing to trust me with it."

Luynes took the lantern on deck, and to the mizzen mast. Now Gareth noted the mast had four climbing steps on it, and, above them, a clever metal hook.

"Hold the lamp for me."

Gareth took the lantern, and Luynes took flint and steel from his pouch. He opened a small door in the lantern, and struck sparks, muttering a few words in a language Gareth didn't know.

"Now, if you'll hang this up there . . ."

Gareth obeyed. There was no heat to be felt at all, and he saw no flame within.

"I think it went out, sir."

"It's fired," Luynes said. "The light it gives is hard to see, except by certain eyes. But we'll be able to make it out by night."

And truly, when it grew dark, a strange, greenish glow illuminated the helm and the men on watch.

"I'm damned," Thom Tehidy said, "if I'll go a-slaving."

"Nor me," Labala said, and there were whispers of agreement from the half-dozen new men around Gareth and his friends. It was the third watch of the night, and they were on the main deck, near the stern, hidden by the main deck above and the bulk of the covered cannon next to them.

"But what choice do we have?" a man asked. "We signed the articles, and I believe if we don't follow Luynes's orders he'll likely bash in our pates with a marlinspike and toss us to the sharks.

"I've never known a slaver before, but I don't think anybody who is, is going to worry a rat's tinkle about somebody like me."

Knoll N'b'ry nodded somberly. "You're likely right. I

saw the way that sheepshagger looked at me, and was damned grateful Gareth gave me that 'shut your lip' look."

"Gareth," Tehidy said, "you've just been listening. What're your thoughts?"

"First is we've got to keep this short," Gareth said. "We don't know if the skipper or any of his friends have any of the Gift for eavesdropping—"

"Not likely," Labala interrupted. "I went and figured out a little spell that should make anybody interested think we're just wondering about the change, and not thinking of doing anything about it."

"Which is pretty true," another sailor said. "What *can* we do?"

"Start with the numbers," Gareth said. "Twenty-five of the forty-one men aboard have never sailed with Luynes."

"But that doesn't mean a good number of 'em won't follow him," a sailor said.

"That's probably true," Gareth said.

"First choice we might have is jumping ship when we make the next port," a sailor said.

"Won't work," Thom said gloomily. "I was polishing the binnacle, and keeping my ears open, and heard Kelch and Rooke talking about the next landfall, and how they're looking to cut loose with some of the slave women they can rent. I wouldn't guess a port that's got slave whores is likely to treat an antislaving swab very kindly."

Gareth nodded.

"Luynes told me, after dinner tonight, we'll be docking for water and fresh provisions at a city called Herti. He told me it isn't one of the Linyati holdings, but it might as well be. He'll be meeting with his Linyati lords for sailing orders.

"A sailor without a ship in a port like that could be

well in danger of getting chained up by the Linyati, I'd guess."

Gareth unconsciously touched the scar on his face. "That's not for me," he said, and saw nods of agreement.

"Second is we can try to seize the ship."

"Mutiny," someone whispered.

"A hanging offense," Labala said. "Even I know that."

"And Luynes hasn't done anything illegal," Gareth said. "There's nothing that I know of on paper about our real trade. And he could probably make a good case, even if he admitted to being a slaver, that we were obeying lawful orders having nothing to do with our cargo."

"The King's Admiralty courts back in Saros *always* back the officers," a man said. "I've seen men hanged along the waterfront for mutiny."

"As have I," Gareth said. "But let's say we could take the ship."

"The odds are close," Knoll said.

"No," Gareth said. "Not if we could take down Luynes and the mates. If we've a leader and a plan, the other men and the bosun will follow us."

"How can you be so damn' sure?" Tehidy said.

"I don't know why I know it," Gareth said quietly. "But I do." There was a sudden touch of steel in his voice.

Tehidy looked at him in surprise, then pursed his lips thoughtfully.

"Assuming all that's true," Thom said, changing the subject, "we're still deep in unfriendly waters. Isn't that weird light you helped put up signaling the Linyati that we're on their side, Gareth?"

"That's what Luynes told me," Gareth said.

"Slaving," a man said. "It's bitter to the mind and the tongue."

"You're right," Gareth said. "But all I can think of

right now is for us to let a little time pass, and maybe a better alternative will crop up."

"You mean *an* alternative," Knoll N'b'ry said glumly. "Right now, we've got none at all."

Gareth woke to the thump of running feet and the shouts of the crew. He pulled on pants, started out of his tiny cabin, then buckled on the sword belt Cosyra had given him and went on deck.

Standing close on either side were two Linyati warships, low, black, rakish hulls with red lateen sails, three guns on a side, two more in the prow, and two sternchasers. The rails were lined with Linyati sailors, some with belted cutlasses, others with ready muskets.

Gareth went to his gun, found someone had already yanked the canvas cover off, and moments later one of the hands trotted up with a stand of balls and another with bagged powder.

"Stand by your guns," Kelch shouted from the quarterdeck. "But don't load. Yet."

The Linyati guns were ready for action, already run out.

Gareth had done some arranging of the watch list, so his friends were on his gun crew.

"Grapeshot, like in the stories," Thom said in a low voice. "Sweep their quarterdeck clean."

"That's stupid," Knoll objected. "Chainshot, for certain. Cut a mast down, and that ship'll fall back in confusion."

"Don't go for easy," Labala said. "Put one of those big bastard cannonballs under his waterline and sink him as he floats."

"Thank you, my admirals," Gareth said. "We'll do whatever the captain orders."

For long moments nothing happened as the three ships sailed side by side.

"Look at that damned lantern," Knoll said.

Its green light flared, now clearly visible in daylight.

A small square hatch slid open in the rear cabin of the nearest Linyati ship. He tried to see who was looking out, but there was nothing but blackness to be seen.

Suddenly a high, ululating squealing came, Gareth thought from the cabin. The Linyati along the railings ran to winches, lines, and the ship tacked right, away from the *Steadfast*. The second ship on the other side did the same, a mirror image, turning away.

"Guess we passed muster?" Gareth hazarded.

"Probably," Thom said. "Wonder what that screeching was. Sounded like somebody doing something awful to a pig."

"Maybe," Labala said, and there was a thin sheen of sweat on his forehead. "Maybe that's something we hope we never know."

An hour later, a lookout sighted land, rolling hills and a desert scape. Luynes gathered the crew, and confirmed what Gareth had heard: Herti was a neutral port, but controlled by the Linyati. There'd be no shore leave for the hands, for they'd be docked for no more than half a day.

Herti was an old, evil city, white, low buildings baking in the wind that came in from the desert behind. Ships of many nations sat at anchor, rolling in the slight swell that came into the wide-mouthed harbor, but many of them were Linyati, either warships or broadbeamed merchantmen, three-masted, triple-deck galleons, twice as big as the *Steadfast*.

Gareth noted this didn't seem to be a trusting port. There were plenty of open wharves, yet most ships preferred to tie up to one of the buoys scattered around the harbor and deal with the landsmen via boats. Most of them also kept swivel guns manned, and aimed at the lighters that came alongside to load or unload.

Luynes seemed to have no fear . . . or, more likely, Gareth thought, was a firm friend of whatever depravity held sway here. He brought the *Steadfast* neatly to a large wharf in the middle of the docks. The wind was blowing from a distant ramshackle building, evidently a fish plant.

Labala wrinkled his nose at the reek.

"Hope those aren't any of the supplies we're layin' in," he said.

"They're not," Rooke said, having padded up behind them. "Purser, the captain and us have business ashore. Have a detail clear out number two hold to take on new provisions. The water hoy'll be alongside in a bit."

Luynes came thudding down the ladder to the main deck.

"*Hern* Radnor, we'll also be taking on some of the . . . tools we'll be needing in our ventures. See they're properly stored in my cabin. You're in charge of the ship, so put out a gangway detail. Armed, if you please. I want no one aboard, not officials, not whores, not visitors, not bumboat boys, without me being on board.

"And I certainly don't want any of the men playing tricks and going ashore against orders. Herti's a tricky place, and matters are a bit delicate for any Sarosian here. If any man disobeys, I'll set him ashore on the spot, with nary a copper nor a weapon to protect him."

"Yes, sir. I understand, sir."

"We'll be back in two, perhaps three, turnings of the glass."

The three went ashore, Rooke hiding a smirk, and

Gareth remembered what the mate had said about cutting loose with slave whores.

But the ship's officers weren't back in three and then four turnings.

The hulk with its fresh water was brought alongside, and men—slaves, obviously—ran hoses across to the *Steadfast*'s tanks, after Gareth had carefully tasted the water and was a bit surprised to find it fresh and pure. The slaves manned pumps, and in less than an hour had finished their task, and lighters rowed the hulk away.

In spite of Luynes's warning, no one approached the ship. A few boys peered at the strange sailors, darted back into the city, shouting.

The waterfront was quiet, very quiet. There were no vendors' cries, no beggars shouting, no orders from the ships nearby. It seemed as if Herti was napping in the heat.

Gareth wondered what would come out at night, decided he wasn't that curious.

Time passed.

Too much time . . . five turnings of the glass.

Gareth, feeling he was probably being overcautious, ordered muskets broken out from the stores and half a dozen men assigned to stand by as reinforcements to the two pistol-armed men on gangway watch.

Luynes's tools arrived, wooden boxes carried by half a dozen men. Gareth ordered them taken to the captain's cabin, and chanced opening one after the porters had left. They were tools indeed . . . ugly tools. Pinchers. Irons. Half a dozen whips, some with metal tips. Manacles. Gareth shuddered, went back on deck.

Another turning of the glass passed.

Then one of the men on the gangway called to Gareth. He ran to the ship's side, saw a man reeling toward them.

He was hunched over, as if he'd been struck in the

side. Then Gareth saw the blood dribbling down his leg, leaving blotches of red on the planking as he stumbled toward them.

The man straightened, and Gareth recognized Kelch, saw the great sword-gash across his stomach. Kelch reeled, clawed at the air, and fell on his back.

Gareth was down the gangway and kneeling beside him.

The man's eyes blinked open.

"Bastards," he managed. "Frigging Linyati . . . never trust 'em . . ."

"What happened?"

"We did . . . what we'd come for . . . got our sailing directions . . . in my pouch . . . and went for wine. Godsdamned Linyati . . . I guess some other faction than the one the skipper'd made his bargain with . . . or maybe ones who just didn't like Sarosians . . . didn't like what we were . . . or maybe what we were there for . . . what we were . . ."

Kelch broke off, gasping for air.

"Bastards, bastards . . . know they killed me . . . kill some of 'em back for me, Pusser . . . they cut down the captain . . . guess they got Rooke too."

"What do we do?"

Kelch managed an awful grin, opened his mouth, and blood poured out. He coughed, turned his head to the side, spat.

"On'y one thing to do, boy. You're in their hands, so you'll have to . . ."

His body contorted and strained back. More blood rushed out of his mouth, and his bare feet drummed on the stone. He jerked once more and lay still.

"Shit," Nomios the bosun said somberly. "Now we're for it."

Gareth ignored him.

"Four men! Carry the mate aboard and to the sail-maker."

Among that man's duties was making a canvas sheath for a coffin.

Gareth stood, trying to figure out what to do next. "Nomios," he said in a low tone. "Have more muskets loaded, two to a man, but keep them hidden belowdecks."

"Yes, sir. What else, sir?" Gareth found it strange that the man, twice Gareth's age and more than that in experience, instantly fell under his sway.

"Take this pouch," Gareth said, picking up the leather purse beside Kelch's body, "and put it in the captain's cabin.

"We won't load the main guns until dark," he went on. "But single up to the main sheet, and have the topmen standing by. We might have to leave in a hurry."

"Aye, aye, sir."

Gareth turned to get back aboard as the four sailors grabbed Kelch's arms and legs and lugged him up the gangway.

He saw three Linyati warships gliding toward him, close inboard. But their guns weren't manned. The ships moved past the *Steadfast* in that eerie silence. None of the Linyati along the rails said anything, showed anything in their expressions.

The three ships put on sail, tacked toward the harbor mouth and the open sea.

Not a half-glass later, a dozen men came down the docks toward the *Steadfast*. All but one wore armor. They carried muskets and had swords at their waist. The unarmed man was a thin, tubercular-looking sort carrying a scroll.

The dozen stopped a stone's cast away.

"Ahoy the ship."

Gareth was on the quarterdeck. He walked to the landward side.

"We hear you."

"It is the decision of the rulers of Herti that, because of a matter of blood, you are required to leave this city at dawn.

"We pride our neutrality, and do not wish to become involved in any private dispute.

"This order is in congruence with international custom, and if disobeyed will be met with the appropriate responses . . . including violence."

He stumbled a little on the last word, then turned, and the formation moved away, a bit faster than it had come.

"And the godsdamned Linyati are outside the harbor, waiting for us," Nomios said.

Gareth nodded.

"We might as well get ready to put on the chains we wuz ready to put other people into," the bosun gloomed.

"No," Gareth said, wondering at his certainty. "No, that'll not happen. None of us will be anyone's slave, not now, not ever.

"Ready the ship for sailing."

Seven

L abala," Gareth said. "You told me once you could bring up a harbor full of mist. Were you yarning, or were you telling the truth?"

"I don't lie," Labala said. "I sometimes just can't keep my memory straight as to tales."

"Good," Gareth said. "Get whatever you need ready. I'd like a spell when it falls dark."

He turned to the crew, who were assembled in the waist. For some reason, he was utterly unafraid, and felt very calm, as if he'd been born to live in this kind of emergency.

"Four men," he said. "No. Three and you, Thom Tehidy. Get five bags of gunpowder, and ten bottles of brandy. Not the good stuff, the raw kind, with the most alcohol.

"At full dark, I want you four to go ashore, just as Labala's mist hopefully rolls in, and burn that fish plant at the end of the wharves. That'll give the locals something to keep them occupied.

"As soon as our bonfire fiends leave the ship, everyone

not on watch get into the armor that's stored up forward. We've already got muskets loaded and ready.

"Rig boarding nets and load the main guns, but we won't run them out until we cast off. The wheels make too much noise on the deck.

"Bosun, plot a compass course that we can use blind to get us out of the harbor.

"Now, set to."

A smile came to Gareth as the crew bustled about its business. Following orders. *His* orders.

Tehidy came to him.

"It'll be a bit of a burden with the four of us and the extra brandy and gunpowder."

"No," Gareth said. "I'll be the fifth man."

Gareth looked at the Linyati lantern on the mizzen mast as it grew dark.

No greenish glare came.

Now, he wondered, was the lantern keyed to Luynes, and had it gone out when he was killed? Or did the Linyati wizards, and there must be some aboard the Slavers' ships still in the harbor, cancel the spell? That might mean they have some kind of contact with the lamp, then. Contact enough, maybe, to use it like a lodestone to locate the *Steadfast*?

He unhooked the lantern, carried it down to the deck, and slipped up the gangway. He left the lantern next to a bollard, came back aboard.

If they're "watching" that, he thought, maybe they'll think we're still at the dock when we're not.

Torches flared along the waterfront, with no human lighter to be seen, and a wind from the land made them flicker. Then, as it got darker, they dimmed slowly. Gareth realized they weren't fading. Rather a dank mist, drifting slowly, unobtrusively in from the water, was masking them.

Either Labala's lucky . . . or we've got ourselves a real wizard, Gareth thought.

"All right," Gareth said to Thom and the three others. "Let's go."

They slid over the gangway, keeping low, and crept along the wharf, rats avoiding the light. Ramps led up toward land, and they followed them.

Gareth, wishing he had some of a soldier's skills, kept peering into the shadows, knowing Herti *must* have sentries posted.

But he saw no one. Maybe these people kept themselves truly disinvolved, and were true neutrals. Or cowards.

Tehidy pressed prickly lips to Gareth's ear.

"We can navigate from here by the smell."

Thom was right. Holding to the shadows, they found the plant, moved along its ramshackle walls, found a sliding door. There weren't any lights visible through cracks in the planking.

Gareth put his shoulder to the door, but it didn't move. Thom pushed him aside, used his strength.

The door came open, with a hinge-rusty *screek* Gareth thought was as loud, and alerting, as a trumpet blast. They froze, waited. But no one responded.

They went inside the long shed a few feet, no further, for fear of stumbling over something with sharp edges. Gareth drew his knife, cursed that it had no point, as every ship's officer he'd known had ordered, thought suddenly and irrelevantly that now he could carry any damned kind of blade he wanted, sawed at the burlap and let powder pool about. He tore off the wire seal and pulled the cork from a bottle of brandy, dabbled some here, there.

Thom was holding out a hooded slowmatch. He saw

the shadows of the four, waiting in the doorway, giving him the honor.

The honor, he thought, of maybe going up in a great ball of flame. He uncovered the slow match and held it to the burlap, saw flames flicker, saw other emptied bags in the growing firelight, touched the match to them.

"Come on," Thom hissed, and they trotted away from the fish plant, flames growing behind them. The flame flashed as gunpowder caught here, then a bigger flare as the wood, soaked in long years of oily fish, took fire.

They ran, then, up the gangplank onto the *Steadfast*. A sailor who'd held a boarding net wide for a passage let it fall.

"Man the guns and send the watch aloft," Gareth ordered. He went on up the ladder to the quarterdeck.

"Very well, mister," Gareth told Nomios. "Put us to sea."

"Yes, sir," Nomios said. "For'rd! Let go the main sheet."

There was a splash as a rope dropped into the water.

"Hard aport your rudder," he said in a low voice to the helmsmen, and the current drifted the *Steadfast* a foot or so away from the dock.

"Set the fores'l and mains'l," and the barefoot men above sidled out on footropes. Yards clattered, and canvas rattled as it unfurled. Sails caught the wind and pulled the prow of the *Steadfast* away from the dock, toward the sea.

"Helmsman," Nomios said. "Th' course is south by south-southeast. Hold firm, and you'll be in the center of the channel."

"Aye."

"Labala," Gareth called down to the main deck.

"What, Gareth?"

"Can you sense the Linyati out there?"

"No," Labala said. "Tried. Didn't work. Sorry."

"Anyone in the waist with good eyes, up to the foredeck," Gareth ordered. "Give quiet warning if you hear or see anything. Anything!"

Gareth closed his eyes, listened, forced his mind away from the *Steadfast*, into the foggy dark. The wind was coming from due north.

"Nomios," he said in a low tone, "correct the steering a point south or so. The wind might blow us a bit wide of the channel on this course."

"Aye, sir. I was just about to do that."

Gareth went down the ladder to the maindeck, called the four gun captains to him, Knoll standing in for Gareth.

"We'll be cutting through the fog sooner or later into clear air," he said. "When we do, if you spot the Linyati, aim your guns, but wait, for the sake of the gods, until I give the command. Maybe we'll be able to slide past them without being seen."

The men nodded, went back to their cannon. Knoll N'b'ry lingered for a minute.

"What're you grinning about?"

"Just about how much you sound like a real captain."

Gareth tried to keep from laughing. "To your gun, sir."

Gareth went back to the quarterdeck, went back to listening. The *Steadfast* was mostly silent, except for the creak of her hull, a quiet splash as a wave broke against the prow now and again, the rustle of the sails.

Labala came up the ladder.

"Gareth," he said, voice low, "I think my damned mist is staying with us!"

"Is that possible?"

"I dunno," Labala said. "I'm making this up as I go along. Maybe it thinks I'm its daddy?"

Gareth nodded. Maybe, just maybe, this would make things easier, and they wouldn't have to—

—He heard a shouted command to starboard, and the clatter of lines through blocks.

A moment later, he could see dim light.

Enough of creeping along, he thought. I'm tired of always running.

"Nomios," he said, "steer for that light."

"But—"

"Do as I order!"

"Yessir!"

The bosun gave quiet orders, and the helmsman spun the wheel.

The light grew brighter. Gareth went to the railing and leaned over.

"What're you loaded with?"

"Grapeshot," came back.

"Good. Aim at the light, and fire when I order. Reload with solid shot, and aim below the light, into the hull, for your second shot."

He went back to the wheel.

The light was very close. The *Steadfast* was closing on a Linyati—at least Gareth hoped it was a Linyati—from the stern, on the Slaver's port side.

"*Ready* . . ." Gareth shouted, and the ship was close enough for him to see startled figures on the ship's deck turn toward him . . .

"Fire!" The two starboard cannon bellowed, and men on the Linyati ship screamed and fell. There was confusion on their deck as the *Steadfast* sailed past, not twenty yards away.

"Bring her about, Nomios! We'll have another taste of that!"

"Aye, sir," and the *Steadfast* came about.

"Bring her down close alongside!"

"Aye, aye."

"Port cannon," Gareth ordered. "You can't miss! Ready . . ."

And the Linyati ship was close aboard. Sailors aboard her jumped back from the railings, afraid the *Steadfast* was intending to ram.

"Fire!" And the two guns crashed. Gunsmoke swirled as the grapeshot scattered across the Slaver's maindeck, and Gareth heard men shriek.

"Load solid shot, and fast," Gareth said, and again brought the *Steadfast* about.

"Ready . . . *Fire* . . ." And this time the port guns slammed their tiny broadside into the Linyati's stern.

"Up her port side," Gareth called.

Just as they closed on the Slaver, one of its sternchasers blasted, and the round whirred past, scant feet overhead, and thudded into the *Steadfast*'s sterncastle. Fire sparkled along the *Steadfast*'s starboard railing, and Gareth saw men—his men—unordered, firing muskets at the sternchaser's crew, and two Linyati went down. His starboard guns fired, aiming low as ordered, and they were even with the Linyati ship just as Gareth saw a small robinet on the quarterdeck fire.

The round came close enough so he felt the rush of wind, then the splatter of something warm on his face, his arm. He glanced up at clear skies, no rain, then saw the helmsman stumble back from the wheel.

He was missing his head, and Gareth knew what the rain had been, tried to keep from throwing up as he took the wheel, steering the *Steadfast* past the Linyati as the Slaver lost headway and fell away to port.

Then the fog was gone, and the sea ahead was clear. Gareth ordered full sail, and a new course:

Due south.

* * *

Two days later, the *Steadfast* lay in the lagoon off a tiny tropic island. The horizon to the north was empty, and there'd been no signs of pursuit after Herti.

The thirty-seven sailors were gathered in the waist. They'd buried Kelch and the helmsman the morning after the battle with the Linyati ship.

Gareth, before he'd told everyone to gather and decide what to do next, had sent a boat ashore to gather limes and a barrel of absolutely fresh water from a creek that purled into the ocean. He ordered the cook to make a cool punch from the fruit, some sugar, and brandy, served a moderate amount to each man.

Knoll N'b'ry had come to him as the others were lined up around the barrel.

"I'm starting to think you're a dangerous man, Gareth Radnor."

"Oh?"

"I think it's most interesting that you take the time to make sure we're all refreshed—with a fruit no one but a nobleman might ever see in Saros—before we discuss the future. A hint of the good things to come.

"Just as I think it's interesting you set the course south after Herti, instead of north, toward home."

"I just figured," Gareth said with an honest smile, "that would be the least likely direction for the Linyati to think we were headed."

"But of course." Knoll sipped from his pewter mug. "I was just thinking about some things you used to talk about when we were boys.

"Do you want it to be my idea, or yours?"

"What are you talking about?"

Knoll didn't answer, but smiled mysteriously, and found a place to sit on a cannon.

Gareth climbed up a couple of steps on the ladder to the quarterdeck.

"All right, men," he said. "I think we've got to decide what to do next."

"Get our sorry asses home," somebody said.

"That's the most obvious plan," Gareth agreed. "The seas are wide and empty, and we should be able to slip past any Linyati. I don't think they'll be looking for us too hard. Or anyway I hope not."

"We go out from Saros," Knoll said in a musing tone, as if to himself, "and then we rush right back, two months later, with our tails between our legs. What proud seafarers we be."

Men looked at him, some frowning in agreement, some puzzled.

"What about the *Steadfast*?" Thom Tehidy asked. "Who owns the ship?"

"I'd guess Captain Luynes's heirs, if he had any."

"I don't rec'leck," Bosun Nomios said, "the skipper ever talking about kin. Though that don't mean he had none."

"If that's true," Gareth said, "we could put in to the King's Courts, and perhaps end up owning the ship, and being able to sell it. Or sail it out again on shares."

A rough-looking man, one of Luynes's original hands, snorted.

"Men like us bein' allowed to own somethin' this fine? Not in Saros, not ever. Likely there's outstanding debts and writs and we'll end up on the beach wi' nothing but our dicks in our hands.

"I'd say we should carry on with the skipper's original plan and go slavin', but I can count noses as good as anybody, and know there ain't no likelihood of that bein' allowed. Even if we could somehow get ahold of whichever

Linyati the captain dealt with, and try to cut some sort of deal again."

"I don't think that'd work," Gareth said. "Plus, I'm no slaver, as I've said again and again.

"Another option is that we could take our chances," he went on, "and stay in these seas, looking for cargo we could barter the swords and muskets for to take back."

"That's an idea," somebody said.

"I've got a better one," Knoll said, and jumped down off the cannon. "We could say screw it, and run up the black flag and make ourselves rich, fast."

There were gasps—from the less experienced men, Gareth noted—and exclamations.

"I've no desire to see a thirteen-wrapped knot about my neck," the ship's cook said. "Or worse."

"Pirating . . ." Gareth said, as if considering the idea for the first time. "But maybe there's a safe way to go about it."

"Like what?" somebody said skeptically.

"What happens if we only prey on the Linyati? Take and loot their merchant ships where we find them. If we're successful enough and the cargoes are rich enough, we keep their ship, if we haven't sunk it in battle, and send it home to Saros with a prize crew."

"Or, better," the rough man said, "we anchor any such ships we take—not that I think we'd have that great a luck—away from Saros, mebbe in Juterbog, till the *Steadfast* sails back. Just in case the king or some godsdamned nobleman thinks of seizing our booty before we reach home."

"I don't understand," a sailor said. "If we just pirate against Linyati, how'll that keep us away from the King's Justice?"

"I think what we'd do is go to my uncle," Gareth said,

"who's got other friends in high places. If we petition the king, and say that we've gone against known enemies of the kingdom—"

"Not to mention offering him a cut of the loot," Labala said.

"That too," Gareth agreed. "We could stand a chance of pulling it off."

"My parents were taken by the Linyati," Thom Tehidy said. "As were Knoll's. And Gareth's were killed. I wouldn't mind cutting a piece out of them. A big piece."

"I lost an aunt in a raid," another sailor said.

"And two ships I used to sail on," one of Luynes's toughs said, "just vanished. I guess m'mates're wearing Linyati chains now. If they still live."

"We'd have to talk more if you like the idea," Gareth said. "Come up with our own set of articles, assuming the majority like the idea."

"What about somebody who doesn't want in?"

"I guess," Gareth said, "he'll just have to ride along with us, and take his chances until he could go back north with a prize crew, or be set ashore in the first civilized port we come to." He grinned. "Pirating, eh? I never thought of that."

"Better think of it," a man shouted. "For I vote you'd best be our captain."

There was a moment of silence, then a cheer.

Gareth came down from the ladder. The waist was a mass of excited, arguing men.

Knoll N'b'ry worked his way through the throng.

"Never thought of that? Gareth, you're still one shitty liar."

"I am not. A liar, I mean."

"I thought it was very smooth, the way I brought the

idea up, since of course you don't know what the hells I'm talking about."

"And I still don't." But there was a peculiar grin on Gareth's face.

"It's just like the old days, when we used to play," Knoll said. "Except this time, the gold'll be real, not bits of carved wood."

He held out his mug.

"Cheers, Captain Radnor."

Eight

Gareth read the pages of foolscap carefully. The writing might have been scrawly, the grammar shaky, and the style florid, but the intent and meaning was clear:

> ... We, the Crewe of the Ship known as The
> Steadfast, do Hereby Agree on the Following
> Artikles of Piracy, Which is Also to be
> Considered Privateering Against the Enemies
> of His Most Gracious King Alfieri of Saros,
> to be Held Proper by All Members of the
> Crew, on Paine of the Most Severest
> Punishment, and Also Pertaining to the
> Divigation of Shares in Our Enterprize ...

No one would receive any money unless they took prizes. Gareth, as captain, would receive five shares, as would the ship itself, for maintenance. The elected mates, Thom Tehidy and a rough-looking older seaman who'd served under Luynes, Froln, would receive three shares each.

Some had wanted Knoll N'b'ry as a mate too, but he refused, saying quietly he didn't know enough to do the job. Perhaps later.

The ship's quartermaster, Galf, being the crew's representative, got three shares. Bosun Nomios had been put up for the post, but violently opposed the idea: "I've never been more'n what I am, and what I am is what I'll be." Gareth took that for no.

Labala was given two shares, and protested that, saying he still wasn't a proper wizard. But he was shouted down, everyone remembering how his fog had saved them and hoping his magic would keep them alive in the future, as well as sorcerously leading them to rich prey.

The ship's carpenter got two shares. Everyone else got one.

Then the wrangling became serious, covering more than three days:

What about sailors on captured ships who wanted to join them? What shares would they get, assuming there'd been prizes taken before they came aboard? Did the crew have to chip in for food and drink, or did that come from the ship's share?

What would be the compensation for a crippled pirate? That was settled as one hundred pieces of gold for the loss of a right arm, fifty for a left arm, which provoked a shouting argument about what that meant to left-handers. The right leg went for fifty pieces of gold, but the left was only good for forty. A finger or an eye, ten gold pieces.

Then came the penalties: death for murder, rape, holding out of any loot. The penalty was to be enforced by shooting or marooning.

Lesser penalties, such as being made to run a gauntlet, fines, or even losing shares were chosen for lesser offenses.

Gareth noted that the men refused to permit the usual penalties to apply: hanging or the lash.

"We'll save that for our enemies," Froln said. "Rememberin'"—and he wriggled his back without realizing it—"how often the whip was laid on us."

By the time matters were settled, Gareth had learned that the term "sea lawyer" wasn't an empty phrase.

He wondered what it would be like if everyone, everywhere, were permitted to choose their companions and their pay, instead of always being at the will of a king, circumstance, or the nearest man with a sword or a title.

And thinking of that matter, he went to the men setting up the Articles and suggested that they write in a phrase saying something like: "All circumstances being proper, we agree that our Gods-Protected Monarch, whom we hold most dear, shall also receive six shares of our enterprise."

This attracted some howls, but one sailor, thoughtfully feeling his neck, said: "Could nay hurt, lads. If it doesn't come to that, it doesn't come to that. But if we're in some dungeon, down with the rats, awaitin' the torturer, the fact we thought good of ol' King Alfieri might stand us good, eh?"

Much argument, but the logic of guarding one's back was accepted by a majority, and so the king was granted his share.

Gareth thought Cosyra would find all this quite interesting and probably funny, and had a sudden pang of loneliness that he was hard-pressed to set aside.

"This might also help our cause with King Alfieri when we sail back to Saros," Gareth said.

"Or else doom us as utter fools," Knoll N'b'ry said

cynically. "Flaunting our villainy in the king's name and all."

The crew examined Gareth's creation that he'd had sewn up by the ship's sailmaker. It was a Sarosian flag—horizontal bars of black, green, white. But where the proper banner would have had the crown of Saros in the center, Gareth had a leering skull, with crossed cutlasses below it.

"If the Linyati are superstitious," Thom Tehidy said, "it'll give 'em a bit of hesitation."

"I'm not superstitious," Labala put in, "and it scares the bollocks off me."

The flag was adopted unanimously as the *Steadfast*'s new colors.

Gareth was happy to let the crew devise its own ways and amusement. He was having enough trouble figuring out the maps.

The contents of Kelch's pouch was, for quite a few hours, a mystery. He'd died saying he had the maps and "directions," whatever they were, in his pouch. But all the pouch contained was a bit of paper and some small paper tubes.

He put them on Luynes's desk to consider, and looked at the late captain's charts. He had roll after roll of maps for regions south of Saros. Gareth noted they were well annotated, showing Luynes's journeys in these largely unknown lands.

He found a projection of the Great Sea, hung it on a bulkhead, and oriented other, more detailed maps around it. Here, up to the right, was Saros, across the Narrow Sea, Juterbog. Then other known countries, which he didn't concern himself with.

Moving south and west were large islands. Gareth knew

of them, hadn't traded with any. Scattered in a spray south of them were dozens and dozens of smaller islands.

One, he noted, had an inked-in name: Freebooter's Island. Interesting.

On south and west was a great dumbbell-shaped continent. The lower bell was Linyati, but it was interesting that the only other chart of Linyati Gareth had seen had nothing but UNKNOWN TERRITORIES across it, and, to its north, the vaguest of dotted lines demarking strange land.

On Luynes's chart, Linyati had named cities, and the upper bell was precisely marked and named as Kashi. But there was very little detail on this part.

Below and to the east of Linyati, in open seas, was a circle, marked SPICE ISLANDS, with several question marks. Gareth made a face. Evidently the location of those islands was to have been part of Luynes's bargain with the Linyati for being their slave transport.

He summoned Nomios and showed him the charts.

"Aye, sir," the bosun said. "Luynes kept them current, as we sailed."

Gareth touched one entry, in the middle of the isthmus connecting Linyati and Kashi.

"That, sir"—Nomios licked his lips hungrily—"that's th' treasure city of Noorat, Cap'n Luynes told. He said th' Linyati raid Kashi for slaves, an' more besides. He said he'd heard there are savage kingdoms there, where gold's nothin' but a dec'ration, and th' people scorn silver as worthless.

"Once a year the Linyati collect all the booty they've stolen to th' settlements along th' coast of Kashi, and a fleet secures these riches, takes them on south, to Noorat, where the tale has it other treasure is brought, from across that isthmus and from the Unknown Seas beyond, all to be taken on to Linyati.

"He thought that'd be a fine taking, if you could convince enough men of spirit to trust each other long enough to sack the city."

"That makes me wonder about something," Gareth said. "If the Linyati have ships of their own sailing up and down the coast, why'd they want to charter the *Steadfast*?"

"Luynes never give me a reason, but I've heard th' wild men of Kashi've got strange ways and sorcery, and are hard fighters. The Linyati lose men—and ships—in th' trade, I was told, especially when they venture into some of th' great rivers, like this one here."

He went to the chart, touched a line leading into the interior of Kashi labeled the Mozaffar River. At its mouth was a dot labeled Cimmar.

"I guess there's enough profit in't so they'd rather hire us to take the risks an' carry their prisoners," Nomios went on. "Certain nobody's ever said Linyati lack courage, even if they like usin' it in groups of a dozen or so."

Gareth looked at another area of the map.

"What's this Freebooter's Island up here to the north?"

"I asked about it once. Luynes said a place of dreams, wouldn't tell me more. He was deep and held his secrets, the cap'n did."

Gareth looked into the bosun's eyes, decided he wasn't lying.

He asked about the tiny rolls of paper from Kelch's pouch, and Nomios shook his head.

"Dunno, sir. Truly I don't."

Gareth dismissed Nomios and told him to ask Labala to come up to the cabin. Maybe he could magic some meaning out of the rolls.

Waiting, he brooded. He'd thought, the Linyati being

his sworn enemies, that he knew something about them. Now he realized he knew nothing—not their tongue, not their habits, not their culture, not their ways of fighting with ships or swords, nothing.

He glumly thought of the other ignorances he'd been confronted with lately, and wondered why he'd had the arrogance to allow anyone to pick him for captain.

He also wondered why at one moment he was very sure of himself, certain of what to do, and the next seeing nothing but a myriad of choices, all appearing bad and dangerous.

Perhaps, Gareth thought, he needed someone to talk to. Such as? He'd heard of the "loneliness of command" and had thought it no better than self-pity. Now he knew its reality.

About the only person he thought he could talk to about things like this would be Cosyra, and she was thousands of leagues distant. Then Labala banged through the cabin door.

"Afternoon, Gareth. What's your need?"

Gareth brought himself back from his dark mood. "Since you're our resident mage, I wondered if maybe you could use your Gift to figure out what these little tubes are that Kelch had. He said he had maps, but these surely aren't them."

"Why not? Remember, the part can be the whole, I've been told, and the Linyati have clever wizards."

"But . . . what kind of spell would you have to say over them to make them full-sized? If there's one, it must have died with Luynes."

"Maybe so, maybe no." Labala picked up a tube, looked at it. "Once I saw a wee toy in a shop. A 'brella, against the rain. Sprinkle water, and *whoomp*, it was full-size. Maybe you touch this with water . . ."

Gareth tried. Nothing.

"Sea water?"

Nothing.

"A dark thought comes," Labala said. "If Luynes was going to have us work a bloody trade . . ."

Gareth took a pin from the chart table, pricked his thumb, smeared a bit of blood on a tube, and thought for an instant he was wrestling a snake, as the tube grew, twisted, and became a large map. He unrolled it, saw unfamiliar writing and scales, but recognized it as a large-scale projection of the isthmus connecting Linyati and Kashi.

"Thankee, sir," Labala said. "M' bill will be sent later. If there's aught else, you have only to whine," and thudded out the hatch and down the ladder, laughing boisterously.

The *Steadfast* couldn't stay in this safe isolated harbor forever. Sooner or later a Linyati with a lookout having sharp eyes, or a curious wizard, would sail by and decide to investigate.

Gareth studied Kelch's charts for long hours, and eventually decided to lie in wait off the city of Batan, which was the first marked settlement north of Noorat, on the continent of Kashi. It wasn't far distant, and there should be passing ships for the taking.

In addition, there were dotted islands around it, which would give the shallow-drafted *Steadfast* lurking places.

He hoped.

He told the crew what he'd decided, and they all voted to back his decision. That was pleasing, but he knew that if no prizes were taken or if they took heavy casualties, Gareth Radnor would be just another foremast hand.

* * *

They reached the mainland of Kashi, far enough north of Noorat to keep from being spotted, turned north, passing through islands, when the lookout atop the mainmast shouted he saw a boat.

Those offwatch crowded the foredeck out of curiosity and saw a long canoe, with twin outriggers and a lateen sail made of matting, scudding across the passage between two islands. There was one person aboard.

Tehidy had the watch, and ordered the *Steadfast* to close on the canoe.

"Maybe he's got fruit aboard, and we'll trade him for bread."

"Or really piss him off," somebody said, "and *give* him ship's biscuit."

"That might not make him angry," a sailor said. "P'raps he's been long without meat, and the worms in the biscuit'll gladden his heart."

The canoe's oarsman was a brown-skinned boy, with very long, very black, very straight hair tied back, wearing only a colorful linen wrap around his thighs. He saw the approaching ship, pulled at his sail's lines, crying out in a high voice.

"He's praying, sounds like."

Then the wind died.

The boy stared at the *Steadfast*, then stood and dove straight overside.

"What the—"

"Poor bastard," Labala said. "Prob'ly thinks we're Linyati, only big ships he's heard of, and prefers drowning to bein' a slave.

"Can't blame him."

By this time, Gareth was on deck. Tehidy looked at him wildly, slid out of his pants and top, and dove over the side.

"For the love of the gods," Nomios said. "And what's he doing *now*?"

"Playin' rescuer?"

The crew rushed to the railing, looked overside. By now, the canoe was almost alongside.

"Drop sail and back the helm," Gareth ordered. "Bring her back on the canoe."

"Aye, sir," the helmsman shouted, and Nomios looked shamefaced at not having given the command himself.

"Look, there he is . . . he's got th' lad."

Tehidy surfaced like a blowing whale, holding the struggling boy under one arm.

"The kid didn't want to . . . *yeowch*."

Boy and Thom disappeared again, and there were bubbles and flurries before Tehidy surfaced, an agonized expression on his face. This time, he had the semiconscious boy by the hair.

"Lousy little bugger," he managed. "Kicked me in the balls and headed for the bottom again. Should've let him drown."

Amid general laughter, Gareth ordered a cargo net retrieved from the hold and a boom rigged. So, unceremoniously, the boy was hoisted aboard the *Steadfast*, his canoe tied alongside.

"Now what?" Gareth asked Tehidy, when he'd finished clutching himself.

"Eh," Froln said. " 'E's not bad-looking. P'raps our mate's getting lonely, and—"

He broke off at Thom's look, and remembered just how strong Tehidy was.

"Damned if I know what we should do with him," Thom said. "But I wasn't going to let him drown on my affair."

"No," Gareth agreed.

The boy spat a stream of words. No one knew what he was saying.

"Interesting," Gareth said. "We don't look like Linyati, but he obviously thinks we're Slavers. That must mean we're in waters they've not traveled lately."

"I think I've a use for him," Labala said.

"Now, Lab," someone shouted. "We've agreed . . . no human sacrifices."

"How'd you like a good swim with a cannonball about th' waist?" Labala suggested. "Gareth, I'm not schooled enough to pull a language spell, at least like a real wizard does it. But I've thought about how it maybe should go. We could try with this kid, couldn't we?"

Gareth nodded, and inside a glass-turning, various herbs—thyme, rosemary, juniper berries, chamomile—were gotten from the cook, chalk marked the deck in three triangles, and Labala had a fresh-caught fish gutted in front of him.

"Brain to brain . . ." he murmured, cutting open the top of the fish's head, prying out the fingernail-sized organ.

He touched it to the boy's head, who tried to squirm away. Labala looked at him fiercely, and the boy stopped trying to escape.

"Now you, Gareth," and Gareth obediently bent his head.

"If it doesn't work," somebody said, "or, rather, if it does, the cap'n's liable to start gaspin' and dive overside, wrigglin' hearty."

"Shut up," Labala grunted. "Like to like . . . I'm thinking now."

He pried the boy's mouth open, the boy tried to bite him, and he clamped his jaws open, touched a finger to spittle.

"Now you, Gareth."

Gareth opened his mouth, and Labala did the same. Labala burned the herbs, and began chanting:

> *"Mind to lips*
> *Lips to words*
> *Words to ears*
> *Ears to mind*
> *Mind to lips*
> *Lips to words . . ."*

Over and over, again touching the fish's organ to Gareth and the boy.

He stepped back, jabbed the canoeist.

"Say something."

The boy glowered, and Gareth heard him say: "Do not touch me, you fat demon!"

"Quiet thy lips," Gareth said, in a tongue he didn't know he spoke. "Be not insulting to the wizard, or he'll change thee into a turtle!"

The boy's eyes went wide.

"You speak the Speech?"

"Of course," Gareth said. "That was what the spell was about."

"I thought he was going to turn me into a fish." The boy looked stubborn. "Thee might as well, for I won't be thy slave, not ever, and I'll get away and be able to drown myself as soon as thee turns thy back."

"No one is going to make you into a slave!"

The boy laughed harshly. "All men with boats like thine do nothing else. I've been taught that again and again by my chiefs."

"Would we have saved you and your boat if we were slavers?"

"No man knows what a demon thinks."

"We'll take you back to your village."

"I'll not show it to thee, for I know thee wants to enslave all of my people. Ah-hah. Now I have thy vile plan. That was why thou saved me," the boy said excitedly. "So I would be thine fish trap, and lead my people into thine nets."

"You're an impossible sort," Gareth said. "I hope you are the son of a chief."

"No. My father is noble, but not a chief, and I see thine cleverness, trying to get me to talk more about my village. I shall say no more."

Gareth shook his head in dismay and turned away.

"And I thought *I* was pigheaded when I was his age. Obviously, Labala, your spell worked. When we capture a Linyati, we'll use the same spell on him."

"But that still leaves the question of what we're going to do with this boy? Pop him back in his canoe?" Knoll N'b'ry asked.

"Pretty much."

An hour later, the canoe and boy were released, the boat piled high with bread, smoked meats and fish, knives, and two of the chopping knives from the cargo. Gareth found a cutlass, dropped it on top, said, "Now, when you're grown, thou will have something to kill Slavers with."

As the *Steadfast* sailed away, the boy stood in his canoe, dropped his wrap, and waved his buttocks at the ship.

"Guess he didn't believe us," N'b'ry said, choking back laughter.

"Guess not," Gareth said. "Forget him.

"It's time for us to go a-pirating."

Nine

The Linyati ship was fairly small, twin-masted, with a pair of small falconets on the quarterdeck. The crew was only ten men, six Linyati, four slaves.

The slave at the helm looked longingly to port, where the dark jungle beckoned. If the Linyati on watch would go below, or nod off, he might have time to put the wheel over and strike for shore, get close enough in to chance the breakers and the sharks.

But the Linyati never seemed to relax that much. The slave wondered gloomily, as he had before, if the bastards were even real men. He preferred to think not, that they were demons, sentenced to this world for sins. But then he thought again: he'd rather be held by men than demons, although what he'd seen the Linyati do to some of his fellows who dared speak rebellion or freedom . . .

He shuddered, checked his heading. The Linyati was looking his way, a cold stare that perhaps read his thoughts.

Then something loomed at them out of blackness. It was another ship. The slave spun the wheel, had a moment to realize the other, larger ship would comb his ship's side to port, and two cannon blasted, shooting high, shooting chainshot, and the foremast cracked and drooped.

The slave let go of the wheel, seeing the mast sway and circle above him, dove for the shelter of the main mast's coat just as the *Steadfast*'s swivel guns on its foredeck fired, and grapeshot cut down the Linyati on watch, splintering the wheel.

Grapnels went across, and the raider was alongside the Linyati ship. Men with cutlasses, whooping, screeching like wild animals, clambered aboard as the five befuddled Linyati in the crew came stumbling up from below cabin in various stages of undress. Two had swords, two pistols. The pistoleers aimed and fired, and muskets flamed. The Linyati staggered, cried out, died.

The slave, peering cautiously around the mast, saw a slender man with a straight sword cut down one of the Linyati, a huge man with a long, studded truncheon crush the skull of another. The tall man was shouting something, and the big man dropped his club and jumped on the survivor.

Other men came up the ladder to the quarterdeck. A man with a cutlass saw the slave was still alive, drew back for a killing blow, was stopped by another.

The slave was on his feet, hands raised high, babbling he was not an enemy, he gave up, and have mercy, please have mercy.

The four slaves cowered next to the stern cabin, waiting for inevitable death. The surviving Linyati was firmly tied to the ladder, and glared hate at anyone who met his eye. Five lanterns illuminated the maindeck.

"Yer orders, sir?" Galf, the quartermaster, said.

"Cut away the mast," Gareth ordered. "Try to jury-rig

some canvas off the stub. Set the sprits'l full, and see how much of the spanker she'll bear before she starts shearing off. I want to beat away from the land. We're too close as it is."

"Sir." And Galf shouted orders, and the men aboard the ship set to.

"Nomios, Tehidy, get a hatch off," Gareth ordered. "Let's see what we've got for our work. But be careful. I don't know what the Linyati might keep below as a surprise."

Tehidy found a mallet, drove wedges from under the hatch cover, while Nomios cut away lashings.

"What about the bodies?" N'b'ry asked.

"Put them overside," Gareth ordered. "I don't remember anyone giving any of ours time for a priest or ceremonies."

A few sailors laughed harshly, and moments later five bodies went spinning out into the night, splashing down into phosphorescence. A moment later, Gareth heard the terrible grunt as a shark slashed into one of the corpses.

"What about him?" a sailor asked, thumbing toward the surviving Linyati.

"Labala! Get your language spell ready," Gareth shouted.

The first time the spell didn't take, and Gareth wondered if the Linyati were impervious. But the second time, after the Linyati had almost bitten Labala's thumb off, and spat rage, Gareth snarled back, "Silence! Or you're dead!"

"You'll kill me anyway," the Linyati said. "There is nothing but war between your kind and mine."

"You aren't the same as I am?"

"Of course not," the Linyati snarled. "There are but

two races permitted, those who rule, and those who are ruled."

Gareth pointed at the slaves.

"Like them?"

"Just so."

"Then what does this do?" He turned to the slaves. "How many of you speak this tongue?"

One man nodded, then the other three muttered they did as well.

"If you were slaves once, I now declare you free," Gareth said.

Utter silence, then a babble of joy from the men. One fell to his knees, and a sailor dragged him back to his feet.

"We kneel for nobody here."

"What do you say to that?" Gareth asked the Linyati.

"It has no meaning," the man said. "You have not the right to name them not-slaves, so slaves they will be again."

"No!" one of the brown men snarled. "Never again. Great man," he said to Gareth. "Will you give us this creature?"

"For what?" Gareth asked.

"To be our slave for a moment, so see how it feels," the man said. "Then to die slowly."

"No," Gareth said. "We probably should kill him, but I'll let no man make another his slave."

He considered for a moment.

"Galf!"

"Sir!"

"Belay my sailing orders for a while."

There were two small boats lashed to the main deck.

"You, you, and you," he said to sailors. "Get both of these boats ready to launch. Enough food and water for, oh, a week in the second one."

He looked at the Linyati, changed languages.

"We'll put you in one now . . . and at dawn let these four men go free. They have information I need, and that'll give you a bit of a start. If they choose to pursue you, or if you've not been able to make shore by then . . . such is your fate."

"Do not expect me to show you mercy if ever we cross paths," the Linyati said. "If I were in your place, I would not do as you are doing."

"I have no such expectations," Gareth said. "I'm not a fool."

"Sir, let's just go shark fishing with his ass," a man said.

"No," Gareth said, a bit reluctantly, then he heard a loud *"Shit!"* from the open cargo hatch, and then a roar of laughter.

Sailors gathered around the hatch as a disgusted Nomios clambered out, followed by a grinning Thom Tehidy.

"Congratulations, my captain," Tehidy said. "You now have five shares of the best dried fruit I've ever seen."

There were moans, groans, and someone said, "For that we could've gotten killed?"

Labala started laughing.

Gareth grinned wryly.

"At least we're learning how to be pirates without getting hurt. And now we've got something to chew on while we're waiting for our next lesson."

Two hours later, the sun was up, and the four former slaves rowed toward the distant shore.

Gareth felt somewhat swimmy-headed: two of the slaves came from different tribes, and now he had three new languages swarming around in his mind. He knew their tongues, but nothing of the people, other than they'd been stolen somewhere in Kashi—there weren't enough details on Gareth's maps, and they didn't know how to read them, anyway—along the coast, taken by raiders and sold to the Linyati who had crewed this ship.

Gareth asked if the crew had owned the ship. Only one of the ex-slaves had known what it meant to own property, and he said he thought not, but he had no idea whose orders they followed.

Gareth watched the small boat course toward the beach, and turned to Froln.

"Now we'll sail this spit kit back into the islands we passed through and careen it. Maybe one of them will have trees straight enough to cobble together a new mast."

"And then what?"

"We'll put a small crew aboard and use it as bait. Then we'll seize a proper cargo to fill its hold with."

Gareth didn't let himself think about the obvious—the second prize had better be more worthwhile, or his men might start thinking their captain was unlucky.

Their first prize's mast was replaced, although lashed-together green trunks were a temporary repair at best, and the five men assigned to her got Labala to make weather charms for them. He admitted quietly to Gareth that he had no idea on how to cast such a spell, but mumbled some words over tiny seashells and gave it to the men anyway.

"At least it'll maybe help 'em stay brave when it comes on to blow."

Gareth thought of naming the ship the *Cosyra*, decided she warranted a far greater ship, called it the *Goodhope* instead, and sent it out to troll the waters between Batan and Noorat, pretending to be a fisherman. He didn't know whether the Linyati ate fish or not, or if their ships had some sort of identifying charm, such as Luynes's had been given. He'd had the *Goodhope* searched from truck to keel and found nothing magical, nor did Labala sense anything.

The *Steadfast* lurked just on the horizon, the *Goodhope*'s mast a thread in the distance, watched by two lookouts with glasses.

On the third day, the *Goodhope* ran up a long banner to the peak of its mainmast, signifying they'd spotted a ship, and the *Steadfast* put on full sail.

"Uh, Cap'n," the sailor said, standing in the companionway. "Th' cargo's nothin' but feathers."

Gareth tried to keep a still face.

"Yessir, feathers, sir," the man went on. He held up a sheaf of brightly colored plumes. "Guess they're used to dec'rate hats or gowns or somethin'."

If there hadn't been three dead men sprawled on the deck, it might have been funny, at least to everyone but Gareth, who could feel the sands of his captaincy running out.

The Linyati ship they'd taken was bigger than the *Steadfast,* a wallowing three-masted twin-decker, square-rigged, with six cannon. The crew had fought hard, and only a handful, all wounded, stood on the maindeck, well guarded. About a dozen slaves were on the other side of the deck, eyeing their former masters malevolently.

Why would anyone have fought so hard for feathers? Gareth wondered. Magical? Religious? Nobody's that weird in their worship. Are they?

He heard a shout from belowdecks, and Knoll N'b'ry pushed past the sailor in the companionway.

"I moved some of the feathers aside," he said, "nicely baled as they are. And below was the ballast."

He held up a rectangular block wrapped in canvas. It was evidently quite heavy.

"Maybe the Linyati are neatness itself," he said, "but I've never seen ballast wrapped like presents. So I unwrapped one."

He let the canvas wrappings fall away, and bright gold caught the sun's dying rays. The crew shouted loud.

"Half the bottom's covered with these," he said, hefting the ingot. "Probably melted-down treasure stolen from Kashi. Now we know why the damned ship sailed like a man trying to walk with a full load in his breeches, eh? And why the bastards fought so hard."

Gareth felt every muscle sag in relief.

Three of the ship's lifeboats were being readied to release the Linyati and the ex-slaves when one of them came to him.

"Leader?" he asked, bowing. He was big, shaven-headed, dignified-looking, and Gareth wondered why his masters hadn't done away with the man. Slaves weren't supposed to do anything but crawl.

"I hear you," Gareth responded, in the man's tongue he'd learned a glass earlier.

"We thank you for freedom, and for the boats. But most of us come from a land inland, up a great river, and far west of where we are. I know where we are, roughly, for I learned to read the sun's position and later the Linyati compass and a map, as many of us have learned the skills of a sailor from the snakes we were forced to serve. I am named Dihr, by the way.

"We have enemies, longtime enemies, between us and home, and, besides, many of us have been years or more slaves, and our women will have remarried and our children finished mourning us and most likely remember not our names."

"You wish, then?" Gareth said.

"You are a man of luck, it is obvious to see. None of us witnessed our masters loading the gold, yet you and your sage, the fat one, who I also see has great power, sniffed their riches out."

Labala made an irked "garumphing" noise, and Gareth realized he must be learning all these Kashi tongues as well, which was all to the good.

"We wish," Dihr continued, "if you would have us, and if you would not be shamed to serve with men of another color and those who wore chains, to join you.

"The most precious thing, we have decided, would be to be able to kill Linyati, many, many Linyati, perhaps ten for each year each of us has spent in bondage.

"What do you say?"

"I must consult with my men," Gareth said. "For my crew is composed of equals, each having a full say in things."

The man looked surprised.

"Hey-up!" Gareth shouted. "Everyone back to the *Steadfast* except you and you, who keep good watch on our prisoners."

Minutes later, the crew had obeyed. Gareth told them the man's proposition.

"It'll cut th' size of our share is the biggest drawback," Froln said.

"So'll gettin' whittled by the Linyati till we can't stand against them or man th' yards proper in a storm," a sailor said. "We lost three today, an' I don't see us goin' back to Ticao to recruit anytime soon."

"True," Froln said. "An' besides, we'll be able to find out more about our prey. I was just thinkin' out loud.

"I vote we take 'em in, at least on a prospect basis, at a share. If some turn coward, or don't work out, we can always put 'em in the boats later, can't we?"

There were only two dissenters to the shouted vote. Gareth went back to the Linyati ship.

"We welcome you," he said. "As for killing Linyati, you kill only those who fight back. We are not yet cold-blooded murderers. And you will be paid equal wages in what we capture, with the rest of us."

The man smiled.

"Now I see why you are lucky. You are not afraid to take chances."

Gareth thought the waters off Batan might be getting warm, and wondered if he'd been right in letting the Linyati he'd captured live, instead of tying a largish boulder to their feet and introducing them to the nearest sea monster.

But he'd done what he'd done.

The three ships, the new prize named the *Revenge,* sailed west-southwest, deeper into Linyati waters. The course of the three ships might be leading into greater danger, but this was where the prizes would be taken. Also, Gareth thought he might be misleading the Linyati sorcerers by such a plan, and they'd not look for him close to their heartland.

The ex-slaves, given language spells in Sarosian, quickly melded with the other sailors, and proved themselves indeed experienced. Surprised that no one used the rope end or worse against them, a few slacked and let others do their work before they realized they could no longer use the stupid expression and drawled incomprehension all slaves use against their masters, and that if they didn't perform a task it might mean their own doom.

He quizzed Dihr and the others over and over about

the Linyati. But their knowledge was amazingly sparse—the Slavers kept their slaves at a distance. Interestingly, slaves were only permitted to go to sea in Linyati or Kashi waters. Slaves aboard the craft trading into foreign waters were nothing more than cargo. The Linyati were indeed a secretive race.

Ashore, the slaves were kept in barracks. No one ever saw a female Linyati, and Dihr thought they might be kept in isolation, "like certain very stupid savages in our own lands do."

One slave reported something chilling: he'd been taken to the ship, when he saw half a dozen Linyati herding some very fat children, brown and white-skinned, toward a low building that reminded the man of a slaughterhouse. "As if they were sheep. And they were fatter than normal children should be, even a chief's son. I thought they'd been caponized."

Dihr added an unsavory detail—he'd seen casks taken from this building to their ship before it set sail, and at certain special occasions a brazier would be set up on deck, a cask broached, and the meat within roasted, with never a morsel offered to the slaves.

Dihr added that none of them wanted any of the meat, particularly after another slave observed thoughtfully that the cooking meat smelled exactly like a funeral pyre.

Gareth swallowed hard, asked for details about the Linyati at sea. They were exceptionally skilled seamen, their officers willing to take hazardous courses without hesitation. When one of the Linyati died or was killed, his corpse was dumped overside without ceremony. At the next port, a replacement would be waiting, and it seemed as if he was already fully trained for his tasks.

Offwatch, they kept to themselves in their own quarters, from which strange singing and screeches which the slaves thought were laughter could be heard. If they worshipped any gods, it wasn't within the slaves' sight or hearing.

They were, as the pirates already knew, utterly merciless in battle and toward any sick or injured slaves.

Sometimes they took their own wizards aboard, mostly seemed to need or want none.

Gareth wondered if they were human at all, if they were demons.

He remembered when the *Steadfast* had first encountered Linyati warships, and the strange squealing that came from the closed stern cabin of one.

"I've heard it," Dihr said. "But only from their ships of war . . . no, once, when this ship sailed with others, going into Kashi, to that great city of theirs, the leader's ship would sail up and down the line, and every once and again the shrieking would come across the water, orders, and the sailors on Dihr's ship would rush to obey."

"Show me on the map where this city is."

"I can try."

Gareth found a marked river on Luynes's main chart about at the midpoint of Kashi, with a dot and a question mark at its mouth.

"Yes," Dihr said. "Their city they name Cimmar, which they built to hold the mouth of the river. The river, wide enough for a hundred ships like this to sail abreast, is the Mozaffar. But it does not stop just inland, as this map shows, but winds south and then east, through my homeland."

Little by little Gareth was learning the measure of their foe.

* * *

They captured four more merchantmen, each with a valuable cargo—silks, brass objects of art, and two carrying spices fully as rich as Luynes had promised.

Gareth knew he had to do something with his fleet before the Linyati came after him. For the moment, he ordered his prizes sailed back with skeleton crews to the cover of that nameless island they'd first found, while he stayed a-raiding with the *Steadfast, Goodhope,* and *Revenge.*

The next ship they sighted was huge, a four-masted triple-decker. There were two of the small, rakish three-masters sailing as escort ahead of the triple-decker.

Froln grinned tightly.

"Wi' guard'yans that'll mean there's sure some'at worth takin' aboard the big 'un, Captain."

Gareth found himself smiling back, and knew his expression was the same as his mate's, a wolfish glee. He had an instant to wonder how much he was changing, pushed the matter away as nonsense, ordered the men to fighting stations, and ran up the *Steadfast's* colors.

The skull flag cracked in the wind, and the pirate formation closed on the biggest ship.

The two warships tacked back, but the three pirate ships refused to close, and raked them with their main guns, aiming for their masts, until the Linyati lay dismasted and helplessly dead in the water.

Then they went after the three-decker. Gareth counted half a dozen guns per side with his glass, and more, lighter cannon in the stern and bow. The ship was a slow sailor, the *Steadfast* and *Goodhope* able to close easily, the slower *Revenge* having about the same speed.

"We go broadside to broadside wi' th' bugger," Froln said, "we're liable to come up second or worse. P'raps we close on th' port side, send the *Revenge* t' th' other, and mebbe confuse 'em or scare 'em a trifle?"

"Better," Gareth said, and gave orders to Froln, signal flags fluttered.

"If this works," he said as the *Steadfast* closed on the huge Linyati ship, trying to ignore the swirlings in his stomach as he saw the bore of the cannon in the ship's stern cabin getting larger and larger, "we'll be rearranging our guns."

Smoke billowed from the Linyati ship's stern, but the balls fell well short.

"Appears she's carryin' bombards or such in the stern," Froln said.

"We're in range," Knoll N'b'ry shouted.

"Ready about," Gareth ordered.

"Sir," the quartermaster called; then, to the helmsman, "Helm a'lee!"

"Helm's a'lee," the helmsman shouted, and the wheel was put down.

"Let go the headsheets . . . let go the spanker," Galf shouted, and sailors ran to obey.

"Stand by the guns to port," Gareth ordered.

"Ready . . . ready," came the reply.

"Mains'l haul!" And the *Steadfast* turned broadside to the Linyati ship.

"Fire when you bear!" Gareth shouted.

A moment later one, then the second demicannon on the *Steadfast* boomed.

"Take her about and do it again," Gareth ordered.

A grim roundelay started, with the three pirate ships sailing up on the Linyati's stern in turn, tacking, firing a broadside, and recovering.

The little *Goodhope* came too close, and one of the

Linyati short-range bombards blew away her bowsprit. She fell back, her small crew swarming up to make repairs.

Then there was a smashing explosion from the Linyati ship's stern, and part of the hull tore away and one of the bombards toppled slowly into the ship's wake.

Gareth ordered the *Steadfast* to close and sweep the quarterdeck with grapeshot, then the *Revenge* to board.

The *Steadfast* came alongside to starboard, through the boiling smoke and red cannon fire, and her men went across as the *Revenge*'s crew leapt over the Linyati's port railing.

The fighting was savage, with no quarter given, but in a quarter glass all the Linyati on deck lay sprawled in their blood.

Gareth winced, rubbed his arm. A pistol ball had ricocheted off a mast and grazed him. Thom Tehidy had a slash down his side, which he was bandaging with a shirt torn from a Linyati corpse. Four men clenched teeth to keep from screaming, two others thrashed in agony, three lay motionless in death.

"Why'd the bastards fight so hard?" he wondered. "I suspect we're rich."

There was a bang as a maindeck hatch came open, and a ghastly stench rolled up, followed by piteous wails and screams.

"Mercy of Megaris," somebody shouted. "We took a slave ship."

And so it was.

There were four slave decks below, each just high enough for a man to sit up on, divided into narrow berths. There were passages down each row, where the Slavers could pass out water and bread when they bothered.

The slaves' excrement slid down between cracks in the bunks, into the bilges.

There were four hundred seventy-three men, women,

children still living, manacled to their bunks. There were another one hundred thirteen bodies in chains.

Labala cast every spell he could think of for perfume, for fresh winds, but it did little good. The sailors cursed the dead Linyati as they carried bodies into the open, where Dihr said a prayer that should help them find a better life, then slid the bodies into the water, not looking at the swirling wakes of the feeding sharks.

Dihr told Gareth that these slaves were "primitive ones, Captain. Not educated, not seamen like us. They've been fresh-taken from their lands and put in this hells-ship for transport to the slave markets of Linyati."

These bewildered, half-starved people were fed as best the pirates knew how, first with delicacies, which made more die, then with simple gruels and fruit.

Labala found himself being their chirurgeon, although he claimed little skills. No one else did, either, but most everyone found himself tending to the sick. Slowly the people began to recover, although children still died, and it tore at Gareth every time he put a small corpse overside.

They sailed back to the island where the rest of their prey lay anchored, and Gareth took stock.

Tehidy and Froln came, asking what he planned next.

"We've got to get rid of these Kashians," he said. "And that ship we took, with its smashed stern, needs better carpenters than we have. We should be deciding which of the ships we've taken are to be disposed of, and in what way. Also, all of our hulls are foul and need cleaning, and our upperworks need rerigging.

"I think we should investigate the charms of Freebooter's Island."

Ten

reebooter's Island was, in fact, a ring of islets, with
jutting skerries offshore and a deep lagoon in the center.

Gareth signaled his seven ships to heave to, while he
sailed around the island to see what was what.

There were gaps in the islets, but he couldn't tell if
the passages were navigable. Two tiny offshore islands had
low-walled forts. But the forts were unmanned, the cannon
stoppered, and he saw no sign of life.

Inside the lagoon were some sixteen ships of various
types. On several of the islands, white stonework gleamed.

A lookout shouted down, saying the passage just off
the beam was guarded by other forts. Gareth glassed them,
saw more cannon, these manned and with open muzzles.

He guessed that passage would be the main channel,
but didn't know what pirate's protocol, if any, was toward
uninvited strangers.

Again the lookout called, reporting a small cutter sailing toward the passage. Standing in its bows was a long-

bearded man wearing a star-studded turban and a thigh-length wrap. He seemed to have no problem keeping his balance as the small boat tossed in the low waves coming through the passage. Two nearly naked, brown-skinned men crewed the boat.

"Helmsman," Gareth called, noting the *Steadfast* had a fair wind abaft.

"Aye."

"Make for that passage."

"Aye, sir."

"Thom, take in all sail but the mains'l, and shorten that. We'll crawl in. Nomios, all hands on deck, and the guns manned but not run out.

"And hoist our colors. We'll find out soon enough whether we're among friends."

The *Steadfast* ghosted toward the cutter, which held its course toward them.

"Ahoy the *Steadfast*," the man in the cutter called.

Gareth started.

"You know us?"

"Aye," the man shouted. "My casting spotted you a day out. Good thing, too. With all your ships, folks around here could get nervous, thinking the damned Linyati had mounted an expedition against us. Or that we're a little slow in hearing of the politics up north and somebody's decided to try to destroy us again."

The cutter dropped sail, and the man jumped easily for the ladder, swarmed up it through the gangway where Gareth, Labala, and the mates waited. He was tall, and at one time would have had the muscular build of a warrior. Now, though, his face was a cheery red under its beard, explaining the great gut he seemed to carry with pride.

"I hight, like they used to say, Dafflemere, once Lord

Dafflemere, now one of the Brethren of the Sea, with a bit of the Gift that at least one among you shares."

"Labala," the large man said. "I'm that man. I think."

Dafflemere made a general bow.

"We greet you, welcome you to Freebooter's Island, wish you all the luck and the best while you're here. I'd guess you're the men who've been playing hells with the Linyati off Noorat?"

"How'd you know that?" Froln asked suspiciously.

"I could be magical, and say I've got my ways, but civilized magic tends to sometimes get fuzzy around the Linyati.

"One of the Brethren was planning on raiding down that way, and was hailed by a neutral he knew from other times. That ship, fresh from trading with the Slavers at Noorat, told him the seas were buzzing like a teased-up wasp's nest, suggested he maybe wanted to seek his benefice elsewhere.

"Don't get angry . . . I know a lot of things, tell nobody. But I don't know your name, sir."

"I'm Gareth Radnor," Gareth said. "Elected captain of this ship and master of the others beyond."

"Pleased. I'll ask your business here, if I'm not intruding. You're welcome whether you came just to drink or sell whatever goods you've acquired."

"Trading our spoils is the first item," Gareth said. "Refitting. Looking for new hands. We've got a ship that needs its stern rebuilt before it can take some people home to Kashi."

"You seized slaves?"

"We did."

"You needn't trouble yourselves with them beyond this island," Dafflemere said carefully. "The Brethren practice complete freedom for all, and there's those who'd be happy to take them off your hands for hard coinage."

"Freedom for all," Gareth said, his voice a bit hard, "except for slaves, you mean."

Dafflemere gave Gareth a chill look. "Some, perhaps most of us, feel slavery is not good. Others . . ." He shrugged. "As I said, all are free to do as they wish."

"Let me ask something," Labala said, changing the subject. "What would've happened if, say, we were Linyati, and had cloaked your magic? What would have happened then?"

"I'm happy to satisfy your curiosity, my friend. First, seizing me is, shall we say, a bit harder than appears, and I'll give you no details, since today's friends may be tomorrow's foes. Second, there are cannon on either side of the passage, with well-trained gun crews."

"We saw them."

"Third . . . well, come here."

Dafflemere went to the railing, swirled in the air with his hand. Gareth found his gesturing hard to watch.

Then a greater swirling in the water below came, and something just below the surface looked at them, a great eye, as big as a man's torso. Two tentacles lifted, curled, almost as high as the *Steadfast*'s mast, splashed down, and a beak came out of the water and clattered.

"There are other of his ilk below," Dafflemere said. "I have learned to call to them, and they think of me as . . . perhaps . . . a friend. Or at any rate someone who ensures they feed well from time to time.

"That is the only caution I must give you. Killing is forbidden on Freebooter's Island, other than in fair duel. And, by the way, the fairness of that duel is open to question by the Brethren. Those who offend are tried by a court of the Brethren, and if guilty become a dainty nibble for my friends here.

"Our other crimes are rape, assault on an unequally armed foe, and theft. The penalties for all are the same as murder.

"Now, if you'll signal to your ships to follow your lead, you can find an anchorage at one of the cables that stretch between the buoys you see. The bottom of this lagoon is far too deep for any anchor chain to reach.

"Again, I bid you welcome, fellow corsairs."

Gareth looked at Thom Tehidy and Knoll N'b'ry, and felt a thrill at the words that went all the way back to their childhood.

Corsairs they were in truth, now.

"Here is what I propose," Gareth said to his men, assembled in the waist of the ex-slave ship. "We shall keep the *Steadfast*, of course, and the *Revenge* and the *Goodhope*, out here for another foray. We'll also keep ownership of two, maybe more, of the other ships, to take what cargo we don't dispose of here to a neutral port to await our homecoming, as we agreed.

"The men, women, and children from Kashi will be taken back by volunteers and set ashore as close as possible to their homeland."

"Damned if I like that," one of the older men said. "They're brown gold ... and I heard that magic-man say we could sell 'em here."

"I've thought of that," Gareth said, "and of our agreement, in the Articles that *all of you signed*," he said with emphasis. "But I wish no grumbling. I'll let go one of my shares, to be split among those who feel wronged, to compensate for the slaves. That is my only offer.

"Anyone disagreeing is welcome to call for a vote on the matter."

Gareth knew he had the majority, and anyone calling for a vote to sell the Kashi men as slaves would, most likely, be cut from the Articles and told to leave the Company.

"Now, as to the cargoes we've taken," he went on, after waiting to see if anyone else said anything. "The first option is that each man can draw his share of raw goods, take it ashore to dispose of as he wishes, on whatever terms he can make.

"The second option is for it to remain with me, for either disposition here for items we either need to continue our voyaging or ones I think will be more valuable back in Saros, or for shipment and sale when we return to Saros.

"The items gotten rid of here will be either traded for or sold for silver or gold. I can safely say that the prices I think I'll get here will be far lower than in Ticao.

"Any of the ship's Company who want their share in gold after I trade or sell can take it here, or, again, leave some or all with the Company."

"Long's I get enough for proper food, a crawlin' drunk, and a couple of women at m' head an' feet, I'll let th' rest stay with you," a sailor said, and, amid laughter, there were shouts of agreement from some, headshakes from others.

"I'll take all I can here," a grizzled seaman said. "For what're the odds of us living to see home again, anyway? Most likely we'll bleach our bones at forty fathoms before we see cold green seas again."

There was an uneasy murmur of agreement from too many of the sailors to that.

The first order of business for Gareth's pirates was getting under the weather, and the residents of Freebooter's

Island, as well as the other corsairs harboring there, seemed quite happy to join in.

The island was a celebration of anarchy. Here someone had put up a building from the island stone, laboriously cut and fitted into shape. Next to it four driftwood logs had been hammered into the sand, given a palm roof and indifferent siding from scavenged lumber. There was a central marketplace, but not much in the way of roads radiating from it.

There weren't many houses—the pirates weren't ashore long enough to build them nor, Gareth suspected, confident enough of their life span to justify the work.

Businesses were trading shacks, taverns, crude inns, brothels, and craft shops, these last run by Kashi natives who'd been rescued from the Linyati and chosen not to return to their homelands.

But Gareth's observations were made in a scattered fashion, as a feast, vaguely in honor of the newcomers' successes against the Linyati, swirled.

Hogs were butchered, dressed, and set on great spits over charcoal to slowly cook, basted with sauces. Chickens were chased down, killed, cleaned, and put into pots with fresh vegetables and fiery peppers. There were salads of strange fruits and bamboo hearts, drenched in spicy dressings.

For drink there was a dozen varieties of liquors, some made on the islands, more the local tipples from northern ports, a few even captured from the Linyati. The favorite among the last was known as Axkiller, not only for its immediate effects but for the way its drinker felt the next day.

About the only thing missing was salt beef and fish, for obvious reasons.

"We wish we could have fresh beef," said a ship's cook, now volunteering to turn one of the roasting pigs, "but th' island won't carry 'em yet. If we had some folks willing to work on land, we c'd clear an' plant one of the other islands, and bring in beeves to graze."

Gareth took a heavy-laden wooden plate and a concoction of various tropical fruits, found an empty brandy keg to sit on, and watched the party as the day turned into dusk:

Here a swarthy, muscled dwarf was juggling half a dozen bottles, pausing now and again to drink from one of them;

Three women were dancing, hand in hand, around a supine, snoring sailor;

Labala was singing in some unknown tongue, half a dozen brown-skinned natives playing instruments like Gareth had never seen, in keys Gareth had never heard;

Thom Tehidy and Knoll N'b'ry were arguing intensely about the correct way to lay nets for sea-trout, using bottles in the sand for their boats and twigs for nets;

Froln, seemingly quite sober, disappeared into a hut with a woman in each arm, gold coins clenched in his teeth;

Bosun Nomios and Dafflemere sat on the sand, playing some sort of board game, but the pieces were small glasses of brandy, and the winner or loser, Gareth couldn't tell which, was required to upend the glass. After a while, Nomios very sedately pitched onto the board and began snoring. Dafflemere got up, tried to dance a victory jig around him, collapsed on the ground and stayed there.

Gareth sat alone, yet quite content, wanting, as far as he could tell, nothing, needing nothing. No, he thought. Not quite. Cosyra would be nice here. That'd be someone who could honestly tell him what Axkiller tasted like.

A brown-skinned boy lounged nearby against a palm tree, a brightly colored flower behind one ear. He was curly haired, handsome. He smiled tentatively at Gareth, who smiled back politely, then shook his head. The boy shrugged, found another's attention, and went up a winding path with him a few moments later.

A quite small, very well built woman, not much more than a girl, sat beside him.

"You are the captain of these?" she asked.

"At the moment," Gareth said.

"A man like yourself, as young as you are, must have much *karaba*," she said. The various languages Gareth had learned swept through his mind. There. *Karaba.* Courage. Manliness.

"Uh . . . thank you."

"I am Irina," she said.

"And I'm Gareth."

"You are by yourself."

Gareth nodded.

"I saw you turn away that boy. Am I better?"

"Uh . . . well, yes, I mean, I'm more attracted to you than men," Gareth stumbled.

Irina preened.

"Then I would be proud to be the consort of a captain . . . for an hour, or as long as you linger here."

"You, uh, honor me deeply," Gareth said. "And I'm enchanted." He wondered why he was sounding like such a bumpkin.

"But . . ." Irina said through her teeth.

"There's someone in Saros that, well . . ."

"What of that?" Irina said. "I'm not offering to company you for eternity, or to bear your brats, now."

"But—"

"Is this woman some sort of witch, that she could sniff out what we do when, or if, you return?"

"No, but—"

Irina gave him a look as good as a broadside, hissed

something untranslatable by the language spells Gareth had learned, and stalked away.

Now what the blazes am I supposed to do about something like that? Gareth wondered. I always thought someone who's given an honest answer about something like this would be, well, maybe not respectful, but at least understanding. And now I've made another enemy.

That woman was behaving like . . . like a man!

Suddenly he found everything enormously funny, burst out laughing, and decided it was time for him to go back to the *Steadfast*. He had to decide how to go about trading. And not think about how very pretty Irina was.

The *Steadfast* was beached on soft sand, and sailors had attached block and tackle between masts and large palms and careened her. Her hull was green, filthy, and already the stink of the dying barnacles drifted everywhere.

"They didn't tell us about this in the romances," Knoll N'b'ry said, then shouted, "All right, men. Off your soft asses and set to."

Crewmen lounging in the shade groaned, got up, picked up scrapers and lit torches, and went back to cleaning the hull. But they worked hard and fast. No man wanted to think about his fate if a Linyati squadron warped into the lagoon, with a ship incapable of fight or escape.

The Linyati slaver, which Gareth had decided to name the *Freedom*—a little irked that he'd already used *Revenge*, considering the ship's purpose and how he intended to use it in the future—was being warped toward the beach as the tide rushed out of the lagoon.

Standing in the shallows was Dafflemere, chanting a spell, wearing only a cut-off pair of breeches. Beside him was Labala, earnestly mimicking the sorcerer's gestures, aping his speech.

There were no more than a dozen men on the ropes, pulling at the ship; steadily, under the influence of the spell, it came closer to shore as if pulled by invisible shipyard winches.

There was a loud scratching as it grounded. Experienced islanders ran close with balks of lumber, braced the ship to keep her from falling on her side.

Dafflemere stopped his spell.

"Now, m'friend," he told Labala. "As I taught you, go in and brace your ship."

Labala nodded, picked up a rock, ran close to one length of timber. He touched the rock to sand, chanted:

> *"As you once were*
> *Be again*
> *Be solid*
> *Pay no need to water*
> *Or wind*
> *Stand true*
> *Stand solid."*

Dafflemere waded ashore.

"A promising sort," he said. "All he lacks is the ability to cipher."

"Which I'm teaching him," Gareth said. "In my copious spare time."

"I'd be willing to take on that chore."

"For how much? You certainly set a price for the services of your shipyard." Gareth politely refrained from commenting on what he thought of a shipyard made up of a long stretch of sloping beach, fifty half-naked men, and a largish pile of lumber, with nary a dry dock or victualing dock.

Dafflemere looked hurt.

"I'll be happy to do that without fee, Captain. For it's always good for a man to have knowledge, is it not?"

Gareth looked at Dafflemere closely, saw no sign of intrigue or mockery.

"My apologies, sir," he said, "for I've become used to everything on these islands being for sale."

"Ah," Dafflemere said cagily, "you fail to understand my subtlety. I'll instruct your wizard, and both you and he will owe me, for I sense that both of you are unfortunately cursed with a sense of morality.

"Sometime in the future I shall need a favor, and you won't be able to begrudge me."

Gareth managed a grin.

"The most I will give you," the man with an eyepatch said, "is two, no three of my heavy falconets for your silks. I expect to go out soon, and will need every gun I have."

"Which is why you've got the falconets stowed amidships, handy for use," Gareth said.

The pirate glowered, played with his eyepatch, poured himself another glass of brandy.

"Let me leave it like this," Gareth said. "Six bales of silks for each gun."

"No. I cannot stand to be dealt with in such a trifling manner," the pirate said. He got up and stalked away from the open-air stand Gareth sat in. But he walked more and more slowly away, waiting for the call back.

"Captain," Gareth said.

The man turned around quickly.

"You didn't finish your brandy, sir."

The man looked angrily at Gareth, then came back and drained his glass. A sheepish smile came.

"You are a hard bargainer, sir. Especially for someone as young as you are."

Gareth shrugged.

"In another life, at another time, were you a merchant?"

"I was apprenticed to one," Gareth said. "And I was a ship's purser."

"Ayee," the pirate wailed. "No wonder I am bested! Take your damned guns!"

Gareth scribbled an instruction on a bit of paper for the ship's prize crew to release the silk.

He considered his accounts, thought he was doing fairly well, not really knowing the worth of anything out here in the unknown.

Another man, this one an island merchant, came up.

"I understand you have spices for sale."

"Not many," Gareth said honestly. "Most are to be shipped home."

"But let us talk about what remains," the man said. "For I have gold to bargain with."

Life on Freebooter's Island was somewhat of a dream for Gareth, when he remembered the cold winds of Saros, the brief summers, and the gray seas heaving around his homeland.

The only clothes needed were a pair of breeches for decency, and food, crispy-fried spiced fish and wonderfully sweet fruits, was gotten by tossing a copper to one of the island natives cooking over a brazier on the beach.

No one cared if you got drunk, as long as you didn't bother anyone else that much. Women were friendly.

The seas were clear, blue, warm, with multicolored fish wriggling through tendrilled seaweed.

Gareth thought of building a house on one of the islets, far enough away from the other pirates, close enough to row over when he wanted company other than Cosyra, who, of course, would be his partner in the idyllic days and soft nights.

Then he caught himself, realizing that half of the charm and the attraction of Freebooter's Island was it was very temporary. Sooner or later, he and the Company would be sailing back out, looking for prey.

If he was forced to live here, doing nothing, for the rest of his life, he'd go mad from boredom within a month.

As, he suspected, would Cosyra.

Gods, but he missed her!

"We're doing fairly well," Gareth told his crew. "We're getting better prices than I'd anticipated and a lot of it in gold or silver. Plus we've signed thirty new men to the Articles.

"As for repairs, the *Steadfast* comes off tomorrow, the *Goodhope* and *Revenge* go on the beach after that.

"The *Freedom*'s stern should be rebuilt within the fortnight, and we can begin thinking about who volunteers to go to Kashi and return the slaves, as we agreed, and then which of our ships should be loaded and start for home, and who'll sail them as prize crews."

"Home, sir?" Nomios said.

"Sorry," Gareth said. "I've been busy . . . and tired. Here's what I think: We'll sell one ship here—I've got a possible buyer—and three others will be packed solid with our treasures and sail for Lyrawise, in Juterbog."

"Why there?" a sailor called. "They may be neutral, but they ain't always been our friends. I've seen Linyati ships sailin' in and out of their ports."

"Better there, for the moment, than Ticao," Gareth said. "As we've talked about before, nobody knows what King Alfieri will think when we come sailing up the Nalta.

"I'd rather keep our loot offshore until we know. If all goes well, then we can bring it upriver for marketing."

"I heard your uncle or brother or such is a Merchant Prince," a sailor said. "No doubt he'll be the one to handle the matter.

"At a goodly profit."

Gareth held back anger. "I've made, and will make, no deals with anyone you men don't approve. I'll let my uncle in on the bidding, unless the Company votes no.

"Is there anything the matter with that?"

The sailor muttered, but turned away.

Trade items that went quickly were Luynes's cutlasses, muskets, and "cutting knives," but Gareth insisted these wouldn't go for gold or silk, but rather on a two- or three-one basis for quality arms, intended for his present and future crews.

Some of them he refused to trade, having other plans for them.

Gareth sat in the *Steadfast*'s longboat looking critically at his ship as it floated in the green, clear waters of the bay. Froln and Galf sat beside him.

"Seems she's a bit bow-down," he said.

"She is, sir," Galf said. "Those demi-cannon are heavy. I moved as much ballast as I dared to the stern, but she still's got a tilt to her."

"She'll sail awkward an' heavy 'gainst a headwind," Froln said. "No question. And fall off quick."

"I'd guess she could hold no closer than, what, six points off the bow, trying to beat to windward?" Gareth said.

"If that," Galf said.

"Awkward," Froln repeated.

"Very well," Gareth said. "My plan doesn't work." He'd wanted to move long-range guns into the bows of his ships, so he could fight the way he'd taken on the slave ship, instead of the ship- and man-wrecking normal broadside to broadside style.

"Or, anyway it doesn't work with the size of the guns we've got," he went on. "We need smaller, lighter cannon. Those two heavy falconets we put in the *Goodhope* seem suitable."

"Pity no one out here wants to trade for guns very badly."

Froln laughed.

"An' you're surprised, Skipper, in these nice, calm, peaceful waters?"

Gareth grinned.

"No. No, I'm not. We don't have any to spare, ourselves. Maybe we'll try this setup again, when we're back in Ticao and there's armories to be called on."

Unlike other pirate officers, who wore a mixture of civilian finery and seaman's garb, this man wore what could have been a uniform, in another time and clime. His red coat was long, split at the back, with gold buttons. His breeches were black, and appeared to have been washed in the last day or so. He wore a ruffled shirt, and a long dirk on one side of his belt, a thin-bladed rapier on the other. He was bareheaded, and fine, carefully brushed brown hair swept almost to his waist.

He sat, unbidden, at the chair in the trading booth.

"Captain Radnor," he said. "I'm Captain Ozerov, of the *Naijak*. Perhaps you've heard of me."

"Not of you, sir," Gareth said politely. "But I certainly know your ship. Well kept, sir, as if it was fresh from the shipyard."

"I believe in discipline," Ozerov said, "and its first part is cleanliness."

"Hard to argue with that," Gareth said. "You're from Juterbog, by your name?"

"Once, a long time ago. Now I work for myself, or, from time to time, those who wish my services."

"How may I be of service to you?"

"Those men of Kashi that you seized," Ozerov said. "I understand you have the noble intent of returning them to their jungles?"

"Such was the vote of my Company."

"I understand it wasn't unanimous."

"No," Gareth admitted. "There were those who see such men as profit."

"You may count me among them," Ozerov said. "As well as my master, in Saros. We have done very well by ourselves not only sailing with the Brethren but, from time to time, purchasing slaves for those civilized nations who keep to the old ways.

"My master, or, more correctly the man whose gold I take, is a most powerful lord, and, since I have been told you and your men largely hail from that land, it might be advantageous to you to do business with me.

"Not just now, in the increased weight of your purse, but in gaining influence with that powerful lord when you return home to Saros, if you plan such, and hope to be taken as a bold privateer rather than a hangable pirate."

"I would be delighted to be seen as such," Gareth said. "Might I ask the name of this great lord you serve?"

"His name is Quindolphin."

Gareth's bellowed laughter brought the puppy sleeping by his feet in the sand up with a yelp, and a few people in the marketplace looked over in curiosity.

"I fail to see your amusement at the mention of such a great man," Ozerov said, his tone menacing.

"My apologies to you, sir," Gareth said. "You could not have known that Lord Quindolphin tried to have me executed for a prank I pulled as a boy, and has since had me hunted across Ticao by troops of his men. Not long before we sailed, his own son tried to murder me.

"I'm sorry, Captain Ozerov, but not only do I not wish to soil my name, my men's name, and the name of my country by dealing in humanity, but I truly prize, especially now, learning the source of his wealth, having the unspeakable Quindolphin as my enemy."

He rose, bowed.

"Thank you, however, Captain Ozerov, for coming to me, even in your misapprehension."

Gareth expected Ozerov to be angry, but the slender man considered Radnor thoughtfully, then stood, returned the bow, and walked away, without response.

Gareth watched him go, and in spite of the midday heat, felt a chill.

The torches flared into the night, and the marketplace rocked with laughter and music.

As usual, Gareth sat to one side, watching the merriment. He'd danced a couple of dances, learning the wild stamping style of the islanders, for politeness, then gone to the sidelines.

He patted back a yawn, wishing that he liked the taste of brandy better, for it certainly enlivened a party, and made the time pass less quickly.

Gareth decided as soon as this song was finished he'd make his way out, back to the *Steadfast*. He'd been talking to the men of Kashi, trying to decide on a proper course and landing place for the *Freedom*.

It pleased him to make careful notes on the pristine blankness of his charts, and he wondered why his country didn't have ships that went out to chart empty seas and lands, instead of leaving matters to merchants and brigands like himself.

A man came out of the shadows, a slight figure behind him. Gareth recognized Captain Ozerov, and his companion the woman named Irina.

He had time to get to his feet, begin a bow, when Ozerov slapped him abruptly, almost knocking him down.

Gareth staggered, recovered.

A woman screamed, a man shouted, and the music broke off into raggedness.

Before Gareth could say anything, Ozerov said, in a loud voice:

"You have offended the dignity of this woman, whom I choose to defend, and I call you to answer that offense in blood."

A sailor somewhere roared laughter, shouted, "Din't know th' slut had any dign'ty. Me an' two others screwed her lights out two nights runnin'."

Ozerov pretended not to notice. Gareth wondered why the farce with Irina, then remembered Dafflemere's cautions about violence on the island, and that a fair duel would be judged by the Brethren.

No doubt defending someone's honor, no matter how slight, would be considered fair.

And of course, if Ozerov killed Gareth, he could name a pretty figure from Lord Quindolphin.

"As the challenged party," Gareth said, "I accept, of course."

"Name your seconds."

That gave Gareth an idea. He smelled drink on Ozerov's breath, and that could give him a slight edge.

"I need no seconds," he said calmly. "We'll fight now. Here."

Ozerov blinked, recovered.

"Very well," he said, but licked his lips. "Set your conditions."

Gareth thought of his own skill with the blade, guessed the rapier and dagger Ozerov carried would be the weapons he was most skilled with.

"Pistols," he said. "At the water's edge, with torches to give us light for the killing."

Gareth shivered in the breeze from the lagoon, even though the night was most balmy.

Tehidy handed him a single-barreled pistol.

"It's fully charged, and I made sure the ball is perfect."

"Thank you, Thom."

"I know you'll win," Tehidy said. "But if not . . ."

"First, have either you or Knoll stand for captain as my replacement. Froln's a good man, but I doubt his judgment. As for me, I'm no gentleman," Gareth said. "Wait until you get a chance and arrange an accident for the good Captain Ozerov that you won't get blamed for, if you can."

"I can do that," Tehidy said. "But don't lose, godsdammit!"

"I hadn't planned on it."

Strangely, Gareth felt icy calm, as he did before a battle.

Fifteen paces distant, Ozerov stood, talking to his second, who was also uniformed.

Dafflemere, who seemed to be the only visible form of the government of Freebooter's Isle, stood a bit aside, holding a pistol in one hand. Two others were stuck in his sash.

"Gentlemen," he called. "It is time. Seconds, stand away from your principals."

The officer and Tehidy moved away.

"This is an argument," Dafflemere said, "that I was told could only be settled in blood. Is this the case?"

Both Gareth and Ozerov said, "Yes."

"Then I shall count three. At the end of that time, you may fire.

"I caution you, seconds, and any others: Do not interfere, or I'll deal with you myself." He motioned with his pistol.

"One . . ."

Gareth lifted his cocked pistol.

"Two . . ."

He breathed long, deep, held it.

"Three!"

His pistol came down, aimed, and fired as Ozerov's gun went off. He felt the ball whip past his shoulder, saw Ozerov stagger and a stain appear, a graze on the outside of Ozerov's thigh.

Tehidy and Ozerov's second ran to their men.

"You hit him!" Tehidy said.

Gareth nodded.

"Blood has been drawn," Dafflemere shouted. "Are you satisfied?"

"I am," Gareth said calmly.

"And you, sir?"

"I am not," Ozerov gritted. "Reload the damned pistols, and I'll set matters right."

"Seconds, you heard the captain's wishes. The duel will go another exchange."

Again the guns were loaded, and the seconds withdrew.

"Again, I shall count three," Dafflemere said.

"One . . ."

Gareth breathed steadily, calmly.

"Two . . ."

He exhaled, held his breath.

"Three!"

Once more Ozerov pulled first. Gareth saw the plume of smoke, felt a dull thud against his upper chest, had a moment of wonderment that it didn't hurt. He staggered, went to his knees.

He saw, through dimming vision, Ozerov whoop in joy, cast his pistol high in the air.

Gareth lifted his arm, lifted the pistol, heavier than lead, heavier than a cannon, and the first wave of pain hit, was pushed back. He extended his pistol at full arm's length and touched the hair trigger.

The pistol bucked, spun out of his hand.

Ozerov contorted, and Gareth saw, above his eyebrows, a smash of red and a gout of tissue.

Then the torches went out, and there was nothing but blackness.

Gareth Radnor fell bonelessly forward into the sand.

Eleven

Fever and its dreams struck Gareth almost immediately.

Sometimes they were pleasant—Gareth saw his parents alive and happy again; sailed into Ticao with a convoy of looted ships in his wake; danced at some great masked ball with Cosyra.

Sometimes they weren't—he relived the day the Slavers came to his village, except this time they dragged his parents away in chains, while Gareth wallowed in muck at the shoreline, unable to rescue them; he sailed the *Steadfast* into the guns of some monstrous Linyati ship, eight impossible gundecks high; on a boyhood prank, Cosyra slipped and fell, screaming, from his grip, to her death.

Occasionally he swam up into consciousness, realized he was on a cot in the shade of a rough lean-to on the seaward side of the island, where the tradewinds could wash away his fever.

There was always someone there to nurse him—Labala, Thom Tehidy, Knoll, Dafflemere. There were women of the island as well, keeping watch through the night. The only one he recognized was, strangely, Irina, who was crying and saying something about she'd thought it was a joke. Once, Cosyra was there, and he knew that was another fever dream, and wept bitterly.

Then the pain would take him, as a shark takes its prey, pulling him back down into the depths, and he could hear himself moaning, no matter how hard he tried to hold back.

Then, one day, he woke, and his mind was clear and the pain was gone.

It was morning, he thought, and Labala was sitting beside him. The big man wasn't looking at him, but was intently copying letters on a tablet, tongue clenched between his teeth in concentration.

"Some nurse you make," Gareth managed, and the tablet spun across the lean-to.

"You live!"

"I think so."

Gareth tried to sit up, and his arm went from under him, and he realized how weak he was.

"How long have I been no better than a lump?"

"Almost a month," Labala said. "Here. Drink some of this."

"This" was a fruit concoction, cooled in a gourd.

"Thanks." Gareth sank back down.

"What have I missed?"

Labala grunted. "And I thought I was all ready, standing by with all the news, waiting for you to come back, and now everything's fluttering about in my head.

"But now I got it in order.

"About a week after me and Dafflemere decided you was going to live, Froln and N'b'ry took the slaves back to where they come from aboard the *Freedom*.

"N'b'ry figured it'd be best to get them out of sight and mind, for fear some others might think, with you down, the vote on whether they was to be freed or not could be reheld.

"They sailed out, were gone a week an' a half, came back a little sweaty."

"Why?"

"Seems there were Linyati all over the waters around Kashi, and they had the hardest damned time eluding them. Knoll said it was like they were looking just for them." He grinned. "Froln cursed me some, saying I should've been along, trying to cast spells of confusion and dismay, instead of playing nursemaid back here.

"But I told them they came back all right, so what's the advantage in whining?"

"How could the Slavers know where to look? It's a big ocean," Gareth wondered, a bit to himself.

"Knoll had the same question. I dunno. But he said the people we sent back went ashore, glad, and one of them said they knew just where to go, how to go up that big damned river, sneak past the Linyati town, and sooner or later they'd be home, with new tales and songs.

"They was most grateful for those swords and such you wouldn't let anyone trade away, and said they knew well how to put them to use. They said they'd pray for all of us until their children's children's children had long gray beards.

"I figure that's about to next week, given most folks' memories and gratitudes."

Gareth drank more fruit juice.

"Anything else?"

"I've saved the best—if that's what it is—till last. See Dafflemere's had a dream. About gold and ships. About the Linyati treasure fleet that sails from Kashi into Linyati waters, stopping in every Linyati port, picking up gold and silver and treasures."

Gareth nodded. He remembered Nomios telling him that Luynes had talked of somehow, someday, finding a way to attack that fleet.

"That—assuming the fleet really exists—would be a proper dream," he said. "But how many ships would it take to attack them?"

"There's been Brethren coming in for resupply, and Dafflemere's been bending their ears hard. We've got twenty-two ships committed, which'd be twenty-six if we go along."

"You mean the Company's been waiting for me to come back before they voted?"

Labala looked away, out at the water.

"We told them they ought to wait. But . . ."

"But they didn't," Gareth said, pretending indifference. "I couldn't have expected them to. How'd the vote go?"

"Most were in favor of sailing with Dafflemere. Some—me, the others who went out as virgins on the *Steadfast*—said we ought to wait till you got better. Others laughed, said if you wanted to come along, as captain, you'd be welcome.

"If not . . . there was just too much gold to wait, and Froln would make a good enough skipper.

"Especially since Dafflemere's been dreaming, constant, about those ships."

Labala looked about cautiously.

"Truth tell, Gareth, that's something I don't like about this deal."

"Why not?"

"The gods send those kind of dreams, mostly to get people into trouble."

Gareth had a thought about who else might have cast those inviting dreams, but said nothing of it. "Well," he said. "I don't guess I've got a lot of choice whether I go in with you, do I?"

Labala shook his head. "Sorry, Gareth. I think you got backed into a corner."

Gareth regained his energy quickly. He was plied with the freshest of fish, pork, chicken at every meal, although there still was no fresh beef to be had. His crews came calling daily, each man with a morsel or a charm that'd help Gareth back to full strength.

Both Labala and Dafflemere specialized in herbal sorcerous potions. Gareth thought both worked on the theory that the more disgusting a medicine was, the better it was for him.

Irina and other island women brought other delicacies, and again Irina apologized for letting herself fall into Ozerov's trap. Gareth told her to pay no mind, she couldn't have known his intent.

She said she'd do absolutely anything to be forgiven. Gareth was sorely tempted, but somehow maintained his nobility. Then, at night, when he saw firelight from below, in the marketplace, and heard women and men laughing together, he cursed his foolishness.

Three times a day he forced himself out of his bed, made himself exercise, walking as far as he dared, then trotting, finally running. He worked out with weapons, keeping them sheathed for added weight.

When he felt still better, he challenged any man to fight him with wooden swords or daggers, a silver piece for anyone who beat him. He lost about twenty pieces of silver, since there were highly skilled swordsmen among the pirates, before he felt his strength at full surge.

Then he moved back aboard the *Steadfast* and announced he was no longer on the sick list and back to duty.

"Permission to come aboard?" the man in the longboat hailed.

Gareth went to the rail, thought he recognized the man in the sternsheets. But he didn't have to guess his identity—the other men in the boat, wearing striped sleeveless shirts and blue breeches, plus the immaculate condition of the boat itself, gave away its identity.

"Come aboard the *Naijak*," he called, and the man swarmed up the ladder.

"Captain Radnor, I'm Captain Petrich," he said. "I, uh, was—"

"The late Ozerov's second in the duel," Gareth said.

"Yessir." Petrich looked uncomfortable.

"Forget about it, unless you propose another challenge," Gareth said. "I doubt the Brethren would consider revenge a just duel—at least, not that sort of revenge."

"No, sir," Petrich said. "What Ozerov did was his own business."

"Then welcome aboard, and come into my cabin for a glass."

"Fruit juice if you have it, or water," Petrich said. "Brandy fuzzles my senses, so I don't drink on duty."

"My taste exactly," Gareth said with some surprise. He and Petrich must be the only corsairs on Freebooter's Island who felt that way.

In the *Steadfast*'s cabin, Petrich came to the point.

"Sir, as you know, our ship was owned by Lord Quindolphin, of Saros. That was why Ozerov challenged you, to gain favor, and most likely gold, with Quindolphin."

"I'd already figured that out," Gareth said, noting Petrich's use of the past tense regarding the *Naijak*'s ownership.

"There are many in the crew who disliked serving Quindolphin, and who feel that slaving is a dirty business, something the gods will hold against us in the afterlife."

"If there are any."

"I believe in them," Petrich said. "And I felt your killing Ozerov, who was one of the most feared duelists I know of, was a sign.

"After his death, we—the officers and men—determined to become true pirates, and sail under the black flag rather than Quindolphin's house banner."

Gareth grunted in surprise.

"To be frank," Petrich said, "it was less a matter of morality than honest greed. Quindolphin's share was half, which is absurd for a man who took none of the risks."

"Interesting," Gareth said. "And, since Quindolphin is one of my enemies, what you say pleases me. But why have you come to tell me this?"

"As I believe in the gods," Petrich said, "I believe in luck. You've proven yourself to be lucky, Captain Radnor.

"The ship's company of the *Naijak* wishes to join your enterprises, and have voted, if you accept us, to follow your lead until we vote to do otherwise, and are willing to accept whatever terms, assuming they're reasonable, you wish to take for such leadership."

Gareth smiled at that.

"That's not the most solid of commitments."

Petrich sighed. "I know. But it appears there is little that is in these waters."

"True." Gareth thought about what Petrich had said. "What experience have you, beyond the seizing of human cargoes?"

"We've taken four or five prizes," Petrich said. "Only

one worth bragging on, and that was a hard fight that cost us more men than I think it should've. Yet another reason to learn under your tutelage."

Ah, Gareth thought. So, now, a bit more than twenty years of age, I'm a worshipful sage.

"I think," Gareth said honestly—though keeping a small check in mind about the hard loyalty of the *Naijak*—"we could be of mutual assistance, if your ship sails and fights as well as it looks. As for my payment, I'd consider two shares acceptable."

"I promise you, it does that," Petrich said. "And I certainly think your suggested share is more than reasonable."

"I should have asked for more," Gareth said.

Petrich smiled, lifted his glass. "A pawky fluid to toast a partnership."

Gareth touched his own mug to Petrich's.

"One other thing," Petrich said. "I . . . we . . . assumed, before we voted, that your ships will take part in Dafflemere's expedition against the treasure ships."

"Such has been decided," Gareth said flatly.

"I tell you, young captain," Dafflemere said, "it's proof that the gods are blessing us that I've had several dreams, each as precise as if it were real life, about the Linyati treasure."

"That is just what I wanted to discuss with you."

Gareth and Dafflemere were in his house, one of the few stone buildings on Freebooter's Island. It was lavishly cluttered with weapons, relics of wrecks, charts, and odd, probably magical, artifacts.

Gareth drank water, Dafflemere a horrible concoction of Axkiller and northern brandy, which never seemed to make him anything other than redder of face.

"You have doubts?"

"Only two," Gareth confessed. "The first is your dreams. Could they be sent as a trap by the Linyati?"

Dafflemere snorted. "To a magician of lesser powers than mine, possibly, although that would still take great wizardry, since I'm not known to the Slavers.

"But I can answer you more precisely, since I've cast spells and found no signs of any foreign thaumaturge's presence. I've used relicts of the Linyati to help me in that search, by the way, which would surely warn me if they were laying a trap."

"That's reassuring," Gareth said.

"I don't mean to be insulting," Dafflemere said, "but is there any possibility your hesitation comes from a bit of jealousy, since this was not your plan?

"I would hardly suggest this," he continued hastily, "if I didn't know you to be a young man of great common sense and skepticism, able to question everything, including your own perceptions. I would hardly have done it with other corsair captains of lesser intellect."

Gareth felt a bit of anger, fought it back, considered Dafflemere's suggestion.

"No," he said slowly. "Or at any rate I don't think there's envy in my caution.

"Perhaps the real reason I'm a bit skeptical is this seems to be a bit of plunging. If we take the treasure ships, all well and good, and we'll be great lords, able, if we wish, to quit reiving forever and be honored, even ennobled, with such riches in our own lands."

Gareth suddenly had a flash of longing for just that, but then it vanished as he thought of the dullness of a country squire's life, or, for that matter, his uncle Pol's.

"But if we fail, if the Linyati are too strong," he continued, "then all this"—and his arm swept the quiet lagoon—"will be shattered."

"Why, lad," Dafflemere said, "none of this was here before we came, now was it? We built this island, intending it only for our own time, for the brief span we're able to strut the quarterdeck, our names a whisper of fear among lesser wights. So who cares if it's washed away as quickly as it came?

"Perhaps my—our—venture is putting everything on a single casting of the dice. What could be grander, Gareth, than that? For what could be worse than living a nice, simple, tedious life in some backwater as if we were proper citizens? Aren't we all rebelling against that fate?"

Gareth remembered what he'd said to Thom Tehidy and Knoll N'b'ry the day the Slavers destroyed his village. There was a bit of a shiver in the memory, but also an honest surge of agreement.

"You're right," Gareth said. "Or anyway my heart says you're right."

"And what else should we follow?" Dafflemere upended his great mug, bellowed laughter.

"All right," Knoll N'b'ry said evenly. "Why me?"

"Because you're about the most level-headed sort in the Company," Gareth said. "Because I think you and Nomios can get the three ships to Juterbog's main port and wait for a suitable amount of time without losing control of the crewmen, nor selling off the cargo for drink."

The two were on the deck of the *Freedom*. Gareth was supervising the placement of four more guns on its maindeck, which would give it ten to a broadside. The ship may have been a slow wallower, but now its punch made it worth keeping rather than sending home.

"I know I can do the last," N'b'ry said. "But I don't know about this crew. Gareth, you've given me every—

well, most every—layabout and rakehelly in the Company."

"Because I don't want them aboard for the raid," Gareth said. "I want men I can trust."

N'b'ry looked at him, and Radnor could tell Knoll was holding back anger.

"So you run off and play, and I've got to take all our loot to a safe place. Just like when we were kids. *Damned* if I like being the dependable one!"

"But you are."

"What about Thom? He's reliable. Oh, I have it. You're afraid he'd throw you overboard if you went to him and said he'd have to miss out on the biggest battle ever."

"There may be some truth to that."

"You know, I could quit the Company."

"But you won't," Gareth said.

"If you'd sounded smug, I might've thrown you overside myself," N'b'ry said. "But you're right. Damn you again."

He looked at the roster, shook his head.

"Why the blazes couldn't this wait until after we've come back from hitting the Linyati?"

Gareth took a deep breath.

"Because there's a fair chance, I think, of not coming back. And the ships you're taking north are the ones I'd like least to put into battle."

"There is that."

"Don't forget," Gareth said, "you and the others are for full shares, whether you're in the fight or not."

"That's a comfort," Knoll said sarcastically. "I didn't go a-pirating with you just to get rich, you know."

"I know," Gareth said. He thought about saying how bad he felt, but knew that would be moral cowardice. He'd been elected captain, so it was his duty to lead as he saw fit, until voted out.

"All right," Knoll said heavily. "Now I'll get the pleasure of telling Nomios. Hoping he doesn't throw me overboard, or take a cutlass to me."

Gareth watched N'b'ry's three ships sail out of the lagoon, wished them safe passage, tried to make himself feel better for what he'd done to his friend. He tried to rationalize, thinking he had nothing to feel bad about; he'd certainly kept Knoll N'b'ry from dying at the hands of the Linyati if things went sour.

That didn't help, and he was late for a conference with his fellow captains on how they should fight the Linyati, when—and if—they encountered them.

Sailing was three days distant when Labala came to Gareth and took him aside.

"My father told me," he began, "that, in our islands, when a witch dreams of sharks, this means there is trouble due."

"And you've dreamt of sharks," Gareth said.

"I have."

"Do you think your dream can stop what another dream's put in motion?"

Labala looked across the harbor, at the ships swarming with working sailors, small boats skittering across the lagoon from ships to shore with supplies, gunpowder.

"No," he said slowly. "Don't guess it can."

Dafflemere, aboard his flagship, the *Thruster,* led the way through the passage, the corsair fleet behind him.

A fair wind blew across the quarterdeck of the *Stead-*

fast, and Galf shouted for full sail; across the blue, white-dappled ocean, canvas slatted down on dozens of masts.

Gareth looked back at the islets, saw, on the headlands, women, children, men, waving farewell.

He turned away, putting the warmth and safety of the land behind.

Ahead lay the open sea, and Linyati gold.

Twelve

The corsairs, in common with merchant sailors, which they'd all been, had a sensible fear of any vessel closer than a dot on the horizon, for fear of collision, and so the twenty-six ships were in a formation that could most politely be called raggedy.

They sailed almost due south, through the island chains around Freebooter Island, then across the open sea toward Kashi, intending to make landfall well west of the city of Batan and wait for the treasure ships.

The two biggest ships were the *Freedom* and Petrich's *Naijak*. The latter, unlike the *Freedom,* was a slender-hulled three-master that sailed handily, rather than butting through the seas. The other pirate ships were either converted northern merchantmen or captured Linyati traders or patrol craft.

The fleet sighted land, turned back to sea, and dropped sail. Dafflemere signaled for a captain's conference, and Gareth ordered his gig lowered. The longboats of Froln, now captaining the *Freedom*; Galf of the *Revenge*; Dihr, the freed Kashi, of the *Goodhope*; and Petrich of the *Naijak* joined as his boat closed on the *Thruster*.

Dafflemere's cabin swarmed with excited pirates, dripping arms and gold-lust. After everyone except Gareth had a mug of brandy from a small, bashed-top keg, Dafflemere hammered for silence with the butt of a—hopefully—unloaded pistol.

"We're here," he announced, "and there's been no sightings of any Linyati or Kashi ships, so we're still unknown in these waters.

"I've cast small spells to divert any magical attention, and shall start other spells to find the location of the treasure fleet."

There was a clamor of agreement. But Gareth stood.

"A suggestion?" he said.

"Go ahead, Cap'n Radnor," a captain said. "You're worth listening to."

"I'm no wizard," Gareth said. "But isn't it possible, Dafflemere, that your spell seeking the Linyati might be discovered by the mages that must be aboard their ships, and sound an alarm?"

"Not likely," Dafflemere said. "I cast with exceeding care. But there's a possibility."

"What about this, instead?" Gareth said. He went to the large map pinned to a bulkhead.

"I'll take the *Goodhope*," he said, "since it's Linyati, and a recent prize, so maybe it doesn't smell as much of pirates as some others, and sail west, along the bight of Kashi. I've noticed that the Linyati like to keep within smelling distance of the land, so I'll do the same.

"As soon as I'm down-horizon, another fast ship comes after me, always keeping my masts, no more, in sight. Perhaps your *Mystery*, Captain Libnah, since it seems fast. Then another when the *Mystery* is almost out of sight.

"When I sight the fleet—which should be easy for anyone who isn't stark blind—I'll make a signal; the next ship repeats it, and so on, back to the fleet, which should give more than enough time to deploy."

The pirates took only a few seconds to consider that and pronounce it a great idea.

"I've got a question, as well," Gareth said. "Dafflemere, do you have powers enough to raise a wind?"

Dafflemere growled in his beard.

"Sometimes yes," he admitted. "But sometimes no."

"Ah," Gareth said.

"Why're you asking?"

"Just curious."

Dafflemere looked skeptical, about to pursue the matter, when another, gray-bearded pirate snorted.

"An' ain't it strange for us hardened whores to be listenin' to a nigh-virgin, now."

"The virgin came in with seven ships, Cunedda," another pirate said. "Last prize I remember you taking was a clamboat."

There was laughter, and, surprisingly, Cunedda had the grace to chuckle.

"So we have an idea," Dafflemere said. "And I can cast passive spells just in case weather or some'at ruins Radnor's observations."

Another round of brandy, and the pirates went back to their ships. Gareth turned the *Steadfast* over to Thom Tehidy, went aboard the *Goodhope,* was away from the fleet within the hour.

The *Goodhope* was—almost—alone in enemy waters. Her only companion was a pair of masts the size of toothpicks on the horizon, the link to the freebooters.

Gareth had Dihr keep the faint smudge of land just in

sight to port. There were four lookouts in the bows, another, precariously, at the main masthead, and Gareth changed them hourly.

He dreaded the thought the Linyati would pass him in a fogbank, or, worse yet, be on a course farther out to sea. But at least they'd be spotted, most likely, by one of the following ships, even though he would be then considered a young, arrogant incompetent.

Labala was hovering anxiously, hoping for some task as soon as the Slavers were spotted. At least he wasn't as prideful as other wizards, making no insistence that *his* spells would never ever alert the Linyati, unlike poor Dafflemere.

Not wanting to sail down the Linyati's throat, he kept the *Goodhope* to a moderate speed. Two days out, Gareth was given a present by the gods he didn't believe in: a lookout spotted a dozen or more fishing boats with strange, triangular sails, that must be Kashi. Best of all, they were slowly moving east.

Gareth ordered all sail except the mainsail down, and that sail goosewinged to keep the *Goodhope* moving just a bit more slowly than the fishing boats.

Another day passed, and there were mutterings of boredom, which Gareth ignored.

Dihr did not:

"You men, I laugh at you," he shouted. "Soon enough there be blood up to your worthless bellybuttons, and then you shall whine to me about too much excitement. What is this madness of sailors that they never are happy with what they have, always wanting more or less?"

"'At's what keeps us goin' from ship to ship," someone answered. "Yer don't think we're doin' this fer pleasure, do you? Man that'd go to sea for pleasure would futter demons just for the pain."

Gareth went to the captain's cabin Dihr insisted he take, pretending he'd heard none of the exchange, and again studied his charts.

Two hours later the cry came:

"Ahoy the deck! Those fishermen're packing on full sail, goin' like stink for the beach!"

Gareth was on deck and up the mast, a glass tucked in his breeches. He clung to the slanting yard and looked out.

"Good call," he said to the lookout beside him.

"Thankee, sir. Looks like barnyard geese when the dog's loose."

Gareth nodded. "Now, keep your eye sharp on the horizon, just there, and you might see the dog himself in a bit. Pass that word on to your replacement when you're relieved."

"Aye, sir."

Gareth shinnied back down, and had the guns loaded and the best men put on watch. Then they waited.

It was midafternoon when the next cry came:

"Sail ho! Sail ho!"

"Whereaway?" Dihr shouted up.

"Two points off the port bow . . . one ship, no, two more of 'em . . . hells, too many to count. Big ships, carryin' full sail."

It was the Linyati treasure fleet.

Gareth gave commands to Dihr, and raised signal flags:

ENEMY IN SIGHT. BEARING SSW MY POSITION.

His original plan had been to make just this report, then return to the fleet. But with a favoring onshore wind, and the lateness of the hour, he chanced getting closer for more information.

The *Goodhope* raced in a long curve until it was due east of the oncoming Linyati, with the lowering sun at her back. Then Gareth eased her closer, under small sail, while he used his most powerful glass from the masthead.

He whistled when he had a count: there were at least twenty ships. Twelve of those were fat, four-masted, awkward merchant ships, like the *Freedom*, except with five decks above the waterline.

These sailed in three rows of four each. In front of the convoy Gareth counted three rakish warships, much like the ones he'd seen when the *Steadfast* first ventured into these waters, except larger. Along the seaward side of the convoy were four more, tacking back and forth to keep from outrunning the merchantmen.

Interestingly enough, he saw only one, possibly two, warships at the convoy's stern, and only a single ship on the landward side, from whence, of course, no attack could ever come.

Interesting, indeed.

But he had enough for the moment.

He came down from his platform, ordered the *Goodhope* to the fleet at full sail.

"Hmm," a captain said, looking at the chart and Gareth's proposed line of attack. "Risky if the wind changes. I dislike sailing close to the shore, especially with an enemy holding the weather gauge."

"That's if Dafflemere's spell fails, at worst," Gareth argued. "They'll not be looking for us inshore of their course, you'll admit."

"I'll admit. Only a fool would chance getting that close to land before a battle."

"A fool," Dafflemere said. "Or a pirate."

There were low laughs at that, less amusement than the hungry meditations of the tiger.

"They'll reach here, where the coastline reaches south,"

Gareth said, touching the map, "in another two days, about dawn. Most likely they'll stand a bit away from the land, which'll give us more searoom.

"Since they're sailing in close company, they've got lights out to keep from ramming each other.

"I'd propose we stand inshore, here, at night and lay to," he went on. "At first light, when they're grumpy and sleepy and changing watch..."

"Then we smash the bastids," Libnah of the *Mystery* said eagerly. "I'm superstitious, so I'm not dreamin' about the grand estate I'll have, and the scandal I'll bring to the neighborhood wif me doxies and carryin' on. But if any of you knows a good land agent, I'll be grateful for the reference."

Cunedda studied the map, nodded.

"It's a good plan, Cap'n Radnor. Something you didn't mention is the dawn wind is generally offshore, which'll help the spell you want Dafflemere to cast. A good plan indeed."

"Do we need to take a vote?" Dafflemere said.

Headshakes, negative mutters.

"Then let's go out and make ourselves into grandees, rolling about in gold," he said, lifting his mug.

"Good luck to us... and a long, slow dying to the Linyati!"

The night was clear, and a waning moon hung overhead. The seas were low, and there was no wind.

The pirate ships, masts bare, rolled in the slight swell, waiting.

Sometime after midnight, the *Steadfast*'s lookout called, said he saw lights off the port bow.

It was the Linyati, trudging along the coast toward Noorat and then into Linyati.

No one was asleep aboard the *Steadfast,* not even the usual fakers who shammed calm before battle.

Slowly, imperceptibly, the darkness faded, and Gareth could see the face of the helmsman across the quarterdeck from him.

A breeze came from the land, and Gareth smelled orange blossoms, swamp muck, the too-sweet reek of flowers he didn't know the names of.

The lights of the Linyati ships were to starboard now, and it wouldn't be long before their lookouts must see the waiting corsairs.

The breeze became a wind as Dafflemere began casting his spell.

"Make full sail," Gareth ordered Tehidy.

"Aye, sir," and wooden blocks whined as halyards were heaved on, and seamen's bare feet slapped the deck as sails opened to the wind.

Tehidy had asked, when Gareth returned from the final conference aboard the *Thruster,* if there'd been some grand strategy developed. Gareth looked at him wryly, and Tehidy started laughing.

"It'll be 'go for the closest and richest' for most of them," Gareth said. "We'll hold to the tactics we've practiced."

Not that Gareth had come up with any subtle tactics, other than strike for the Linyati ships' sterns, and for his five ships to hang together in the initial attack.

"We're seen," Tehidy said.

That was obvious as Gareth glassed the Linyati. They, too, were putting on all the canvas they carried in a rather futile attempt to escape. Two of the warships in the convoy's fore were tacking back to support the single ship guarding the landward side of the convoy.

The pirate fleet swept out, spreading as captains chose a target.

The air was salty and sweet to Gareth as they closed on the Linyati. He touched the three pistols in his sash, made sure they were half-cocked and ready, and his sword loose in its sheath.

The closest of the huge hulks saw the five pirates coming down on him, and someone panicked—strange for the Slavers. Its helm went hard to port, and the ship strained onto a new course, directly across the convoy lines.

"They'll be ruinin' themselves an' all we'll have to do is watch," someone on the *Steadfast*'s maindeck shouted, and so it was as the veering merchantman smashed into the stern of another ship.

"Signals to *Freedom* and *Naijak*," Gareth snapped. "Attack those two ships first," and flags went snapping up the mast.

"We'll take . . ." Gareth considered, "that fat one on the rear. Signal to *Revenge* and *Goodhope*."

"Sir."

"Helmsman, we'll go close under her stern."

"Aye, sir."

"Run out the guns!"

Gunports banged open, and the wooden trucks of the gun carriages squealed on the deck. The *Steadfast* closed on the Linyati ship. White smoke plumed down the Linyati's side, and moments later the dull thud of her cannon rolled across the water.

"Still out of range," Tehidy said. "And whoever laid those guns is as blind as a flop-eared pig."

Gareth nodded absently, watching the Linyati ship.

"Gunners," he shouted. "This one has a lower gundeck in her stern. Break that up for me."

Gun captains crouched over their cannon, motioning

to gunners to muscle the gun left, right, using handspikes to adjust the elevation.

Tehidy chortled, and Gareth glanced over, to see a broadside from the *Thruster* smash into the convoy's sole landward escort. A moment later, the ship exploded. White, then black smoke boiled, and Gareth could see things—Linyati, masts, cannon—spinning through the air.

"Thank you, Dafflemere," he murmured. "But there's no gold sinking warships."

"Nor much of anything else on that one," Tehidy said.

The Linyati merchant ship was very close, and again, the gunners in the stern deck fired too soon, and balls arced past, well in front of the *Steadfast*'s bows.

"Stand by . . ." Gareth called. "Bow guns, fire when you bear."

The small falconets barked, and one of the *Steadfast*'s main guns as well. That premature ball thudded into the Linyati amidships, but Gareth saw the smaller balls of the falconets smash into the stern deck, and he imagined he heard screams.

"Damn that gunner," Tehidy said. "You, Gun One, if you can't fire when you're s'posed to, I know a man who can."

"Main guns . . . fire at will," Gareth shouted, and the only cannon bearing blasted into the Linyati.

"Bring her about," Gareth ordered, "and hit her again!"

The *Revenge* was just behind the *Steadfast,* and its broadside slammed into the Linyati stern as well. The little *Goodhope,* unnoticed by the Linyati, cut under her bows and, her cannon at full elevation, blasted the foredeck of the Slaver's ship with grapeshot, skittered out of the way.

"Good," Gareth said. "We'll strike her again, then lay alongside for boarding."

Again the cannon boomed, and as the *Revenge* cleared

the Linyati, Gareth ran down the ladders, across the main-deck, and up to the foredeck.

He could feel his heart thudding wildly as the *Steadfast* drove into the Linyati stern. There was someone at a cabin window, aiming a musket, two other Linyati behind him. The falconets, firing grape this time, banged, and there was no one in the window, and smoke poured out.

"You men with the grapnels," Gareth said, and the two muscled sailors swung the hooks about their heads, let them go, and they thunked solidly into the Linyati ship.

A musket fired, and a man beside Gareth went down, and he saw a Linyati leaning over, trying to cut the grapnel's rope with a bill.

"I don't think so," he said aloud, a pistol leveled across his forearm, and it went off. The Linyati, face still expressionless, leaned farther and farther forward and fell into the closing space between the two ships, and his corpse was crushed.

"Away boarders away," Gareth shouted, and leapt for that window the musketeers had been shot away from. He caught the splintery wood with his forearms, pulled himself up, and rolled into the cabin, spinning away, not giving anyone inside a chance to kill him.

Gareth was on his feet, but he realized there was no danger as his eyes adjusted to the darkness. The falconet's shot had blown the three Linyati apart. The dripping walls and overhead looked as if they'd been freshly and carelessly painted, and the color was dark red. Gareth made out some pieces that might have been men, felt nothing as his fighting rage built, going across the room and kicking the cabin door open.

There were other pirates coming up behind him as he burst out onto a gundeck with six guns to a side. Linyati sailors saw him, shouted, and some of them had daggers or swords out, rushing him.

"Getcher ass outa the way," someone shouted, unceremoniously pushing Gareth to the side. There were half a dozen men with muskets, kneeling, and they fired, and the Linyati reeled back. Another rank fired as the first reloaded, and the Linyati fled up a ladder toward the main deck.

Gareth and the boarders went after them, broke out onto the main deck.

He blinked in the tropic sunlight, flinched as the sailor beside him screamed as a musket ball ricocheted off the deck and smashed his kneecap.

Gareth shot down that Linyati as the Slaver scrabbled with ramrod and powder, dropped the empty pistol to the deck. Someone handed him a loaded weapon, and three Linyati rushed him. He shot one, who collapsed into his fellow. Gareth ran that Slaver through, parried a cutlass slash from the third, and put his own blade through the man's neck.

The Linyati's momentary panic had vanished. The maindeck, already littered with bodies, was a clash of steel and the snap of muskets and pistols. The Slavers were covering behind masts and cannon, firing steadily. Four Linyati rushed the companionway Gareth had come up, slammed the hatch and barred it.

Reinforcements cut off, the Linyati shrilled glee and closed on the pirates.

A man wearing finery on the deck above was shouting orders. Gareth saw an unfired musket on the deck, had it, knelt, and shot the officer down.

But the Linyati's fighting calm didn't break.

The pirates were forced back, toward the bow of the merchantman.

"A hand here," Thom Tehidy shouted, pushing at a

squat cannon. Labala, unnoticed blood dripping from a sword-slash across his chest, was beside him, helping.

Laboriously they pulled the gun back from the battery. Tehidy slashed the breeching rope, and they turned the gun around, pointing across the ship's main deck.

Someone tossed a torch through the air, and Labala had it, rammed it against the cannon's touchhole just as Gareth wondered if the thing was loaded, and the squat cannon belched fire across the deck, grapeshot scattering the Linyati.

Pirate gunners sheathed their swords, and hurriedly began reloading the gun.

Gareth heard a high squealing he remembered from his first encounter with a Linyati warship, just as the *Revenge* came alongside and reinforcements poured over the railing.

A cabin door on the deck above the fighters slammed open, and a nightmare burst out.

It was an enormous, tailless lizard, half again as tall as a man, with a long, fanged head like a crocodile. Its skin was composed of rainbow-hued scales, and it carried a forward-curving sword in each four-clawed hand. It moved impossibly fast, leaping down the ladder, slashing into pirates, spinning away from counterthrusts and lunges, squealing all the while.

Gareth shot at it with one of his pistols, missed, and, guts clenching, went for the monster with his sword.

Then the cannon went off again, and balls riddled the creature. It fell, but was up again, and then Labala came from nowhere with a huge ax and smashed it into the reptile's skull.

It shrieked, writhed, and fell. Labala, not taking any chances, yanked the ax free and smashed it down again, beheading the monster.

Very suddenly, the battle was over. Surviving Linyati seemed to lose all heart. Some dropped their weapons and slumped to the deck; more ran for the side and leapt overboard.

Gareth paid no mind. He gaped at the dead monster as its muscles curled and spasmed.

Labala was shaking.

"That's their god?"

"Or demon," Gareth managed.

"Forget him," Thom said. "He's dead. You and you, put this overside, just to make sure."

The two ordered pirates, pale-faced, picked up the creature, staggered to the railing, and rolled it over. Then one looked at the slimy ichor on his hands, and threw up.

The companionway was opened, and the bottled-up crew of the *Steadfast* stormed out, to find no one left to fight.

Gareth went to one of the Linyati, pulled him to his feet. The man slumped as though he was boneless.

"What was that?" Gareth demanded.

He had to ask twice more before the man looked at him.

"We call them Runners," the man said slowly, dully.

"What are they? Your gods? Demons?"

"No."

"Are they your priests?"

"No."

"Magicians?"

"They have great magic, but they aren't just our wizards."

"Then what?"

"Runners," the Slaver said.

"You follow their orders?"

The man nodded.

"Where did they come from?"

The man shook his head.

"Why do you follow them?"

"Because," the Linyati said, "they made us."

"They created you? Are you not-men?"

"We are men," the Linyati said.

"What do you mean, then?"

But the man refused to answer any other questions.

Gareth was considering whether he could stomach putting the man to torture, thought the Linyati still wouldn't answer, when someone shouted.

"Cap'n Radnor! Come below!"

He put the matter aside to think on, followed the voice down a ladder into the hold.

Three pirates with torches stood, gaping.

The hold gleamed silver, gold, other colors at them. Carefully lashed down was an incredible treasure, from golden ingots to strangely wrought, small statues in metal Gareth had never seen to hand-worked ceremonial weapons in gold.

He picked up a small, perfect onyx statue of a naked woman, then heard the burble of water.

"We holed her," he said. "One of our shots must've gone low."

He went to the hatch, called up to Thom Tehidy.

"Thom, get men down here! The ship's sinking, and we'll not let it go down with *this* cargo!"

Pirates streamed down and the riches were cut free, passed to the deck, and overside into the *Steadfast* and *Revenge*.

Two Kashi went overside to see if a sail could be fothered to seal off the hole the cannon had made. They surfaced, shaking their heads.

"The gun tore away several timbers," one called up to

Gareth, "and the sea has taken others away. This ship is dying."

Gareth thought of stripping off and diving down to see for himself, decided there wasn't time.

There were still other Linyati ships to be taken.

Within moments after the corsairs had streamed back to their own vessels the great Linyati merchant ship began listing heavily, going farther and farther over as each minute passed. Its railing went under, and the sea flowed, unchecked, into the open hatch. The hulk rolled, and its stern lifted, showing the cannon wound that had doomed her.

Then her nose went down, and her stern rose high in the air, and she slid under.

"Now, let's look for another victim," Gareth ordered, and they raised sail and turned east.

The shattered Linyati convoy was a melee of ships, some still with headway, fighting with their cannon or trying to flee. These were being pursued, or brought to battle with gunfire or boarding.

The battle was not one-sided. Gareth saw a ship with the black flag at its truck sinking, a scattering of boats pulling away.

There was no question of stopping to pick up survivors while the treasure ships were still to be taken. After the battle there'd be time . . . and riches . . . enough for mercy, and no pirate expected otherwise.

Gareth wished he had something better than signal flags to let Dafflemere know about these Runners, and to try to bring them down, for it seemed, mostly, to break the Linyati's spirit.

But not always.

The *Freedom* and the *Naijak* found them. They'd boarded the two Linyati who'd rammed each other, and also found great treasure, although the *Naijak* had been swept with two broadsides as the boarders were going across, losing men on its gun deck and its mizzen mast.

But there were no Runners aboard, so unless the monsters had gone overboard, or hidden, they weren't always to be found. But these Linyati fought to the last man.

Again, a puzzlement, and for another day.

This day was for loot.

The *Revenge* and the *Steadfast* caught up with another merchantman, this one less full of fight than the first. They stood off and cannoned its guns into submission, the little *Goodhope* nipping here and there like a terrier after a bull.

Again they boarded, and this time the Linyati dropped their arms and stood, waiting to be killed, after a few minutes. But they found no Runner, and Gareth wondered if there was only one with the treasure fleet.

One of the handful of surviving Linyati warships attacked, and the *Revenge* fired chainshot, bringing down its main mast in a clutter of canvas and wood, leaving it dead in the water.

They looted the merchantmen, filling their holds with gold. Now they disdained unknown metals and silver, keeping only gold and jewels.

Gareth watched his men pass treasure into the *Steadfast*'s hold, noticed that the wind had changed, and now was blowing onshore. Dafflemere's spell must have broken. But the change would bring no good to the Linyati— the swifter, more maneuverable pirates could chase them right to the beach.

"This," Labala said, "is a day to remember. I guess my dream of sharks was false, or that we are the sharks."

"It is a great day," Gareth said. "We'll have a worthy homecoming, and—"

He was interrupted by a cry from the masthead:

"Sail ho! Many ships to port!"

In these waters they could only be Linyati.

"More treasure for the taking," Labala said.

"Maybe," Gareth said, and went to the lookout's position with a glass.

They weren't merchantmen, not with the three rakish sails of the Linyati warships. But these were bigger than any he'd seen.

He counted fifteen, in two inverted V formations, creaming waves at their prow, the wind at their stern, sailing hard toward the battle.

Gareth went down the mast quickly.

"Cut away from that ship," he ordered Thom Tehidy, who looked bewildered, then saw the onrushing Linyati.

Gareth ordered signal flags up to alert the other pirates and found a speaking trumpet.

"All hands! All hands!" he shouted. "Back aboard your ships, and make full sail! We've fallen into a Linyati trap!

"Now it's our turn to run!"

Thirteen

The pirates, no longer wolves but the broken herd, fled in all directions under full sail, all organization broken.

"What orders, Cap'n?" Tehidy shouted.

The wind, possibly magical, was driving them toward shore, favoring the attacking Linyati who, offshore, now held the weather gauge.

"Due east," Gareth ordered, and the *Steadfast,* flanked by the other four ships in his Company, drove away from the battle.

They weren't sailing at top speed, all of them heavy-laden with treasure. The *Naijak,* missing its aft mast, was trailing to the rear.

"Look there," Tehidy said, passing Gareth a glass. Gareth saw the *Thruster,* Dafflemere's ship, being attacked by three Linyati warships, then something more important:

Five of the Linyati, holding close formation, were coming after him.

"Labala!"

"What?" the heavy magician shouted up from the main deck.

"Can you manage a weather spell? I could use a nice steady wind a bit off the port bow. We can sail closer to the wind than they can."

"Dunno. Those spells are bastards, especially if there's magicians on the other side, and I'm still studying. But I'll try."

"Steer a little to port," Gareth ordered the helmsman. "We'll run before the wind till we close on land."

He thought of telling the watch quartermaster to be wary of steering close and being taken aback, then caught himself. The sailor was experienced and knew that if that happened, the Linyati might be down on them in less than a glass.

Thom Tehidy came close, so as not to be overheard. "Interesting the Slavers hit Dafflemere's ship, then came after us. Far as I know, Dafflemere and Labala are the only magicians a-pirating around here."

"You're thinking their wizards sense our magic, and track us?"

"I'm not thinking anything," Tehidy said. "I'm just worrying."

"Let's hope you're wrong," Gareth said, "and they're merely after us because we look organized."

"Let's hope," Tehidy agreed. "And as long as we're hoping, let's think good thoughts about being able to out-sail them."

Two turnings of the glass later, and hope was running short: The Linyati ships, their triple lateen sails full, were closing, the lead ship not half a dozen cannonshots distant.

Labala's weather spell had not, so far, begun to work, although the weather had begun to worsen, the onshore wind gusting, and the seas choppy, which slowed down the less handy Linyati a bit.

But the *Naijak* was falling astern, in spite of all possible sail clapped on its two remaining masts.

Within another two glasses, it'd be within range of the Linyati. And then . . .

He was still watching the *Naijak* when he saw its foremast sway, crack, and fall, carrying all sails overboard. The ship rolled, out of control. He saw men with axes swarm the welter of canvas, wood, lines, trying to cut away the debris.

"Dismasted," Tehidy said. "She's done."

Gareth nodded absently, thought a moment, made a decision, thought he was a softheaded fool.

"Put her about," he said. "We're going back to take off her men. If we can."

Tehidy looked at Gareth, started to say something, then began shouting orders.

The hands stood, stupefied, then moved to obey. Except for one man, who came to the foot of the quarterdeck ladder.

"Cap'n, what the *hells* are you doing?"

"Saving some shipmates."

"Screw them! They barely even signed th' Articles. What about our own asses?"

"Would you want someone to leave *you* for the Slavers?"

The man hesitated, heard the growls from his shipmates.

"Awright," he said. "We'll do it. But you'd best get away with it . . . *Captain*."

Gareth ordered signals hoisted to the other ships, telling them to steer north-northeast, making for Lyrawise, Juterbog's capital, as they'd agreed.

He'd catch up as he could, when he could.

"Labala! Get me some kind of casting on that Linyati . . . uncontrollable itching or desperate fear or pubic lice."

"I'll try."

Gareth was pleased with his crew's steadiness, hearing laughter at his command.

He ordered new signals hoisted to the *Naijak*, then there was little to do for some minutes except remember his geometry. He calculated the closing triangle between the *Steadfast*, the *Naijak* and the forward-most Linyati.

"Main guns, load chainshot," he called. "Bow and stern chasers, load grape. Gun captains, we're going alongside the *Naijak* on her port side. Sta'board guns, shoot high when you've got something to shoot at. We want to dismast that first one if we can. Port, when we clear the *Naijak*, pick the same targets.

"You men in the bow and stern, sweep me their quarterdeck if you have a chance!"

The *Naijak* was close, and, beyond her, the Linyati.

"Grapnel men to the rail," Gareth shouted, then ran to the rail with his speaking trumpet.

"Ahoy the *Naijak*! I'm coming alongside to take you off! Bring what you can carry, no more!"

Petrich, on the quarterdeck, shouted something back, which was lost in the wind. More minutes rushed past, and the other ship was very near.

"Stand by to back the helm," he ordered. "Thom, back all sails and have your grapnel men ready to throw."

"Aye, sir," and the *Naijak* was looming close on them, its rail about three feet above those of the *Steadfast*.

"Let go!" Tehidy shouted, and three grapnels arced through the air, dug into the *Naijak*, their ropes quickly lashed around bitts, and they were tight with the cripple.

The first *Naijak* hand appeared, teetering on his railing. He was carrying a bar of gold in each hand, a cutlass stuck in his waistband.

"Come on!" someone shouted, and the man jumped, then a stream of sailors followed, all laden with treasure snatched from the hold of the doomed ship, none worrying about inconsequentia like their gear or provisions.

Gareth heard shouts, turned, saw the Linyati ship round the stern of the *Naijak*. Its guns boomed, and three balls whistled across the *Steadfast*. Someone was hit, and screamed, the scream cut short.

The *Steadfast*'s main guns couldn't bear yet, nor did the bow guns have a target, the Linyati stern blocked by the *Naijak*.

Gareth saw two of the *Naijak*'s officers, then Petrich, leap down onto his ship. The grapnel men, not needing orders, cut the grapnel ropes, and the *Steadfast* was free, just as the two swivel guns in the bow had a target.

They banged, and grape swept the Linyati quarterdeck. The helmsman and a man beside him pitched sideways and fell.

The Linyati guns slammed again, and the *Steadfast* reeled, taking solid hits just above the waterline.

Then Gareth's main guns bore, and they crashed. The mainmast of the Linyati broke, fell overside, then, from nowhere, the little *Goodhope* swept in, and fired a broadside from its light guns, well aimed, that smashed into the Linyati gundeck.

"Reload, grape," someone shouted, and the *Steadfast*'s guns went off again. The Linyati, hit hard, heeled, its helm over, and turned away from the battle.

"All sail," Gareth shouted. "And below, Thom, with three men, and report on the damage."

"Aye, sir."

"Then pick our best hands and make repairs," but Tehidy was gone.

They were in the clear, and Gareth saw the other four Linyati closing. He had his trumpet up, shouting to the *Goodhope,* "Thanks!"

Dihr, not needing any assistance, bellowed back:

"We pay our debts," just as his popguns went off again, and more Linyati dropped aboard the warship.

Then something strange happened aboard the Slaver, as their crewmen looked away from the two pirates, seemed to see something on their port, and shouted warnings. A gun went off, firing into emptiness.

That could only be Labala's spell.

Tehidy was back on the bridge.

"Everything looks above the waterline, Gareth, and as long as you don't heel over too sharp, we won't take on much water. The carpenter said he'll have the holes patched in a watch, maybe two."

Gareth took a moment, breathing the sharp air of the wind coming across the bows, feeling life surge through him; he noticed Petrich beside him.

"Thanks, Captain," he said. "I didn't expect—"

"Forget it," Gareth said. "I'm just sorry to see all that gold go to the sea bottom."

"Forget the gold," Petrich said. "We can always steal more of it, being still alive, can't we?"

"Alive we are," Gareth agreed. "And let's try to stay that way. But I could use some of your hands below, repairing the damage."

"You've got them," and Petrich hurried away. Labala came out from below.

"I couldn't give you a weather spell," Labala said. "But I magicked you a couple of monsters, even though they're most likely fangless."

"That was what the Linyati were screaming about and shooting at?"

"Surely was. I modeled them after Dafflemere's beasts, the ones we saw when we first sailed into Freebooter's Island. Thought maybe you'd prefer them to crabs, eh?"

"Good," Gareth approved.

Labala breathed heavily. "Poor damned Dafflemere. Now we'll never be able to repay that favor we owe him."

Gareth nodded somberly.

"I just wish I could've come up with a good storm," Labala said. "I need to do more studyin'."

He slumped off the quarterdeck.

A sailor's head appeared at the top of the maindeck ladder, the same one who'd questioned his orders.

"Cap'n? Sorry I said what I said."

"Don't worry about it."

"You've got battle luck," the man said. "Real battle luck."

"Tell me that when we find the others," Gareth said, a bit uncomfortably. "We've still got four of the Slavers after us."

"Aarh, the hells with 'em," the sailor said confidently. "We'll lose 'em in a watch."

But by nightfall the four Linyati were still there, as the swells grew higher and the wind sharpened. Just at dusk, the lookout aloft reported sail dead ahead, and they were closing on the rest of the Company, their progress slowed by the unhandy *Freedom*.

The next day, the wind and waves had worsened, but the wind stayed generally from the east, so they weren't being driven back on their pursuers nor toward Kashi. The squalls kept the seamen busy, blowing in a fan shape, so the sails required constant trimming.

Gareth was able to exchange occasional communication with his three other ships. Some of the crew wanted to go about and sail down on the warships, given even odds.

"No," Gareth said decisively. "It'd be not quite one to one, considering how small the *Goodhope* is. And with our cargo, we're not as maneuverable as we should be. Even if we sank them, we'd still lose members of the Company."

Someone muttered that the shares'd be that much larger, but he said it with a smile.

Gareth went up to the masthead at least twice a watch. Slowly his ships were pulling away from the shallow-drafted Linyati.

But they still kept up the pursuit.

Labala had talked to every man in the crew, asking him what was the first thought that came, after fear, when a storm hit.

When it was Gareth's turn, he thought, then said, "How much saltier the air is when the wind blows spume up from the water."

Labala thanked him, scribbled on his tablet in the writing he'd half learned from Dafflemere, went on.

Later that watch Gareth was below, making sure the patchwork on the hull was holding. On his way back topside, he passed by the small compartment the crew had rigged for Labala as his own quarters—less, Labala told Gareth later with a snicker, "due to respect than they're 'feared I'll mistake a spell and there'll be nothing but mice scurryin' about the deck."

The curtain was open, and Gareth glanced in. Labala had a large candle and was muttering words, sprinkling incense into its flame then blowing it out. He'd relight it, mumble, and blow it out again.

Gareth, having no idea what Labala was doing, and being, like most sensible people, leery of anything resembling wizard's business, went on his way.

"I relieve you, sir," Petrich said.

"No," Gareth said. "I'm still doing fine."

"You've been on the quarterdeck for three straight watches," Petrich said firmly. "What reserves'll you have left if the Linyati suddenly come on us?"

Gareth realized Petrich was right.

"Only long enough to freshen up," he said, feeling the repressed fatigue come to in a wave, hitting him in the knees and back.

"That, and have something to eat, and get your head down. I promise I'll call you at the changing of the watch."

"Or if anything—and I mean anything—happens."

"Very well," Petrich said. "Oh. One other thing, if I can take a moment."

"Go ahead."

"I've talked to my fellow officers and warrants, and we think it would be appropriate if you set us ashore in Lyrawise. I do not think I want to have to stand before Lord Quindolphin and explain first why we decided to run up the black flag after Ozerov was killed, second why I chose to serve under your banner, third why we went a-pirating instead of staying in the nice, safe slavery trade, and last where in the hells his damned expensive ship is.

"None of those questions do I have answers for, at least not ones that would turn away the Lord's anger.

"We'd already decided we wouldn't be taking the *Naijak* up the Nalta River into Ticao for all but one of those reasons."

Gareth laughed. "Of course, Petrich. First, if we reach home with the gold we've already gotten, every man jack of us is rich, so we can do what we want and not worry about Quindolphins."

"What I want," Petrich said, "is go a-shopping in Lyrawise for another ship. Then, when—or, rather, if—you decide to sail out again, I wouldn't mind taking another shot at the Slavers, under your command."

"I thank you, sir. But I have no idea of my future plans, other than"—and Gareth yawned jawcrackingly wide—"a bar of soap, a nice quiet time in the jakes, and perhaps some lemonade."

Naturally, he'd barely emptied his bowels—sitting in the open head in his gallery off his cabin and almost getting washed overside for his daintiness—and decided he'd best wash, when another wave of exhaustion struck.

He got to his feet, stumbled a few steps, and fell facefirst on his bunk.

Needless to say, Petrich didn't waken him that watch, nor the next.

When Gareth was shaken awake, there was warm soup and, somehow, fresh-baked bread, drenched in salted butter, waiting.

And news the storm was worsening.

The day was bleak, the sky and sea an indistinguishable wall of gray, perforated by white here and there as the wind tore wavetops away and dashed them against the hard-pressed corsair ships, all laboring under reduced sail, barely making headway.

Gareth had gone aloft, scanned the horizon, wiping his glass every look with a wet chamois. Of the Linyati he saw nothing.

He tried to allow himself hope, went back down, the wind trying to pluck him from the shrouds and whirl him away to his doom.

*   *   *

It was just at the changing of the watch when the lookout shouted he had signal flags from the *Freedom*. Everyone on the quarterdeck tried to read them as they whipped and flapped in the gale.

". . . water . . . forehold," Gareth made out.

"Taking is the top signal," Tehidy said. "And I can't make out the one below that. But the two others are "request assistance."

"I have the third," Petrich said. "Sinking."

"Hands to quarters," Gareth ordered. "Here we go again."

The *Freedom* wallowed, visibly bow-down. The *Steadfast* was to her starboard, *Avenger* to her port, and the little *Goodhope* in her wake, ready to pick up anyone who went overboard, although in this storm any victim would have little chance.

The *Freedom*, like other Linyati slave ships, was a pig at best in a seaway, intended only for sailing close to shore, scurrying for shelter at the slightest storm. But the ship's behavior was far worse than it'd ever been before.

A signal from Froln, her captain, explained all. Evidently during the battle she'd been struck well forward in her hold, and no one had seen the damage until it was too late.

Gareth sent back asking how much longer the *Freedom* would stay afloat, hoping they'd be able to stand by until the storm abated, then attempt salve or rescue.

Froln's signal said he'd go down within the watch.

Gareth didn't know what to do. Then Tehidy called attention to a long series of signals from the *Avenger*. Galf had vastly more experience before the mast than Radnor and had an idea.

The first stage would be to take off as much of the cargo as they could.

Her crew struggled to bring up portable pieces of the Linyati treasure to the deck, and lashed them into the nets used to keep boarders off.

Then the *Avenger* came as close as she dared as a seaman hurled a line across. The line was run up to a cargo boom. The line was taken up, then men aboard the *Avenger* yanked at the boom's lines, bodily pulling the net up and out. The *Avenger* rolled as a wave came across the maindeck; the net full of gold dipped below the ocean, and Gareth heard the moan on his own ship.

The net came back up, dripping but intact, and was hauled by main force aboard the *Avenger.*

Then it was the *Steadfast*'s turn. As the men took up the slack on the boom line, the *Freedom* yawed, almost colliding with the *Steadfast.* The helmsman put his wheel over, and the ship pitched away. The line to the cargo net on the *Avenger*'s deck yanked the net across the deck, smashing the railing and into the water before it, too, was safely brought aboard.

"Enough of this," Gareth said. "Gold isn't worth lives."

Now the real risk came, as both pirate ships came close aboard the sinking *Freedom* and once again used grapnels on long lines to secure to the other ship. This time the nets were slung out, below the railings, over the seething waters, to catch anyone who jumped for safety and missed. Four men went in them first, and three were pulled up to safety.

The last missed the hand reaching for him, fell back toward the net, and struck its headrope. He scrabbled for a hold, had one for an instant, then his hand slipped and he dropped into the foaming surf between the two ships.

But the other hands aboard the *Freedom* made it across,

with no more loss. Then they cut the grapnels free and put their helms hard over—just as the four Linyati ships, in close formation, broke out of the howling sea mist at them.

The first fired from its bow guns, then the others, and a ball came close to the *Steadfast*. Others smashed into the abandoned *Freedom*.

They were caught quite cold, cannons unloaded, unmanned and stoppered, and the gunports closed against the storm.

Gareth wondered how the Linyati were able to man their guns on those ships with their gundecks barely above the water line, fought to keep from ducking as gun smoke swirled from the Linyati ports, and a pair of cannonballs smashed into the *Steadfast*.

Men, waist deep in water, were struggling on the main deck, trying to get the guns loaded, keep the powder dry, get a slowmatch up from the galley without it being drowned out. Gareth saw a man drop a cannonball on his foot, scream in pain, not seeing the wave that came aboard and took him away, still screaming.

Then he saw Labala on the foredeck, leaning out. He was stripped to the waist, heedless of the storm whipping about him. He was waving something as he paced back and forth.

It was the candle Gareth had seen him studying—somehow, in spite of the gale, it stayed lit.

Labala leaned over the candle and blew hard, harder.

Gareth heard, above the shriek of the storm in the rigging, the howl of a great blast, started to cry to the quartermaster to get all sail down, but felt nothing.

But the boiling seas ahead of the *Steadfast* whipped high, as he'd seen only once in his life, and that safely ashore, from a headland.

The wind, from nowhere, was more than a gale, more

than a hurricane. Its blast caught the four Linyati ships. Masts aboard the first two Slavers snapped like toothpicks. The third, less fortunate, had sturdier timber, and the wind knocked the warship on its beams, as a child's toy boat is knocked over in a pond by a zephyr.

The wind took the fourth ship's sails, tore them from their masts, left it dead in the water.

It came once again, veering to a different quadrant, bringing waves up before it, over the Linyati ships' sides, drowning their cannon and cannoneers and leaving the ships dead in the water, sinking.

The *Steadfast* came close to one of the Linyati ships, and Gareth looked over, saw Slavers fighting for their lives, for their ships; he knew it was useless.

He felt a moment of pity, then hardened his heart.

Labala pulled himself up the ladder, a grin dividing his face almost in half.

"I couldn't do a weather spell," he shouted. "But at least I got you a gods-damned little breeze, didn't I?"

Fourteen

Two months later, at the beginning of autumn, the *Steadfast* rode up the Nalta River into Ticao on the rising tide.

Gareth Radnor was making his homecoming.

The Company had fled east for two days after Labala's storm, tending their wounded and burying and mourning their dead. There were far too many of both for it to be easy to rejoice over the gold in the ships' hulls.

Gareth had signaled heave-to when Labala said he sensed no signs of pursuit, then called for a conference of captains and a representative from each ship of the men of Kashi.

He offered the ex-slaves the *Goodhope* to return to their native lands, along with their promised shares, lessen the price of the ship.

The Kashi men went back to their ship to report the offer to the others. Dihr returned to the *Steadfast*.

"We said once we'd been corrupted by seeing things other than our own jungles," he said. "Now, having spent time with you evil men of the sword, we can hardly return to innocence." He grinned. "So, if the Company will still have us, we'll sail on with you as pirates.

"Unless your lands have some hatred for men of color?"

"I know of none," Gareth said truthfully. "Especially not rich men of color, which you all are. Thanks for your faith, even after the disaster."

Dihr shrugged. "The plan was not yours, nor a bad one. As the saying goes, some days you slay the dragon, some days the dragon burns you alive."

The Company had no troubles on its long passage from the seas of Kashi across the Great Ocean to Juterbog. They'd had a joyous, and drunken, reunion with the prize ships in Lyrawise.

When sobriety finally set in, they'd given Petrich and the other men of the *Naijak* their shares of the Linyati gold, and their hope of seeing them again, when the winds blew soft, the seas were azure, and the Slavers had more gold to take.

Thom Tehidy had wanted to scrap Gareth's precautions and sail directly for Ticao with the full fleet. But Gareth held firm and ordered N'b'ry to keep charge of the five other ships until his word. Those men who wanted to be paid off, who couldn't bear waiting anymore, could be given their shares and signed off.

Then Gareth, with a picked crew, sailed across the narrow straits for home.

Gareth saw little of the passage, leaving the deck to Froln and N'b'ry while he stayed below, writing two full accounts of their passage.

When they reached Nalta Mouth, he hired couriers to take those accounts upriver, the first to his uncle, the second to Cosyra. With Cosyra's, he sent a wonderfully cast, stylized solid gold and gem-set icon of a Kashi eagle, and the note:

> *Buy oysters. Buy many oysters. I've decided I love you.*

They'd begun the tedious sail upriver to Ticao, endlessly tacking, sometimes anchoring to wait for the tide to turn. Gareth had tried to keep his sailors away from the dockwallopers and layabouts at Nalta Mouth, so his tale would arrive fresh in the capital, but doubted he'd had any success. Keeping a sailor from yarning was almost as hard as trying to keep him sober.

He stood on the quarterdeck, seeing, about a quarter league ahead, his uncle Pol's wharfside factory. Even from here he could see it was freshly painted, so his uncle had seen continued prosperity.

There was a crowd along the quay, he hoped waiting for him.

This was the homecoming he'd dreamed of when he was a boy. He knew he looked his best, darkly tanned from the tropics, hair bleached to a dark blond, hanging in ringlets to brush his shoulders. He wore thigh-top, loose boots, dark velvet breeches, and a deeply veed white silk blouse worked with golden thread, that'd been made from captured Kashi cloth. Cosyra's dagger and sword swung at his waist in richly worked leather.

"*Hern* Froln," he ordered. "Bring her in to the dock. Smartly, if you will. We've an audience."

"Aye, sir. Back all sails," Froln called, then gave orders, till the foresail caught a bit of the wind and slowly the *Steadfast* moved toward the dock.

"Berthing party, for'rd!"

Hands, wearing the colorful garb they'd had made up

in Lyrawise, went into the bows with lines, where men waited to catch them and draw the ship neatly to its berth, tying the ropes to bollards.

Gareth scanned the crowd, remembering the surprises of his last landfall, was surprised to see no one he recognized—not his uncle or family, and not Cosyra.

The gangway was lowered, and Gareth descended.

Two men, both with swords ready, moved forward, and others in the crowd, wearing red and black livery, tossed back concealing cloaks and lifted muskets, steadily aimed at the sailors.

Gareth recognized one of the two, slender, a bit taller, pinched lips over a beard that had filled out a bit since he'd seen him last.

Anthon Quindolphin!

"Gareth Radnor and crew," he said in his grating voice. "In the name of King Alfieri and in the name of the King's Justice, I order your arrest on the charge of high treason, and also order the holding of your men as witnesses to your incredible crimes as well as possible accomplices, in which event they are also to face the King's Justice. I have this warrant, ordering you, Gareth Radnor, to be taken immediately into custody, to await the stern pleasure of our king, and you others to be taken to a common prison.

"Do not resist us, any of you, or we'll use deadly force without hesitation."

There was utter silence but the plash of the river waves against the *Steadfast*'s hull. Then snarling laughter came, and a man rode out of an alleyway.

He was big, solid, clean shaven, in late middle age. Gareth had never seen him before. But his tight lips and glaring eyes made it easy for Gareth to realize he had finally been taken by his worst enemy: Lord Quindolphin.

"Seize them," he ordered, and the men moved forward.

The sailors looked for succor, but there was none. Suddenly there was a splash from the *Steadfast*'s stern. Gareth turned, saw a large brown arm sweep up, then another, and watched Labala swim strongly away.

"One of them jumped overboard," Anthon reported the obvious. "Shall we go after him?"

"Don't worry about him," Quindolphin said. "We have their leader, the others do not matter."

"There's enough who've been in the Great Dungeon once who come away alive like you did, Lord Radnor," the warder Aharah said. "And none at all a second time, it fears me to tell you."

"There's no lord to me," Gareth said, looking about his cell. If it weren't for the bars on the balcony, it could be taken for an expensive set of apartments. "Why'd you grant me the title?"

"We've—the whole damned city has—heard of what you done to the Slavers."

"Including Lord Quindolphin, evidently."

"Word spreads," Aharah said. "We was expecting you to be given the King's Freedom of the City, an' a title, but . . . nobody knows how, but you angered the king somehow.

"Not that hard to do, these days. He's gettin' old and fearful, some say. But we—the rest of the warders and me—don't consider this what we'd call a proud moment."

"I thank you," Gareth said.

"There ought to be more like you, out cutting those damned Linyati's throat strings for them, and taking their gold. Is't true you've got great treasure to show for your raiding?"

Gareth smiled, didn't answer.

"What did I do to deserve a cell like this?" he said,

looking at the alcove with a double-sized bed with unbelievably clean linen, a lounging divan, a table with matching chairs that would seat a dozen, a fireplace to keep off the chill that was coming with the late-afternoon fog rolling off the river, a writing desk and books.

"You don't answer my questions," Aharah said, "I don't have to answer yours.

"We'll let it be a s'prise."

Gareth had a visitor within the turning of the glass: Lord Quindolphin, and six heavily armed retainers.

The door slammed open, and two warders ushered the nobleman and his retinue in. He looked about the cell, pursed his lips even more, but said nothing about the furnishings.

"You'll forgive me if I don't bow," Gareth said. "But I only acknowledge gentlemen."

One of Quindolphin's escorts growled.

"Pay no mind," Quindolphin said. "The villain can speak as he likes, considering he'll have but few days to use his tongue.

"You see, Radnor, there are none who can stand before me for long. Eventually I have my revenge on those who've wronged me."

"Even if it's got to be done in secret, by night," Gareth said. "Exactly what I'd expect from a slaver."

Quindolphin whitened.

"What is that canard you spoke?"

"No lie," Gareth said, noting the expressions from the two warders, and even one of Quindolphin's men. "We encountered your ship, the *Naijak,* in our voyages, and Captain Ozerov explained what purpose he had in the Southern Seas."

"You lie!"

"You might be interested," Gareth said, "that I killed Ozerov myself. Also that your fine ship seems to have sunk in a storm in those waters, so your investment has come a bit of a cropper, hasn't it?"

"I did not come here to be slanged by a traitor!"

"No," Gareth agreed. "But it's happening, isn't it?"

Two of the men started forward. Gareth moved very quickly, kicking a chair into their path, grabbing an end table and snapping off two of its legs. One in each hand, short staves, he smiled tightly.

"Come then," he said. "Let us play."

One man grabbed for a pistol in his belt, and Gareth hurled the length of wood, jagged end first, between the man's eyes. He screeched, stumbled back.

"Here now," one of the warders said, drawing his dagger. "Enough of that. This man awaits the King's Justice, and he'll see no harm before then!"

Quindolphin's flush died. He glared at Gareth, turned, and stalked out without another word. His men dragged their bleeding fellow after him.

"I'm sorry, Warder, about breaking your furniture," Gareth said. "When I get some funds I'll pay for its replacement."

He was breathing hard, but joy surged through him. He wished he'd thrown that stave into the lord's face, but found consolation in that at the least he'd finally been able to take direct action against his enemy.

"Don't worry about the table," the warder said. "But next time we come, there'll be more than just the two of us. You're a right dangerous man, Lord Radnor."

Aharah's "surprise" was explained at dusk.

Two men in ceremonial half-armor, flanked by a grinning Aharah, brought covered trays into the room, then pushed a wheeled cart in after it, followed by a small wicker case.

"What does all this mean?"

No one answered Gareth, and the three went out. Gareth had an instant to puzzle, and the door came open again and Cosyra burst in.

She was even more beautiful than he remembered. Still with short hair, she wore a green silk tie around her neck and breasts. Her midriff was bare, and she wore baggy, wide-bottomed pants with ankle boots. The tiny golden eagle he'd sent from Nalta Mouth was on a chain at her throat.

"We have until dawn," she said.

Gareth did not remember going across the few feet from where he'd gaped to take her in his arms, nor the next few minutes as they kissed.

He started to say something, kissed her again. He heard the cell door close, and the locks grate, but paid no heed.

Gareth picked her up in his arms, carried her to the bed, and lay down, half across her. Then the wave took them both, lifted them, and finally let them down, sweating, weak, naked, legs entwined.

Neither could manage coherency for a long time. Then Cosyra whispered, "So that's what it's like."

"With you, that's what it's like," Gareth managed.

"You wouldn't know, never having been with anyone else before, like me."

"Of course. You're right."

"Do you know how much trouble I went to to get the freshest oysters, and two dozens of them? Now they're going to go to waste."

She squealed suddenly.

"Oh. You aren't going to need them, are you?"

* * *

"Wasn't there something about love?" Cosyra said sometime later.

"There was."

"You still just think?"

"I'm sure. I love you."

"Then let me try something I read about, dreaming about you when you were far away, and see if I know how to do it properly."

"I assume it was your gold that paid for all this," Gareth said.

"Of course," Cosyra said. "A noblewoman of my standing wouldn't consider losing her virginity in anything other than the most perfect surroundings."

"Even if it is still a dungeon."

"That will make it a story I can tell my grandchildren about, won't it?" she said. "Although I may have to leave out some of the . . . more interesting parts."

Quite naked, Gareth considered the dishes Cosyra had brought in. The covered vessels had spells on them, so the food was as if it'd come fresh from the oven.

Besides the small, utterly succulent oysters, on the half-shell with horseradish and lemon, there was a beef filet in pastry, buttered new potatoes, and lemon tarts. But the dish Gareth prized most, beyond the oysters, was a simple dish of sliced fresh tomatoes with chopped chives, oil, and cracked black pepper.

"There are things," he explained between mouthfuls, "the Southern Waters never give you."

Cosyra, as naked as he was, was sprawled on the shambled bed.

"There had best be *many* things the Southern Waters never gave you."

"Would I have picked out that eagle I sent you if there weren't?"

"I don't know," she said. "You rogues always know the way to a girl's heart."

"Speaking of which, how long will mine keep beating?"

Cosyra turned serious.

"The king is between the rocky Mount he lives on and a stone wall. He was livid when reports came—from Lord Quindolphin, incidentally—of your raiding against the Linyati.

"Then their ambassador complained in court about you, and other equally murderous renegades, and cleverly shamed the king into promising he'd make a response."

"Which will be?"

"I do not know," Cosyra said. "He's been very secretive about you, and none of my friends have been able to draw him out. If I didn't know Alfieri, I'd think his conscience was bothering him." She laughed grimly. "But kings give that up when they put on the crown, it seems."

"So what will happen with me?"

"At the moment, nothing. There's been no mention of a trial, or summary justice, or anything."

"What about my men?" Gareth asked.

"I've done what I can," Cosyra said. "They've been moved out of the main prison and are being held in a separate yard that's normally used for debtors, so there'll be no nonsense with whips or things like that."

Gareth looked at her with new respect.

"Milady, I knew you were noble, but I didn't think you were that noble. Or had that much muscle."

"That's a nice, gentlemanly compliment," Cosyra said, clearly changing the subject. "To tell a lady, who's just given her all and then some, you like her muscles. Would you like me to climb a rope or tuck a sail or whatever it is you pirates do to gain further respect?"

"So all this means we can do more than wait on the king's pleasure?" Gareth asked.

"I see no other options," Cosyra said, a little bitterly. "Now you know what the reality is of being at court. Everything is at the pleasure of his Majesty, sometimes including breathing, I think.

"I'll let you know as soon as I know anything, and the warders are well bribed in the event of their learning aught."

Gareth thought.

"Since Quindolphin came here to gloat, with some of his bullyboys, I don't think this prison is exactly safe, ignoring your charming presence as yet another indicator. I've known sieves to be less leaky.

"I would give a deal for some kind of weapon."

"If you'll lift up the tray the beef is in . . ." Cosyra murmured.

There were two knives under the tray, with leather sheaths as plain as their hafts and handles.

"The armorer I bought them from said the short one can be tied to your inner thigh to be hidden, the longer one down the center of your back, on that chain that appears ornamental."

Gareth hefted them.

"Good." He grinned at himself. "Perhaps I've spent too much time in the company of rogues to feel naked without a weapon. But . . ."

"And who is to say Saros is any less deadly than anything you've seen?" Cosyra said. "Now, if you've finished making an utter pig of yourself, freshen your mouth from that small bottle, take away my plate, and pour me another glass of the wine you've been ignoring for that terrible water. I see even pirating hasn't improved your tastes."

"And then what?"

"And then come here again, so I can see if your boasts hold true.

"Dawn comes early enough for us."

A week and a day passed. Cosyra was able to visit Gareth in his cell nearly every day, her men posted outside to guarantee privacy, but couldn't chance any more full nights.

She did report that poor Lord Quindolphin wasn't at court these days, having been struck with a plague of boils.

Gareth laughed, thinking of Labala's escape, and explained to Cosyra, who found it equally funny.

"It's a pity," she said, "your wizard doesn't know how to bring on leprosy, however. Fast-acting leprosy."

His uncle Pol came visiting, and was, surprisingly, quite cheerful. Gareth noted that he now wore a golden key around his neck, asked and found Pol had, indeed, been made a Merchant Prince in Gareth's absence.

"A just reward for my life of honesty, purity, and never chancing the law," he said. "Unlike some *others* I can name." But he didn't sound terribly critical.

"Both you and Cosyra seem quite unconcerned by my presence in this dungeon," Gareth said, just a bit angrily.

"Certainly," Pol said. "It isn't *our* necks the headsman is measuring while sharpening his ax."

"Uncle, have you taken to having wine at lunch?"

"Normally, no," Pol said. "But I received a piece of excellent news, at least I deem it to be such, to justify a glass or two this day."

Gareth waited, but Pol didn't continue, so he assumed it must have been mercantile.

"Now," Pol went on, "I've visited your men in their

own durance and found one, your Tehidy, to be quite reliable.

"He informed me there are five ships lying in Lyrawise waiting for clearance, and those ships are laden beyond riches."

"This is true," Gareth said. "I thought—quite correctly as it happened—it might be overly easy for certain royal personages to seize them if they wished, as they've seized me, after having listened to those"—and Gareth almost broke his practice and used profanity, but caught himself in time—"Slavers and that Quindolphin."

"Tut," Pol said. "All things work themselves out, given a sufficiency of common sense, some gold, and a bit more of silver, which I'll no doubt be recompensed for, with appropriate interest, when I become your agent and dispose of your acquisitions."

"Which means?"

"Which means I'm most impressed with you, Gareth, for your caution as well as your evident success. I'm truly saddened you didn't choose to become my heir apparent."

"At the moment," Gareth said, "considering my present situation, so am I." He paced to the barred window, stared out at the Sarosian fall, and the river flowing away to the lands of dreams, then turned back.

"But I will admit," he said, "prison becomes easier the more familiar I become with it."

"Try not to let it become *too* familiar," Pol said. "For we know what familiarity breeds, and such carelessness could serve to introduce you to that man with the ax we were referring to earlier."

"Which means, even though I'm charged with high treason, I'm not to face death?" Gareth asked.

"I don't know precisely what the king is thinking about

you," Pol said. "But I anticipate your men will be freed within a day or more.

"And there's already been a petition put forth in your name that if you are condemned you be allowed to die not in these gray stone walls, but near the river you so love."

"The river I so love?" Gareth was a bit slow, then got it. "Oh."

"Exactly," Pol said. "It's very hard for someone to make an escape from this dungeon. But out in the open, along the Nalta, where there might be some boats lurking nearby, with desperate men aboard who care little about the King's Guards."

Gareth smiled at that. "Which would truly make me a pirate in these lands."

"To the last degree," Pol agreed, standing. "I merely came to cheer you, my nephew, and to say that tailors will be visiting you shortly for some new garments, suitable for your presentation at court."

Gareth's eyes widened.

"At present," Pol continued, "they won't be the sort some men are unfortunate enough to need, with easily unbuttoned collars and front so the cloth can be pulled back to give the axman good aim."

"That's my uncle, always full of good cheer."

"That is me," Pol agreed, going to the door. "Warder! Open this up!" He turned back. "One final thing I just remembered that no doubt will sadden you, as it does me.

"Poor Lord Quindolphin has a terrible case of boils."

"So I heard."

"They are not improving," Pol said, his voice most sorrowful. "In spite of the best chirurgeons and wizards, who swear the plague might have come from distant shores for all they're capable of curing him.

"The plague seems to have centered on his lower regions, so he's unable to ride or even sit comfortably, and as a man who loves the hunt that distresses him utterly.

"The second home for these carbuncles is his face, so that even his mistresses are too appalled by his features to keep him company. A pity," Pol said, as Aharah opened the cell door.

"A pity indeed," Gareth agreed.

They came for Gareth just at dawn. There were six of the King's Guards, Aharah, and a mousy little man who said he was named Quish, one of King Alfieri's chamberlains.

"And what would you have of me?" Gareth demanded.

"Your presence is demanded at court," Quish said. "You have a chance to bathe and put on proper clothing. But make no moves of resistance, I warn you."

Gareth quickly washed from his basin, noticing the other men turned away to give him a semblance of privacy, but Quish kept casting interested looks at him.

He thought of tucking the shorter of his knives somewhere, but thought better of it. He was a pirate, not a regicide, and would take his fate as it was offered.

When he was dressed in a sober black suit Pol's tailor had made up for him, he was told to extend his hands. A thin silver chain was fastened about them, and a spell whispered by Quish.

"Do not attempt to escape," he said solemnly, patting a small ceremonial dagger at his waist. "For I am armed, and will have no hesitation in using this if necessary."

Gareth nodded solemnly. "You have my vow, and I quite realize what a dangerous man you are."

They went down the endless stone stairs into the courtyard, where a coach in the royal colors waited.

Gareth was put in the back, and Quish sat across from him.

The coach moved off, the Guardsmen mounted beside, and Gareth saw through its window the gates to the prison clang open, and felt hope building.

The streets were packed. Gareth thought at first it was normal midday traffic, then he heard the shouting:

"Damn the Linyati!"

"Death to the Slavers!"

"Free our Pirate!"

And:

"Gareth . . . Gareth . . . Gareth . . ."

The throng was for him, and Gareth wondered who'd organized the demonstration.

The mounted Guards drew closer to the carriage, and Gareth overheard their words through the open window:

"Looks like more damned trouble," the first said.

"Mebbe," the second said. "But not likely. Don't see any staves or clubs or knives on the ends of sticks being waved about."

"You're right. But I don't trust crowds."

"They can turn ugly on you, can't they?" the second agreed. "Especially when there's some justice to what they're raving on about."

There was a boil of noise, and Gareth couldn't make out what they were saying, then:

". . . again and again, till our villages are stripped bare. Is that what the king wants?"

"Hells if I know," the other one said. "But the army'll send out an expeditionary force, I heard, to patrol the coasts and wait for another raid."

"Shit," the first said. "That's no response, riding here, there, and everywhere, always late, always missing their damned smash-and-grabs. The only proper thing is to put the navy out in strength after the Linyati, not here, but down in their damned homeland.

"Burn some of *their* villages, cities, a hundred for the dozen of ours they've ruined, and let them see what it's like to be on the sharp end of the sword. For all I care, sell 'em to any demons looking for fresh meat. I'm against slavery, but I'm willing to make exceptions."

"There'd be few object to that," the second said. "Hells, I'd likely volunteer myself to go down amongst them, if I were a sailor. Especially since I hear they're arse-deep in gold."

The coach creaked on once more and the horsemen moved away.

Gareth looked at Quish.

"Have the Linyati been raiding our coasts again?"

"I'm instructed to have no conversation beyond the necessary with you," Quish said, and Gareth was fairly sure he knew the answer to his question.

The palace held the top of the Mount, its stone walls elaborately worked, parapets with ready cannon, gold and white banners flowing, and, over them all, the great black, green, and white flag of Saros, the royal crest embroidered on it, showing the king was in residence.

The central courtyard was full of milling courtiers, and a double line of King's Guards, their weapons ready.

Gareth saw Cosyra, didn't think he should wave, was hustled down the line and into the palace.

There were a scattering of guards here and there, but the halls were almost vacant otherwise.

Gareth was taken to the hall's end, past the tattered banners of battles fought and won over the centuries. A huge double door opened silently in front of him, and

Gareth entered a huge chamber, whose vaulted ceiling was high overhead.

"Unloose him," a voice said.

The only person in the room, besides Quish, Gareth, and two Guards, was a thin, fretful man in his late fifties. His beard was graying, rather tattered, hardly fitted to the rich ermines he wore and the jeweled crown on his head.

Gareth ignored Quish's fumblings at the chain and knelt, awe surging through him.

The chain came away.

"You may rise," King Alfieri said. At least his voice was deep, sonorous. "And you may approach us.

"Guards, Lord Quish, leave us."

"But—"

"Such is our command. This man is our faithful subject, and we shall come to no harm."

Quish and the Guards scuttled out.

"You are the famous Gareth Radnor," Alfieri said.

"I thank your Majesty, but don't know if I'm famous."

"Oh, you're famous all right. Famous for having pirated all over the Linyati realm, famous for having put us in a quandary, with that double-damned ambassador of theirs threatening what might happen to our truce if you weren't brought to the proper justice and all.

"It should have been most simple," Alfieri grumbled. "We should have been able to seize your loot as a proper penalty, have our best executioner give you a nice, painless death, put your ever so obstreperous men into the coastal guard or navy, explain to the Linyati there had been some misunderstanding, and peace would continue to reign.

"Don't think we're a weakling, Radnor. But we swore to our father, when we returned from fighting in Juterbog as a young man, we'd allow no war to take our subjects' lives, and we've kept that vow for thirty years.

"You don't know what war's like, Radnor. Anything is better than that."

Gareth said nothing.

"You don't agree, of course. Go ahead. We'll not kill you just for speaking. It was in the olden days when we could do that," Alfieri said, a bit forlornly. "When kings had *real* power. Go ahead," he said once more. "Tell us why we're wrong."

"I can't say you're wrong, Sire," Gareth said. "But I do think there're things that are worse than war, and must be stood against. Slavery being one."

Alfieri's lips went thin, and he looked down. "The Linyati bastards do not make keeping the peace easy," he said. "Particularly when they want a certain corsair pulled limb from limb, and then have the temerity to raze a dozen leagues of coast, taking away our people into chains and leaving nothing but wasteland behind."

Gareth remembered what the two Guardsmen had been talking about, thought about giving thanks to some god he'd have to pick out later.

"The *damned* Linyati," Alfieri went on. "Plus there are petitions from a certain noblewoman in our favor, a Merchant Prince, some of his friends, and even some of the firebreathers in our own navy. And then that son of a bitch Quindolphin.

"And now our own people are running here and there, shouting your name and calling for us to do something about those Slavers.

"Let me ask you this, Radnor. We said you are our faithful servant."

"That is true, Sire," Gareth said.

"Then let us talk about this treasure you seem to have acquired from the Linyati. I don't suppose there's any hope you'd make life easy for us, and simply arrange for it to be transported from whatever hiding place you've got it hidden in, is there?"

Gareth didn't answer.

"Hmmph," King Alfieri growled. "We didn't think so. But let us ask. How much is there?"

"In gold, Sire, enough to build a palace, half a dozen palaces. Gold and jewels such as no one in Saros has ever seen, enough to fill the holds of two ships to foundering.

"There's enough other goods—silks, spices, and such— to fill the holds of three prize ships I sent north before attacking the Linyati treasure fleet."

Alfieri stared at Gareth, licked his lips.

"We understand you pirates have your own covenants and such."

"Yes, Sire. We call them Articles."

"When you were setting up these 'Articles,' did you consider your monarch?"

Gareth gladly remembered the section he'd forced down his crew's throat.

"Of course, your Majesty. We unanimously decided to grant you six full shares, more than anyone else."

"You decided?" Alfieri said. "But you were captain, correct? Couldn't you just dictate the terms you wished?"

"No, Sire. As with everything else, what we did was decided by proper vote."

Alfieri stared at him closely.

"No wonder they say pirates are more dangerous even than they appear," he said. "Now, as to this share, we were thinking that a quarter of your booty would be more appropriate."

Gareth had one tiny moment of objecting, then remembered three quarters of something to a free man is far more valuable than everything to a corpse. He bowed.

"We would be honored to make such an arrangement."

Alfieri smiled.

"You don't seem to think it is necessary to consult with your crew about the matter?"

"I think," Gareth said, "considering the circumstances, there's no need for that formality."

Alfieri nodded, paced back and forth.

"Crowds in the streets . . . gold concealed on some distant shore . . . those arrogant bastards the Slavers . . . Damn, but we hate to be manipulated!"

Alfieri didn't seem to be talking to Gareth at the last.

"But we've been proud that we always know what to do and when to do it."

He walked to a stand of halberds, took one out, and Gareth felt a moment of alarm. Alfieri crashed the halberd's butt on the flagstones three times.

Gareth, who knew better than to turn his back on his ruler, heard a door open, and Quish's voice: "Sire?"

"You may allow our court to return."

"Sire!"

"As we said before, we don't like to be manipulated, and we dislike even more when we have to admit to being . . . not fully apprised of a situation.

"We hope that damned Quindolphin's boils suppurate him to death!

"Come here, Radnor, and let's get this over with. We have more than enough other work than to concern ourselves over a single pirate."

Gareth, completely perplexed, followed Alfieri to the end of the room, where a high-backed, jewel-inlaid throne sat atop low steps. Alfieri went up the risers and turned.

Gareth heard a throng yammering into the room, the echoes of their excitement against the high apse.

A great sword in a sheath hung against the back of the throne.

"All kneel," someone shouted as Alfieri picked up the sword by its belt, and Gareth and the others went down.

The sword hissed out of its sheath, and Alfieri came forward. Gareth noted that he carried the weapon easily, as a man who knew what its real purpose was.

"You may rise," Alfieri said, his voice a boom. "Except you, Gareth Radnor."

Gareth waited, having no idea what was about to happen.

"Do you acknowledge us, Alfieri, as your king, as the only ruler you follow, and acknowledge you will obey any and all commandments given you by us, or by our officers?"

"Of course, Your Majesty."

The sword came out, and Gareth almost flinched as its edge touched his shoulders, the top of his head.

"Rise then, Sir Gareth Radnor, the newest of my Servants."

Gareth Radnor—Sir Gareth Radnor—almost started crying.

Fifteen

"eautiful, is it not, Sir Gareth?" the little round man said proudly, waving his hand around the horizon, his words almost lost in the keening wind.

Gareth, still not used to the title, considered what he was looking at. The stone house just behind him was huge, four-storied, with square towers at either side. It sat in a slight vale, just low enough to block the strongest winds from the sea. Behind it, protected by plane trees, were out-buildings and a formal garden. Strangely, there was no wall around the estate, front or rear, and the grounds were carefully maintained so that anyone in the house had a clear view—or shot—in any direction.

Gareth noted two small cannon atop each tower.

"The former householder liked to feel safe," he said dryly.

The round man cleared his throat nervously.

"The lord had his enemies . . . 'tis a pity he chose to live as he did."

"You mean, die," Cosyra said, hiding mirth.

"Yes, well, he should not have defied King Alfieri."

"Or," Cosyra put in, "if he was going to tell the king he was an idiot who not only didn't deserve his taxes, but his fealty either, he should've at least stayed mewed up in this castle rather than return to court."

The skull of the land's former owner, still with bits of clinging flesh the ravens hadn't gotten around to, now decorated a spike over one of Ticao's gates.

"Don't forget," said the round man, who was the agent for the land, "the price not only includes these grounds, but almost two thousand hectares, some worked, some open lands, plus two hamlets you cannot see from here, and, of course, the village below.

"The river we crossed coming to this house, which you also control riparian rights to, has a small hand-built tributary behind the house, there, that feeds into your fishpond. The river itself falls into the ocean just beyond that bluff.

"You'll reap a hundred pieces of gold from the sea-fishing per year, the land produces enough for all your people to live on, plus there's fallow acreage should you desire to have produce for sale. The uplands have no sheep on them, but they could easily be added, and your herd of prime cattle, about forty-five head, could also be increased without stressing the land.

"There's deer for the taking, only half of which are the king's, fowl, and great fish in the ocean for the sport.

"Your yeomen, several hundred of them, are all stout lads. The merchants will stand behind you four-square, and there's no sign of plague or other evils.

"There's one witch in the village, and she's a most agreeable creature, well thought of by all. There's no chirurgeon, unfortunately."

The village nestled at the bottom of the twisting track that led down to the sea. Fishing boats bobbed at anchor around the half-dozen stone piers, and gaily painted houses lined the winding, cobbled streets. There were half a dozen businesses as well: small stores, a tavern, a fish plant.

Gareth nodded.

"Reminds me a trifle of our old village," Thom Tehidy said.

"Ee-yes," Knoll N'b'ry agreed. "If you buy it, Gareth, you'd best consider putting in a pair of guns . . . moyane or pykmayone culverin to give you the range up here to reach out to sea, and perhaps a pair of lombards down on the wharf for anyone closing on the village, and training some of the locals to fire them."

"And aren't you three the most worrisome sort of pirates?" N'b'ry's companion, a lovely, very young, black-haired trader's daughter named Suel, laughed. "Who'd be likely to attack any of you, Knoll, particularly if you and Thom do as you talked and built your own houses on either side of this monster?"

The three looked at her, didn't comment. They all knew why the cannon might be necessary, remembering the village they'd grown up in.

N'b'ry had told Gareth he was very fond of Suel, and not for her prized conversation; Cosyra had rolled her eyes and agreed that was obvious.

Tehidy's partner on this outing was a chubby shop-keeper's daughter, Myan, quick-witted and always cheerful.

"And I don't believe, come to think about it," Suel went on, pretending a pout, "these brave bold swordsmen standing around talking about the yield of land as if they were common landsmen! That's *not* what I expected."

"Now there, at least," Cosyra added, "I agree with you. Riches have turned all of them into conservative, cautious sorts, haven't they?"

She wasn't the only one to pretend disappointment in

the corsairs' behavior. When the Company's fleet and cargo had been brought upriver and, as agreed, given to Pol Radnor for disposal, Ticao licked its lips and prepared for the greatest madness in its history.

Each share, even after the king's creaking, heavy-laden wagons had trundled off to the palace's treasury, was worth what a hard-working merchant might realize in twenty years' labor.

Now it would be for the spending, as the crews were paid off and the Articles dissolved.

But things, mostly, did not work out that way.

Labala came to Gareth as he was making out the paperwork for the sale of all ships but the *Steadfast*, which Gareth had decided to keep for his own for reasons he thought were wishy-washy, sentimental, and not worth telling anyone about.

"Gareth," the big brown man complained. "None of these bastards I sailed with are worth sour owl crud."

"Why not?"

"Here I am, full of spunk and the money to pay to let it go, and I can't find anyone to roister with, at least anyone worthwhile. All the ones I thought sturdy bastards are counting their gold and thinking about buying a shop, or a farm, or a fishing boat, or something for their godsdamned dotage.

"Godsdamned disappointing, I call it, especially when none of them are likely to live that long.

"Somebody told me once Saros was nothing but an island of shopkeepers looking for an apron to tie on and butcher paper to scribble accounts on. I never believed it before, but I sure do now.

"Hells, I'd ask you to go whoring with me if I didn't know you don't drink and have your own lady now."

Gareth had thought for a bit.

"Why don't you take your gold and find a nice sorcerer to study under? That and finish learning how to read."

Labala turned serious. "Talking of that, and the man who started teaching me magic, if I were more of a seaman, I'd buy me a scow and go see if poor godsdamned Dafflemere is still alive.

"But I'll wager the bastardly Slavers got him, and hopefully killed him. I'd a lot rather think about that than him in Linyati chains somewhere."

Labala sat mournfully for a few moments, then heaved himself to his feet.

"Fat lot talking to you did me," he said. "So I guess I'll do what you and everybody else has told me. Get a couple of doxies to keep myself warm in this damned upcoming winter of yours, and learn more magic. It's either that or find my way back to my own islands, wherever they are. Except I don't remember anyone using gold to get by on, but something like seashells on strings, of which I have none.

"Damn, but they never told me being rich meant being bored."

And he grumbled away.

In truth, Gareth Radnor felt about the same. What did he need with as much gold as he had? He had Cosyra; was in the king's graces, as much as anyone could remain in the mercurial ruler's favor; knew no riches could buy off his enemies the Quindolphins, nor did he wish that easy an ending to the feud; was healthy and happy.

As soon as he thought that, he could feel the tapping of boredom at the back of his mind, and bethought himself of various excitements, which he discussed with Cosyra.

Hunting? A poor deer was no match for a man with a musket, and he was hardly fool enough to go after the great

bears of the north with only a spear, as some loons did.
Besides, after hunting men, even a bear would be tame.

Fishing? He'd done that for a living as a boy and hated
it, so how could there be much amusement in the sport?

Whoring? With Cosyra? Hardly.

Gambling? He tried that once, lost a dozen gold pieces
and felt mildly sick to his stomach.

"What you're going to do," Cosyra said, "with my able
assistance, is buy a nice piece of land somewhere."

"Why?"

"Because people who have a tendency to end up in
the Great Dungeon, as you seem to, are far better treated
as landed gentry than as an unwashed sailor with hairy
toes."

"My toes are not hairy," he protested, but her instructions took him, Cosyra, N'b'ry, and Tehidy along the coast,
looking at properties.

This near-castle, with its villages, farmlands, and fish-
eries, was the best they'd found.

"And how much will this fine plot set me back?"

The round man named a price, and while Gareth swallowed hard, added hastily, "And the title Lord Newgrange
can be had atop it all for only . . . oh, another thousand
pieces of gold."

"The title," Cosyra put in coldly, "will accompany the
estate."

"But—"

"*I* am Lady Cosyra of the Mount," she said, "and am
well familiar with the tradition of the heraldic college."

"Oh. But of course. I merely meant there's a certain
amount of paperwork, and some money accompanying that
generally leavens things, and . . ." and the round man sputtered down into embarrassed silence.

Gareth leaned close to Cosyra.

"Am I supposed to bargain? I mean, being one of the King's Servants, and I've never bought any land before."

"You thank him," Cosyra said, "we return to that little inn that's given me fleas, and then, tonight, in writing, we make a counteroffer of, oh, half what he mentioned."

"That's still more gold than I could ever dream of," Gareth said.

"So?" Cosyra said coldly. "Aren't you the one who prattled on to me about how meaningless gold is?"

"Yes, but—"

"Congratulations, my love," she said. "You're already learning the hypocrisy of the very rich. Now you can learn to be bored in utter isolation and moan about how much you miss Ticao."

Two days later, after offers and counteroffers, Newgrange was his.

Tehidy and N'b'ry had already consulted builders and made offers on other pieces farther along the coast; Gareth had written to Ticao's best foundry and ordered two cannon, mentioning that he thought he might have further business for them in a while.

"Never thought we'd end up like this," N'b'ry said. "Owning *anything*, let alone almost as far as I can see . . ."

"Magical," Tehidy murmured. "Did you know, speaking of magic, the person who took quickest to my lectures on the fine art of gunlaying was the witch?

"Odd world we live in."

Gareth smiled, and scratched hard.

That damned inn *did* have fleas.

Gareth wrote a long, unsigned report about that final raid, skirting facts that might be unpleasant for the highest nobleman to have to consider, focusing on the utterly inhuman reptiles that appeared to control the Linyati.

He gave it to Cosyra, with instructions for her to give it to the current Lord of the Admiralty, whom she had known from girlhood.

The King's Navy, such as it was, should know how the Slavers fought, thought, and operated, as much as Gareth had been able to determine.

"I'm most proud of you, Gareth," Pol said, reflexively pushing a decanter of brandy across his littered desk. "From a mere seaman to a knighted, hmmph, well . . ."

"Go ahead, Uncle," Gareth said, amused. "I'm not ashamed of being a pirate."

"Maybe so, maybe no," Pol grumbled. "But it's hardly a dignified term, now is it?"

"I never planned on being dignified."

"Perhaps not. Uh, the reason I asked you to visit me, was to inquire as to your future plans?"

Gareth started to give a flippant answer, then turned serious.

"I don't know, sir. I never planned on having more money than I could ever spend, and thought I'd always be working at something, maybe in the end to have my own merchantman or something.

"I can't see going out to Newgrange and turning into one of those bucolic fatbutts, worried about when his prize mare's going to drop or whether his marrows will take the top prize at the district gala."

"No," Pol said. "I may have my country estates like Priscian wanted, but she's the one who's welcome to spend more than a few weeks away from Ticao.

"If I had to spend the rest of my life out there, damme, but I'd rust solid within the year!"

Gareth walked to the window, looked out at the Nalta and the ships moving steadily up- and downriver. He glanced at a ship model on a shelf, recognized it, with a bit of sadness—then anger as he remembered her fate—as the lost *Idris,* of his first voyage. He wondered why his uncle had the model built, then returned to the subject at hand.

"I don't know," Gareth said again. "Perhaps I'll wait until war starts with the Slavers, which must happen before I'm too old to fight.

"I still don't have satisfaction for my parents, and would welcome a good, honest war to settle their accounts."

Pol harrumphed.

"Do you have a suggestion, Uncle?"

"I do not, and must not," Pol said. "For what I might be thinking is against the King's Justice, not to mention Priscian would have me toasted and buttered for even thinking about anything that might put you in danger.

"You know, she quite wants to see you and Lady Cosyra, well, married. And I beg your pardon for intruding in your own affairs."

Gareth wasn't offended, and thought of telling Pol of Cosyra's views on marriage. He decided not to. "You mean, go a-pirating once again?" he asked instead.

"Well . . . no, or, rather, actually I've discussed the significant profits you returned with some of my fellows, including, naturally, my father-in-law, and they are most . . . well, jealous is the proper if somewhat discourteous word."

Gareth was about to pass the subject off and suggest they go out for the midday meal when an idea came.

"Jealous enough to invest in such an enterprise?"

"Oh, certainly," Pol said. "Some of them—and breathe not a word of this—have been bold enough to think of setting out privateers of their own. But of course such raiders not only are generally unlucky, but become hellish independent, and have a terrible tendency to go off on their own and never pay their share and end at a rope's end, of no profit to anyone."

"I know that," Gareth said. "But let us say a certain enterprise is suggested, one which would require a fair investment."

"How large?" Pol asked cautiously.

"Oh, let us say, twenty to thirty ships."

Pol winced.

"Some warships, some transports, some merchantmen. And soldiers. At least three hundred, I'd prefer half a thousand. Remembering that the enterprise I'm thinking of is still no more than a dream."

"When would you sail? I won't ask where for the moment, since you're being mysterious. It would take time to prepare for something this great," Pol said.

"No sooner than late spring, more likely early summer," Gareth said.

"That many soldiers," Pol said. "With our tiny army, I don't know if we could muster that many from those discharged or from adventurous youth."

"The men would have to be trained before they fought, for their first battle would likely be the deciding one."

"Then we'd have to go across the Narrow Sea, and hire in Lyrawise and other of Juterbog's cities. And how we'd manage that without word getting out to . . . I assume you're talking about striking against the Linyati?"

"There could be ways," Gareth said. "All it would take is money. And don't panic, Uncle. I'm not even sure I want to take part in something like this. It's a bit too much like putting all your wealth on the single turning of a card.

"And it would require a deal of camouflaging," he finished.

"And what would we, I mean the investors, reap from such an extravaganza?" Pol asked.

Gareth smiled.

"Perhaps riches to make what I brought back this time look no better than a beggar's copper."

Cosyra got up from the bed, padded over to where Gareth stood looking out the bay window.

"What's so fascinating?"

"Just watching the lights of the village go out," he said.

"You're lying."

Gareth pretended injury.

"How can you tell?"

"Because I'm starting to know you a little bit . . . and there's the ocean out there, beyond the village. What were you thinking?"

"I was just wondering what comes next," Gareth said slowly. "And about how I'm several kinds of a damned fool for not being satisfied with what I've got."

"Why should you be?" Cosyra said after a moment, and there was an edge to her voice. "Do you think I am? I may be Lady Cosyra of the Mount, but my whole damned life is predictable."

"Thanks a lot."

"I'm sorry, Gareth," she said, "but you *are* part of it. Say I disgrace myself, and run off with you. Say, even, that I'm willing to marry you, and you're willing to marry me, which isn't a hint, by the way.

"Then I'm supposed to sit here and make babies, just like I would have to do for anyone else I married.

"It'd just be that you're more interesting, and better in bed, and better-looking than Lord Mushmouth, who was my alternative before.

"Damn, but I wish I could run off to sea," she said

vehemently. She remained for a while, then: "It looks freezing out there."

"It is."

"The fishpond froze over last night," she said. "I was going to show it to you when you rode in, but you had . . . other things on your mind.

"It was nice, looking down through the water, like a windowpane, seeing the fish move slowly about. I wonder what fish dream of, in the winter, when they sleep?"

He moved behind her, put his arms around her, slid them up to curl around her breasts.

"Am I being in a sour mood?" she asked.

"You're in some kind of mood," he said. "Maybe if we made love again."

She turned, put her arms around him.

"It certainly couldn't hurt, could it," and the last of her sentence was muffled by his mouth over hers.

"I've decided," he said the next morning over breakfast, "on a scheme."

"Butter me a muffin," Cosyra said, "and tell me more."

Gareth obeyed, after checking in the serving pantry to make sure none of the servants was listening.

"My, aren't we dramatic?"

"Shut up and eat your muffin. I've decided to go after the Linyati again."

Cosyra yawned. "That's supposed to be news?"

"I just decided it for certain this morning, in the bath," Gareth said.

"*I* knew you were going to do it last week."

Gareth eyed her thoughtfully. "You're sure you have nothing of the Gift?"

Cosyra smiled mysteriously, cut a bit of the seasoned ham, put it on her muffin.

"I've even decided what of your outfits—all twelve of them, you overdressed lordling, we *must* buy you some more clothes—we'll take back to Ticao with us so you can start organizing."

Gareth was at the King's Court, looking for his uncle and one of the possible investors, when he saw Lord Quindolphin. Quindolphin was in deep conversation with the man Cosyra had identified to Radnor as the Linyati ambassador.

Interesting.

Very, very interesting.

A deal of camouflaging . . .

A certain hack was hired, and two weeks later, a pamphlet was in all the bookshops:

A True
Account of
A Fabulous Journey
To
The Great, Rich
Frozen Kingdoms
Of the Far North
Beyond Any Man's Reck
Together With
A Full
Description of the
Gold and Treasure
To Be Found There
Together With
A Narration
Of Their Most
Barbaric Ways

And Brutal Government
No Civilized Nation
Should Countenance

Gareth sent for Labala, told him what he wanted. The man snorted.

"For this you bring me from my studies?"

"I've heard of your studies," Gareth said dryly. "It's not possible to futter every maiden in Ticao, you know."

"It's still a great goal to set your life after," Labala insisted. "But you don't need sorcery for what you want. All you need is a handful of gossips, a bit of gold, and the right taverns to gossip in."

"The last of which I'm sure you know."

"The ones I don't, Thom Tehidy does," and Labala departed on his task.

Within the week, "everyone" in Ticao knew that Sir Gareth Radnor was preparing a new expedition. And, breathe not a word of it, but it would be to the far north, to the great kingdoms "everyone" knew were beyond the frozen cities Saros already traded with. Relieving them of a greater part of their gold would be only right, considering the monstrous lords who ruled those lands.

Another story spread, this one easily verified: more than twenty ships had been chartered or bought by an unknown person and were being modified with heavier cannon, larger provision lockers, high bulwarks in the bows suitable for keeping off the icy northern seas, and extra canvas and rope for campaigning in a harsh climate.

"Two days at sea," Gareth told his uncle, "and we can strip off the wood on the prows and use them for the cook's fire.

"Everything else"—and he wasn't aware of how sharkish his smile was—"will be put to *very* good use."

Very quietly, agents for a dozen of the richer Merchant Princes of Ticao started buying fur clothing.

"Do you know," Pol said, "what your camouflage is doing to the price of hides? Catskin for gloves is up to two pieces of silver a skin, and you would not believe what a martin-lined coat sells for.

"What am I to do with all those damned pelts and coats and such I've got hidden in that warehouse?"

"Wait until next fall," Gareth said. "Well after we've sailed. Then you'll have a monopoly on the market and can persuade everyone this year's style will be furs, from head to foot. Sell at your cost, no more, and quickly, and all the idiots who drove the market up will be broken."

Pol eyed his nephew thoughtfully.

"Perhaps it's a good thing you *didn't* join my firm. Your ideas are entirely too slick."

"So you aren't going to follow my suggestion?"

"I didn't say *that*."

Agents in the cities of Juterbog busily interviewed experienced soldiers, and one of the most important qualifications they sought was experience in winter warfare. Those accepted were given enough silver to make their way to Lyrawise, report to a factor there for quarters and armament, and wait for transshipment.

Gareth pulled his cloak closer as he went out the shipyard gates. It was just dusk, midwinter, with a gale coming upriver from the sea.

He looked back to the *Steadfast* in the ways, studying his ship in the growing dimness. A day before, the foundry had delivered the first of the guns he'd had designed and built—long-barreled, small-bore culverins, intended to mount in the bows of a ship, much like the small swivel guns that'd been mounted there before. But these, fifteen feet long, were heavier, throwing a shot of eight pounds out a thousand yards, intended to smash the stern of a fleeing enemy or cut down masts and rigging.

He'd tried the idea back on Freebooter's Island, but the guns he had available were too heavy and put the *Steadfast* badly out of trim. But these new guns looked as if they would be ideal for a pirate going about his business. His other ships would be similarly fitted.

It was brutal cold, and he'd told off his carriage earlier in the day. The streets would likely be icing, and he'd rather chance his own footing up the winding hills to Cosyra's house than any carriage, even one with cleated wheels. He could have taken a horse out that morning, but he liked the animals little better than he ever had, and distrusted his abilities to stay in the saddle in hard weather.

He was considering whether there was any further way to deceive the Linyati when the wagon hurtled out of a passage at full speed.

It was a heavy freight wagon, with six horses drawing it, and was coming straight at him.

Gareth shouted a warning, then saw the driver was not only cloaked, but masked. The wagon, closing, almost filled the narrow lane, and Gareth looked for an alley to duck into. There was none—the driver had chosen his spot well, with a walled house on one side, and a brick building on the other, flush with the street.

Gareth saw but one chance, and leapt into the middle of the street as the wagon closed. He jumped, had the lead animal by the halter, pulled himself clear of the ground, and had hold of the harness. He heard the driver shouting curses, felt the sting of the man's whip on his shoulders, then, feet flailing, found footing on the wagon's tongue, and was steadying himself, no worse than being on a yardarm in a gale.

The driver, not ten feet distant, was pulling a pistol from the depths of his cloak, and Gareth dragged out his dagger with his free hand, braced, and threw the knife, hoping for luck, knowing at knife-throwing he had little.

The blade spun once, and the haft took the driver in the face—not glamorous, but near as deadly. He screeched and threw his hands high, fell off the wagon to the side, and the wheels crushed him.

Gareth ran up the wagon tongue and pulled himself into the seat. There were two bravos in the back of the wagon, just realizing their murder-scheme was going astray.

The driver's pistol, cocked, lay on the wagon seat. Gareth had it up, aimed, and fired. One of the rakehellies shouted in pain, grabbed his midsection and stumbled back, back, and fell off the rear of the wagon bed.

The last was pulling a dagger, and Gareth, sword in hand, leapt into the bed. His stance was easy, for this was no more than the deck of a rolling ship. The man swept at him with the blade, and Gareth ran him through, let him drop.

He turned back to try to stop the wagon's careering course and saw, just ahead, a tight curve the wagon would never make.

Gareth sheathed his sword and leapt off the cart, into a small wind-battered tree, still with some of its leaves.

The wagon smashed into the stone wall of the curve. Gareth heard the horses scream and thrash as he crashed down through the branches, his cloak and clothes tearing, spinning down to land, breathless and staggering, on his feet.

He didn't wait for the hue and cry, but saw a byway, darted into it, and was gone.

He'd had more than enough of Lord Quindolphin's games, he decided, and the time had come to think of recompense.

"I don't like this," Cosyra said.

Gareth waited. He was getting used to Cosyra's sometimes-oblique way of approaching things.

"There's been a man snooping around my house for the past couple of days," she said. "Waiting until the servants go out on an errand, then offering them silver to satisfy his curiosity."

"About what?"

"About you and me."

"Mmmh," Gareth said. "I dislike pryers myself. Who do you suppose he's spying for? Quindolphin?"

"That was my first thought. I hid beyond the gates, planning to wait until one of my servants indicated him, then I'd follow him to his lair and, possibly, have some of your men kidnap him and find out his master's purpose. But I didn't need any such romance, for I recognized him.

"Or, rather, I remembered where I'd seen him. In court, as one of the King's Chamberlain's agents."

Gareth blinked.

"What does the king want to know about us?"

"I don't know," Cosyra said rather grimly. "But I do know that the less you come to King Alfieri's notice, the better off you are."

Sledges thudded, and the *Steadfast* moved in its ways, sliding backward. She hit the river stern-first, and water gouted.

"And I hope," Labala said, finishing his incantation,

"the demons of the sea and the air keep you safe, and whatever the gods of corsairs are, look over us."

"It's not a proper launching," Thom Tehidy said. "For which thank the gods, for the brandy'll not get wasted bashed over her prow, but tucked safe inside, where it belongs."

"That's what I like about men," Cosyra said. "You're so damned romantic."

Wherries moved in on the *Steadfast* as N'b'ry, on the quarterdeck, shouted orders and lines went across. The ship would be towed cross-river for rerigging, then would join the twenty others waiting in a basin below Ticao.

"That man," Gareth said, looking at N'b'ry, "is going to be a captain this time, whether he wishes it or not. We'll not spare talent for its modesty."

The day was bright, and there was a false hint of spring in the air, and he was nearly ready to sail.

"The name's—"

"Kuldja," Gareth interrupted. "You were a foremast hand on the *Revenge*. A good one, too, as I recollect."

He sat at a crude desk—a pair of salt beef kegs with a plank between them—on the main deck of the *Steadfast*. There was a line of sailors across the deck and down the gangplank. Behind him were Froln and Galf, who'd already signed aboard.

The man, a stubby, hard-muscled, bowlegged tough, looked surprised, then knuckled his forehead.

"Aye, sir. Heard you was signing on again. Th' same Articles as afore?"

"Pretty much," Gareth said. "It's a little more complicated than before, since we've more sponsors. There'll be soldiers on some of the ships, but they're working for hire. But you'll be down for a full share, as before."

"But th' treasure'll be richer, too, up north?"

"I wouldn't be sailing if I didn't think it were," Gareth said, and passed the quill pen across. The man scrawled an X, and Gareth neatly wrote in his name next to it.

"Good signin' with you again, Cap'n, and hopin' we'll have more of your luck."

"Thanks. You can move your duffle into the fo'c'sle any time you want here. I'll be stationing you on the *Steadfast*, not one of the other ships."

"I'll be doin' that tonight," Kuldja said, turning to go.

"How'd your time ashore go?" Gareth asked.

"Not bad," Kuldja allowed. "Got married. Bought the old bitch a sweetshop."

"But you'd rather come aboard now? Things not going well?" Gareth was being, he realized, nosy. But he was very curious as to how his men had weathered their time ashore.

"Goin' as well as anybody c'd 'spect," Kuldja said. "But bein' in a bed that don't move gets tiresome. An' th' old bitch has two kids afore me."

"Welcome back," Gareth said, and turned, hearing a chant:

> "*Up the rope he will go*
> *He will go*
> *He will go*
> *Bein' hanged the best he should know*
> *He should know*
> *He should know . . .*"

Four very drunken men stumbled up the gangway, carrying a fifth, who dangled between them, snoring loudly.

"P'mission t' come 'board," the first one said, touching his forehead, almost falling. He and the others didn't wait for an answer, but jumped down onto the main deck, the fifth man's head clonking loudly against a bulwark.

Gareth knew all of them as rogues and competent rascals. All five looked badly battered and were shabbily dressed.

"Lookin' t' sign aboard, bein' out of money an' with the watch prob'ly on us," one said, then sighed and slid to the deck.

"Froln, do you fancy these relics?" Gareth asked, grinning.

Froln shrugged. "Why not? At least three of 'em made it aboard on their own feet. Better'n the last group we took."

The five were guided to the side, waiting for one of the ferry boats to take them to Froln's new ship, the *Seawrack*.

"Cap'n," Galf said. "Here comes our backbone."

Gareth went to the rail, saw a tight knot of brown-skinned men coming down the dock, trying to stay in some kind of file and step. At their head was Dihr. All of them wore fresh, clean whites, striped collarless shirts, and had matching dunnage.

"Permission to come aboard, sir?" Dihr called. "Got a crew of men here, looking for berths if there's any left."

"Come along, my friend," Gareth said. "I was hoping you men of Kashi hadn't decided to buy a town somewhere and turn your backs to the sea. A thousand welcomes to you."

There was no trouble filling the lists. Many of those who'd sailed with Gareth before came back, other experienced seamen followed. There were also boys and young men looking for adventure, and a goodly share of others, men running from something—a harsh master, the law, a bad marriage, the grinding toil on land, mostly themselves.

Some gave their proper names, others thought hastily, found another label to live under.

Gareth took all that were hale and hearty, caring little where they came from or what laws he was breaking by not inquiring as to their past.

The sea would forgive . . . or forget . . . all that came before.

"What is it you found?" Gareth asked.

"A clever thing indeed," Labala said, unwrapping the glittering green cloth. "Here you have a bit of sulfur, nestled in some kindling. That'd be paired to some other kindling by the wizard who built the package, for an easy job of arson. Here is what I think's a dried-up worm. Enliven that—which takes a good magician to bring anything back to life, even a worm—and that'll be at your food or the wood of your hull.

"Here's something that might be poison, which I didn't taste. Hells if I know how it'd be conveyed into a barrel, and multiplied.

"Gunpowder, this, with a little vial of water. Perhaps those could be charmed into life, and take kin with the gunpowder in the magazine.

"All things a master magician would come up with to destroy a ship a day—or a month—distant at sea," Labala finished.

"Pitch it overboard," Gareth said.

"I'd rather not," Labala said. "It's been rendered harmless, I think, and it might have some uses in the close by-and-by."

Gareth reluctantly agreed, asked, "Where'd you find it?"

"Cuddled down like a babe in the sail stowage, right here aboard the *Steadfast,* under everything where it'd never be found 'til it worked one or another of its evils."

"How'd you find it?"

"Well, Gareth, meaning no offense," Labala said, "I know you've got sentries aboard all our ships, and others rowing around all of the day and night.

"But I spent too much time on the docks not to know there's always a way aboard a ship, any ship, so I planted little charms, little warners, here and there aboard them all, nice little spells on them that'd twig me if someone of evil intent came aboard.

"Damned hard spell to cast, if I do say so myself," Labala went on. "Considering the villains and footpads you've been signing aboard.

"But one yapped to me, like a small but fierce watchdog, and so I came.

"I've spent the last few hours prying at it, not just with my fingers, and I can give you a direction its caster might be found in. Matter of fact, I took an hour and tracked my casting, and I doubt if you'll guess who most likely laid it."

"I rather think I will."

"Perhaps we should never have gone pranking with those pigs?"

Gareth could feel the simmering anger boil up. "Perhaps so, perhaps no. But I think it's now time to make a call on the Lord of Pigs' wallow."

Lord Quindolphin's "wallow" sat on the royal Mount, an ornate, crenellated stone mansion, with high walls and spiked ironwork atop them, most defensible against warders or the mob.

The gate yawned open invitingly.

There were twenty men standing with Gareth, carefully chosen men of the *Steadfast*. None appeared armed.

The street outside the mansion was thronged with

passersby, many of them wearing cloaks, none looking interested in the sailors.

"Well," Gareth said. "Into the lion's den and see what develops."

The men moved forward. Labala stepped aside.

"I think I might be of more good out here."

No one argued—few questioned magicians' thinking.

The courtyard was cobbled with variegated stones, and to one side were stables and, in open sheds, various carriages. The yard was deserted.

Gareth led the way to the main entrance steps, and, suddenly, the open iron gates banged shut, with no one visible shutting them.

"Stop," a voice boomed. "Quite far enough."

Lord Quindolphin stood on a balcony door to one side glaring down.

"I don't believe you were stupid enough to walk into my grasp, Radnor."

"I am merely a citizen who feels wronged by you and seeks recompense."

"Recompense?" Quindolphin laughed humorlessly. "You sorry bastard, do you think you're still in the land of pirates, where someone can do exactly as he pleases if his sword is sharp enough?"

"Why not?" Gareth said calmly. "You seem to."

"You have luck," Quindolphin growled. "Otherwise, the shame you brought my family would have been blotted out years ago.

"But now the balance shall be finally evened. You've entered my grounds with hooligans, and all laws say a man has the right to defend himself.

"Dessau, attend me!"

A man appeared on a smaller balcony next to Quindolphin's. He had long silver hair and beard, carefully tended, and wore a loose black tunic and pants.

"Yes, Lord?"

"Destroy these trespassers who intend harm to my family and myself!"

Dessau smiled thinly. "It is my pleasure, Lord Quindolphin."

He looked down at the sailors, and Gareth heard someone moan in fear. Others drew hidden long knives and pistols.

"A proper defense . . . I've always been fond of fire. *Most* fond," Dessau purred.

He held out his right hand, finger pointing at Gareth, and his left hand moved in strange arabesques:

> *"My beauty*
> *My pride*
> *My friend*
> *My sword*
> *Come to me*
> *Bring your power*
> *Your terror*
> *As I order you*
> *Strike!*
> *Strike now!"*

A tiny ball of flame appeared at the tip of his finger, grew until it was the size of his head. Again, Dessau shouted, "Strike now!" and the flame shot away from the wizard, then stopped in midair, coiling back on itself like a waking cat, and lashed back at the wizard.

It flowed around his arm like quicksilver and Dessau screamed, pawed at himself, fell back out of sight.

Quindolphin gaped in astonishment.

"You have attempted to kill me," Gareth shouted, playing as much to witnesses as Quindolphin had. "I charge you, my loyal men, to take this man into custody to face the King's Justice!"

Out of an alley a dozen men ran, carrying an iron-butted length of heavy wood. They smashed the ram into the iron gates, and they pinwheeled apart. The men, openly armed, trotted into the courtyard, others, casting aside their cloaks and the role of idle street wanderers, behind them.

"Guards!" Quindolphin shouted, his voice cracking. "To me!"

Doors slammed open, and men crowded into the courtyard, all wearing dark red and black livery, all heavily armed.

"Take them!" Gareth cried, drawing his sword and pulling a pistol from inside his coat.

He ran for the mansion steps, and two men blocked his way. A pistol banged behind him, and one guard dropped. The other lunged, and Gareth parried, put his blade in the man's chest.

He butted at the mansion doors, then Tehidy was beside him, and the men with the ram. The door smashed into flinders, and he was inside.

"Harm no one who doesn't try to stand against you," he called. He saw stairs, and ran up them, looking for Quindolphin, hoping that when he found him, he'd fight rather than surrender to very questionable arrest.

A fat, middle-aged woman was at the landing, holding towels. She shrieked, fainted, and Gareth leapt over her body, went up a flight, then another, to the level the balcony was on.

A young woman's face peered from a doorway, then the door slammed and he heard bolts snicking. Paying no mind, he ran on, saw an open door, looked inside.

Sprawled on the floor, his arm blackened, the wizard Dessau writhed.

"Please . . . please . . ." he moaned.

Gareth heard a door bang, footsteps, ran on. He rounded a corner in time to see a door bang closed, heard the heavy bar being dropped in place. He slammed at it hard and bruised his shoulder, without effect.

He started back the way he'd come, hoping to catch Quindolphin below.

Labala stood in the corridor, looking at the burned wizard.

"I looked into your little packet," he said to the fallen man. "And thought the devices you'd had your dogsbody plant might be some of your favorites. So I built some counterspells before we came here.

"Next time we meet, wizard, don't be so damned sure of yourself.

"And cast your spells with your left hand."

He laughed nastily, and Gareth had him by the arm.

"Come on, Labala! Help me find Quindolphin!"

"Certainly, Gareth," the big brown man said calmly. "You have but to ask."

They clattered downstairs into chaos.

There was a knot of terrified servants in a corner of the great room, and every now and then a pirate would survey one or another of the younger maids and lick his lips; but they obeyed orders and harmed no innocent.

Things were different for Quindolphin's guards. Their bodies were scattered across the courtyard, moaning wounded lying here and there. Gareth grudged them their courage, grabbed men and told them to look for the lord and, come to think of it, for his son.

But neither Anthon nor the lord were found, having

either a snug bolthole somewhere in the mansion, or a secret back passage to flee the grounds.

After an hour, Gareth ordered his men away.

There was no fire, but the mansion's interior was thoroughly wrecked. Furniture was broken, art ripped, statues smashed, food and wine splashed around walls, crystal crunched underfoot.

"Your crew's a barbaric bunch of bastards," N'b'ry observed, considering the damage, not intending humor.

"They are," Gareth agreed. "And I suppose I'm a barbarian amongst them, for I can't summon a tear for anything other than I wasn't able to get Quindolphin at the point of my sword."

N'b'ry looked at him and shook his head.

Cosyra did much, much more.

"I don't believe you had the temerity to go after a great lord like Quindolphin so openly! Gods, Gareth, you can't do things like that!

"We're a civilized country here. It would have been all right to hire an assassin, or a poisoner, or a wizard to give him a deathspell, or even a gang of footpads to waylay him when he goes out. We're realistic about sometimes having to go beyond the law.

"But making open threats, sacking a nobleman's house in the middle of the capital, in daylight, killing two or three dozen of his household guards and terrifying his staff? You really want to go back to the Great Dungeon, don't you?"

Gareth's fine rage had subsided, and he sat sheepishly, letting her savage him.

"I should never let you out of eyesight," Cosyra said.

"It'll be a fine matter now, when the king hears about this! I'll get a dungeon bag packed."

His uncle also ripped into him, saying that no man had

the right to indulge himself so basely, particularly when the wealth and investments of so many others depended on him.

Gareth, logically knowing he'd been in the wrong, took all the abuse humbly. But no matter how he tried, he couldn't suppress a savage red joy at finally striking at Quindolphin, although he knew the king's slow-grinding justice would eventually find him.

But none of the King's Guards appeared with a warrant, and though the wrecking was the awed talk and eventual laughter of Ticao, no summons to the palace came.

Nor was anything heard of Quindolphin or his family, and no one saw them in the capital.

Gareth waited a couple of days for the king's doom to crash down, then went back to getting ready to sail, as men swarmed about the merchant ships that had been converted into either transports or warcraft in the basin.

Labala was forced to hire another pair of magicians, casting spells of safety around the ships and men. But nothing magical attacked them.

Once the Linyati ambassador was seen, sitting at ease in an expensive watercraft, appearing to be doing no more than taking the air and casually watching the bustle. Gareth had him followed until his boat went back upriver.

Finally spring brightened into summer, and Gareth's ships were ready.

He set a sailing date, had it posted in the city's taverns.

Two days before, the king's summons finally came.

"So now you seek riches to the north, Lord Newgrange," King Alfieri said. The two were, once again, alone in the throne room.

Gareth thought of lying, changed his mind.

"No, your Majesty."

Alfieri's eyes widened, but he said nothing.

"I'm sailing against the Linyati again, Sire. This time I'm intending to seize their entire treasure fleet and bring it back to Saros."

"We rather wondered about your purported target," the king said. "We must remind you, in spite of difficulties, we remain at peace with that kingdom."

It was Gareth's turn to be silent.

"By the way," the king went on. "We read the report you prepared for the First Lord, and we were truly shocked. It is bad enough for Man to be ruled by ignoblemen in far too many lands, far more terrible for the Linyati and their slaves to be governed by these strange demons you called Runners. That fact alone has altered our entire perception of how the Linyati problem might be solved, or at least brought under control.

"Just what is your plan for attacking them? We can assure you this room is completely empty, and even our usual hidden listening posts are bare," Alfieri said.

"Once before, we struck them at sea, and were counter ambushed while savaging them," Gareth said. "This time, my plan is simpler. I've hired mercenaries—"

"We know this," Alfieri said. "For a brief moment we were worried that you were planning an insurrection against us."

"Sire! I shall always be your faithful servant," Gareth said.

"So we thought. Go on with your plans."

"I plan on using the old pirate lair of Freebooter's Island for a base after we reach the Kashi seas," Gareth went on. "Hopefully, we'll not be discovered. From there—" He broke off. "I wish I had a map to make my explanation easier."

"You need not fear losing our attention," Alfieri said. "We're aware—more than aware, due to recent events—of the lands the Linyati control."

Gareth hid surprise at the king's interest, went on.

"We'll land somewhere on the isthmus between Kashi and Linyati, and seize their treasure city of Noorat by land, before the annual treasure fleet works its way along the coast of Kashi.

"We'll be waiting when it arrives. I'll have the harbor forts secured with my gunners, and my fighting ships hidden, somewhere at sea, to close the jaws of the trap.

"With luck, their captains will surrender, rather than fight, and we'll have transport to bring the treasure home. But I'm taking enough ships of my own to handle even the worst disaster."

King Alfieri sat thinking.

"A bold, but very simple plan, which is always to the good," he said. "And you've done very well in keeping it concealed. We're impressed. The only reason we guessed the northern expedition might be a hoax was, as we said earlier, we've had trusted men of ours investigate the lives of you . . . and your friends."

Gareth guessed that was why the King's Chamberlain's man had been digging into Cosyra's life.

"A bold plan, indeed," Alfieri said. "One that could bring this kingdom great riches, and, this must be kept most secret, a measure of acceptance for a war that we fear is inevitable, given the intransigence of the Linyati." He sighed.

"Something you should be aware of. The Linyati ambassador has made several approaches to us, saying, with some degree of arrogance, that the pirate Gareth Radnor must be given into their hands, or the wrath of the Linyati might be loosed against all Saros.

"Diddly-damned fool idiot! Doesn't he know threats are to be made by men of war, not diplomats?

"We were further irked when Lord Quindolphin sought an audience, some months back, asking for your head. We refused, and we gather he took other steps for revenge.

"But we must say, we are not amused by your ruthless sacking of his estates! Especially in full light of day, and making no attempt to conceal who you were.

"Tsk. We doubt me that you'd make much of a statesman."

"No, Sire," Gareth said. "I'm afraid I would not."

"Then please, a favor. Do not embarrass us any further," Alfieri said, a bit mournfully. "At least not here in Ticao or anywhere else for a space."

"No, Sire," Gareth said. "I promise."

Alfieri walked to a long table, opened a drawer, took out a wax-sealed parchment scroll, and gave it to Gareth.

"This is our most secret Letter of Marque, giving you our permission to strike against the Linyati Slavers, to maintain the safety of the seas and the peace of our beloved kingdom of Saros, by any means you deem necessary."

Gareth, overwhelmed, bowed deeply.

"I thank your Majesty."

"We assume you're not naive enough to think," Alfieri said, "that should you be taken by the Slavers this will grant you freedom.

"The best you could expect is a moment of hesitation, perhaps, which might give you time to escape. Or die nobly fighting rather than in their torture chambers."

Gareth put the parchment safely inside his belt pouch.

"One other thing," Alfieri said. "As we said, don't embarrass us. Which also means, don't pirate any of our closer allies. I have not given you open season on anything lootable."

"No, Sire," Gareth said. "My only foe is the Slavers."

"Then go seek them out." Alfieri shook his head. "We never dreamed we might be using a corsair to further the demands of this kingdom. At least you're not a common pirate, even though certain, shall we say, habits, might well complicate both our future and yours.

"Go out and do well, and you shall be rewarded beyond your dreams when you return."

Gareth bowed again. Alfieri nodded, turned away, and Gareth backed out of the royal presence.

He found his tunic soaked with sweat once he was outside the palace, and wondered what Alfieri had meant about his habits.

But there was no one, not even Cosyra, to ask that of.

Saying good-bye to Cosyra was wrenching, but she seemed to take it almost lightly. They made love fiercely that last night, and in the morning, as they were dressing, she told him there'd be no playing about with brown-skinned Kashi women.

"For there are many spells a woman knows, and I want you to be sure that I'll always have my eyes on you."

"I give you the same promise I gave the king," Gareth said. "I'll consider no foolishness, not ever."

"Hmph. A pirate's promise!"

Gareth's twenty-five ships glided downriver carrying more than six hundred and fifty men, their sails stained gray, their hulls gleaming with fresh paint.

They were escorted by a great flotilla of onlookers. It looked as if half of Ticao had rented boats, and the other half ridden or walked out along the shore to watch the expedition depart for "beyond the frozen cities of the north."

In the lead was the *Steadfast,* and Gareth stood, trying to hold back pride, on the quarterdeck.

The river gave the ships to the sea, and the swell was gentle, the wind strong from the north, and the summer sky blue.

The crowds at Nalta Mouth cheered, and the people aboard the motley boats echoed the cheers before they turned back toward Ticao.

Above Gareth, at the tip of the mizzen mast, fluttered the black, green, and white banner of Saros. Once they'd gathered up the mercenaries waiting in Lyrawise and were beyond land, that would come down and Gareth's own corsair banner run up.

Then all would be reduced to the simple matter of fight hard, fight canny, or die.

Sixteen

The weather continued fair across the Narrow Sea, and ships' officers had a chance to begin training the new men and assigning others their duty stations.

There were only a few ships around them. Once a rakish yacht almost flew past the *Steadfast*, and Gareth wondered why he hadn't used some of his riches to buy such a wonderful toy.

Gareth was pleased to have his friends aboard the *Steadfast*: N'b'ry, Tehidy, and Galf as watch officers, Nomios happily back as bosun, Labala as wizard.

Gareth would have wanted more strength in the magical area, but for some reason, really competent and experienced wizards hadn't wanted to sign aboard, possibly content with their lot in Ticao, possibly accustomed to adventuring in other, more rarefied spheres, possibly terrified because the pamphleteer might have done too good a job writing about the terrible thaumaturges of the frozen north.

He'd done some last-minute arranging to give Dihr and his men of Kashi a light scouting three-masted caravel he'd had rerigged with lateen sails to look like a Linyati patrol ship. They named it the *Return*.

The fleet made port in Lyrawise. Waiting were the 300-plus mercenaries that had been signed, plus various officials with bills for the various taverns that had been ruined, citizens who'd been outraged in one way or another, not to mention unpaid charges at other taverns, armories, tailors, and inns.

Gareth paid without too much complaint, thinking that this was exactly how he'd read soldiers would act, and he shouldn't be upset.

He also thought soldiers didn't behave much differently than sailors, except their weapons would generally be more ready at hand, and hence their depredations would be bolder.

At least during the wait Gareth's agents had divided the mercenaries into squads and companies and appointed officers. They could drill on the decks of the transports to keep them somewhat out of trouble, although Gareth was glad he'd had those ships crewed by large, belligerent-looking sailors.

Before boarding the soldiers, he gathered them on dockside and read the appropriate parts of the Articles—those that dealt with discipline.

A rather beefy, dark man in half armor chortled something about having a child for a leader, and Nomios cracked his skull with a belaying pin. The men around the prone soldier seemed to understand the illustration that discipline afloat would be quick and harsh.

Naturally, the night before they sailed, half a dozen soldiers changed their mind and went overboard, swimming frantically for the shore. Gareth didn't have them pursued, for there'd be no other penalty but shooting for desertion, and he didn't want to do that. Besides, even if he'd forgiven their crime, they'd most likely make indifferent warriors.

The anchors came up, men chanting at the windlasses, the fleet put the land behind, and Gareth got seasick for half the day.

A day and night later, after Juterbog was well astern and they'd passed through a fleet of small fishing boats, the signal went up on the *Steadfast* for all ships to heave to and all captains report.

The sea was flat, and the sun was a bronze disk as the boats scuttled, like so many water bugs, over to the *Steadfast.*

Gareth, looking very much at ease, inwardly with stomach churning, sat on the top step of the quarterdeck ladder smiling down at the officers and mates in the waist below. The watch behind him was armed with hidden pistols, and there were men concealed forward with muskets loaded. In addition, a swivel gun was unobtrusively mounted on a railing, loaded with grape.

Gareth had no idea how his officers would take what he was about to announce. Tehidy had greeted each officer as he came aboard and given him a sealed envelope.

"First things first," Gareth said, and his voice carried across the water. He nodded to two sailors at the mizzen mast, and Gareth's banner, the Sarosian flag with a skull and crossed cutlasses, soared to the mast.

"Now we're flying under our true colors," he said.

There was a bit of a cheer.

"You can open your envelopes now," he said.

Some of the men obeyed, and read the identical instructions within. Others looked uneasily about, fingers touching their swords.

There was a sudden curse here, and a grin there, as

the more geographically inclined officers understood the instructions.

"Yes," Gareth said. "I've lied to you all these long months. We're not sailing north against any great kingdoms. As far as I know, the only thing beyond the frozen cities of the north are polar bears and ice up to your bum.

"But I do know where treasure lies."

He reached behind him, picked up a piece of Kashi sculpture of solid gold, exotically shaped. He tossed it down the ladder, to bounce dully on the deck. An officer picked it up reflexively, gasped at the weight.

"That's one piece of the treasure the Linyati steal from the Kashi every year.

"Last year, I stole a little of it away from the Slavers. Some of you shared in the riches, and I'm sure you all saw my men, from common deckhands to mates, lording it about Ticao.

"Now I propose to go after all of it.

"I invite all of you to change your ideas, your plans, and go with me after real treasure, treasure I've seen, handled, looted for myself."

There came that wolf-growl from some of the officers. Dihr and his first mate were grinning happily. Froln had moved to one side, was leaning casually against a bulwark watching his fellow officers, hand nonchalantly draped on his sword grip.

"This is outrageous," one captain sputtered.

"It is, isn't it?" Gareth agreed. "Just the kind of thing a pirate would do."

The captain harrumphed; then, in spite of himself, a grin came, and he laughed aloud. "Glad to be with you, Captain Radnor."

But another officer wasn't amused. "We signed aboard

for one duty," he said. "I'm no seabag lawyer, but I'd guess this change invalidates the Articles I signed."

"Possibly," Gareth agreed. "But the deceptions were intended to deceive the Linyati and their agents in Ticao. It would be a disappointment, would it not, for you to return, barely two weeks after you sailed out so boldly, to announce all was a fraud?"

The man thought, realized what was behind Gareth's words, paled.

"Just for m' own knowledge," Froln called, "what do you propose to do with someone who wants out?"

Gareth had given hard thought to the matter, and the answer had been given by a close study of his charts.

"I'll not murder him," he said, "nor force him to sail, unwilling, after gold he'd probably hate to possess."

He went on, through the laughter. "About four days' sail from here there's a certain island that used to be inhabited. There's still supposed to be huts, and fishermen leave dry food, in the event they're wrecked there.

"My solution for anyone opting out at this point is to maroon them there. By the time the fall storms come, and fishing vessels might pass by the island, the Linyati will already know of our presence, by the bloody grip we have on their throats!"

There was silence except for the creak of the ship and the wind rustling through the rigging.

"You're very damn' clever, Captain Radnor," someone said. But his tones were admiring, not critical.

"Thank you," Radnor said. "Before you leave the *Steadfast,* be sure and advise me, or one of my officers, if you plan to defect, so we can make the proper arrangements.

"And don't think of returning to your own ship and

then attempting to break away from the fleet, for I promise you, all our lives will require us to pursue and destroy you.

"I'm sorry," he said, not sounding sorry at all. "But this is a hard world. Now, to continue our plan against the Linyati . . ."

"I was watching their faces," N'b'ry said. It was about two turnings of the glass later. The captains had departed, and the new course, almost due south, had been ordered and sail set. The two were in Gareth's cabin, relaxing for a moment.

"I saw only three or four who're afraid of the Slavers or whatever," he went on, "and the more they thought about the fortune we brought back, the less they wanted out."

"That's what I expected," Gareth said. "Or, so I don't sound arrogant, hoped, anyway. All the officers we interviewed for command had a bit of the rogue in them, or at least the opportunist, in my eyes."

He sat down in a hand-carved chair, put his feet up on his chart table, and stretched mightily.

"Now, with any luck, things will go easily, at least until we reach Freebooter's Island."

"That I'm looking forward to," N'b'ry said. "There was that small woman with the boldest eye. Perhaps she's no longer with that one-eyed scoundrel who's half again bigger than me. I think—"

There was a hard rap at the door. Gareth swung his feet down to the deck.

"Enter."

It was Galf. "Sir, we've got problems."

Gareth sighed. "Of what sort?"

"We've found a stowaway—or rather, the stowaway's come out of hiding up forward."

"I don't see any problem requiring me," Gareth said.

"Anyone who wants to be a corsair badly enough to stow away should just be signed on the Articles."

"Sir, it's not a he. It's a she."

Gareth made a sound in his throat.

"And she refuses to be put ashore, sir, but demands a hearing under our Articles."

"Now there's a bold wench," N'b'ry said. "And as I recall, we don't have anything in the Articles forbidding women in the crew. Nobody ever thought that would be a problem."

"Do not be absurd, Knoll N'b'ry," Gareth said, buckling on his sword belt. "Come on, and let's deal masterfully with the situation—although I don't have a damned clue what we should do.

"Thank the gods for the Articles and the crew having the vote in the matter. I suppose, after it goes against her, we can turn back and put her aboard one of those fishing boats we passed. It's most unlikely she would have heard of our change of plans, nor would a single unknown be believed back in Ticao."

Gareth thought he'd developed a bit of command presence, the ability to handle any situation, no matter how deadly, how bizarre, without showing his real emotions.

But seeing Lady Cosyra of the Mount standing defiantly on his main deck shook him to the core, and he was later sure he'd turned pale, or green, or something.

Even though she was more than a bit travel-worn and in need of a bath, she was still striking, wearing close-tied kneeboots, dark blue pants, and a deerskin tunic, laced at the neck.

She also wore a sword belt with a thin-bladed rapier and, just behind it, a narrow, single-edged dagger.

"Good morrow, Captain," Cosyra said in a merry voice. "I'm thankful to be aboard your vessel."

Some of the crewmen, who'd recognized Cosyra and knew the relationship between the two, snickered.

"I wish I could say the same, Cosyra," and Gareth was disturbed enough to swear, "What the *hells* are you doing here?"

"I stowed away in Lyrawise," she said, "intending to serve with your fleet, Captain."

"You can't do that!" Gareth said.

"Why not? I've read your Articles, and there's nothing forbidding women to join your crew."

"'Tain't reasonable," a beefy sailor, Shenshi, Gareth remembered, growled. "If th' cap'n's whore can git aboard, so can mine."

Cosyra's half smile vanished, and she turned to the sailor.

"That is once," she said coldly. The man, about to say something else, saw the look in her eyes, and stepped back. Cosyra turned back to Gareth.

He still felt numb-witted.

"How did you get to Juterbog ahead of us?" was the best he could manage.

"Easily. I hired a ship."

Gareth remembered the yacht that had distanced them days before.

A sailor—Kuldja—was on a barrel head.

"Why can't she sign?" he shouted. "If there ain't rules against it, she should be able to join us if she can hold her own wi' a cutlass or a halyard."

"An' where'd she sleep? She'd be welcome in my hammock," a crewman said. "But folks might talk."

There was laughter.

"She can sleep where she damned pleases," another crewman said. "Same as the rest of us."

"Damned woman'll do nothing but make trouble," another said.

"The hells I will," Cosyra said. "Tell me there's none among you who've gone into another's hammock aboard ship for comfort. Does anyone spit on them the next morning?"

There was an uneasy shifting. Sailors far from land and women traditionally found comfort with one another or by themselves, but it wasn't something that was talked about.

"The problem, young woman," a bearded pirate said, "is that you must be able to carry your weight, both literally and figuratively, with the rest of us. Have you experience as a sailor?"

"No," Cosyra admitted. "But I'm agile, and have no fear of heights. Aren't there men—boys, even—signed on this ship who think the bow is called the 'pointy end'?"

There were chuckles.

"Aye," the bearded man admitted. "We train men for the trade. But what about fighting? I see you're armed. Is that for show?"

"I've been trained," Cosyra said. "And blooded."

Gareth remembered the fight with Anthon's bullies, and nodded involuntarily.

The deck was now filled with men, some in agreement, others shaking their heads vehemently, others, undecided, arguing back and forth.

"I still say the cap'n's lady should be allowed on," Kuldja returned. "And if she chooses to share his cabin, what of it? Aren't officers given some gravy?"

"Gravy ain't what we're talkin' about," Shenshi said. "At least, gravy's not what I leave in my doxy."

Amid the laughter, Cosyra walked deliberately to Shenshi.

"That was twice," she said clearly, and the laughter died. "There is no third time."

Her hand whipped, hard, across his face twice. He lifted a fist, and Cosyra jumped back, very fast, and her blade was in her hand.

"Now," she said. "You've been challenged. Make what you want of it."

A sailor shouted:

"There's no fightin' aboard ship! Grounds for marooning!"

Another: "But she ain't a crewman. Let 'em fight! Never seen a woman 'gainst a man. I'll give . . . two, naw, three to one for Shenshi."

"Done an' done," another shouted. "I saw her leap, an' Shenshi's 'bout as quick as a stalled ox."

Gareth turned to Tehidy.

"In my cabin. Get two pistols."

Thom nodded, slid away.

Gareth saw Labala move unobtrusively to the foredeck railing overlooking the waist, a belaying pin ready.

"Wait," the bearded sailor said, holding up both hands. "Maybe this solves our problem. And gives some amusement.

"Let these two fight. If she wins—or even shows herself handily—then perhaps we ought to admit her to the Company. If not . . . well, then, the problem is solved, is it not?"

There was a roar of approval.

Gareth started forward.

"Captain," Nomios said. "Stay your course. This one's beyond you."

Gareth looked around helplessly. A sailor was already coiling a long length of rope into a circle on the deck below.

"Yer steps outside this, drop yer guard and get back

inside," he said. "No fightin' beyond the round. Keeps things from gettin' compelcated, an' dancin' around on steps an' such like in th' romances."

Cosyra nodded understanding.

Shenshi had a large cutlass in one hand, testing its edge with his thumb.

"Won't be much of a fight, boys," he called. "Get your silver on me, an' watch me smash that titty blade of hers, then it'll be interestin'. Real interestin'."

He pulled off his shirt.

"You goin' do the same?" he called, and winked to the applause. Sailors were calling bets back and forth.

Tehidy was beside Gareth.

"I've got the pistols. You want me to shoot him?"

Gareth shook his head helplessly.

"Let them engage, or we'll have a mutiny on our hands," he decided. "If Cosyra doesn't go down the first time he hits her, I'll try to break it up then."

There were two sailors standing in front of him. Both had sheath knives drawn.

"Captain, we's sorry. But th' Articles apply, an' you'll have to stand by and let what happens happen."

Gareth, lips in a thin line, didn't reply. Tehidy moved to one side, one hand casually under his shirt—on, Gareth knew, a pistol butt.

"Very well," the bearded sailor called.

"Are both of you ready?"

Cosyra, rapier in her hand, nodded.

"Ready-ready," Shenshi said. "More'n ready."

Cosyra was in a half crouch, moving, careful steps, to Shenshi's offside. The big man's blade came up, and he slashed at her, going low. Cosyra jumped back, almost to the rope's edge, then jump-lunged.

Her blade flicked out once, twice, a third time.

Shenshi yelped, then looked down at his chest, as blood oozed out. There was another wound lower down, just below the first, below his lungs, and a third in the biceps of his sword arm.

Shenshi's eyes widened, his mouth fell open, and the cutlass clattered down.

"I . . . she . . ." and he stumbled forward and fell to the deck, facedown.

There was utter silence on the deck.

Gareth looked at Cosyra, who managed a weak smile. He suddenly and strangely thought he'd never loved her more than at that moment.

The bearded man walked to Shenshi's sprawled body, looked down at the twin wounds in his back, he knelt, then stood.

"He's still breathing," the man announced. "Mayhap he'll live. Perhaps, magician, you'll tend to him? He's not the brightest man we have aboard, but he'll do in a melee."

Labala tossed the belaying pin aside, came down the ladder, bent over Shenshi.

The bearded man inclined his head to Cosyra.

"Congratulations, milady. That was as pretty a piece of work as I've seen in years."

He turned, looked up at Gareth.

"Captain, I think we've added another corsair to the Company. Perhaps you'll have her sign the Articles?"

And so Lady Cosyra of the Mount became a pirate.

Seventeen

The paradise of Freebooter's Island was shattered. The twin forts guarding the channel were blackened ruins, and sunk in the lagoon were half a dozen ships the pirates had left behind on their massive raid. The houses looked as if a giant had trampled them in a rage.

Gareth thought he could smell smoke, but that wasn't possible. The Linyati had come and gone time past.

"They must've used their wizards to track where we sailed from," N'b'ry said. His expression was stricken, and Gareth remembered what he'd said about the small woman with the boldest eye.

Without waiting for orders the pirates had manned the guns, and the lookouts were scanning the land, looking for attackers, or just a sign of life.

But there was none, until a parrot burst, squawking, from a tree, and everyone jumped.

"Nomios," Gareth said. "Two boats with a landing party."

"Sir."

"And signal to the others to stand by, without entering the passage. Have their guns manned and run out."

"Sir."

"Labala," Gareth said. "I want you with us as well, smelling for any magic."

The big man nodded.

The plash of the oars was very loud as the boats moved toward shore. The water was still crystalline, the wind still soft, the sands gleaming white.

But the island was dead.

Gareth jumped into the shallows, waded ashore, hand near a pistol in his sling.

Nothing moved except tattered vegetation in the cool breeze.

Here, where the pirate's market had been, was nothing but waste, the buildings ripped apart or fired. Even the handful of stone buildings above it had been smashed by cannon fire . . . or magic.

"Hallooo," Gareth shouted. "We're friends."

Echoes came back without reply.

Gareth called again.

"Knoll . . . Thom . . . search around the settlement in the bush. Maybe someone's still alive, still here, and too frightened to come out."

Tehidy and N'b'ry pointed to men they wanted. Other pirates got out of the boats, pulled them higher on the sand, their keels scraping loudly.

The search parties were about to start up what had been the main "avenue" when an amused laugh came, seeming from nowhere, from everywhere.

Gareth found he was having trouble breathing; he had his pistol cocked and his sword was in his hand.

The laugh grew louder, and the wizard Dafflemere came from behind a tumbled wall of coconut logs.

He was barefoot, and wore tattered pants and, incongruously, an iron breastplate with no shirt under it. He had a cutlass thrust through a rope belt, and, hanging from it, a hunting knife. His beard was longer than ever, but now was a dirty white, boiling in ignored tangles over the armor plate to his belly.

He had an easy smile on his face.

"Greetings, Gareth Radnor."

"Uh . . . good day to you, Dafflemere."

Gareth shot a quick glance at Labala, who was looking troubled.

"No, I'm hardly a ghost," Dafflemere said. "In the flesh, though it's been hard keeping it together the last year, or month, or however long it's been since the bastards took the *Thruster* and put me to the torture."

"The last we saw of you," Gareth said, "was hard off the coast of Kashi, sore assailed."

"Sore, indeed," Dafflemere said, still sounding amused. "It took three of them to clear our decks, and every one of us was wounded.

"But in the end, they took us.

"And that night, after they'd sailed about, finishing off any of our ships that were still afloat, picking up those of us who weren't smart enough to breathe water and go to an untroubled doom, then they gave themselves pleasure.

"They rafted their ships, and then vied to see who could give their prisoners the slowest death. They started with the boys, then the men, then the officers.

"It was then I saw the horror that rules them." Dafflemere shuddered. "Like lizards scuttling about, but huge, reeking of musk and evil.

"They loved, even more than the men or half-men they rule, seeing our pain and death."

"I saw them, too," Gareth said.

"One of the Linyati wizards—at least that's what I suppose he was—bent over me," Dafflemere went on, "as I lay in chains, and said he knew that I organized the sally against their treasure fleet.

"Myself and you. They wanted to know what I knew of you, and where you were, and I answered honestly nothing, that I'd been busy with my own troubles when the battle was joined.

"But they didn't believe me, and so they heated their pinchers and prods, and made sure they had their heaviest ropes ready.

"But I fooled them."

Again, Dafflemere's laughter rang.

"I escaped."

"How?"

Dafflemere's smile vanished, and he looked troubled.

"I do not know. I tell you true, I do not know. All that grows dim, as if I'm viewing myself through a mist, a seafog.

"Someone . . . something . . . must have saved me. I don't know what, or who.

"But when I recollect clear, I was back here, on this island. Time must have passed, for the Slavers had come and gone, taking all who didn't fight to the death with them.

"I gathered bodies, burned them here on the beach. There was food, and game to be hunted, and all I had to do was wait, for I knew someone, and I guessed it would be you, would return.

"Or else another generation of freebooters would come, for as long as kings and noblemen keep men in chains, there'll be men to run to sea to find freedom and revenge, and I would help them, as I propose to help you, for my powers are even greater than they were."

"How did they grow?" Labala said.

"Again, that is something I don't know. But I can feel the strength within me, biding its time for the moment to strike, in terrible ways the Linyati cannot dream of."

"I scent you," Labala said. "But I smell no evil. If you are a demon now, or a spirit in thrall with the Linyati, I think I would be able to sense that."

"You would," Dafflemere agreed. "For you've always had power, even though it was latent, half-buried; power enough to scent if I was a puppet."

"But who took you from the decks of that Linyati ship?" Gareth persisted. "Who rescued you?"

"As I said, I do not know," Dafflemere said, untroubled by Gareth's prodding. "Perhaps one of my friends?"

He waved a hand at the lagoon, and, suddenly, tentacles came up, thrashing the calm water into white foam and as rapidly vanished.

"Oh yes. I still have my friends," he said. "And my magic, as I said.

"Now, I would appreciate some food such as I've not had for months, food I thought I'd never long for. I want ship's biscuit, salt beef, wine or beer. Preserved fruit of the north, if there is any.

"I think that was all that kept me from going mad while I waited, dreaming of what I did not have.

"Or perhaps it didn't stop me from madness. But that doesn't matter, so long as I am allowed to sail with you, sail with you against the Linyati.

"Perhaps they have stolen my soul, for I sense something lacking within me.

"Or perhaps not.

"Perhaps I am simply mad, and perhaps the Slavers let me live, brought me here and left me marooned, thinking that amusing.

"Perhaps, perhaps.

"But may I sail with you, Gareth Radnor? You owe me a promised favor from times past.

"I can provide my magic . . . and those creatures I showed you before."

Dafflemere smiled, but his smile was harsh, showing teeth that might have been those of a shark.

"Yes, Dafflemere," Gareth said, ignoring the alarmed looks from N'b'ry and Tehidy, as Labala nodded in approval.

"You can sail with us . . . against the Slavers."

Eighteen

S omewhat damned impressive," Knoll N'b'ry whispered, although the Linyati fort was at least a third of a league distant. "I doubt if any of our cannon can elevate enough to reach the fort, let alone break through those walls. What we need is a damned great bombard, which I somehow forgot to pack in my seabag."

Gareth squashed a mosquito, nodded.

"A master wizard—which I'm not . . . yet—would have to come up with a bogglin' spell to break those walls down," Labala agreed.

Gareth didn't respond. Making a task seem harder wasn't a very good way to find a solution.

"Could we just sail into Noorat down the middle of the passage?" N'b'ry said. "Maybe their cannon can't reach to midchannel."

"Care to bet our ship . . . or anyone's . . . on that?"

"No."

The city of Noorat had been built at the midpoint of a great, rocky C in mid-jungle. The land rose to promontories at either side, and on these, stone forts, with thick walls about forty feet high, had been built.

Gareth had begun by spying out the fort on the west side of the bay, now this one.

"How the hells did they get those stone blocks up here? Slave power?" Tehidy wondered.

"Magic," Labala suggested. "And then haulin' those big damned guns up after them—what are they, anyway?"

"I'd guess big culverin, which'll give them range, and maybe some perrier, lobbing high over the bay," Tehidy said.

Gareth noted, however, that the only direction those cannon were facing was to sea.

The city inside the bay beckoned to Gareth, with warmth, civilization, and, most of all, gold. Gold now, more gold for the taking when this year's treasure fleet arrived.

"Mmph," he said at length. "Let's go."

"Did you come up with something?" N'b'ry asked, as they slithered back down the knoll and started downhill to where their boat waited.

"I did," Gareth said. "All I had to do was discard the impossible, and what was left over was what we'll attempt."

"Which is only . . ." Labala asked.

"Preposterous," Gareth said.

"I think," Tehidy said, studying the map, "I'm most glad to be a sailor, instead of an infantryman."

"My deepest sympathies," Gareth said sorrowfully. "I deeply regret having to tell you every man not required to keep the ships afloat suddenly shines with soldierly virtues. Or hadn't you noticed that our bills of lading included packs, canteens, slings, weapons belts, and great clonking boots for all of us, not just the soldiers?"

"Including me, I hope?" Cosyra said. "I'm starting to feel, no offense, like you're keeping me in cotton batting."

Gareth hesitated. He was in fact wanting to keep her from harm's way. Which he'd better not continue, he realized.

"You'll be marching right in front of me," Gareth said.

Tehidy studied the crude map again.

"I'm too fat to be doing this kind of thing," he complained.

"Who isn't?" Gareth said. "I'll want you here, on the eastern side. You and Froln will be in command of that landing force, with mates from the other ships to back you up."

"And you'll be over here on the west?" Tehidy asked.

"Yes."

"Having all the fun, while we dance around, diverting the Slavers—and probably getting our asses shot off."

"I hope so."

The pirates had made their approach cunningly, steering well east of Noorat, almost to Batan, then holding close to the coast while sailing along the isthmus. Dafflemere and Labala had cast the most powerful weather spells they could devise; powerful yet subtle, so the wizards of Noorat hopefully wouldn't scent them out.

Labala swore he'd done no good, but the weather had been ideal for their purposes—hazy and squally, with visibility no more than two or three leagues. Gareth felt a little proud that he'd thought to have the fleet's sails dyed gray, even though most of the ships' bosuns had muttered, wanting to at least sail out in perfectly tidy form.

Then he fell into his usual moroseness, going over his intentions, and how the Linyati would inevitably destroy him, again and again. Cosyra noted his moroseness, asked if he was always this moody before action.

"Probably," he said, remembering other times, other glooms. "I guess it's my way of praying for luck. If I don't believe in gods, then not believing in luck would be one way of praying, wouldn't it?"

"You, sir, are a loon," Cosyra announced.

Once Gareth had a plan, and it was a little too complex to make him happy, he brought his captains together. The fleet was hidden behind an island, about half a day's sail away from Noorat.

The ships' officers muttered for a while after Gareth had finished, feeling they were liable to take far too many casualties in the assault, and that no one who knew anything of battle ever split his forces. But no one could come up with a better way to seize Noorat.

So, that night, half the fleet, with two-thirds of the troopships, raised anchor. Well clear of land, they sailed east. Then they turned back until they closed on land, and found a somewhat sheltered anchorage. It would be a long hike back to the eastern fort for the landing party, but they wouldn't be seen. Hopefully.

Gareth and the others waited for a day after Froln and Tehidy's departure, in case the eastern party had problems and was delayed. Then they, too, closed on Noorat, and, in the depths of the night, the second landing party went ashore.

The mercenaries formed up, cursing under their breath, being cursed when they fell or raised their voices by bosun mates and their own officers and warrants.

In a sweating line, they crept toward the promontory through the depths of the jungle.

It was hot and sticky, and the ground under Gareth's unaccustomed boots was muck. He heard strange cries he hoped were animals or night birds, and the night was full of ominous rustlings and whispers. Mosquitoes and other biting insects hummed around, and he wondered what they fed on when there weren't nice, succulent pirates to nibble on.

He held as close to the beach as he could, just in the fringes of the jungle. The men behind him, unaccustomed to moving as a unit, accordioned back and forth as the column snaked along.

It was quite dark until after midnight, when the moon came out and then they could move faster. They encountered no guards, no patrols, and Gareth hoped the men to the east were having equal luck.

The promontory loomed, and the ground rose in front of them, the trees reduced to a scatter of brush.

That was far enough, and they held in cover. Now all there was to do was wait.

He wished the forts were manned by normal men, who might get sleepy or lackadaisical, not Linyati. The Slavers would be as alert, guarding this fort where nothing ever happened, as if it were the first time the post had been manned. But, his mind reminded, if wishes were fishes, we'd all have some fried.

If all went well . . . and since when did that ever happen in battle, Gareth thought, and pressed Cosyra's hand for morale's sake.

The sky had just begun to lighten when Gareth heard, across the water, the thud of musketry. The eastern force was attacking the fort on the other promontory.

That was his cue to move forward, with twenty men, all sailors, to the foot of the fort's walls. He crept around the side until he could see the sallyport.

Again, he waited.

Across the mouth of the bay, white smoke billowed,

then came the louder slap of a cannon. Gareth made a face. Either he'd missed a cannon on the landward side, or the Linyati across the water had a field gun that could be easily muscled about.

A metal gate rattled open at the sallyport, and Gareth shrank back into cover. Two groups of Linyati—Gareth hastily counted them, got around thirty—hurried down the hill to a dock, where a dozen boats were moored.

After a time, he chanced another look, saw the boats moving steadily across the bay's mouth to reinforce the eastern fort.

Above that fort, a dark swirl formed in the sky. Everything was going as planned. That was Dafflemere and Labala's casting, a smallish cyclone, hopefully able to pluck a man from a wall and drop him to his death.

The swirl moved across the fort, and Gareth thought he could hear screams.

Now Tehidy and Froln should be retreating. Instead he heard the musketry grow louder, and the field gun bang once more. The deception appeared to be turning into a full-scale attack.

He trotted back to where the sailors waited, and motioned. They spread out, unslinging the grapneled lines wound over their shoulders.

A sailor cast. His grapnel didn't find a hold, but grated against the stone and fell back. Gareth winced, knowing the sound must have alerted the remaining Linyati within, but there was no challenge.

Nomios threw next, and his hook caught firm, then another and another grapnel arced up. As soon as a sailor's grapnel caught, he swarmed up the knotted rope. Other men came out of the jungle, and went up the ropes behind them. These carried other ropes, with loops for the unhandy soldiery.

Gareth had no time to watch, was climbing up, hand over hand. He saw a olive-complected head peer over the parapet, cry the alarm. A musket barrel came next, and fired down.

Gareth heard a grunt, saw, out of the corner of his eye, a sailor release his hold and fall limply down onto the fort's talus.

That Linyati made the mistake of looking at the results of his shot. Gareth had a precarious toehold and a pistol out when Cosyra, on the next rope, fired, and the Linyati sprawled, motionless, over the battlements.

Other ropes were tied off by sailors and dropped down, and bundled, loaded muskets were pulled up as Gareth reached the top of the wall.

A Linyati ran at Cosyra, pike leveled, and Gareth shot him down, pulled a second pistol from his sash.

The fort was simply constructed, the walls sheltering a barracks at one end, a magazine at the other, a cookshed at the third, and a small drill ground on the last.

Pirates swarmed over the walls as the Linyati formed a wedge, came up a ramp to the parapets. Musket fire volleyed down at the Slavers. They fell back, came again, were shot down.

Discipline like this was completely foreign to the sailors, and with a yell, in spite of shouted orders from officers, they charged down into the square into a vicious melee, no quarter asked or given.

Gareth grimaced at his men's independence, and knew he had to be at their forefront. He ran halfway down the ramp and leapt into the rear of a knot of Linyati. He shot down two with his remaining pistols, realized he should have reloaded before he jumped, and then a giant Slaver was on him, swinging a double-bitted ax, face wide in battle-madness. Gareth knew better than to parry with his thin blade, and back-rolled into the dirt, across a body. The Linyati came in again and Gareth heard the crack of a pistol, and the Slaver's throat vanished in a spray of blood.

Cosyra was behind him, dropping her empty pistol and pulling her rapier. A Linyati came at her, and she brushed his sword aside, drilled him neatly through the heart, pulled her blade free as another attacked shouting something.

Gareth, from behind, put his sword into the back of the man's skull. He spasmed like a headless chicken and went down, as another Slaver cut at Gareth, and Radnor slashed his guts open.

Then there was no one left to kill, and even the wounded Linyati wouldn't let themselves scream in pain.

Gareth spotted N'b'ry.

"Look for Runners on that side," he shouted, grabbing a freshly loaded musket from a man who'd remembered his orders, unlike the others.

"Come on," Gareth ordered, pointing. "You—you—you—check for any survivors. We could use a prisoner."

They quickly combed the barracks, then the cookshed, found no Linyati alive, none of the dominating Runners. N'b'ry shouted the cookhouse was clear as well.

Gareth ordered him to take more men and make sure there weren't any manholes or secret rooms, remembering the cleverness lizards had in hiding themselves while waiting for prey. But the only living beings in the fort were the pirates.

And the flies, swarming in, smelling blood, as the sun rose higher, turning the fort into an oven.

Gareth told Nomios to raise the flag he was carrying wrapped around his midsection, and moments later, the pirates' banner lifted over the fort.

Gareth went to the battlements with a glass he'd found

in the barracks, peering across the water at the other fort. Smoke still boiled, and he heard the crackle of musketry.

He wondered why Froln and Tehidy hadn't withdrawn, as the plan ordered, and why the Linyati cannon had fallen silent.

A pirate with very sharp eyes pointed across, and shouted in glee.

Gareth hastily refocused his glass, and saw his black, green, and white skull-embroidered flag float into sight, above the other fort's parapets. He heard cheering from behind him.

Now they had the Linyati, Gareth thought. With both sides of the bay controlled, there would be nothing for the Slavers to do but surrender.

Which brought a host of other problems to mind.

But first was celebrating . . . and counting the price.

It was high. Almost seventy-five soldiers had been shot down charging across open ground outside the other fort, the Linyati grapeshot sweeping their line. They'd paid no mind to the plan of withdrawal once the shooting had begun, but kept attacking. Eventually a man had scrambled to the top of the wall and held the parapet long enough for others to clamber up.

They jumped down into the courtyard and opened the gates for the rest of the attackers. Fifteen seamen had died in that struggle.

Gareth didn't like it, but if Froln and his men had withdrawn, as planned, they'd still have to attack that fort sooner or later.

In his own attack, twenty-five soldiers and eleven sailors were casualties. Labala and one of the two chirurgeons with the expedition were busy treating them.

Gareth ordered the fort's guns loaded and run out, and

gunners were detailed to the cannon. Then there was nothing to do but wait, and meditate on what to do next.

The problem was, no one really knew very much about the Linyati. Gareth, because of his interrogation of captured Slavers, knew more than most, and realized how ignorant he was.

On the voyage out, he'd quizzed Dihr and the other men of Kashi who'd been Linyati slaves, and found out how secretive these people were.

None of the slaves had ever seen a Linyati woman or child.

All of the men from Kashi had served in the Linyati cities along the Kashi coast, none being taken to the homeland.

None of the slaves knew anything about Linyati social customs—slaves were used, unlike in other countries, strictly for outside work and manual labor, so there was no one who could provide information on the Slavers' private lives. Once they disappeared into their blank-walled houses, all knowledge stopped.

So Gareth had no idea what to expect inside the low walls of Noorat.

He chanced taking a small boat with a white flag toward the city—but he crewed the boat, a very quick little cutter, with sailors with boat racing experience. Of course, he was behind the cutter's tiller.

The sea was calm, the sky clear, and the white stone walls were silent. He saw no sign of life as the cutter closed on Noorat, nor was there a response to the white flag.

Not for a long moment, until he saw smoke boil up from one of the walls. A cannon ball flew overhead, and Gareth put the tiller hard over and, zigging, fled back to the mouth of the bay. Other cannon fired, and Gareth noted with interest they were all small bore and short-ranged.

So the Slavers wouldn't be logical and surrender.

Very well, it would be a fight. But it would have to be won quickly, for Gareth estimated the treasure fleet would be due in about a month.

The pirate fleet sailed into the bay, and the transports anchored under the cover of the forts' guns.

The warships went on line and sailed back and forth, just out of range of Noorat's cannon, slamming broadsides over the city's walls. But again, there was no sign of surrender, and the only mark of infliction Gareth could see was an occasional plume of smoke.

Small groups of men were secretly landed, and reconnoitered the land around Noorat. To the east was tropical forest, to the west, swamp. Only to the rear of the city were there fingers of land, leading into the unknown interior.

So the Slavers' city would have to be taken the hard way, by main force.

Cosyra came to him the night before the attack, as he was pacing the quarterdeck of the *Steadfast*.

"About the fight?"

"Yes?"

"We break into the city . . . and then what?"

"We put anyone who resists to the sword," Gareth said. "And seize whatever gold they've got stored, like good pirates are supposed to do."

"What about the Linyati women?"

"We don't even know if they have any."

Gareth saw Cosyra was looking at him steadily in the light from the binnacle.

"What if there are?" she asked again.

Gareth shifted uncomfortably. "Do you mean they'll

come to harm? I'm afraid so," he said. "I don't think there'll be holding my sailors back, let alone the soldiery, if they see the chance for rape."

"Even if you ordered anyone doing that to be shot?"

"Cosyra, I won't . . . I can't . . . do that," Gareth said. "My men wouldn't stand for that order, and I know very well the mercenaries would either hoot and ignore me—or shoot me down where I stand."

She looked at him, then at the scattering of lights from Noorat, said no more, but went below.

At dawn, a dozen warships sailed as close as they dared to the wall marking Noorat's eastern border, and began shelling it. The shelling lasted all day, and the Linyati began moving their guns to that wall to respond.

All that night, the cannonading kept on. At the second glass of the first watch, soldiers boarded boats, and, with a sorcerous fog covering them, closed on the city's western wall.

But the Linyati magicians saw through the casting, sent a counterspell, and, just at false dawn, the fog lifted suddenly and the Slavers' small guns opened up, as soldiers were leaping into the low surf and charging the wall.

Grapeshot swept the beach, and the soldiers flattened, pinned behind low dunes.

The *Catspaw*, a small sloop, took it on herself to close on the city, and, with very accurate shooting from her bow guns, smash at the city gates.

Gareth sent flags up to tell the *Catspaw* to pull back, she was within range of the Linyati guns, but her captain ignored the signals, turned broadside and opened fire.

Balls smashed into the heavy timber, and Gareth could see it begin to sag.

At that moment, flame shot high on the *Catspaw*, and

an instant later its magazine caught and the ship was no more than a ball of dark smoke and fire, timbers cascading through the air.

Wishing he was a man of profanity, Gareth sent up flags ordering two of the larger pirate ships to follow his command, not knowing if they were obeyed as he ordered the *Steadfast* to close on the bits of smoking ruin that had been the *Catspaw*.

"When you're in range," he called to Tehidy, in the bows with the two culverins, "do me more damage."

"Aye," came the shout back, then cannon balls splashed into the clear water just short of the *Steadfast*. Tehidy's cannon boomed, and Gareth could see little of Noorat's walls, which made him grateful, not particularly wanting to see the inevitable doom.

Other, bigger guns slammed to his left and right, and Gareth saw the two ships he'd ordered in firing away.

He heard a shout from the foredeck: "Th' gates're down!"

Gareth paid no mind, but ordered the *Steadfast* about, and away from harm's way. Chainshot—at least that was what he guessed it was—whirred overhead, and a yard snapped, crashed down, and Gareth heard someone scream.

Then his ship was out of danger, the other two back-watering as well, almost grounding.

The soldiers ashore were up, running, pouring through the gate, and Noorat's defenses were breached.

"Stand by to put a landing party ashore," Gareth called. "Nomios, take the deck."

He ran down the ladder to the main deck where boats were being hoisted out, and Cosyra was ahead of him, clambering over the rail, teeth bared in a hard grin.

Noorat was very alien. The buildings, most of them two- or three-storied, had domed roofs. What Gareth called houses were generally clustered around two or three larger buildings. Stores? Community halls? He didn't know.

The streets were wide, and curved, so there was never a clear view for long.

Here and there were odd obelisks, commemorating who knew what.

Noorat was not only alien, but almost deserted.

Gareth wondered why—had the city been built with the expectation of colonists who never materialized? Was this where the Slavers based their raiding expeditions, and the Linyati were off at sea? Again, no answers came.

The pirates moved systematically through the city, clearing as they went. Mostly the buildings were empty, but sometimes a knot of Linyati would explode out into battle.

They asked, and gave, no mercy.

There were others in the city. Slaves. These were chained in low barracks, and when the doors were broken in, cowered, expecting death at first, then exploded into hysterical joy when their chains were struck off and they were allowed to arm themselves.

Instantly, they became the most savage hunters of their former masters.

Most were men from Kashi, although there were a few bearded white men, speaking no known language. Gareth tried to talk to two of them, got nowhere, and didn't have time to find Labala and have a language spell cast. He could find out where they were from later.

So far, no one reported encountering a Linyati woman or child, and Gareth was deeply grateful.

Gareth entered the building cautiously, sword in one hand, pistol in the other.

"Naught to worry about," the pirate with him said.

"There was but one of 'em, and he's down in his blood right there."

Gareth nodded absently, looking around the house, ignoring the sprawled corpse, trying to understand his enemy.

There was a table and four chairs, simply designed, but with elaborate gold and silver inlays. More gold relics hung on the walls, but the room didn't look as if it were lived in. The next room had a dresser and cot, in the same style as the other furniture. The third was tiny, and had a hole in the floor, and washing buckets on a bench. Gareth leaned over the hole, heard rushing water below.

He made a note they'd have to find the entrance to the sewers and make sure the Slavers—or their masters, the Runners—weren't using them as a hiding place.

The last room was a kitchen, with a cupboard of various grains and a simple charcoal stove. Half a dozen pots hung on wall pegs.

That was all. It almost could have been the cell of a hermit or priest withdrawing from the world.

Gareth investigated other houses, found them equally bare.

Had the Linyati no pleasures? Abroad, in his trading days, he'd seen them in taverns, entering bordellos, although he had no idea what they did, had never been curious enough to bribe a whore and ask.

Again, the Linyati were a puzzlement.

A pirate broke into a warehouse expecting to find treasure, found something more valuable—thirty wheeled cannon, very light, very portable, moyen weighing no more than four hundredweight.

Gareth sent for gunners, and had the enemy guns dispatched to the companies in the city, with powder, solid, and grapeshot.

Now, when a houseful of Slavers was found, the pirates could stand off at street's end and smash it with a dozen balls, forcing the Linyati out into a charge, to be mown down by grapeshot.

The sun was overhead, and Gareth wondered where the day had gone. Seconds later, enormous thirst took him, and he was delighted to come upon a pair of mercenaries rolling a keg out of a building into the street. They turned it on end and smashed the wood in with their musket butts.

"Have a go," one said.

"Nay," the other said. "I'll wait for you. You're the elder."

"Here," Gareth said, pushing one aside and dipping a finger into the liquid. He tasted, made a face.

"Poison, 'tis," one soldier gasped. "As I feart."

"No," Gareth said. "It's beer. Good beer, I'd guess, but I'm not a drinker."

The soldier whooped and buried his face in the barrel.

Gareth, almost preferring thirst, drank two cupped handsfuls, could stomach no more, and went looking for water.

He was feeling his head start to swim when he came on a square with a bubbling artesian well and drank himself silly and sober before he went on.

All of the sailors were silent, in awe, as if they were in the cathedral of a great god.

Perhaps, pirates loving what they do, they were.

The building was filled with gold. Ingots were stacked, ceiling high, to one side. On the other were still unmelted statues, wall decorations, even small pieces of furniture, many with inset jewels.

But these were of lesser matter:

The room was dominated by a gigantic golden wheel, half again as tall as a man, worked with abstract designs, with strange creatures here and there.

The wheel was almost a forearm thick, and Gareth wondered what it was meant for, what unknown city it had been looted from, even how it had been transported to Noorat.

He saw Dafflemere smiling lovingly at the wheel.

"Rich, rich, rich," he said quietly. "Now I can buy back the lands I lost, and my title . . . and still have enough to lose in every gambling hell Saros offers, and be mad, without a soul, in highest fashion."

No one had reported seeing a Runner, and Gareth was wondering if there were none of the monsters in Noorat, which would make no sense—or, rather, as little sense as everything else about the Slavers did.

Then a messenger came, calling for Gareth to follow him.

He heard the high keening of a Runner before he came into the tiny square, now an abattoir. Half a dozen Linyati lay sprawled in their blood outside a house. In front of them were twenty dead soldiers and three or four sailors, almost as if they'd been cut down in formation.

At their head lay a soldier with a plumed hat, Gareth guessed one of their officers.

Cosyra and ten pirates were crouched behind a low wall.

"Bastard came out of nowhere, ambushed them," she said, and shivered. "Gods, Gareth, you told me they were awful . . . but not that awful. He was butchering the last of those men when we came up.

"We had time for a couple of shots, no more, and he

fled back into that house. I'm not even sure we wounded him."

Gareth turned to the messenger.

"Go back, and get two of the small guns up here."

"Aye, sir," and the man darted off.

"We'll blow his nest down around his ears," Gareth said. "If he's got ears."

But there wasn't time. Gareth heard the shrilling get louder, louder still, heard Cosyra shout for the sailors to get on line and fire on her command.

The Runner bounded down an open staircase into the open. He came across the square in leaping bounds, a sword in each claw.

"Fire!" Cosyra shouted, and the muskets went off in a ragged volley.

The Runner fell hard, rolled, was back on his feet, and Cosyra, shouting, ran toward him, sword held like a lance.

Gareth went after her, his ears a roar of blood fever and fear.

The Runner swung one of his blades at Cosyra, and she ducked, thrust once, jumped aside as his other sword lashed. Again she lunged, this time taking the monstrous lizard below his fanged jaws.

The shrilling became a scream, and the Runner staggered, jaws wide open, and Gareth shot the creature in the mouth.

The Runner went down, and Gareth thrust his sword into the demon, if that was what it was, where a heart should be, saw a dark, almost black, ichor welling.

Cosyra was panting, and sagged against him.

"Always strike what you're most afraid of," she managed. "My mother told me that."

"And what am I supposed to do?" Gareth said. "Stand and cheer?"

"Hells no," Cosyra said. "You're a bold vagabond. Protect me from this stupid idea of playing hero."

"I promise." Gareth kissed her stained, sweating forehead.

Cosyra pulled away from him.

"You," she said, pointing to a sailor, and authority was strong in her voice. "Go find me a magician. On the double."

The pirate gaped twice, then nodded and ran off.

Moments later, Labala ran into the square.

"Ah," he said, without surprise. "You've got one of 'em. There's been two more winkled out. Nasty sorts they are, who take a deal of killing."

"I want a spell," Cosyra said shortly. "Something that'll give warning on these monsters, so we don't get ambushed again."

"Mmmmh," Labala said. "Since we have a body to play with, should be simple 'nough."

He opened a bag he carried at his waist, took out small vials.

"Now, if someone can find me some bits of wood . . . ah, the handle of that halberd will do fine, especially since it's a war tool.

"You there. You look strong enough. Break that wood up into five or six lengths."

The sailor grunted, obeyed.

Labala bent over the Runner's corpse, dabbed a finger in the beast's gore. He drew a six-pointed star on the cobbles, put a daub of blood inside each point.

He opened two of the vials, sprinkled dried herbs in the center of the star. The six pieces of wood were dipped in the Runner's ichor, laid in the star's center. Then he chanted, three times:

> *"Scent, ye hounds*
> *Track what lives still*
> *Death seeks life*
> *Death seeks life*
> *Your nose what was before*
> *Seek*
> *Find*
> *There are no shadows*
> *There is no night*
> *There are no hides*
> *Seek*
> *Find."*

The sticks stirred, coming to life. Labala gave them to Cosyra, who took them with a bit of reluctance.

"Here are your hunting dogs," he said. "They'll do what you task them to."

The mercenary captain found Gareth an hour or so later. He was pale, looked shocked.

"Sir," he said, trying, without success, to keep a tremor from his voice. "We tracked some of those damned lizards to a lair with one of those magic sticks Lady Cosyra gave us. They attacked, and we killed them, but they fought with such a damnable frenzy we thought they were protecting something important."

He swallowed hard. "I guess it is. I didn't know what to do, and one of your ship captains said you'd best see for yourself."

"What is it?" Gareth asked.

The soldier shook his head. "I'm not sure . . . or, better, I don't want to be sure."

Gareth followed him down winding streets to a large building with big doors gaping. In front of it sprawled half a dozen Runners, and three times that many soldiers. The demons *had* fought hard.

Gareth started inside, and the soldier hung back.

The building was one great room. In its center was obscene horror.

It was pale yellow, the color of pus, a wide blob that resembled a pudding left in the sun, ten yards across. It moved, waves pulsing across its surface. Here and there, things were slowly emerging from its skin.

Gareth smelled an unpleasant odor, like rotting flesh.

He swallowed hard, walked closer. The things were half-formed adult Linyati, covered with a glistening slime. Their eyes were open, but blank, and their limbs moved spasmodically.

There were half a dozen complete Slavers lying on the floor around the hulk, moving senselessly from time to time, alive, but empty-eyed, as if waiting for souls.

Gareth felt bile rise, turned away.

Now he knew why no one had seen Linyati women or children.

He went outside, trying to keep his face under control.

"Sir," the soldier asked. "What is it?"

"A Linyati breeder," he said, unable to use the word mother. "Find pitch, or anything that burns. Fire the monster, and make sure none of those things lying around it are still alive.

"If you find more . . . kill them too."

"Sir."

They found three more of the Linyati "mothers," burned them; killed fifteen Runners, a dozen Linyati magicians, and over a hundred Slavers.

Then the city was quiet, except for the pain of the

wounded, the yip of the sea dogs as they looted, and the crackle of flames.

Noorat was theirs.

Now all the pirates had to do was wait for the treasure fleet.

Nineteen

Gareth paced back and forth, envying the softly snoring Cosyra in the bed nearby. He had a bad case of what his mother had called the frets, unable to sleep.

He went to the window, looked out at the tropic night. The pair of guards below, outside the building he'd commandeered, paced their rounds in a somewhat military manner, almost as if they were soldiers instead of discipline-be-damned pirates.

Gareth's first fret was that the Linyati ships were at least two weeks late, by his reckoning from the previous year.

Beyond the city, gentle, phosphorescent waves touched the beach. The pirates' ships were anchored around the bay, most with no more than a skeleton crew aboard.

In the distance, atop the promontories, the lights of the forts winked. Those were fully manned and would give the signal when the Slavers hove into view, more than enough time for the pirates to be roused and man their ships.

One of the forts blinked a signal, echoed a moment later by the second. Purely routine.

Fret two was that Labala had come to him three days ago and said he'd begun dreaming of sharks once more.

He'd set Dafflemere and Labala trying to discover if enemies were close, or if someone was casting a spell against the expedition, but they found nothing.

Dafflemere had returned to his favorite pastime—sitting with a glass of watered Axkiller, staring at the high-piled riches of the Linyati, and drawing, endlessly, on a map of Saros's north, just what estates he planned to purchase when they returned.

Labala's self-chosen post was at the infirmary.

That was fret number three.

Labala and Cosyra, who'd become his tutor in reading, had discovered why Noorat was so thinly populated. Just beyond the city were row after row of graves, first uncovered by the burial squads dragging dead Linyati and Runners to a common grave. The Slavers gave no more ceremony to their dead than the pirates, their graves being no more than long ditches.

Gareth had been about to disinter some of them, trying to decide what poor sinners would be put on that detail, but Dafflemere said magic would do a better, less smelly job of finding the cause of the deaths.

By the time his incantations worked, Gareth already knew what had killed the Slavers, for it was sweeping his own ranks:

Fever. Half a dozen men reported swimmy heads, vomiting, and bloody discharges. Three of them died, and a dozen more were down.

The sickness swept through the pirates' ranks, killing thirty. Dafflemere said the flux was the same that had killed the evidently more susceptible Linyati.

Then it was gone. For the moment. Gareth dreaded the thought that it might return just as the treasure ships arrived.

Gareth growled at himself. Brooding, even though this always seemed to come to him before action, was no way to make himself sleepy.

He lay back down and thought in another direction, of the vast wealth that was—he hoped—pushing through the green waters toward Noorat.

That led him to plan, once more, his tactics. Should he have his ships waiting, cloaked by magic, in a bight of the bay? Or should he be more subtle and, if there was sufficient warning, have his fleet slip out to sea, and, after the treasure ships sailed into the bay, have them sail back to put the cork in the bottle?

Or was that too complicated, too likely to be spotted?

Better the ships should enter, or at least close to within range of the forts' great guns. Then, once a few of them had been hit, or, better, once they'd all entered the bay and were trapped, then he could . . .

Gareth forced his mind away, but sleep was still distant.

He tried thinking of distant things, of Ticao, of Newgrange, of the manor house with Cosyra and the downs sweeping to the sea, the village below. But that didn't bring sleep either.

Very well, he decided. I'll put my thoughts far away, across the isthmus, into the unknown seas. Labala had worked a language spell with the white slaves, discovered they came from lands far east, beyond Kashi/Linyati, where there was a vast sea with islands great and small. One of the ex-slaves said he'd seen slaves brought to his land by the Linyati, who spoke a strange language like Gareth's. Those women and children were highly thought of by his people for their handsome features, intelligence, and sophistication often beyond their masters.

Gareth thought of exploring these distant seas, looking for Sarosians to free. His mind chuckled, and asked if he wasn't also thinking about the possibilities of loot and gold. He tried to curse himself for having become too much the pirate, then, considering these distant lands were in league with the Linyati, smiled, refusing to accept the sin. But, once again, sleep had eluded him.

He got up for a glass of chilled, limed water from the pitcher on the window table, was pouring, staring idly out to sea, and saw a new phosphorescence in the waters dancing toward the city.

Gareth smiled, remembering a Festival of Lights in Ticao, just after he'd come to the city, and how the watermen had paraded the river, boats alight with torches. Children had launched paper boats, with candles and wishes scribbled on bits of paper, into the torrent in imitation.

Then he jolted fully alert.

The lights in the bay weren't phosphorescent, but something else.

He grabbed the telescope on the table.

Sailing into the bay were a hundred tiny boats, each with torches flaming fore and aft.

One was sailing close to an anchored ship, and Gareth saw the watch aboard trying to fend it off. But the boat touched the ship, and exploded in a blast of flame.

Fireships, sent by Linyati magic!

Another ship roared into ruin, and then a third.

Somehow the Linyati had discovered Gareth's trap, used magic to keep from being discovered as they closed, and now were sending in these boats to destroy their enemy.

He swore he'd never do anything other than run the next time Labala dreamt of sharks.

Others in the city had seen the fires and improvised alarms; pots and muskets were sounding as Gareth's men came alert, stumbling out of their quarters, weapons in hand.

"What . . . whazzat . . ." a sleepy Cosyra managed, sitting up.

"Get dressed and arm yourself," Gareth said, pulling his clothes on, grabbing his weapons belt. "The Slavers have stolen a march on us!" He went to the window, called to the watch below: "Get Dafflemere and Labala to me!"

The soldiers ashore were assembling near Noorat's sea gate.

The seamen ran for the boats beached along the strand and pulled for their ships. All too often those had already gouted into flames, bringing near daylight to the bay.

Gareth paced with his officers, trying to decide what to do next.

"I can't say why," Dafflemere told him, "but we missed them. I thought I had wards out in all directions . . . plus my ocean creatures, sufficient for at least two or three days' warning. But . . ." his voice trailed off helplessly.

Gareth, trying not to show anger, looked to Labala, who shook his head, having no answers, and looked away.

"So we let them trap us again," he said grimly. "The question now is how do we get out of it. I count no more than half a dozen of our ships still intact.

"I assume the Linyati wizards used sorcery to prepare, conceal, and then guide those fireboats to their targets."

"Likely," Dafflemere said, staring out at the bay. "So somehow they scented us, and no doubt, the treasure fleet is now holed up in some Kashi port, or else bypassed Noorat for Batan or a Linyati port.

"My riches, my estate," he mourned. "All gone."

"Screw your estate," Cosyra said. "The question as I see it is what comes next for us?"

"Hopefully the forts will be strong enough to hold the Slavers outside the bay, maybe even destroy some of them if they try to force a passage," Gareth said. "Then we'll have to wait them out, until winter storms drive them off, or until they run out of provisions. That's completely passive, but I don't see anything better at the moment."

"And then," Knoll N'b'ry said, "the only problem we'll have is fitting all of us into howsomemany ships are left, and then skulking back to Saros with our heads between our legs to face the king."

"As long as they're still connected to our necks, we'll figure a way to take care of him," Thom Tehidy said. "Right now, all I care about is trying to get a boat to take me to the *Steadfast*, which I pray is still afloat. That damned Nomios put out before I could get to him."

"Aye," Gareth said. "We can worry about what happens in Saros when . . . if we reach it.

"Look," he said suddenly. "Signal lights from the western fort."

N'b'ry had his eyes shaded reading the flashes.

"Linyati . . . attacking. Will fire as they close . . . *Shit-fire!*"

A great flash lit the bay, momentarily blinding Gareth. A huge blastwave swept down from the promontory and across the bay. When the afterflare let him see again, he made out a black, fiery cloud where the western fort had been.

"Godsdammit," Dafflemere said. "They used some kind of magic to set off the magazine up there . . . either that, or else they managed to get inside the fort and—"

Again, all of them ducked reflexively as another explosion rocked them.

"Both forts," Cosyra said grimly. "Now we're naked."

Gareth shouted for the ranking infantry officers.

"We'll move those little cannon to the waterfront," he decided. "Bring whatever ships are still afloat back toward the city. The Slavers will have to make a frontal attack on the city, as we had to do, since the land outside won't permit anything else, and we'll drive them off then."

"I'll start building spells," Labala said.

"No," Dafflemere said. "I doubt if your plan will work, Gareth. If they've powers enough to see us, and determine how we deployed our forces, don't you think they'll have had brains enough to bring enough of their damned soldiers to overwhelm us? I doubt we'll be able to stand against the numbers they'll land.

"The only chance is to flee. Maybe take that land passage, those paths through the swamp to solid land, then turn east. Maybe you can lose them in the jungles, and find some Linyati town to steal some ships to get home."

Gareth gnawed at a lip.

"You're right." He thought, had an idea.

He saw a couple of the Kashi ex-slaves in the soldiers' ranks, called them to him, asked hurried questions in their language, thanked and dismissed them, and turned back to the others.

"All right," he said. "A better idea. Maybe. No one has any idea what lies east of here, in Kashi, and I'd as soon not face any more Slavers for a time. But some of these men of Kashi know the isthmus, and what lies west. They'll be our guides.

"We'll leave Noorat and go west into Kashi, looking for ships that we can buy or steal. The damned Slavers won't follow us there."

Someone shouted there were boats coming back, and from out of the night, a scatter of ships' boats came. Some held two or three men, some were packed. All the men were filthy, smoke-blackened, exhausted, defeated.

Gareth saw Nomios being helped out of one boat by men he recognized, and felt his guts clench, knowing the *Steadfast* was no more.

Froln came out of another boat, with the crew of the *Seawrack,* and stumbled to Gareth.

"We tried, godsdammit," he said, wiping tears away with a torn sleeve. His face was seared raw. "Godsdammit, we tried," he said again. "But their damn' fire had magic behind it, and you'd sand it out one place, and it'd spring up in another."

"Never mind," Gareth said. "You're alive, and there's always other ships."

Froln managed a twisted grin.

"Aye, sir. Thanks."

"Put signals out," Gareth ordered. "Take Nomios with you. I want all men off the ships, with whatever gear they can carry for a long march, and the ships' magazines set with slow matches."

"Sir." Froln started away. "Damn, but I hate being beat by those friggin' monsters!" Then he was gone.

Gareth turned to N'b'ry.

"I want you . . . and Cosyra . . . to take charge of the march. Keep west until you can find a town worth taking that's got ships or seaworthy boats. Or even a shipyard."

"And where do you plan on being?" Cosyra demanded.

"Someone will have to hold them here long enough for you to make a clean escape," Gareth said.

"That will be my job," Dafflemere said. "Mine and my friends."

"We . . . they'll need all the magic they can on the march," Gareth said. "No."

"Sorry," Dafflemere said. "I failed twice now. At least I can succeed at this. I'm staying."

"I'll stand with you," N'b'ry said firmly.

"That's my task," Gareth said. "I'm the one they elected captain."

"Just damned so," N'b'ry said. "There's going to be many a league of trouble before anyone sees Saros. Use common sense, Gareth! Where do you think you'll be of most use? Any fool can stand behind a line of cannon and die nobly. Not that I have any intention of hanging about for the Linyati to have their fun with."

"He's right," Cosyra said. "Stop feeling sorry for your-self and wanting to play martyr."

Gareth flushed, realized they were telling the truth.

"There," Tehidy said. "Now we've got some sense wrung into you. Now, let's get ourselves ready to"—and he winced—"hike for a few lifetimes or so, with happy, happy smiles on our faces."

It was an hour before dawn. The Linyati ships had made no attempt to enter the bay.

The Slavers' field pieces had been muscled outside the walls and loaded. Labala had cast a spell on them and given a catchword to N'b'ry so they could be fired all at once on a command with a talisman.

The soldiers and surviving sailors, about three hundred fifty strong, were drawn up and ready to march. Rations and durable clothing had been issued.

Four of the small, wheeled Linyati cannon were in the line of march, their trails with long ropes for men to haul them.

More important for many, the treasure vault had been opened, and the men were told to take anything they wanted that they could carry.

Gareth looked again at that huge golden wheel he'd hoped to give the king for his throne room, found two small, intricately worked statuettes, and stuffed them in the pack he'd made from a pair of breeches.

Then he went to Dafflemere, who was standing to one side, sipping a glass of Axkiller as if waiting for a party to begin back on Freebooter's Island.

"I don't envy you, Gareth," Dafflemere said. "Your way will be hard."

Gareth forced a smile. "I'm sorry."

"Why?" Dafflemere said. "My friends are out there"— he waved his hand at the bay—"wanting battle, for the Slavers damage creatures as well as men. They've never really had a chance to wreak revenge, you know.

"I count myself proud to stand with them.

"There's some beings as good—mayhap better—than any man I've dealt with, even though they affright the eye."

Gareth's eyes were smarting a little, and he nodded farewell, hurried to N'b'ry.

"You remember what Cosyra told me about martyrdom?"

N'b'ry grinned, seemingly unconcerned.

"Tell that to the fastest runner in all Saros; the man, I must remind you, who consistently outran you up hill and down dale. I need no reminder, and I'll catch up to you spavined sailors inside a day after I fire up these bastards' bums.

"Now, get you gone, or all this stupid nobility and fine sentiment will end up wasted."

It was just dawn, and the Linyati fleet was sailing into the bay.

Gareth ordered the men to a halt. They were on a knoll

half a mile beyond Noorat, just high enough above the jungle to see the city and bay.

The Linyati ships were the three-masted great warships that had attacked before, but there were far more than fifteen now.

They sailed in the center of the passage in threes, moving as if chained together.

Gareth counted fifty through his glass, guessed the Slavers had decided to deal with the pirates massively, killing mice with sledges. He wondered if Lord Quindolphin had somehow discovered the expedition's real destination and alerted the Slavers to play this trap.

But if so, that, too, had to be set aside for the present.

He saw a swirl in the middle of the column and gaped.

Something that might have been a squid, but with three beaked heads, came out of the water. It was twice the size of the ship it was next to.

He saw the smoke of cannonfire as the monster's tentacles curled over the ship's rail, had its mast, and overturned it, spilling cannon and men into the bay.

Sharks swirled up—even bigger than basking sharks, but with the tearing savagery of blues, ripping into the swimming, drowning Linyati.

There were other creatures, sea serpents, long eels with plumes and great fanged jaws, monsters like the swimming dragons of mythology. Gareth had a moment to wonder if these brutes were natural beasts, tamed by Dafflemere, or created or brought from other, nightmare worlds, and realized he'd never know the answer.

Now the sounds of battle came: screams of dying Linyati, the shrilling of Runners, and the howl of Dafflemere's fiends as cannonballs took them and they spouted blood, rolled over, dying, proving they were as mortal as any.

Other beasts, equally fabulous, swarmed at the Linyati, but the Slavers' magic struck, and they writhed in convulsions. Gareth somehow knew Dafflemere was dying with them, a brave man, among the bravest, whether the Linyati had stolen his soul or not, whether he was a ghost or demon.

A wave of smoke appeared along the shore, and then the shockwave of N'b'ry's broadside rolled toward them, the treetops waving as if tossed by a hurricane.

Gareth saw ships hit, swaying out of line and crashing aground as the last of Dafflemere's "friends" savaged the Slavers.

"Come on," he ordered. "Let's make sure their dying gave us the time we need."

And they began the long march toward home.

Twenty

The column marched appallingly slowly. The sailors weren't used to marching, weren't used to soldiering, weren't used to jungles, and weren't used to obeying growled orders from sweating sergeants.

The mercenaries, never a civil lot at best to seamen, who in turn ragged them unmercifully aboard ship, were snarling beasts before the company had gone more than two leagues.

Slow though they were traveling, at least, thought Gareth, they were moving, and away from the coast.

He wanted to keep the men as close to the ocean as possible on their march east. When they were close to Batan, he'd chance sending scouts to see if the city was alerted, which he assumed it would be. They'd then have to continue on to the next settlement, Kashi or Linyati, to find ships or, in the worst case, seize and hold a town long enough to build them.

He tried to keep his mind on the future, on what they

should do, to keep himself from mourning poor Knoll N'b'ry.

Cosyra was marching close behind. She forced a smile, and said, "Why didn't you tell me about this part of pirating?"

Gareth tried to think of something flip, saw Tehidy, tears having cut runnels down his smoke-blackened cheeks, and said nothing.

At dusk, Gareth had the column make camp along the narrow animal trail they were following, then summoned all of the infantry officers, all ships' officers, Dihr, and any of the men of Kashi.

"Things have changed, as you see," he began.

Some of them managed a bit of laughter.

"You soldiers, now we're in your hands, and will have to learn to fight by your rules," he said. "I want you to divide your men into small fighting units, which would be . . ."

"The smallest that's practical for fighting is about twenty," an elaborately mustachioed giant of a man said. Gareth remembered his name was Iset, and that he was a captain.

"Twenty men," Gareth repeated. "Then break your men down into ten-man groups, and you'll have ten of my sailors to train in each group."

"I don't think," Iset said, "we'll be able to make up a proper contingent. We've been hit hard, y'know."

"Then five men and fifteen sea dogs," Gareth said.

Iset made a face.

"A problem?" Petrich, once captain of Quindolphin's *Naijak*, said.

"Meaning no offense, sir," Iset said. "But that doesn't give us much in the way of experienced fighters."

"Sailors have no trouble fighting," Gareth said. "Especially not my roughnecks."

There was a ripple of amusement.

"You'll have to train them to do the rest," he went on. "Scouting and knowing how to make attacks and like that. And we'll scatter officers, mates, and bosuns through the column. They may not know how to march or make a flanking attack, but they know how to order men."

The sailors nodded, waited for Iset or one of the others to disagree.

"Parlous times," Iset said instead. "But I suppose there's no other option."

"When we march, we'll alternate units, so everyone gets experience breaking trail," Gareth went on. He explained his plan.

"Dihr, I want you and any Kashi men in separate units behind the men in front, then scattered through the column," he said. "We'll need your knowledge."

"There's only a couple of us, men who we freed in Noorat, who know these jungles," Dihr said. "Just because we're all brown doesn't mean we're the same."

"Of course not," Gareth said, a bit impatiently. "And don't think I'm judging you quickly. But you might have a bit more knowledge in common than you think. What sort of plants are around a swamp. What noises a little animal makes, and those of a big killer one.

"Maybe even what fruits we can eat, or plants we can boil."

"Mmmh," Dihr said. "Sorry, Cap'n. I spoke too fast."

"Break your men into . . . oh, ten-man units," Gareth went on. "Put men who've served for a while in charge of each team."

"That can be done."

Gareth was about to continue when he heard shouts.

Men were on their feet, grabbing muskets, swords, when the call came up the line: "Two men, coming up from the rear. They're not Linyati."

"Tehidy," Gareth said. "Take five men and go collect those stragglers."

"Sir."

Cosyra unobtrusively held up crossed, hopeful fingers, and Gareth nodded.

"The rest of you, back to your men," Gareth went on. "One more thing. Anyone with any experience cooking, send him up here. We're short on provisions and won't be able to afford separate messing like we did aboard ship."

A few minutes after the officers had dispersed, Knoll N'b'ry and one of his volunteers came into the middle of the camp.

"Evenin'," he said, as casually as if he'd encountered Gareth strolling along the banks of the Nalta River after evening meal.

Gareth might have been willing to play along, but Cosyra wasn't.

"*Damn* you," she said fiercely. "You can make someone worry."

"Now, now," N'b'ry said. "Didn't I promise I wouldn't let them get me?"

"I'm glad you're a man of your word."

"I am that," N'b'ry said. "But I had to come along in a bit of a hurry. It seems you've got friends."

Gareth's smile vanished.

"After the broadside, my friend here and I took off at our best speed in your tracks," N'b'ry went on. "Which was a very good thing, for the damned Linyati landed, took no more than an hour to search Noorat and realize it was empty, then their troops promptly found our trail, like they were damned hounds or something, and are only about three hours behind.

"Moving slow, but steady," he said. "About a thousand, maybe fifteen hundred of them. All soldiers, with armor and muskets and all."

"Son of a bitch!" Cosyra said.

"Perhaps," N'b'ry said, "about dawn, you'd like to go back and have a look?"

"I think," Gareth said, lowering his glass, "Cosyra spoke for all of us last night."

Labala, without asking, took up the telescope, peered through it.

There were the two of them, plus four soldiers for security, Iset, and Thom Tehidy.

Just on the far side of the great swampy clearing, the Linyati wound into sight. There were three columns, moving parallel with the rough animal track Gareth was following, which slowed them down a bit, but was intended to keep them from being ambushed.

Even Gareth could tell they were trained infantry, wearing breastplates, knee boots, and curved, open-faced helmets. They were heavily armed, and Gareth had seen six Linyati men staggering along under the weight of a tiny, short-barreled moyen carried in a cradle. He counted five other guns.

"The thing that I don't like," Gareth said, "besides their being here at all, is that they were able to mount the pursuit so handily. Labala?"

"You're right," the big man said, lowering the glass. "I see men in robes, muttering as they walk. They've got wizards scenting us."

"Can you block them?"

Labala thought, then grinned, not pleasantly.

"If I can consult with the good captain Iset for a moment, perhaps I can come up with something nasty."

The creek was just too deep to wade across, and a dozen and a half feet wide, with steep banks. Just downstream, the water shallowed into a deep swamp, and upstream the banks were higher and the trees thicker.

There was more than enough evidence of the pirates' crossing here. The Linyati put out a line of muskets along their bank and ordered a handful of scouts across.

They slid into the water, splashed, flailed, and one of them showed near-humanity, shrieking as he went under.

The Slaver's commander sent two men downstream to try to rescue him, and had a man doff his armor and go across with a rope.

The scouts tried again, pulling on the rope, naked but for their sword belts, and this time made it across.

They went, as ordered, a dozen yards into the brush, then came back, reported the crossing was clear.

The commander put a company on the other side, and by that time the rest of his formation had closed on the river, packing the banks. Five ropes were over, and soldiers were pulling their way across.

"Now," Iset whispered, and brush was ripped away from the mouth of the two cannon just upstream from the crossing.

Grapeshot tore into the packed Linyati, and they shrieked, panicked, and wallowed back.

Tehidy and his gunners reloaded and men with muskets moved past them, sent a volley, then another, into the Slavers on their bank.

They, too, broke, dropped their weapons and jumped into the water.

The cannon blasted once more, one into the far shore, the other into the men in the water.

"Go," Gareth said, and men took the ropes of one cannon and began pulling it away, back onto the trail.

"You too," he told Labala, who stopped muttering words and went after the cannon.

The second cannon fired another blast, then it, too, retreated with the covering soldiery.

Gareth, following Iset and Labala's plan, had dropped off two cannon, the magician, and three groups of soldiers, and ordered the column to march on, leaving as wide and sloppy a track as they could. The cannon had been moved back to the ford, and the men waited for their target, while Labala cast what he called an "easy dissemblance . . . Dafflemere taught me this one."

"That little ambush we laid," Iset said, "is called a buttonhook."

"Thank you, sir, for your invaluable illustration of an obscure principle," Gareth said politely.

"It damned certain discourages anyone on your trail from closing too fast," the soldier said. "I think we put it to them well."

"Let's make sure they've learned their lesson," Gareth said.

Twice more that day, but without the balky cannon, picked men fell out of line, waited for the Linyati to approach, fired one volley, then ran before the Slavers could charge. By nightfall, Gareth had taken only three casualties, all wounded, with no idea of how many Slavers he'd killed.

Then it was the Linyati's turn. They must have picked a small unit, no more than fifty men, and marched all night until they closed on the pirates' circled camp.

At dawn, as men were waking, stumbling about, they fired once, then charged with pike and sword.

The corsairs fell back in shock, then regrouped and counterattacked, shattering their foe.

If any Linyati lived through that, they must have fled quickly. The Slaver infantry must have been accustomed to fighting primitive tribesmen, not trained men-at-arms.

But Gareth still had twenty men down, ten killed.

They made stretchers for the wounded and pushed on.

Gareth considered his musketry, had a rather evil idea. Men who were known for their shooting ability were left behind in hides. They would snipe the Linyati when they hove into sight.

But Gareth had made things a little more sophisticated: the musketeers were to shoot down any Linyati carrying the cannon, any Linyati in robes, anyone who seemed to be giving orders, and of course, any Runners.

Iset added another category—anyone who walked in second or third place behind the Slaver at the point of the column. These, he explained, would either be officers or experienced soldiers taking a breather from being on point themselves. The point men would also be shaken.

Gareth went back with a three-man team, was offered a shot when the Linyati were in sight. He shook his head. It seemed, illogically, a little too much like cold-blooded murder, even though he knew the Linyati weren't human at all.

What they were, he didn't know yet.

His high moral resolve broke as he saw a Runner. He took a musket, aimed, fired, missed.

The other three, cover broken, shot quickly at the center of the column, then ran, seeing skirmishers move out from the main column.

*   *   *

As the days passed, the sailors grew leaner, more able to keep the march. Gareth thought they were moving just a bit faster than the Slavers, and allowed himself a bit of hope.

Labala announced that he had a new skill: blister mechanic.

The snipers reported seeing two, possibly three other Runners with the column; they tried to shoot them, but they seemed to be charmed.

They'd marched eight days from Noorat, and each patch of jungle, swamp, small clearing, seemed exactly the same. If it weren't for their compasses, Gareth would have thought they were marching in circles.

According to his plot, the pirates were now even with Batan, but with the pursuit, he dared not turn to the coast, for fear of being trapped.

Labala rubbed out the triangles scrawled in the dirt, blew out the smoldering brazier.

"All I can give you, Gareth, is my feeling. Which isn't good. The wizards with them are seeking a specific person with our column."

"Me?"

"No," Labala said. "So you needn't come up with another noble self-sacrifice. Nor me, which was my next thought."

"Who, then?"

Labala held out his hands, perplexed.

"This," Tehidy said proudly, "is mine own creation."

He pointed up thirty feet, to the crotch of a tree. In it,

on end, was a log about as big as a man's trunk. Stuck into it were sharpened lengths of wood.

"Now, you see," Tehidy said proudly, "a poor Linyati comes loping along this path, probably looking all about for one of our shooters, and he never sees this little vine across the trail.

"He kicks it—please, Gareth, don't get too close, I don't trust your coordination—and the vine, which runs around that branch and up to yon log, which is poised most delicately, yanks said log down, swinging all along the track, impaling the first, probably the second, and possibly the third man in line.

"No waste of gunpowder, or of men," he said. "Now, the new man in front will be watching the trees, and he won't see the pit we've dug farther up the trail, with spikes at the bottom."

"Ingeniously nasty."

"From you, that's high praise. Now, my friend, I'd like to comb out all ships' carpenters and have them form a rear element, building these traps as we go."

"Do it," Gareth said.

The traps, of various styles, worked to a greater or lesser degree.

But the Linyati kept coming.

"This pirate's life isn't as romantic as it should be," Cosyra said, using a smoldering ember to tease a leech fastened to her leg. It dropped off, and she stepped on it, grimacing.

"I had romantic images, even back in Noorat when you decided we were going to take a little hike, of pastoral campfires at night, me dancing some sort of wild dance in the firelight, while the pirates clapped in unison.

"Then we'd go off into the shadows, where you would have built a leafy bower, and make mad, passionate love."

"That's hardly fair for the others," Gareth said. "Ignoring the fact I'm not even sure what a leafy bower is, let alone how to build one."

"Screw the others," Cosyra said. "You're the one I'm in love with."

"Speaking of which," Gareth said, "have you considered what you want to do when we get back to Ticao?"

"That's why you stay captain," Cosyra said. "It's your incurable optimism.

"But I've given it a thought. Assuming my fellow lords don't want to have me up before the king for some sort of malfeasance, running off with a rogue like you, maybe I'll consider marriage."

Gareth gulped.

"Or maybe not," she said. "Speaking of which, I've arranged things so I've got third watch, at the head of the column."

"Glad to see an officer doing her duty," Gareth said, not sure if he was glad of the change of subject.

"Duty my left nipple," she said rudely. "There's nobody around at that time of night, and I don't think we're likely to be attacked from the front, so you might come visiting.

"Also, you'll note my hair is a little wet? I slid off and dunked myself downstream in that creek we're getting water from. So *I'm* clean.

"Doesn't that suggest, o my captain, you might do the same? Pirates don't have to be stinky all the time, you know."

The animal track they'd been following crossed a definite path the next morning. That would make easier going for the column ... and for the Linyati. Also, it led further into the interior, rather than to the coast, petering out in a tumble of abandoned stone shacks less than a mile east.

Gareth thought a moment, then decided that any semi-civilized people in this wilderness must, of course, be enemies of the Slavers.

He ordered the troops to take the path west, then consulted Labala.

"I've sensed more watchers," the wizard decided gloomily. "Different from the Linyati."

"Friendly? Enemy?"

"Dunno," was his reply. "Guess we'll have to wait to see whether we get hit with rocks or posies to find out."

The men at the head of the marchers also reported eerie feelings of being watched, invisibly.

The first watcher was seen, or perhaps sensed, by Labala, who looked up into a tree, yelped surprise, and swarmed up it, moving with incredible speed for a man of his bulk.

The young man squatting in the tree, watching, gape-mouthed at the monster coming at him, fumbled an arrow out of his quiver, and then Labala had him in an armhold.

Squirm as he might, the man couldn't get free, and Labala brought him to ground. The young man was roped to a tree, and Gareth and Cosyra came forward.

The man's eyes were like saucers in his brown face, especially looking at an armed woman.

Dihr and his crew tried all the languages they knew, but without success.

Labala used his language spell on himself, Dihr, and Gareth.

"Who are you?" Gareth asked.

The young man shook his head violently.

"I am Gareth," Radnor said. "I lead these men. We mean no harm."

"Then why my name?"

"It is our custom."

"Magic men want names," the young man said. "It gives them power over you."

Gareth muttered.

"Very well. We'll call you . . . Wind, for if it weren't for our wizard, you could have blown right past us."

"That is not a bad name," the man grudged. "I will allow that."

"Godsdamned big of you," Froln growled.

"Where are your people?"

"My people? Half a day march, in a direction I will not name. My masters? Two days up the path."

"Masters?"

"Masters, with strong powers, like you must have, to chance these cursed jungles and their demons."

"But you did the same."

"Only because I heard you coming, and my curiosity bit me, and my village knows me to be a fool at times. Now I'm doomed to be your slave."

"We have no slaves."

Wind looked skeptically at Dihr.

"Then who is he? Dark men like me with light men are always slaves."

"I am one who chooses to march with these men," Dihr answered. "But I was a slave once. Of the evil ones who wear metal hats."

"I know them," Wind said excitedly. "They come into our land, take slaves, burn our villages. Sometimes our Masters can fight them with their magic, but mostly the Masters are too taken with their own business, or are too lazy to come help us, for they consider us far beneath them.

"I should not have said that," he said. "I will be punished if you tell my Masters I said they were lazy."

"We will tell them nothing," Gareth said.

"Poor timid bastard," said one of the pirates, Shenshi, the one who'd lost a duel to Cosyra. "Scared of us, scared of his damned Masters, scared of the jungle . . . but you can't blame him." Shenshi picked up the bow Wind had carried, took an arrow from the quiver.

"Look at this damned toy," he said.

"No, no," Wind protested, trying to reach for the bow.

"Keep a quiet tool, there, sonny," Shenshi said. "I won't hurt your little toy." He fiddled with it, shook his head.

"No more'n, what, ten, maybe fifteen pounds pull? Arrow's about as straight as my old woman's lies. Feathers don't look like they even came off the same bird. Not even a stone or metal point, just sharpened wood." He touched the tip. "Ouch. Sharp, though. Guess it'd do for monkeys or birds. Small birds. Haw."

"Forget about that," Gareth said. "Wind, what are your Masters like? Do they look like you?"

Wind shook his head violently. "No, for I am little, and they are great."

"Are they the same color?"

"Of course. All proper men look like me."

Labala and Dihr grinned at each other.

"Lad's got common sense," Dihr said. "I'll wager that—"

There was a gurgle of agony. Gareth spun, saw Shenshi stagger, gasping for air, hands clawed. He took two stumbling steps, fell face-first, lay very still.

Labala knelt, turned him over. Gareth looked away from the agony-stricken, flushed face, the bulging eyes.

"He's dead."

"What could—"

"The arrow," Dihr said. "Poisoned."

Gareth cautiously picked up the arrow, noted a dark stain at its point.

"I guess he ain't as harmless as he looks," Froln said. "Hard way to find it out, ain't it?"

"Do not harm me," Wind said. "I tried to stop that man."

"We won't hurt you," Gareth said. "What Shenshi did was of his own foolishness. Nomios, take four men and bury the idiot, which should remind all of us to watch ourselves closely in this unknown land." He turned back to the native.

"Wind, about your Masters? You said they strike against anyone strange, and that they—all of your people— hate the ones we call Slavers."

Wind looked at the corpse on the ground, then at Gareth.

"Yes. That is true."

"On the theory that the enemy of my enemy is my friend," Gareth said, and changed back into Wind's dialect, "we want you to take us to your Masters."

"Oh no," Wind said. "For surely they would kill me for disturbing them."

"Then take us to where we can find them for ourselves," Gareth said.

Wind looked at the armed men around him, slowly nodded.

"I will do that, for I sense I must. I will take you to the great city of Herti."

Cosyra shook her head.

"Enemy of my enemy? Considering how afraid he is of his own rulers, if that's what they are . . . Gareth, I hope your logic, if that's what it is, works back of beyond."

*　　*　　*

The path wound through the jungle, almost imperceptibly getting wider, until it was a road. Dihr pointed out that the jungle on either side of the track was now scrubby, secondary growth.

Gareth suddenly realized the road was now paved, with overgrown, untended cobbles.

He ordered Iset to put flankers out.

"Hells fire," Thom Tehidy remarked as he passed with a scattering of mercenaries, "it do appear to us country folks, we's approachin' civi . . . civi . . . eddicated folks, it do, it do."

Then, on a crest, they saw stone buildings beyond—huge, flat-topped, shallow pyramids.

Civilization, indeed. But as they drew closer, they saw the pyramids were overgrown, vines curling up the buildings' steps.

Gareth asked Wind about that.

"We used to be much greater," he explained. Then he glanced around to see if anyone was listening, lowered his voice. "Some say the gods have turned against us . . . or that our magic has become weak."

He clamped his mouth shut, looked frightened.

Gareth, feeling a chill, made sure the men had their weapons ready, and the four cannon were loaded and their gunners close at hand.

Now the road wound between these pyramids, and Gareth could see they were honeycombed with tunnels, the disused entrances half-blocked.

There were scattered megaliths, some toppled and broken.

A scout called an alarm, and a spotted cat, as big as a lion, growled from atop a pyramid and bounded away.

They moved on, more slowly.

Tehidy ran in from one flank.

"Gareth," he called, beckoning. Gareth and Cosyra followed him.

Tehidy stopped beside a raised circle, like a well only larger, and pointed down grimly.

At the bottom wasn't water, but stacked bones, human skulls scattered among them.

"Sacrifices," he guessed.

"Sort of," Tehidy said. "Look at them more closely. Notice how they've all been cracked, for their marrow?"

Gareth felt his stomach turn.

"I suppose," he managed, "that's one reason for a population decline."

"Why," Cosyra said, "am I thinking we ought to turn around and hustle back the way we came?"

"There's some say," Gareth said, "the Linyati also have their favorite dishes."

"Mercy," Cosyra said, with mock enthusiasm, "what a *great* adventure this is turning into."

They still saw no one, but the pyramids were no longer abandoned, and other roads crossed theirs. Low buildings appeared, also of stone.

They rounded one and came to a gate. Its uprights were two huge scorpions, the crosspiece held up by their poised tails.

"This is as far as I can go," Wind said. "I have come too far . . . those are forbidden to be seen by my people."

Before Gareth could argue, Wind spun and ran, ducking through a narrow passage between buildings, and was gone.

Gareth and Cosyra looked at each other, said nothing, and went on.

Quite suddenly, from nowhere, a man was standing in front of them. He was big, taller than Labala, and wore what looked like snakeskin pants, paired with golden sandals and a snake vest that showed off his heavily tattooed chest. His face, also tattooed, carried the arrogance of long-held power. He had a tall staff in one hand and wore a circlet of gold around his curling, black hair.

He spoke. Gareth held up both hands, not understanding.

The man tried another language, then a third, both incomprehensible.

He frowned in anger, then said, slowly, in the tongue Wind had spoken:

"I am Baryatin, chief mage of Herti. What brings you, without invitation, to our lands, for you are not welcome?"

"We did not come by choice," Gareth said. "We are pursued."

"By the Raiders from the Sea?"

"Yes."

"That is the second group my spell showed me." He shook his head angrily. "I do not like using this speech of under-men. Extend your hand."

Gareth obeyed, hearing from somewhere behind him the clack of a musket being cocked.

Baryatin held out his staff, touched Gareth.

"Now you understand the speech of proper men," he said in a different tongue. "Is there anyone else this might be useful for?"

Gareth pointed to Labala, Cosyra, N'b'ry, and Tehidy.

Baryatin grunted.

"I see you are a man with little real power, if you must have all these underlings to listen to my words of wisdom and make judgments. But have them do as you did.

"Except for the woman. I refuse to lower myself to her level."

Gareth held back anger, motioned the three forward.

As Labala came back, he winked at Cosyra, whose lips unpursed. Good, Gareth thought. Labala can pass the language along. We'll have every one of us learn His Haughtiness's tongue before nightfall and have three hundred eavesdroppers.

"So, pursued, you say," Baryatin said. "Since you evidently encountered one of those the gods gave as my servants to bring you here, you no doubt know the Raiders are little liked in this kingdom, and are slain, or sacrificed, whenever we can seize one or more of them."

"So I learned," Gareth said. "We wish no more than a day or two's shelter and provisions for our march while these Raiders seek without finding us, then a guide to your borders, if you would, to a path that will lead us on east and eventually back to the sea, for that is also where we come from."

Baryatin's face was motionless for a moment, then he nodded abruptly.

"We can at least shelter you. Then I and my fellows will decide on your future."

"Enemy of my enemy, hmm?" Cosyra whispered. "Thank several gods for the cannon."

As they followed Baryatin into the heart of the city, the signs of neglect grew fewer, although they saw no indication of new construction.

The streets were lined with people watching the foreigners. No one smiled, no one laughed, and even the children were cold-faced, staring.

Iset came up from the column's rear.

"Notice," he said, stroking his mustache, "what they're armed with? Bows and arrows. No muskets, and I saw no sign of cannon. This is very, very good, I think."

"You think we may have to fight our way out?" Gareth said.

"Labala told me what that wand-shaker said, about them deciding on our future. Where I come from, that isn't generally regarded as an expression of true love."

"No," Gareth agreed.

"And don't these charming folks—yes, I'm smiling at you, you old fart with the beard and the glower," Iset went on, "while I'd as soon slit your weasand for you—don't they look like they're just itching to invite us home for dinner?

"Wanting us for the main course, I mean."

The city was studded with small lakes, which kept the temperature cool in spite of the bright sun and stonework. Baryatin led them down a causeway to a flat islet of bare stone with two long buildings on it that looked like barracks.

"These are your quarters until we inform you otherwise," he said. "You may clean yourselves and rest. Tomorrow night there will be a meal, when my fellows will have assembled to evaluate you and pass judgment. Bring only your ranking officers."

Without waiting for a response, he stalked away.

"Officers, to me," Gareth called, and the men ran up.

"I don't like this at all," he said. "There looks to be only one way off this island."

"But only one way on," Iset said. "We'll put two guns covering the causeway and let 'em charge."

"Until we run out of powder," Thom Tehidy said.

"Another thing, Gareth," N'b'ry said. "Did you look close at those buildings? And see the bars on the windows?"

"I hadn't before," Gareth said. "Get the carpenters to

work. Loosen the bars from the inside, so we're not quite as trapped as we look. And have them mousehole the walls on all sides, without breaking quite through, so we won't be held to the doors if we want to make a fast exit. Instruct them to work quietly, so our friends on the other shore don't figure out what we're doing.

"Labala, get your language spell working.

"Froln, get a couple of swimmers and go for a bath. Find out how deep the water is, especially from here to that avenue over there. It looks wide enough for a quick retreat out of this wonderful city."

"I'll do that," Froln said.

"Thom," Gareth said, "pick your best gunners for the other two cannon, and have all four loaded with fresh powder and shot, fully manned at all times. Also, grab enough men to move those guns anywhere on this flat little mantrap. Save on our grapeshot, and load them with the rubble the carpenters dig out of the buildings—busted rock can kill just as dead."

Tehidy grinned tightly.

Gareth caught himself. "Wait a minute. Iset said he saw no sign of guns or even muskets. Did any of you see any gunpowder weapons?"

Headshakes, denials.

"A strange thought comes to me," Gareth said. "Baryatin didn't seem to pay any attention to our guns. I wonder if he knows what they're for? I wonder if we could bumfoozle him for a time.

"Thom, when the guns are out, have your gunners dance around them every now and then, as if they're some sort of idols, or sprinkle them with flowers or something."

"Nobody's that stupid," Tehidy said.

"So what's the harm in doing what I suggest? It'll keep the gunners angry at me, and keep them from stiffening up."

"I'll do it," Tehidy said with a sigh. "I hope you're going to do something equally stupid."

"Probably," Gareth said. "I'm going for a swim. As soon as it's dark."

Armed men brought food to the island . . . and a miserable-looking man who, a guard told Gareth, was their food taster. "So you will know we do not seek underhanded ways of destroying our enemies."

"I take that to mean," Cosyra said, "that they seek underhanded ways of destroying their enemies."

"Most likely," Gareth agreed. "But that poor man looks as if he could use a good meal."

The foods were dressed fowls, corn, eggs, spiced peppers, a rather sour beer, and fruit.

"Makes you wonder," Tehidy said. "If these cheerful fellers aren't in the habit of entertaining, where'd they rustle up the rations so quickly?"

"That ain't hard," Froln said. "They did a house-to-house and yanked everybody's dinner out from the table."

"Makes sense," Tehidy said. "You notice the men with the bows didn't vanish after making their delivery, but are manning posts on the other end of the causeway?"

"I noticed," Froln said. "I noticed."

One end of a barracks was a cookhouse, and the seacooks set to work while the rest cleaned up in shifts, weapons at hand.

Cosyra splashed about happily.

"I think," she said, "if I soak for, oh, another week and a half, I might get most of the jungle muck off my skin."

"Don't work too hard," Gareth advised. "Remember, we jump back in it in a few days—assuming these rockpilers we're guesting with do something civilized, like replenish our supplies."

"You know," Cosyra said, pointedly looking away from Gareth, "to change the subject away from people who I'm pretty sure want us dead, I've been thinking about this marriage idea, and am not sure I like it all that much."

"You've gone back to the way you used to think."

"*Think*, I think, is the correct word, I think," she said. "This damned love business muddies your mind.

"However, pretending I'm a rational adult, I *did* decide to do something when we get back to Ticao.

"I was never keen on finding out who my father is, I guess for fear he'd turn out to be some piece of noble slime like our friend Quindolphin.

"But I'm going to be a big girl, and put inquiry agents to work when we get back."

"What'll you do if you find him?" Gareth asked.

"That I'm not sure of. Probably, after I finish crying my eyes out, slap the old bastard silly for hiding from me all these years."

Gareth moved through the water slowly, smoothly, keeping his legs and arms below the water, as he'd learned as a boy, hand-spearing sharks lazing near the surface of the ocean, never splashing, never alarming.

A light rain drizzled the lake, making it harder for him to be seen.

He knew the corsairs were being watched, most likely by watchers in the shadows and magic, and had taken precautions before setting out. Ten men had jumped into the lake, splashing noisily, but only nine had surfaced close to the island.

Gareth swam to the mucky bottom, about ten feet down, then as far as he could underwater. He surfaced, took a breath, went on toward the far side of the lake. It turned out to be larger than he'd thought, curving around in a large C.

On the far side of the lake, just beyond sight of Gareth's island, was another causeway, this one floating.

He saw nothing on the shore worth investigating and was about to swim back, then he swam to the causeway and examined it carefully. It was a series of lashed-together rafts of heavy wood, each raft about fifteen feet by twenty feet.

Gareth floated on his back, thinking, planning. Interesting, he thought, as he began the slow, careful swim back. Very interesting.

Gareth and Cosyra had been given a corner to themselves, and someone had hung blankets on a rope for privacy.

They lay close together, listening to the rain as it drummed harder on the tile roof.

"Very strange," Cosyra whispered, "sleeping indoors and all."

"Mmm-hmm. Do you think it'll become popular?" Gareth asked.

"Probably not," Cosyra said. "Ouch—I'd gotten used to my nice soft mud and all. This floor magnifies all my corners."

Gareth whispered a suggestion in her ear, and she giggled and rolled on her back.

"I do love you, you know," he said, as his hands moved over her body.

"Nice to have *something* to depend on," she murmured.

* * *

Gareth dreamt that night, and his dream was terrible, for he knew it was truth.

He hung over dense, uncleared jungle, seeing nothing but the furtiveness of the forest creatures as they came and went. In the distance was the sea. Slowly, tribes of hunters, slash-and-burn farmers moved into the region.

A fierce tribe of warriors came from the south, fleeing some strange demons. They cleared and planted the jungle, warred on the tribes around them, subjugated them.

These slaves labored, building great pyramids, while the warriors went out, again and again, bringing back captives from afar.

Some of these were made slaves, others were sacrificed in larger and larger lots. The wizards of this people grew stronger with the deaths.

They became creative in their killings, slowly dismembering their prisoners, slicing them slowly to ribbons, or, worse yet, closing them in intricately wrought iron scorpions over fires. When the screams stopped, the magicians fed on the scorched human flesh, and pronounced this good, that they were gaining the strength of these defeated soldiers.

Then came a time when there were no more enemies to fight or raid, and so the wizards turned on their own people.

The sacrifices grew ever more elaborate, more brutal, and the magicians seemed not to care that the jungle was slowly regaining its ground as the population shrank and seemed to lose their spirit.

The evil of these people hung over them and their lands like a dark, dirty fog, and then Gareth woke up in the dimness just before dawn.

Cosyra woke at the same time, looked at him, started

to say something, then got up and hastily went out and
threw up into the lake. He followed her out.

She rinsed her mouth, asked, "Did you dream? About
these bastards?"

Gareth nodded.

"That wasn't a dream," she said. It was not a question.

"No," Gareth said.

"Did they . . . their magicians . . . send it?"

"I don't know," Gareth said. He saw Labala coming
out of another door. "If they did, why'd they send the last
part—the part about their decadence—if they're trying to
frighten us."

He noticed Labala was shaken.

"You, too, dreamed of these around us?"

"I did," Labala said. "And more. I saw something,
some sort of vision, after I'd seen these people's slow
dying.

"I don't think it was intended. Maybe I was riding on
the spirit of one of these wizards here, like you can launch
a canoe through the surf more easily in the backwash of
a great wave.

"I hung over this island and saw us sleeping, some of
us moaning in our sleep, for many of us were dreaming
the dream.

"Then I was outside the city, a day's travel, beyond
any of the buildings. I saw the Linyati in their camp, and
two Runners were talking to a man who looked like that
Baryatin and another dressed like him.

"Then I woke up."

Gareth considered. "Not good," he said. "Assuming
you dreamt true, and there's no reason you didn't, that
means they're negotiating with the Slavers.

"Their enemies."

"The enemy of my enemy could be my friend," Cosyra reminded him.

Gareth nodded. "Maybe they're thinking they could buy the Slavers off from their raiding by delivering us, all trussed up for the slaughter."

"I think," Labala said, "I'd best be preparing some spells, and we had better start packing for a very sudden journey."

"What about that dinner tonight?" Cosyra said.

"I don't think we'll have any choice," Gareth said. "We'll just have to go well armed, and hope if they start something we can fight our way back here."

"And then what?"

"I don't know," Gareth said. "We'll have to find—and seize—the opportunity when it comes."

"If it comes," Cosyra corrected.

Gareth was looking for Iset, and found Knoll N'b'ry, Froln, and Nomios in deep concentration. N'b'ry had drawn some sketches on the rock wall of the barracks with a stone.

It was various views of a ship.

"Now that'll give these Hertis something to puzzle over once we leave," Gareth said, amused.

"Here," N'b'ry said, "just the man we need. I've been thinking about the way we go a-pirating, and there's things wrong with it."

"No fooling," Gareth said. "The way we got euchred out of that treasure fleet still rankles."

"The first thing we're doing wrong," N'b'ry went on, "is we're using the wrong kind of ships."

"He's tellin' us we ought not just grab the first merchantman we see, or, we build one like it, but with guns, like the old *Steadfast*," Froln said. "Look at this."

The drawing was of a long, slender, two-masted ship, with a bow like a knife-blade. But what caught the eye was the amount of sail it carried—two huge gaffsails on each mast, plus triangular sails between the foremast and the jib boom. Also, small squaresails reached above the angled gaffsails.

"Enough sail there to drive her under," Gareth said.

"Not with that shape," N'b'ry said. "She'll cut through the water, not push her way like a fat-butted marketwoman. Also, see the rake on the masts, to take the strain."

Gareth considered the design.

"Looks like it ought to sail close to the wind."

"Just so," N'b'ry agreed.

"We kin flash our arses in front of any escort," Nomios said, "run downwind, then tack back, not wearin' ship, and be on the merchantmen like the wolf."

He stared out the door, and Gareth knew he was seeing open ocean and clean sky, instead of gray, evil stone.

The air that day was still and humid, as if waiting for a storm.

A runner came, just before the midday meal, to tell Gareth that Baryatin wished the woman to attend the feast as well as his officers.

"I wonder why the change?" Cosyra wondered.

"The wand-waver wants a little beauty—besides mine, I mean—to liven up the affair," Tehidy suggested.

Cosyra looked at him and snorted. "I think I'd best go sharpen my dagger."

Twenty-one

No, Cosyra," Gareth said slowly. "Sharpen your dagger if you wish, but you'll not be using it to slice a roast. We'll not be attending this feast."

Froln grimaced. "'Twould be a declaration of war, with us trapped on this damned rock."

"Better that than dividing our forces," Gareth said. "Kill the officers at the feast, hit this island at the same time—that would make things just too easy."

He sent for Labala.

"You told us that the Linyati are pursuing one of us in particular, with no idea who, right?"

Labala nodded. "I've done other divinations since then, with still nothing to shout about."

"Try this, though there's no magic in it," Gareth said. "First Baryatin won't deign to give his language spell to a mere woman. Then, half a glass ago, he sends word that Cosyra must attend this feast of his. And Labala had a vision of Baryatin or somebody with a pretty serious case of the tattoos talking to the Linyati.

"I'm just evil-minded enough to think the Slavers have made a deal—give us Cosyra, and we'll help you kill off the pirates and stop raiding your lands. Baryatin is too arrogant to realize the alliance will last about a minute and a half after they have what they want—then it'll be back to business as usual."

"That's a big jump in logic," N'b'ry complained.

"Starting," Cosyra added, "with the fact nobody's got the slightest idea why they supposedly want me, rather than, say, a chubby brown wizard or this cute devil with a beard."

"I'm not chubby," Labala protested. "Just . . . firmly built."

"Maybe so, maybe no," Froln said. "I'm not botherin' with that, all I need is the truth that we'd be easy to take out if we split up.

"I vote with you, Gareth—and I know damned well so will the men.

"So what do we do?"

"Pack up," Gareth said. "Try to keep it from being obvious. Ready to move in two hours. And give me ten good swimmers right now."

Tehidy took a deep breath.

"This is good," he announced. "Ever since we've been in Herti, it's like the walls are closing in on me."

"Aw," N'b'ry said. "Him wants his widdle jungle back."

"Damned right I do," Tehidy agreed. "And I want it *now*."

He stamped like an infant. Everyone grinned, and started preparations for the march out.

Gareth waited with the swimmers inside the barracks until the pirates were ready to move. The four cannon were left in position, in the hopes that the men of Herti, even though the Slavers also had guns, still didn't know what the shiny brass tubes were intended for.

Iset reported the column was ready. "Straight across the causeway in a charge, move two guns with us, set up a bridgehead, and then—"

"No," Gareth said. "I've got to believe, if Baryatin's double-dealing us like I think, he's got to have soldiers— maybe the Linyati, too—in position over there waiting for us to do the obvious.

"That's why I wanted the swimmers. We're going out a different way—but as soon as they figure out what I'm intending, that'll have torn it, and the shooting will start, so be ready."

He told his officers what he intended, then motioned to the swimmers.

"Let's go for a bath."

Gareth stripped naked except for a long, sheathed knife on a belt. The others did the same.

He took a deep breath, ran out of the barracks, flat-dove into the lake, and swam hard around the islet, toward that floating causeway.

He made the causeway, pulled himself up on it.

A man pulling a small cart across saw him, yelped in alarm, and started running as the other swimmers came out of the water, the cart overturning and bananas scattering in all directions.

"Four of you to the near shore, where that thicket is. Cut eleven straight saplings and strip them for poles. The rest of you, start cutting these rafts apart."

As the men went to work, Gareth heard shouts, war cries, and saw Herti soldiers running down to the water-front, toward the unseen solid causeway to the pirates' barracks.

He thought he spotted the curved metal helmets of the Linyati to one flank, but wasn't sure.

One of the pirate guns slammed, and the ball crashed through a file of Herti soldiers. They hesitated, and Gareth realized his hope had proven true—as solidly grouped as they were, they had no familiarity with artillery and the tactics it made necessary.

Another round of grape swathed through the ranks. Gareth saw one of the Slavers' stubby moyens being pushed into view from behind a monolith, powder and shot bearers behind it.

"We're ready, Cap'n," a swimmer called, and three rafts floated free. They took poles and began pushing the rafts through the shallow water toward the island.

They rounded the curve just as a mass of Herti soldiers charged across the causeway. Both stationary guns cracked, and swept the causeway clean.

A Linyati moyen went off, and Gareth saw the cannonball bounce across the water and skip across the islet without hitting anyone.

The two mobile guns were aiming at the moyen when another, unseen gun fired. The closest pirate gun was struck, knocked spinning into the lake, its crew shattered by the ricocheting bits of the ball.

Then the two mobile guns fired as one. They hit just behind the moyen, in the powder supply, and it exploded in a gout of black smoke.

The Herti tried another charge, and this time the corsairs let them get within musket range before firing.

Then the rafts were at the islet, and Gareth was shouting orders to get aboard, get the guns on the rafts, move, move, we're on our way out of here!

A Slaver cannon fired, and its ball cut through a knot of soldiers, gore splattering for yards.

Fire was returned, and the Linyati pulled their gun back into the shelter of a pyramid.

A gunner cleverly aimed at the low, square building next to it, blasted grapeshot. Evidently enough of the small balls ricocheted into the hidden Linyati gunners, for Gareth heard shrieks of agony across the water.

The pirates and the three surviving guns were packed onto the rafts, and the polemen set to, sweating in the bright sun, back the way they'd come.

Herti and Linyati soldiers saw Gareth's intended landing and poured around the shores of the lake as the Slavers' cannon were pushed into the open and fired at the rafts.

Now the benefits of Gareth's sniping were evident, for these gunners, not the first nor the third set who'd carried the guns until shot down, couldn't seem to strike a moving target.

"Dammit, dammit," Gareth heard Tehidy mutter as one of the pirate guns fired. "And where are we going to find more gunpowder, dammit, dammit!"

The rafts banged ashore. Iset and his officers shouted orders, Iset stroking his mustache as calmly as if this were a familiar drill. As the Herti ran toward them, the corsair formations counterattacked as they'd been trained.

They slammed into the motley throngs in a wedge. Pistols and muskets cracked, and men screamed as cutlasses slashed, were parried by spears, and knives cut into flesh.

It was quickly apparent that the Herti, as the dream had showed, had had no serious enemies for many years. Here a knot fought bravely until cut down, there half a hundred were charged by ten pirates and screeched into a panicky retreat.

There were Linyati on the field, holding firm, carefully aiming, shooting, loading, but no more than a hundred so far.

"Don't chase them," Gareth was bellowing. "Pull back and form up!"

The pirates reluctantly started back, and then thunder rolled across the cloudless sky.

There came a great roar, but no beast showed itself.

Instead, the front line of the corsairs seemed to go mad, throwing away their swords and muskets, pulling at their clothes, then leaping on their fellows, ripping and tearing with clawed hands and teeth, as if they'd become jungle cats.

The skies were filled with maniacal laughter, and Baryatin appeared in front of the Herti soldiery. He spoke, but his voice came from the heavens:

"Now, evil invaders, see that you cannot stand against my magic. Let your greatest wizard try to save these men as they ravage their fellows, then writhe on the ground, dying, as if their guts were snakes, tearing at their bodies."

And, indeed, the afflicted pirates were on the ground, screaming in utter agony, now tearing at themselves, dying a horrible death.

Once more the laughter rang.

"Very well," Labala said quietly, and walked out in front of the lines. "Gods, and Dafflemere's spirit, be with me."

He lifted something on a chain around his neck, and Gareth saw it was a shark's tooth.

Labala called out words, but none that Gareth knew, words that hurt his ears.

Now it was the Hertis' turn to howl in frenzy as something invisible struck at them from the empty air, and blood spurted. One soldier ran toward the pirate lines as if pursued, and then something took him, like a great white shark takes its prey, and tore him in half.

But in a flash, the sharks, if that was what Labala had brought up, were gone, leaving only a dozen or so rent bodies on the dirt.

"You have some power, fat witch," Baryatin called. "But I broke your spell. I have a creature of my own, needing but one, who thrives on the blood of wizards. Now, see your doom, and the doom of others, for once summoned my demon will not vanish until he's had his fill of blood."

Baryatin's hands moved, and Gareth smelled the reek of a slaughterhouse, the stink of burning bodies.

He began chanting—not words, but primal grunting noises, the summonings of some terrible beast.

Something swirled in the air between the armies, who stood as if paralyzed, waiting, watching.

Something like a cloud appeared, but more solid, with twisting colors of excrement, decay, rottenness; it, whatever it was, shrilled in delight, borning.

There was a sharp crack from behind Gareth.

Baryatin's incantation stopped, but his mouth stayed wide open. Then blood gouted in a solid stream. The wizard took two stumbling steps, lifted his hands to his throat, but the blood kept pouring.

He twisted and fell.

The apparition between the armies vanished.

Cosyra stepped forward, her still-smoking pistol gripped in two hands.

"Sometimes," she said, voice shaking, "lead beats magic."

Then there was chaos in the Herti ranks. Men turned and ran in complete panic, no matter if they were in the first or the last rank, trampling their fellows.

The Linyati held firm for an instant.

"Wake up, you sorry bastards," Iset shouted. "Volley into the Slavers!"

Muskets cracked, first singly, then in a volley, and the Slavers, too, broke and ran.

"I think," Cosyra said wearily, "the way is clear now."

"I know you won't let me marry her," Labala said earnestly to Gareth. "But I'll accept lifelong slavery for her saving me."

"Oh stop it," Cosyra said. "You men were standing around with your fingers in your poop, and somebody had to do something."

They were outside Herti, marching through overgrown pyramids and abandoned farms.

"Well," Thom Tehidy said, "at least we've seen the worst of what Kashi can offer us, even if those frigging Slavers are still on our track."

He made a face. "Anyway, I can only *hope* we've seen the worst."

Twenty-two

A month later, they'd left the jungle behind and were crossing a high, grassy plain dotted with occasional groves, springs, and pools.

There were less than three hundred of the corsairs left. Both chirurgeons had been killed in Herti, so the casualties either healed with what sorcery and rough medicine Labala and the two assistants he was training could offer, or else died, were buried, and the column marched over the grave, to leave no trace for the still-pursuing Linyati.

Twice Gareth laid an elaborate ambush, but the Slavers now seemed able to sense danger, and turned away before entering the killing zone. At least his rear scouts were still able to snipe a victim now and again, and sometimes waylay an unwary skirmisher. But they were still outnumbered more than two to one.

They'd encountered half a dozen empty monolithic cities before leaving the jungle. They'd sheltered in one against a storm, but the horrible dreams that came made the driving rain welcome, and they'd not chanced entering another.

Gareth wondered whether these cities, which showed signs of fire and battle, had been destroyed by the warriors of Herti or by Slavers.

As they climbed higher, still holding east, still hoping to somehow elude the pursuit and turn back to the coast, they'd found empty villages, and even seen the villagers fleeing in panic with what they could carry.

"In these parts," Dihr said, "the white man is a slaver, no better."

Gareth had ordered the villages left alone, but pirates being pirates, four men had slipped away from the night's camp, looking, their friends said later, for women and drink in the nearby village, ready to pay with either gold or steel.

After midnight, the sentries had jolted to full alert, hearing terrible screams from the village. At dawn, Gareth sent a strong patrol in to look for the fools.

They found nothing but patches of blood on the ground, pools larger than a man's body should contain. But there was no sign of the four men, and the column marched on, into the grasslands.

The weather was hot, but not as muggy as it'd been in the lowlands, and it rained every day or so, gentle showers that the men welcomed.

Their clothes were ragged, and those with seaboots had long since cut them into sandals. They had no problem with provisions, the land being thick with game animals.

The biggest shortage was gunpowder. The best musketeers became hunters, and prided themselves on never needing more than a single shot to bring down an animal.

One day, the scouts reported springs ahead, an ideal campsite. But the second report returned they were sulfurous, poisonous, and stinking.

Cosyra mentioned wistfully that great Sarosian ladies paid well to visit a resort and soak in the sulfur springs, and perhaps they could pause for a day.

Gareth looked at her skeptically, and she burst into laughter, having gotten the rise she wanted. Tehidy and Labala came and asked if they could stop for a few hours while they had a work party mine some sulfur, which they refused to explain the reason for.

Gareth approved, which gave the sailors and soldiers a chance to mend their gear and break from the ceaseless marching. The work party came back with crude sulfur bricks wrapped in leaves. Everyone was to take a brick and put it in his pack.

Why? "Magical reasons," hissed Tehidy, while Labala nodded agreement, and that was enough to stop questions from most.

When they marched on, Gareth sniffed Cosyra's hair. Sulfurous. She smiled blandly and said any noblewoman worth her salts could always find a way to slip away and do what she wanted, regardless of man's intent.

The nonsensical catchphrase "Is this Tehidy's worst?" ran up and down the column, no matter whether the event was good or sour. Gareth felt the morale was as good as could be expected, but not much better. The Linyati, always behind them, always a threat, drained the men's spirits. They needed a victory, or at least a change away from these utterly foreign grasslands—well-watered deserts to most.

Labala crafted small amulets, gave them to the scouts, and told them to feel the amulets from time to time and notify him if they grew warm.

A day later, they camped near a small river. The scouts had chased a small herd of antelope into nets and butchered them without wasting shot.

For once there were no problems reported, and Gareth lay in the shade of a tree, Cosyra's head pillowed on his chest. He had a mug of cool water beside him and could smell the succulence of antelope roasting on nearby spits.

"This is too good," Cosyra said, and moments later was proven right as a sentry yelped alarm.

Far out, in the grasslands, Gareth spotted movement. The air was still, but the high grass was waving, as if some hidden creature was leaving a wake. But the wake was impossibly long.

No one could see what was making the track, but Gareth ordered everyone to stand to, weapons ready.

Two more of the wakes were reported. But they did no more than circle the camp, then disappear.

Gareth told the night watch to be very wary, knowing he needn't have spoken. The men were watchful, jumpy, as night came.

No alarms were shouted, but the morning watch guards, going out to relieve the graveyard sentries for the last shift before dawn, reported one man vanished, with never a bloodstain or outcry.

They moved on, and again saw the marks of these unseen creatures, tracking them. Labala tried to cast a spell to find out what they were, and got nothing.

That night, two more sentries vanished.

Gareth considered what might be done. He was assuming their enemy wasn't human or a demon, but some fleshly creature. His skin crept at the plan he arrived at. But he had only the one, and he couldn't ask or order anyone to take part but himself.

He chose the campsite well for that night, on a low knoll above the grasses. He had one cannon loaded and pointed at a spot about twenty yards distant, near two boulders. Then he consulted with Labala for a charm.

Guards reported, as it grew dark, the "wakes" once more, closing on the knoll.

The sentries were in threes, stationed close to the rest of the fully alert men.

"You are one damned fool," Cosyra raged at Gareth.

"Maybe," Gareth agreed. "And I'm the captain."

"Which means you've got to go down there, waving your bottom as bait? Why can't you ask for volunteers?

"Never mind," she went on. "I know the answer. Because you're the captain. I'm starting to figure it out. Well, kiss me, and try not to get vanished, all right?"

"I'll definitely do my best."

Gareth had two pistols in his belt, a cutlass, and a musket. He went downhill, to the cannoneers. He gave one end of a cord to Thom Tehidy, who would be his lead gunner, and tied the other around his wrist.

"I hope you're well laid," he said, dry-mouthed.

"I am," Tehidy said, wanting to make some sort of jest, not finding any.

Gareth went on down to the boulders, and waited.

It grew dark, darker still, as the column's fires above him were banked, and the minutes stretched like hours.

He was as alert as his fear and Labala's spell could make him.

Time dragged, and clouds scudded across the moon.

Twice he started before realizing it was only a mouse or some other harmless creature scurrying to his front.

Then his palms were sweaty, and he sensed something was out there—something big, something dangerous. He licked his lips, waited, knowing it was closing on him.

Close enough, his building terror shrilled, and he dove into the shelter of the boulders, yanking on the cord.

A moment later, the cannon fired, flame spurting toward him, grapeshot spanging off the boulders above him, and something screamed.

It was more than a scream—a shriek of agony to the gods. Gareth forced himself to his knees, saw something like a snake looming high above, thrashing down as he ducked; the snake's body, if that was what it was, was as big around as a man's torso.

He had the musket up, fired into the writhing bulk, tossed it aside, and was scrambling back to the shelter of his gun.

It was reloaded, waiting, as he rolled past it. Tehidy held the match to the touchhole, and again it fired into the night.

The scream had never stopped, and now it burbled, like a great fish gaffed through the gills, and the thrashing faded, as if the monster was rolling away in its death agonies.

Gareth found his hands shaking, made his way back to the center of the camp, ordered the fires built up.

Cosyra came to him, pale-faced, and kissed him, holding him close, not saying a word.

At that moment Gareth wished he could be like other men, and find solace in drink—then remembered they had almost none.

He tried to sleep, only to wake shaking once more from a dream he did not want to remember. He sat up next to Cosyra, who was busy pretending sleep, for the rest of the night.

The dawn showed the grass where Gareth had lain as bait flattened, and the ground torn up. There were splotches of a disgusting-smelling yellow ichor here and there, and the ripped ground formed a trail.

No one volunteered to follow it to see what might lie at the end.

The column went on, and they were not troubled again by the nightmares, whatever they were.

"And am I not a genius," Thom Tehidy boasted, ducking out of the narrow cave the scouts had located.

"The genius, sir, is I," Labala said. "For was it not I who built the amulets that scented out your cave and your saltpeter?"

"A mere device, a tool," Tehidy said, "with the inspiration provided by the real brains behind this stumbling bunch of yahoos."

"As Captain Yahoo to you scum," Gareth said, "would you two mind explaining what wonderful feat you've accomplished?"

"Seventy-five parts of saltpeter," Tehidy said, "five parts of sulfur, and if you'll observe the banks of yon creek, you'll see willow trees, regarded by us artillery experts as the finest source of charcoal—five parts—and there you have it.

"Gunpowder, Gareth. All we need do is mix up our ingredients, with my colleague here's slight sorcerous assistance. I learned from the Royal Cannoneers back in Ticao, once I realized you'd stuck me behind a gun forevermore, a bit of the noble trade of killing folks with large guns, and found gunpowder's a bit chancy."

"I'm not th' one for gettin' my head blown off," Nomios grumbled, "while you two lackwits fool about."

"'Tis seldom gunpowder fails in that regard," Tehidy said. "Unfortunately. More likely it fizzles like a damp squib. So, as I was saying, we gather our ingredients, wet them down a bit so they'll mix thoroughly, which is termed corning, add a bit of ensorcellment, and *bang*."

"Bang 'tis," Nomios agreed. "And bang it can always be, for I'll keep m' distance from both you loons."

"Oh ye of little faith."

For once, everything worked, although Labala and Tehidy were up most of the night experimenting, making vile smells and fizzles before, around dawn, they produced a nice proper bang that brought everybody up, scrabbling for a firearm and cursing.

And they had gunpowder, almost twice what they'd had before. It wasn't as strong as the powder they'd carried with them, requiring almost half again as much for the same power, but it worked.

Gareth felt that maybe his boasted luck, which had been more than a bit in abeyance, might be returning a trifle.

Gareth, trying to keep from thinking about how many paces before him until the day's march ended, trying to think of something to get them off this cursed treadmill they were trapped on, plucked something that looked a bit like the dandelions of home, except far bigger, and green. He blew it at Cosyra, watched the bits of fluff blow away.

"Did you make a wish?" she asked.

"I did," he lied, taking another step.

He looked up at the sky, and saw, very high, a huge bird drifting in the wind, drifting north, toward the distant sea. The northerly breeze blowing down here on the ground must be stronger up there. If he had wings, if Labala could ensorcell a bird, he could get an idea of where they were, where they were heading, rather than pursue this blind travel east, trying to guess when they might turn north and look for a settlement that would have ships for purchase or theft.

Perhaps it was high adventure, sailing into the unknown, making your charts as you went. But he was a corsair, and his world was the ocean, not these damned swamps and plains and jungles!

He had a bit of an idea, considered it over another fifty paces, thought it might have some merit. He dropped back to where Labala marched with Tehidy, in front of the column's lead cannon, to ask if it might be possible.

"You realize, of course," N'b'ry said cheerfully, "the whole Company thinks you—and your pet magician—are madder than a pair of pigs in clover.

"Collecting butterflies, indeed," he said.

"Shut up," Gareth said. "The idea sounds daft enough without your contributions."

"Shut up is right," Labala said. "Dewinging a dead butterfiggle's hard work.

"Now, Gareth, take these wings, and touch them to your eyes. Gently, dammit. I don't want to have go chasing around for more of 'em when it gets dark."

Gareth obeyed.

"Now, drink this."

"What is it?" Gareth asked suspiciously.

"A draft I concocted which will make you sleep ... and dream. But it won't be dreaming. Vile-tasting, it is."

Gareth swallowed, choked. "You aren't understating the case."

About half the column was sitting around the grove, watching, while others assigned to cooking or sentry duty busied themselves elsewhere.

"Now, finish it off, and go beddy," Labala said.

Gareth yawned mightily, leaned back on his rolled blanket, and closed his eyes. In a few seconds, he let out a bubbling snore.

"I want a bottle of that," Cosyra said, "for when he gets the broods and can't sleep—and, worse, won't let me nod off either."

"A magician's specialties should never be taken for that of a chirurgeon's," Labala said loftily.

"And I remember when you were no better than a long-shoreman, living off coppers and what you could steal," Cosyra said.

"Cosyra," N'b'ry suggested, "don't remind him of how he's inflated his position—he's, *hem-hem*, inflated enough as it is in reality.

"Labala, that's a question," he went on. "How in the hells is it, when all about you are starving, that you appear to be just as, well, nobly built as when we were aboard ship?"

Labala tried to look evil. "Haven't you realized where those men we keep missing are going?" He licked his lips. "Learned some interestin' things from the Slavers and those pricks with their pyramids. Nothing finer than thin-sliced, unwashed pirate. Yum."

He reached over to Gareth, peeled back an eyelid.

"He's well under, so the rest of you clamp your lips and let me set to work and show you what powers I've inherited from the unfortunate Lord Dafflemere." His expression turned serious, then he forced the past away.

"Now, we gently crumble these butterfly wings, like so. Now, we touch these assembled twigs—notice how they flicker and flame into life, with nary a match nor ember, which is yet another benefit a master sorcerer can provide.

"Into the flames we put rue, skullcap, chohosh, other herbs of benefit."

Labala half closed his eyes, began chanting:

"Your eye
Is in these shards
Like unto like
Taking on

Taking on
Other powers
Other ways
Your eye
Lifts
Sails
Travels with these bits
Up into the wind
Travels with the wind
Seeing all
Seeing all
North
With the wind
Land far below you
Seeing all
Seeing all
Then returning
Remembering
Sight
What was below
What was seen."

He repeated the incantation three times, then held the crushed wings over his head and let them go. The smoke from the tiny fire caught them, whirled them up, and then the wind took them away.

He opened his eyes.

"Now we wait to see what happens. And, perhaps, start thinking about evening-meal."

Without surprise, Gareth looked back and down at his camp, far below.

He realized that he was drawn in the direction he was "looking," so he somehow changed his view, without understanding how he did it, to the east and to the north as he rose higher and higher.

It appeared as if the grasslands ran on forever, but then, not too far ahead of where the company rested, he saw the beginnings of a spring that became a creek, and grew into a small river.

It cascaded down from the plateau into the jungle in a great waterfall. It pooled, grew wider, and was a river, growing ever larger as it ran toward the waiting sea.

Somehow Gareth could see the spring as if he were standing beside it, as well as from high above it, how the river grew, washing toward the distant ocean. He hoped it was the Mozaffar, with the northernmost Linyati town at its mouth, for he remembered from freed slaves that it was navigable far into the interior.

He could even make out jungle villages along the banks of the river, and, through haze, the river mouth and the longed-for sea that would take him home from these strange lands. He even thought he could make out ships, sails set, leaving the city at the river's end.

Sadly, he realized it was time to return, although he could have stayed here aloft, without body, without cares, caressed by the wind, forever. If only there was a way for Cosyra to be with him. Perhaps, when it came time to die . . .

Gareth's eyes snapped open, and he was lying on his blanket, Cosyra beside him on one side, Labala on the other.

"About time you returned," the magician said. "Or else there'll be no dinner for you at all."

"What did you see?" Cosyra asked, and behind her Froln and N'b'ry crouched, listening intently.

"I saw the birth of the river we'll follow to the sea,

and the city with the ships we'll need to take," Gareth said. "Not more than three or four days' distant."

Froln got to his feet.

"A cheer, boys," he called. "For we'll not die in this stinkin' damn' wasteland after all!"

Twenty-three

I like this but little," Froln grumbled, looking over the cliff, paying little regard to the spray from the nearby waterfall drifting past.

"Nor I, sir," Nomios agreed. "Th' tackle's worn and in bits. And I doubt me if there's enough for a full run down to th' cliffbase. The rope'll wear on the rocks, for we've no decent timber for a windlass. It'll all be shit, sweat, and yo-heave-ho, like in the old days before men discovered leverage."

The column had reached the place where the river dove over the side of the plateau, crashing down and down, more than a thousand feet, to deep pools below.

"It'll be a scramble for the able men," Froln gloomed. "And it'll take care to slip the stretchers with our sick and wounded down without losin' anyone."

He and Bosun Nomios looked at each other.

"As for the rest . . . like you said, we haven't sheaves, windlasses, capstans, hoists, or levers," Froln added gloomily. "It shall be a bitch."

"We'll need magic for the cannon," Nomios said.

"Or a damned great friendly bird," Froln agreed.

Gareth, only half listening, had been studying, foot by foot, the rocky, brush-covered precipice.

"We can do it," he announced.

The other two seamen waited.

"We'll do it in stages," he said. "First from here down to that outcropping, then from there—the longest drop—to where the water bounces next to that ledge. We'll carry the guns along the ledge, and make a short lower there—where that scraggly tree comes out of the cliff face—and then straight down, to that beach, and we're home."

The other two considered.

"Just possible," Nomios said.

"We'll link the ropes we've been using to pull the guns with, and, Labala, is there a strengthening spell you could cast?"

"I could," Labala said. "But with no guarantees on how long it'll hold true. Our ropes are damned near as worn as we are, Gareth."

"I know that," Gareth agreed. "First, we'll put the sick and wounded down, the same way the guns will go. Froln, detail ten men for each position and get them headed down.

"Cosyra, would you do the honors of taking charge of that? Take Thom Tehidy as your assistant."

"Gladly."

It took the rest of the day to get the stretchers, and the men who were walking wounded, to the bottom of the cliff. Next went half the supplies. Gareth, not liking that his force was split, put musketeers down, to guard against anything coming out of the nearby jungle.

"I want steady officers at each landing," Gareth said. "Froln, here at the top. Captain Petrich, you'll be in the worst position, down on the ledge."

"Thank you," Petrich, once of the *Naijak*, said. "I thought you'd forgotten me."

"Nomios, you can order the lowering from where that tree is, and Knoll, take charge of landing the guns down on that beach, moving them out of the way, and remounting them on their carriages."

"What about you, Gareth?" N'b'ry said.

"I'll stay up here and chew on my fingernails," Gareth said. "Even though I've got my best seamen on the cliff."

Those soldiers who hadn't gone down the night before were put on the lashed-together ropes for brute muscle.

The rest of the supplies, then the gun carriages, powder, and the rest of the matrosses' tools, went down. Sailors were stationed at each level, helping the rest of the soldiery to the bottom.

"Clear below," Gareth bellowed, and the first of the guns, tied in a skein of ropes, slid over the edge, lowered by double ropes.

"Handsomely, you men," he shouted, and the soldiers, moving slowly, obeying the command, walked the ropes to the edge of the cliff.

The cannon rested on the rocky outcropping. The ropes were released, and men took them down to where the gun waited. Again, the gun went down, but this time there were fewer men to lower it, and twice it almost got away from them.

But it came down safely, and was carried along the ledge, and once more was lowered, then again to the cliff's bottom.

Gareth, in spite of the cool spray drifting across from the waterfall, was sweating hard.

Nimble topmen scrambled the ropes back to the top, and the second gun went down, again without incident.

Gareth noted Labala standing at cliff's edge, lips moving in what he hoped was an incantation, feared was a prayer.

On the last lowering, the men were tired. The gun slid over the edge of the cliff a little too fast. Gareth was about to shout for them to hold at the first landing, the outcropping, and rest for a spell before continuing. But he was too late. The soldiers were letting it down too fast, reacted to Froln's angry shouts and braked too suddenly. The cannon jerked to a halt, and that was enough strain for one rope to let go, then the other.

The gun dropped, and crashed off the outcropping, shattering the arm of a sailor who was bravely trying to stop it, then rolled over the edge. It spun twice in the air, tarnished bronze casting the late-morning sun, and smashed down onto the ledge, crushing Petrich and another corsair, then bouncing, rolling, clanging like a horrible bell, and smashing apart on the rocks at the bottom of the cliff.

No one said anything, no one made any accusations.

The men on top and on the cliff ledges climbed down, and someone said a prayer for Petrich and his fellow.

Then they made up their packs and lifted the two surviving guns onto their carriages and set off into the jungle.

Its familiarity welcomed them, but no one rejoiced.

There were small animal tracks the pirates had learned to recognize and exploit, and they followed them, keeping close to the river as it grew larger, making crossings of the tributaries when they reached them.

On the third day of march the scouts Gareth had left at the waterfall rejoined the column.

There'd been no sign of the pursuing Linyati, and now there was cheeriness. All they had to do was continue on the leagues, who knew how many: a hundred, two hundred, maybe less, maybe more. Sooner or later, the river would get wide and deep enough for them to build rafts, and then, afloat, in their own world, all would be well, even though fresh water wasn't nearly as comforting as salt.

They would find or take some ships somewhere along the way, maybe from those damned Slavers with their city at river's mouth, and then home to Saros.

Men started making jokes, thinking maybe they'd live, considered what they'd do with the treasured gold each still carried in his pack.

Then, on the fifth day of march, the scouts reported they were being watched by men armed with muskets.

Twenty-four

By the time Gareth reached the head of the column, the watchers had vanished. Gareth ordered them to march on, but slowly, with flankers out as far as the thick jungle around them permitted. He stayed near the head of the march, along with Labala and Iset.

For the rest of that day, they were watched. But no one shot at them or made any hostile moves, and so Gareth ordered his men to hold their fire.

That night—before it got dark, not wanting to give the watchers out there in the jungle a silhouette to aim at—they posted double sentries, and cooked their rations, now not much more than whatever could be gathered on the march, plus dried meat and various wild fruits and vegetables the cooks had decided were edible.

No one talked much, and everyone kept his weapon at hand. The officers around Gareth were tense, waiting.

"They *could* always surprise us and be friendly," Cosyra offered. "Doesn't it make sense that *somebody* in these damned jungles has to be?"

"I think," N'b'ry said cynically, "everyone in Kashi who was a decent sort got devoured a dozen generations ago." He stood up, stretched. "Well, I guess I'd best get my head down and have a nap before the shooting starts."

Four men suddenly came out of the brush, somehow having bypassed the sentries. They were unarmed except for belt knives, and held up empty hands. They wore elaborately worked short leather jackets, and knee pants.

Instantly, two dozen muskets were aimed and cocked.

The men remained motionless, and the pirates relaxed—slightly.

One of them walked forward, very slowly.

"I am Riet," he said in a language Gareth vaguely remembered, pointing to N'b'ry. "I think you are the man who returned me here to my homeland. Do you remember me?"

N'b'ry recovered.

"No . . ."

"I was afraid not," Riet said. "But it was your ships . . . yours and some of these other men, I think, that took me from the chains of the men who called themselves Linyati."

Froln walked forward.

"Yes," Riet said. "And you are another."

"Sunnuvabitch," a pirate murmured. "Goodwill sometimes does pay off. And I would've sold these bastards for a handful of gold."

"Shut up," someone hissed.

"Why are you men of ships and deep water here, in our jungles?" Riet said, obviously not understanding Sarosian.

"We sailed from the island you knew us on, against those Slavers," Gareth said. "We took one of their cities, far west of here, and were waiting to seize their treasure ships."

"We heard tales of a great battle," Riet said. "But little more than fireside stories without details." He looked around. "I would guess you were defeated, and lost your ships."

"We fled that city, our ships burning behind us," Gareth admitted, "through the jungles and across the high flatlands, with the Slavers pursuing us.

"When we thought we had lost them, we turned north, determining to follow this river to its mouth, and somehow find ships to return us to our homeland."

"You would chance the Slaver city of Cimmar, as they call it? You are brave indeed," Riet said.

"Desperate men can be called brave," Gareth said.

"Well, you are safe now, at least for as long as you remain with us," Riet said. "Our scouts reported strangers in the jungle days ago, and I decided to come with them and see if we would have a chance to destroy some more Slavers, arrogant in their gold lust, for chancing travel this deep in enemy lands. From my unfortunate experience with those creatures, my people now think of me as a war leader, although war is a disgusting thought to all of us.

"Now there shall be great rejoicing and feasting, for there are many who remember being slaves, and being hopeless, thinking they would never see their lovely jungles again, and remember your freeing us, asking never a hide in payment, nor any of the gold, gems, or silver we work for amusement that seem to drive the Slavers mad when they see it."

Froln licked his lips unconsciously, hearing the word "gold."

"Yes, and we shall do all we can to help you in your journey downriver," Riet went on. "But first is a time, as I said, to feast and rejoice."

* * *

The town, a respectable settlement of more than two-hundred score people, sat on a tributary that pooled, then ran into the Mozaffar. The Kashi who lived there, who called themselves the Sa'ib, farmed the fertile land behind the town and raised fish in pools. Hunting was now just a hobby for them, and Gareth got the idea the Sa'ib looked a little down on anyone who hadn't figured out farming was a far more stable way to live than lurking in bushes for a passing deer or knocking monkeys from trees with slings or bows.

The feast, Riet said, would be in three days, rather than immediately. The next two days would be for rest and recovery.

The pirates were given their own compound, and food and drink were provided. Some of the pirates talked about going out and looking for women, but Gareth noted when night fell the collection of huts fell silent except for ex-hausted snores.

Gareth sat beside the sleeping Cosyra for what seemed to be half the night, unable to sleep, listening to the night, waiting for hostile sounds. He decided he was too tense to get any rest, but thought he might lie down with his eyes shut.

It was late the next afternoon when he awoke, feeling differently than he had for . . . for months, he realized, feel-ing some of the strain slip away.

"Get your dirty body clean," Cosyra advised. "You're hours behind the rest of us."

And so it was.

The pirates' filthy clothing was piled and burned. New garments were provided like the ones Riet had worn, styl-ish jackets and pants sewn of various animal skins, lav-ishly decorated. Even sword belts and pistol slings were worn and cracking, and Riet had tanners making replacements.

Most of the men went to the river to bathe, although there were a few, as always, who boasted of liking the way they smelled. The men came back laughing, for the women of Sa'ib had been eager spectators, and made comments that were easily understandable, although not many of the corsairs had been given a language spell by Labala.

That night, too, ended early, although there were some hardy souls—Tehidy, Froln, others—who sat up drinking the palm beer they'd been given and talking quietly.

The next night, all was abandon.

Gareth had wondered if the Sa'ib were intensely private, for no one except Riet and the men who brought food had disturbed them thus far.

Now he found otherwise.

The compound gates were thrown open, and it seemed everyone in the town swarmed in, eager to meet these white-skinned strangers, each with a small present.

There was a constant flow of food, everything from tidbits to huge roasted fish from the river, seasoned with hot peppers.

There was drink—the palm beer that some liked, wine made from fruit, and even some fruit brandies, for the Sa'ib knew the art of distillery.

And there were other pleasures.

The tough little foremast hand, Kuldja, staggered up to Gareth, tears in his eyes, and swore he'd stay here for the rest of his life, and the hells with being a pirate.

"The women don't want money, or even a present to lie with me," he said. "Not like any damned port town I was ever in, not even like Ticao, where everybody has to pay one way or another."

He hiccuped, saw a rather plain, but smiling, woman wink at him, and stumbled after her.

"Poor bastard," Cosyra said.

"That's one of the worst things about being a sailor," Gareth said. "You come ashore, and only have a few hours.

"We brag about our independence," he said, a bit melancholic. "But that means no home but a foc's'le bunk, no food but that in a waterfront dive, no love but—"

"But you don't know anything about that, remember," Cosyra said. "You were a virgin before you met me, and now you don't need anything else."

Gareth's momentary sadness vanished. "I could not agree with you more, my Lady Cosyra of the Mount."

"Damned well better," she growled, kissed him, and they found their way to the outskirts of the town, and a quiet glade.

At dusk, the real feast began.

Long tables were set up, and a steady stream of courses and drink arrived. It wasn't possible for the human stomach to hold that much, but some of the pirates tried.

Riet and other Sa'ib made speeches about how glad they were to be able to repay the pirates for what they'd done, and how they wished they could do more. But the Slavers were so evil, so skilled with weapons, no one except great warriors like the corsairs could ever stand against them.

Gareth thought of saying that if someone never tried to fight, they could never win, but that wasn't for this night. Besides, he had no right to feel superior to people who were constantly in fear of a Linyati raid, who'd seen relatives torn away, not just once as Gareth and others had, but year after year after century. His speech was nothing but praise and thanks for their new friends.

And so the party went on, great fires roaring, driving away the jungle darkness around the town.

Drink poured down gullets in unbelievable quantities, and Gareth, again, was almost sorry he didn't favor alcohol.

Cosyra sat beside him, sipping a glass of wine.

"So much for piratical abandon," she said. "Welcome to a life of sobriety, Cosyra, doing what your love does." She hiccuped, proving sobriety was a matter of degrees this night.

Labala wandered up, and Gareth was a bit surprised to see him quite sober.

"You're not feeling well," Cosyra said. "Or is it magicians, as they grow in strength, become more abstem . . . abstem . . . they don't get drunk anymore?"

"Maybe I am getting sick," Labala said. "Or maybe I just can't relax, and keep expecting something to happen."

"Such as?" Gareth asked.

"Such as I don't know," Labala said.

"Look," Cosyra said. "See that woman? She's smiling at you. Why don't you go see *why* she's smiling."

Labala forced a smile.

"Thanks. Maybe I will," and left.

The feast seemed fated to go on until dawn, or until there was nothing left to eat or drink.

Riet had slumped under the table, a happy smile on his face.

Gareth saw two naked women, screaming laughter, drag a pirate into a hut, pulling at his pants, noted Froln very earnestly peeling and tossing fruit to an amazingly big and multicolored bird, and having what must have been a most meaningful conversation.

"Shall we?" he asked, jerking his head toward their hut.

"I think so," Cosyra said, yawning. "And I think you wore me out this afternoon. I'm ready for sleep, no more."

Gareth had barely fallen asleep when the Linyati attacked.

Twenty-five

The shots woke Gareth. He was on his feet, brain not working, but his hands automatically fumbled for a sling of pistols and his sword belt.

He found his breeches, yanked them on as another volley rang and he heard screams of men dying. Cosyra pulled on her breeches and a man—not a man, Gareth realized, seeing the curved helmet, but a Slaver—burst into their hut. Gareth had a pistol out, shot the Linyati in the face, saw others in the flaring torches outside the hut.

A musket cracked and the ball whipped past him, and a torch was hurled into the hut.

"Now!" Gareth shouted, and the two plunged out of the hut as it caught fire. Gareth cut down the Slaver reloading his piece, ducked a thrust from a swordsman and slashed at him. That one went away, and there was another Slaver with a musket aimed at his breast; Cosyra shot him before he could fire.

The compound was like a flame-lit day as pirates staggered awake, still drunk, trying to fight back.

There was a Runner amidst them, a cutlass in each clawed hand. Some pirates saw the monster and charged it, screaming rage. Froln came in from a flank, lunged, and cut the Runner's leg open.

It shrilled pain, rage, spun on him, knocked Froln's blade away. The pirate went flat, and the Runner's slash missed.

Dihr was braced against a hut, and Gareth saw blood runnelling down his leg. But his hold on his musket was very steady. He fired, and the ball took the Runner in the throat. It thrashed about, dying.

Women, screaming, ran out of the huts, and the Slavers showed no mercy, killing them to get at the corsairs.

Gareth heard a howl of rage, and Riet and other Kashi, Cosyra at their head, attacked the knot of Slavers. He lost her in the melee, then she burst out the other side, her blade black with blood in the firelight.

There were soldiers then, heads still muzzled with drink, but forming an unsteady line and attacking.

No one fled, no one hid. By now, there were no cowards left among the corsairs.

A Kashi woman, arm half severed, used a Slaver's pike to impale a Linyati in robes, then twisted and fell herself.

Two Slavers attacked Gareth. He knocked one's thrust away, slashed at his legs, then pain burnt across his chest as the other Linyati's thrust almost went home. Gareth spun inside the Slaver's guard, smashed his face in with the pommel of his sword, kicked him into his fellow. As they stumbled back, his blade flicked once, twice, and they both were down.

The night exploded and Slavers, Kashi, pirates were cut apart as Linyati cannon fired into the throng, not caring who they killed.

Gareth saw Tehidy pushing a cannon from behind a hut, flanking the Linyati guns, and ran toward him.

Cosyra was shouting for a rally, and a Runner saw her, leapt over two Slavers, dropping one of his swords, and grabbed at her. Cosyra back-rolled, came up under the monster, and drove her sword straight up, through the Runner's chin into where a brain should be.

Another Runner darted at her, and Kuldja swung at him from the side with a ramrod that was somehow afire. The Runner staggered, and then the fire touched him and he burned as if he were made of tar.

Kuldja whooped joy, and Cosyra grinned at him. A Linyati cannon banged, and Kuldja was ripped like a cloth doll.

Cosyra, untouched by the shot, found a loaded musket in the dirt, had it up, aimed, and killed a Linyati gunner.

Gareth pushed the second gun into line beside Tehidy, and Knoll N'b'ry was beside him, helping.

N'b'ry grunted oddly, stood up, and blood poured from a small hole above his ear. Eyes wide, he fell limply, and Gareth didn't need to look to see if he was still alive.

Blood rage surged, and Gareth pulled a slow match from a gunner's hand, bent over the cannon. It bore, and he held the match to the touchhole and the cannon fired, Tehidy's an instant later.

Grapeshot swathed through the Linyati gunners, and the survivors fell back from their guns for a moment.

Gareth, screaming rage, ran into their midst, knowing nothing but a killing frenzy, seeing men's faces come up, go away, seeing Linyati, thrusting at them, again, killing another, and there were men beside him, fighting, killing, some white, some brown.

Labala was shouting a spell from somewhere, and Gareth saw dropped weapons stir, lift, and thrust at Linyati, with no human hand to control them. A Slaver wizard was calling a counterspell, and a brush knife spun through the air and took most of his head away.

The Slavers broke, tried to flee.

But there was no safety, no mercy, and the pirates and the Sa'ib slaughtered them as they ran.

There was nothing but blood and death for Gareth, and then he recovered, kneeling beside N'b'ry's body.

He remembered Knoll's japery, friendship, the ships he wanted to build, and now there was nothing but death on a nameless jungle town's dirt street.

He thought of telling Suel, the woman Knoll had companioned, far away in Saros, of N'b'ry's bravery, tasted ashes and knew courage was meaningless compared to the vast emptiness he felt.

Gareth got up, staggered, but paid no attention to his wound. Cosyra, Tehidy, Riet, Dihr, Froln, others were before him. He saw Kuldja's unrecognizable body lying nearby, other bodies of pirates, soldiers, Kashi.

"This was a beginning," he said, voice calm. "We have destroyed those who pursued us. Now, we shall journey downriver, to Cimmar.

"That means you, Riet, and other men of Kashi. We shall recruit as we travel. It is time for the Kashi to stand and take back what is their own.

"Our plans have changed. No longer are we going to be content with just stealing the Linyati ships at the river's mouth.

"We are going to sack Cimmar, take its treasure, burn it to the ground, kill everyone within its walls, and the Mozaffar shall belong to the Kashi.

"Death to the Slavers!"

Twenty-six

The long, slender canoes slid into the water silently. Kashi paddlers at bow and stern took the stroke and steered the dozen boats toward the lights of Cimmar, less than half a league distant.

The other men in the canoes were Gareth's most skilled gunners. They were heading toward four dark bulks, Linyati ships sitting at anchor.

Their faces and clothes were darkened with charcoal; they were barefoot, armed with daggers and swords. Gareth, in the lead canoe, wished he had greater trust in men—and, for that matter, machines—to have allowed the pistols in their waistbands to be loaded.

But one accidental discharge could ruin their carefully laid plans.

After the desperate fight in the jungle town, the pirates had built rafts and, with native canoes, moved downriver. The Sa'ib had provided twenty recruits, Riet at their head.

At every river village they stopped, waited for the

panic-stricken Kashi to realize these white men weren't Slavers and come back from their hiding places in the jungle, and asked for volunteers.

"Only five men is all I'm asking for from your town, just as I'm asking the same from every village we come to," Gareth cajoled. "Less than you lose a year when the Slavers come through. We'll train you how to stand, how to soldier. Now is the time to fight back!"

But his words were less effective than the arguments offered by Dihr, other ex-slaves, and the Sa'ib, for the men of Kashi could see the examples, and didn't have to worry about the words.

By the time they closed on Cimmar, they had six hundred men of Kashi with them.

The battle in Riet's town had cost the pirates dearly. There were less than two hundred left, and many of those were wounded. But Labala's spells and the Sa'ib herbalists were rapidly curing the injured.

Each night, when the motley convoy of rafts and canoes pulled ashore, Iset and the other soldiers would train the Kashi in drills and mock battles, making sure that the natives did better and better each day. Confidence grew, and the men began boasting of how they would destroy the Linyati and bring long-lost pride back to the people of the jungle.

"Right you are," the warrants would cynically agree. "Pride an' honor it is, lads, as long as you don't give 'em time to recover. Keep movin', keep killin', and we'll all be heroes. Live heroes."

Gareth and Cosyra had something else to ponder: Labala's spell determining the Slavers had been after Cosyra had been accurate, considering the Runner that had tried to take her alive during the battle. But no matter how they considered, neither had any explanation whatsoever.

Labala sensed Slaver magic the closer they came to the river mouth, spells intended to detect anyone hostile. He cast subtle counterspells to make the wizards careless, confident that no one would dare approach them.

They'd made a final camp half a day above Cimmar, and Gareth and his officers moved close to the city, planning the attack.

Cimmar was about the size of Noorat, on the eastern bank of the Mozaffar, built close to the waterfront, with walls keeping back the jungle's dangers.

When they first arrived, there had been only one ship anchored in the roadstead, barely enough for the men, let alone the gold they stubbornly carried and the loot they hoped to take.

But a day later, three more of the great treasure ships sailed in, and Gareth wondered if the fleet was assembling for its annual passage down coast to Linyati.

He liked the plan they eventually came up with. It was very simple: the pirates would seize the ships offshore, while Iset, his soldiers, and the remaining Kashi would attack the city from the north, the river-mouth side. Gareth thought the Linyati would least expect an attack from that direction.

The force was moved into final attack position and took up hides on the final day.

"Let's not do anything stupid," Cosyra said.

"I'm never guilty of that."

"I mean, like getting killed."

"Not in the plan at all," Gareth said.

Cosyra chose her words carefully. "So don't get angry when the fighting starts."

Gareth started to do just that, remembering the debt he still owed for the deaths of his parents, his village, Knoll N'b'ry, others, then realized what she meant.

"Sorry," he said. "I'll be cuke as a coolcumber."

Cosyra grinned and kissed him. "Stay calm, and let them lose their heads," she said.

"My romantic lover," Gareth said, and kissed her back.

At dusk, the soldiers moved out, around the city walls, and at full dark the gunners put out in their boats.

The pirates kept looking worriedly at the city walls as they closed. But Gareth had learned from Iset that men looking out from a well-lit place into darkness weren't likely to spot much, especially not craft as small as those the pirates rode.

Gareth's canoe closed on the first ship, the rowers never making a splash, and the bow oarsman grabbed the anchor chain. Gareth slipped past him and, dagger between his teeth, went up the rusting, slimy links. He stopped at the top, his head below the ship's railing. Slowly he peered over, saw no one on the foredeck, and slid over the rail, Cosyra behind him.

Other pirates followed, boarding soundlessly. Then, knives ready, they spread down across the ship's deck.

There were two men on watch on the quarterdeck. Knives thudded home in their backs, and they gasped, their dead forms eased to the deck.

Gareth loaded his pistol in case there was a Runner aboard, went through a hatch into the officers' quarters, the rest of his murderers behind him.

But there was no monster, only sleeping men, who never woke. Next were the crewmen, asleep in their hammocks along the lower gundeck. The pirates sheathed their knives, went in with cutlasses. Three men woke, hearing their mates gurgle into death, then joined them. There'd been only one outcry, and that muffled, before the ship was theirs.

Tehidy and Gareth made a quick investigation of the

guns. There was nothing unusual about them, nor about the powder, fuses, and shot in the magazines. Tehidy made the interesting discovery that the Linyati ship carried explosive shot. He grinned at Gareth.

"This'll help out when the excitement starts."

Gareth nodded. "First broadside, though, should be solid," he said.

"Don't tell a farmer which end of a seed goes down," Tehidy sneered, and gunners began loading the cannon.

Other sailors, helped by the Kashi in the boats, were lowering the ship's second, emergency anchor off the stern.

A dozen men were left aboard this ship, commanded by Froln, and the raiders moved on to the second, which was also taken in silent blood, as was the third. On them as well, the guns were loaded and run out and a second anchor dropped off the ships' sterns. Dihr was put in command of the second ship, Galf the third.

Someone got careless, or was becoming sick of the butchery, and missed the anchor watch aboard the last ship. He cried out, seeing steel glint against the thin moon, and went down. But his outcry was enough to alert a Slaver on the quarterdeck. He had a musket aimed and fired it at the first pirate up the ladder.

The shot brought the ship's officers alert. It was too late for them, but the sailors aboard had time to roll out of their hammocks and grab weapons.

The pirates were outnumbered about two to one, and belowdecks was a slashing, shouting brawl before the last Slaver went down, weltering in his blood.

Gareth saw a hooded lantern ashore flickering a question at their ship.

"Load the guns," he shouted, as the men tossed the bodies of the Slavers overboard.

Again, the lantern flashed.

"I can hit it with two shots," Nomios shouted from the main deck.

"Stand by, then," Gareth shouted, turned to Cosyra. "Signal the others. We're ready."

Cosyra unwrapped a torch, whispered the spell Labala had taught her, and the torch seared into life.

"Damn! There went my eyebrows," she said, and began waving the torch back and forth.

Gareth jumped as a gun on the deck below him barked, then the others volleyed.

The other ships fired, and Gareth saw cannonballs slam into the buildings on the shore.

Men on the capstans set to work, wearing the ships about, until the guns on the other side bore, and these, too, sent a broadside into the city.

Next they loaded with explosive shells, the master gunner lighting the fuse on each ball before it was gingerly rammed down the barrel.

It was easy to mark these shots when they hit—smoke and fire boiled up, and often the fire took hold.

Gareth could hear screams and shouts from Cimmar, and then they grew suddenly louder. This could only mean Iset had attacked the eastern wall.

Moments later, he saw a cloud of fire lift over the wall—more of Labala's fire magic, carried by the wind.

Cimmar was alive, the streets swarming with Linyati as the soldiers swept through. Now it was harder to find an open target, as fire built and smoke boiled high.

"All right," Gareth called. "Cease firing!"

There was a final bang, then silence.

"Men of the watch, take your posts," Gareth called. "The rest of us, back in the boats and ashore!"

* * *

There were two dozen or more dead Linyati on the rocky beach, sprawled around boats. They'd been launching an attack on Gareth's ships, which he'd not seen, and some keen-eyed or lucky gunner had cut them down.

Cimmar was chaos. Linyati ran here, there, sometimes attacked when they saw a pirate, sometimes ran away, sometimes dashed past, as if they hadn't noticed.

Even Runners were taken by the hysteria, charging any human they saw, whether one or ten.

Somewhere in the night's bloodiness, Gareth found Labala, who told him the attack on the wall had been expensive. Iset had been killed, as had almost half of his soldiery. The Kashi had fought well, but, as always with new troops, suffered heavy casualties. Riet of the Sa'ib was among them.

But Cimmar was crumbling, as the fires tore at it from one side and the pirates from the other.

The treasure room was huge, and the high-piled gold and jewels winked and beckoned to the pirates standing in the open door.

But that wasn't what held Gareth and the others' attention.

One entire wall was taken up with a great relief map of what must be the entire world, including lands completely unknown to any Sarosian. Gareth looked at lands he knew and realized the map was far more accurate, even in its small scale, than any chart he had.

The base material used for the map's land was gold, the oceans were what looked like sheets cut from an enormous aquamarine. But that gem was always tiny, Gareth knew; he couldn't imagine one huge enough to be shaved for this enormous map.

Other gems were set here and there for other cities.

Gareth looked at Saros, saw Ticao, and Lyrawise across the Narrow Seas. Over there, on the peninsula connecting the continents of Linyati and Kashi, was a gleam for the treasure city of Noorat that they'd sacked.

But that wasn't what caught and held his and the other mariners' attention.

The map was alive.

An unknown island to the south-southeast of Linyati glowed with red light. Then the red flashed in three places on Linyati's south coast and spread around the continent's shores, a fever-blotch. It spread until all of Linyati glowed, spread through Kashi.

This was the Linyati's chart of their conquests, terrifying in the speed of its spread.

Even more horrible were the splotches that touched on other, unknown continents—even a bit of red in Juterbog.

Here was where the Linyati must have come to dream and boast, and think of the days when all the world would be red.

Gareth wondered on those first three marks where the Linyati must have appeared. *Appeared*, he realized, was the most appropriate word, not *were born*. But where had they come from? Another world like the one they'd come to? The haunts of demons? Or is this where the gods or devils had brought them to life?

He shook his head.

All he knew for sure was this chart showed clearly the intent of the Linyati. They intended to occupy the entire world, and Gareth sensed there would be no place for man once they did, not even as slaves. The Runners would merely create more and more Linyati to mindlessly do their bidding.

In that smouldering ruin he knew to the bottom of his guts:

It must be either Man or Linyati.

Blind rage came, and he seized a gold statue in one hand: a statue of a monster he had never seen, hoped existed only in Linyati fever dreams.

He threw it with all his strength against the chart, destroying its prediction, and the map shattered, golden fragments coming down with spinning gems and bits of aquamarine.

The weariness fell away, and Gareth was ready to go out into the flaming streets, ready to kill on, denying the Linyati menace.

He walked out of the palace as the pirates shouted to form a loading party before they lost the gold to the fires.

Cosyra was waiting. She started to say something, saw his expression, remained silent.

Gareth felt heat sear him as the flames from the fired city roared closer, knew the building would be engulfed before long. He glanced at the flames, brighter than the rising sun.

"I think," he said to Cosyra, "that perhaps, this night, we've struck a match that will shine all the way to Saros and the king's throne."

"There," she agreed, "and to Linyati."

"Let it bring them awake," Gareth said fiercely. "Let them know us for their desperate enemies and sharpen their swords and magic. Because when they come, we'll be ready."

Twenty-seven

There were three coastal guard ships driving down on the wallowing treasure ships.

Gareth watched them through his glass, grinning at their obvious confusion: Ships, obviously Linyati in design, but flying Sarosian colors. Not quite Sarosian, but with a skull and crossed cutlasses below the device.

A signal ran to the masthead of the lead guard vessel:
WHAT SHIP? WHAT NATION?

"Make a signal back," Gareth said. "Sir Gareth, Lord Newgrange of Saros. With gold for the king."

"Aye, sir," Nomios said with a grin, picking banners from the flag bag, attaching them to the halyard and sending it aloft into the snapping breeze.

The passage had taken two slow months, sailing within days from the ruins that had been Cimmar. The surviving Kashi swore they'd not rebuild and occupy the city, but leave the rubble as a signal to the Linyati to never more venture up the Mozaffar. But in case the Slavers were slow learners, the Kashi would maintain guard posts a day's travel upriver, ready to ambush any slaving ships that chanced the passage.

And so, with tears for the dead and promises to meet again in the future, Gareth's four ships had set sail for the north.

The Linyati ships were pigs at best, but they held an enormous amount of cargo. The four were filled to the gunwales with the Slavers' treasure.

They'd sighted Saros's most southerly reach just at dawn, and as they closed on the homeland, there'd been a lively discussion on the quarterdeck.

"I think," Thom Tehidy said, "I'm going to buy a title to go with my new prominence. Perhaps marry Myan. And maybe we should rename Newgrange N'b'ry, if you see fit, Gareth."

There was a sad silence for a moment.

"I'm going to continue my studies," Labala said. "But this time, the wizards'll come to me. If I decide they're pompous asses, I'll double their fees and pitch them in the river."

"I," the helmsman said, unbidden, "am going to throw the world's biggest drunk."

"Which, m'boy," Nomios put in, "will eat up, oh, the hundredth part of your single share. What'll you do with the rest?"

The helmsman pondered for a minute, trying to figure what could be done with money beyond his avarice, then brightened: "After that, I'll throw the world's *second* biggest drunk."

The lookout aloft called down, "Sail ahoy, hard on the port tack," and a moment later, "Three sails to port. I have them clear. Flying the Sarosian banner."

Now the lead guard ship was close enough for Gareth

to see real turmoil on its quarterdeck. Another, longer signal went up, letter by letter:

IS LADY COSYRA OF THE MOUNT ABOARD?

"Send back affirmative," Gareth said, and looked at Cosyra, who made a face.

"I guess they figured out where I went, hmm? I'm grateful we're bringing back enough treasure to blind even the king, or we might both end up in a cell in the Great Dungeon by tomorrow." She sighed. "I guess my great adventure is over and I'm back to being chained to society, forever more twinkling through life." She put her arm around Gareth. "But it was fun, wasn't it?"

Gareth thought of Knoll N'b'ry, and hundreds of others, rotting in unmarked graves in a strange jungle land. But they'd chosen to go, had they not? And didn't all men have a death due, sooner or later?

"It was," he agreed.

"Sir," Nomios said. "The strangest reply to my signal. They sent back one word—Hallelujah, letter by letter—and requested permission for their captain to come aboard."

"Strange. Since when do the coastal guard need permission to board any vessel but the king's?" Gareth said. "Of course they can. Order a heave-to."

The three guardships lowered their sails as they closed on Gareth's ship. A boat was launched from the lead ship, and rowed rapidly across to the treasure ship's boarding port.

The guard captain came up the ladder in a sprightly manner, even though he was a gray-haired, pudgy man.

Gareth went to him, extending his hand.

The officer saw Cosyra, ignored Gareth, and went to his knee.

"Thank Megaris and all our other gods," he said. "You live, Your Grace."

Gareth was astonished to see tears in the man's eyes.

"Uh . . . get up, man," Cosyra managed. "And what's this Your Grace nonsense?"

The man remained on his knees.

"Then I have the greatest honor of my life, Your Highness, in telling you that you are now the queen of all Saros."

Someone behind Gareth uttered a shocked obscenity that sounded like a prayer.

"I said get up, man!" Cosyra said. "And what's this queen business?"

Finally the guardsman obeyed.

"Ma'am," he said. "When you left, with Lord Newgrange here, Alfieri still . . . still sat the throne. But not a month after you were discovered to be missing, he fell from his horse, riding along the waterfront. Some said he was looking for you.

"He never regained consciousness, and I can promise you, his rites were the finest any historian could discover that had ever been held in the kingdom."

"You are taking a very long-winded way through your explanation," Cosyra said, and Gareth could feel her held-back anger.

"When his testament was read out, milady, it announced that you were his daughter, born . . . well, out of marriage, but now acknowledged as his rightful heir."

"Son of a bitch," Cosyra said thoughtfully. "So *that* was Mother's great secret."

"Yes, my lady," the guardsman said, obviously not understanding. "All Saros went a little mad, realizing their new ruler was not only out of the country, but in the heart of enemy seas and lands as well. Especially since relations with the Linyati have worsened, and we're very close to war."

"So," Gareth mused, "when Quindolphin the snake

heard about your running away with me, he immediately told his allies, who went after you either to hold as hostage or to use as their puppet. Explains a lot, doesn't it?"

Cosyra didn't answer, but turned and looked out at the dim line that was Saros.

"I shall be *dipped*," she murmured, and the guardsman hid a wince at her language.

"I think," Gareth said, fingering the sea eagle he still wore about his neck, "we might be in for some interesting times."

Cosyra turned back and put her arms around him.

"You're telling me," Cosyra, Lady of the Mount, Queen of Saros, said thoughtfully.

"Interesting, indeed."

CHRIS BUNCH is the coauthor (with Allan Cole) of the Sten series and the Anteros trilogy for Del Rey. As a solo writer, he is the author of the Shadow Warrior and Last Legion science fiction series. Both Ranger and airborne-qualified, he was part of the first troop commitment into Vietnam, a patrol commander, and a combat correspondent for *Stars & Stripes*. Later, he edited outlaw motorcycle magazines and wrote for everything from the underground press to *Look* magazine, *Rolling Stone*, and prime-time television. He is now a full-time novelist.

VISIT WARNER ASPECT ONLINE!

THE WARNER ASPECT HOMEPAGE

You'll find us at: www.twbookmark.com then by clicking on Science Fiction and Fantasy.

NEW AND UPCOMING TITLES

Each month we feature our new titles and reader favorites.

AUTHOR INFO

Author bios, bibliographies and links to personal websites.

CONTESTS AND OTHER FUN STUFF

Advance galley giveaways, autographed copies, and more.

THE ASPECT BUZZ

What's new, hot and upcoming from Warner Aspect: awards news, bestsellers, movie tie-in information . . .